HEART of the HIGHLAND WOLF

TERRY SPEAR

sourcebooks
casablanca

Copyright © 2011 by Terry Spear
Cover and internal design © 2011 by Sourcebooks, Inc.
Cover design by Dawn Pope
Cover images © Astra Potocki/Alamy, Daryl Benson/Getty Images,
WrightLight/iStockphoto.com

Sourcebooks and the colophon are registered trademarks of Sourcebooks, Inc.

Published by Sourcebooks Casablanca, an imprint of Sourcebooks, Inc.
P.O. Box 4410, Naperville, Illinois 60567-4410
(630) 961-3900
FAX: (630) 961-2168
www.sourcebooks.com

Printed and bound in the United States of America
RRD 10 9 8 7 6

"Another great story sure to amaze and intrigue readers… sensual, passionate, and very well written… Terry Spear's writing is pure entertainment."

—*The Long and the Short of It Reviews*

"Riveting and entertaining… makes one want to devour all of the rest of Terry Spear's books."

—*Fresh Fiction*

"Full of nail-biting suspense, sexy scenes, and plenty of hot alphas… Terry Spear knows exactly how to extract emotions from her readers… and keep them riveted."

—*Love Romance Passion*

"Typical of Ms. Spear's wolf shape-shifter books: great plots, fascinating characters, and wonderful love stories."

—*Star-Crossed Romance*

"Terrific suspense and enough action to keep a reader fascinated."

—*Night Owl Romance*

"Spear's trademark of using realistic wolf characteristics and behavior remains refreshingly delightful."

—*CK2's Kwips and Kritiques*

Praise for *Seduced by the Wolf*

"Gently laced with just enough wolf detail and werewolf lore, this action-packed story crackles with mystery, adventure, violence, and passion; a worthy addition to Spear's beautifully imagined werewolf world."

—*Library Journal*

"Ms. Spear's werewolf stories keep getting better and better. You will find yourself lusting after the sexy alpha hero and cheering for the heroine."

—*Night Owl Romance*

"Terry Spear really knows how to ensnare her readers! *Seduced by the Wolf* has everything a paranormal romance reader wants: sensuousness, adventure, excitement."

—*Ramsey's Reviews*

"I love, love, LOVE this novel! Cassie and Leidolf steam up the pages with a delightful courtship dance, and the subplots of secondary characters are just as intriguing and well developed. All the realistic wolf behavior shows the author has done her homework and adds depth and color that makes the action leap from the pages."

—*CK2's Kwips & Kritiques*

Praise for *Legend of the White Wolf*

"Spear's latest novel is bursting with romance, suspense, and heart-pounding excitement… *Legend of the White Wolf* will leave you howling for more!"

—*Love Romance Passion*

"WHEW!!! What a thrilling, engaging, wonderful ride… Great characters and a riveting plot, a total page-turner."

—*Seriously Reviewed*

I dedicate Heart of the Highland Wolf *to my Highland ancestors who inspired me to write about love immortalized in the Highlands of Scotland and to readers all over the globe who find happiness in fictional tales of romance, adventure, mystery, and enduring love.*

Chapter 1

THE GHOSTLY FOG MADE JULIA FEEL AS THOUGH SHE had slipped into the primordial past. She couldn't believe she'd made it to the Highlands of Scotland where a castle beckoned, filled with secrets, intrigue, and hunky Scots—*with any luck*. Hopefully, none of them would learn why she was really here and put a stop to it.

Nothing would dampen her enthusiasm as she and her friend Maria Baquero headed for Baird Cottage, within hiking distance of Argent Castle—and the *end* of her writer's block.

At least, that was the plan.

After flight delays and missed luggage, they'd had trouble getting their rental car at Inverness Airport—following a mix-up when a Scotsman declared their car was his. Another man had creeped Julia out when she realized he was watching them, and she'd felt apprehensive at the way his thin lips hadn't hinted at a bit of friendliness. But then she dismissed him as she and Maria finally set off in late afternoon with Maria driving the rented Fiat into the deepening fog.

The laird of Argent Castle, Ian MacNeill, had been a royal pain to deal with concerning filming the movie at his castle. Luckily, as assistant director, only Maria had to do business with him. Pretending to be Maria's assistant, Julia was to watch from the sidelines and take notes. But not for the film production. For her breakout

novel. Julia Wildthorn was one of the United States'
most successful werewolf romance novelists and the
only one, she was sure, who had ever suffered a writer's
block like this one.

Dense fog obscured the curving road as it ran through
rocky land on either side. Pine trees in the distance faded
into the thickening soup, which offered glimpses of
quaint dry-stone dykes that must have stood for centuries, snaking across the land and dividing someone's
property from another's.

Despite Julia's enhanced wolf vision, she couldn't
see any better than a human in the soup.

Eyes widening, she caught sight of something running
in the woods. Something gray. Something that looked a
lot like a wolf and then melted into the fog like a phantom.

Heartbeat ratchetting up several notches, she tried to
catch another glimpse, her hand tightening on the door's
armrest as she peered out the window, her nose almost
touching the glass. "Did you see anything?" she asked
Maria, her voice tight.

Maria gave her a disgruntled snort. "In this fog? I can
barely see the road. What did you think you saw?"

"A… wolf." Julia strained to get another glimpse of
what she'd seen. "But it couldn't have been. Wolves
here were killed off centuries ago."

Off to Julia's left, the mist parted, revealing older
aspen, the bark covered with dark lichen stretching
upward, while tall, straight Scots pines and stands of
willowy birch clustered close together in the distance.
But no more signs of a wolf. Julia blinked her eyes.
Maybe because she was so tired from the trip, her eyes
were playing tricks on her.

Julia straightened and faced Maria. "Maybe it was a *lupus garou*, if I wasn't imagining it." She smiled at the thought. "A hunky Highland werewolf in a kilt."

She'd never considered she might run across a *lupus garou* in Scotland. Not as elusive as their kind were, hiding their secret from the rest of the world. Unless she bumped into one and could smell his or her scent, she wouldn't know a *lupus garou* from a strictly human type.

"Hmm, a Highland werewolf," Maria said thoughtfully, sliding her hands over the steering wheel, "although getting hold of a Spanish conquistador would be just as intriguing."

An Iberian werewolf whose ancestors had been turned by a wolfish conquistador, Maria was a beauty with dark brown hair and thick, long eyelashes.

Being a redhead with fair skin, Julia turned heads on her own, but the two of them together often stole the show.

Maria was still stewing about the laird who was in charge of Argent Castle. "Laird Ian MacNeill is being a real hard ass about the filming particulars—restricting our use of the castle and grounds, the times, the locations, and who knows what else when we arrive."

"Maybe he won't be so bad once the filming begins." Although Julia didn't believe that—and the sour look on Maria's face said she didn't, either. Julia pulled the laird's photo from her purse. Maria's boss had paid a private investigator good money to obtain the picture. "Exactly how did the guy get a picture of the laird like this if it's so difficult to catch a glimpse of him?"

"The P.I. followed him to a Celtic festival. The laird was surrounded by his men and a couple of women, so the detective snapped one shot right before the laird took part in a sword-fighting demonstration."

"Who won?"

"The laird and his men. According to the P.I., the MacNeills had a real workout against the Sutherlands. Bad blood has existed between them for centuries. The fighting looked so real, he thought organizers of the show might step in and stop the demonstration."

In one word, Julia summed up Laird Ian MacNeill's appearance: *dangerous.*

It wasn't his handsome features—his short, very dark coffee-colored hair, the rich color of his eyes, the rigid planes of his face, and his aristocratic nose—that made him appear that way. Not his broad shoulders or firm stance or unsmiling mouth, either. It was his unerring gaze that seemed so piercingly astute, like he could see into a person's very soul.

That worried her.

In the photo, the man was prime hunk, wearing a predominantly green and blue kilt, an ermine sporran belted in front, and a sword sheathed behind him. From the looks of the hilt partially peeking over his shoulder, the sword served as a warning that he was armed and deadly, much more so than just his looks. He wore a shirt belted, hanging open to the waist, and revealing sexy abs a woman would love to caress. At least this woman would. Just as rugged, his castle sat in the background, formidable, commanding, and resilient.

She could just imagine him wielding that lethal sword against his enemy.

Maria shook her head. "He's arrogant, hard-nosed, too far above us, and on top of that, we're Americans and working—or at least he'll think you're working—with the film crew he so despises. So just remember that in case you're getting romantic notions from that picture of him. He's too wickedly sexy for his own good... or maybe I should say, for *your* own good."

Maria was probably right. Julia wanted to see the laird up close and personal for the sake of writing her manuscript, but she didn't want to hear the disparaging things he might say to her. That would ruin her image of him as the hero type. And if he looked at her the way he did in the picture, she feared he would see right through her.

Just then, they topped the hill and faced a sea of white, curly fur blocking their way. Maria gasped and slammed on the brakes. Julia's heart rapped a triple beat, and she grabbed the dashboard. Like a pastoral scene from an old-time painting, the mob of sheep was making its way to the other side of the rocky glen. Several sheared sheep—ewes, a curly horned ram, and lots of lambs—crossed the road, along with a sheepherder with a gnarled walking stick in hand and his collie.

Instantly, Julia thought about the wolf.

Once the sheep had passed, Maria started driving slower than before and cleared her throat.

"As soon as we drop off our carry-on luggage, I have to drive over to the estate for a meeting."

Harold Washburn, the producer of the film, and most of the staff were staying at a local mansion. Maria had insisted on leasing Baird Cottage, citing its closeness to the castle. In truth, it was to hide that she and Julia were *lupus garous* and that Julia wasn't truly working for Maria.

"At this rate, I'm not going to make it in time. I haven't seen a sign in a while, and... I thought we would have been there by now," Maria continued.

Julia strained to see into the distance, searching for another road sign, but the fog that had parted in places for her to glimpse the trees was again too thick to see a thing.

A shadow of gray bolted across the road. *The wolf.* A gray wolf.

Maria gasped and slammed on her brakes. Julia's mouth dropped open, but the squeal died in her throat as headlights reflected off her side mirror. The headlights barreled on top of them. It was too late.

Rubber and brakes squealed behind them. Heart pounding, Julia braced for the crash, the wolf forgotten.

Bang! The rental car flew off the road like an airborne mini-plane. Then it landed hard, tearing down the incline. Bouncing. Jolting. Teeth jarring. A white cloud filled Julia's vision and she gasped.

A shotgun blast! A horrible jolt. Another bang!

Before Julia could process what had happened, the white air bag deflated, and a snaking wall of rocks loomed before them only a couple of feet away in the fog.

"Hit the brakes!" Julia screamed.

⁓

As soon as he heard the explosions ahead, Ian MacNeill slowed his car and watched the road and the shoulders, looking for signs of a collision. Some poor fool must have been driving too slowly in the fog, while another had been driving too fast, hence the horrendous noise in the distance.

His youngest brother, Duncan—which being quadruplets meant only by minutes—peered out the passenger window.

"It had to be a car wreck," Duncan said, his tone concerned.

"Aye." Ian watched for lights that might indicate vehicles ahead. Their wolf hearing was so enhanced that the sounds made could have been some kilometers distant.

"I don't see anything, Ian. Not a thing. No tire skids, no broken glass. But the explosive sounds were loud enough that the vehicles had to have damage."

Unease scraping down his spine, Ian agreed.

Duncan leaned against the passenger door and then motioned toward the incline. "Taillights in the fog, down there."

"And scraps of red metal from a vehicle up here," Ian said as his headlights glinted off pieces of metal and part of a taillight reflector.

He pulled off onto the soft shoulder, turned off the ignition, and exited the vehicle. With Duncan at his side, he hurried down the incline toward the cherry-colored fog.

"Hello, anybody hurt?" Ian called out, his dark voice traveling over the glen. He took a breath and swore he smelled a hint of the acrid odor of gunfire.

No one answered his call, and another trace of unease wormed its way into his blood. Then he heard a moan. A woman's moan.

"Hell, probably a woman driving way too slow and got hit," Duncan growled, quickening his run.

Duncan should know since he'd smashed into the rear bumper of a woman's car just the month before for the same reason. Ian hoped to hell no one had life-threatening injuries.

The odor of burning tires, scraped raw metal, and refrigerant gas leaking from the car's air-conditioning system drifted to them. Then smoke.

"Smoke," Duncan said, racing to the car.

"Hello!" Ian called out again as they scrambled to reach the vehicle smashed into the dry dyke, the front bumper looking like an accordion, the red metal crumpled against the windshield. Glass everywhere sparkled like diamond shards on the ground. The windshield was shattered, and the driver's side window, a spider web of cracks. White sheets of material covered the shattered dash—deflated air bags.

The two rear tires had blown out, and the rear bumper was smashed and the metal torn from its moorings, one end now touching the ground. But Ian didn't see telltale signs of another vehicle's paint on this one. Yet after considering the rear bumper, he assumed someone *had* to have hit the car *hard*.

Ian reached the driver's door first, but the frame was so badly bent that the door wouldn't budge. He peered in through the window as Duncan reached him. No one inside the vehicle. He glanced around, raised his nose, and smelled... petrol, hot and burning.

"Duncan!" Ian grabbed his brother's arm and yanked him away from the car.

Boom! The forceful explosion threw them several meters away, heat singeing their eyebrows and zapping the moisture out of the cool, wet air. His ears ringing, hearing deadened, eyes and nostrils filled with smoke, Ian lay still in the grass, dazed. Then he jerked to a sitting position and looked for his brother.

Duncan was sitting nearby, shaking his head as if clearing the fog from it. "Hell. The driver had better sense than we did." His black clothes were now covered in gray soot and splotches of brown mud.

Ian agreed. "The car had a couple of small suitcases—someone on holiday."

"A lass from the looks of it," Duncan added.

"Aye, one of the suitcases was pink, and I glimpsed a handbag sitting on the center console."

They both watched as orange flames consumed the car. No worry of anything else catching fire, as damp as it was. The rains that morning had turned everything to mud, which Ian's light khaki-colored trousers were now soaking up. Ian stood and wiped the mud off his hands and onto his trousers. "You okay?"

"Aye. Can't hear anything worth a damn. Your voice sounds a million kilometers away. And my head is splitting."

"Same here. Come on. Let's find the woman. She's probably in better shape than we are." Ian cast Duncan a dark smile. "You look like hell, brother."

Duncan snorted. "You don't look much better."

Ian slapped him on the back, and the two made a wide circle around the car, looking for any indication of where the driver would have gone. Heel marks. Not one, but two sets of prints. "Two," Ian said, pointing to the tracks. "Lassies, both of them."

"Do you smell something?" Duncan asked.

"If you mean burning rubber, petrol, smoke, hot

metal, and mud, aye. Was there something else you smelled then? A woman's perfume, maybe?"

Duncan tilted his head up, took another deep breath, and then coughed. "Let's move away from the fire. I can't smell anything but smoke. But I thought..." He shook his head.

"What?"

"Nothing."

Ian moved away from the burning car, but something in Duncan's voice made him take another long look at his brother. Duncan was frowning, concentrating, and sampling the air, trying to locate the women.

"Blood?" Ian asked, thinking maybe Duncan had smelled an injury and was concerned about it. The smoke and burning petrol were wreaking havoc with his own sense of smell now.

"Aye, well, that and..." Duncan looked at him with an odd expression. "...the faint scent of wolf."

Chapter 2

"I STILL THINK WE SHOULD HAVE STAYED WITH THE car," Julia grumbled under her breath, limping in her heels, her ankle throbbing. She held onto Maria for support as they hurried away from the wreck as fast as possible.

The sound of an explosion at their backs made Julia jump. But they were far from there now. And they heard no more shouts, which worried Julia as her heart thundered spastically. What if the man who had come after them had been injured?

The sweet, earthy smell of rain preceded the start of a shower. Then the raindrops poured down on them in earnest, the plants and earth offering up a cleansing scent.

They would be drenched before they got much of anywhere, even though they weren't letting up on the pace, despite their minor injuries. Julia wished she hadn't taken off her pantsuit jacket to keep it from getting wrinkled by her seat belt. The jacket, being in the backseat, hadn't been on her mind, not when they'd discovered Maria's door was jammed tight and Julia had to help her over the console. Now, the shell of aqua silk Julia wore was plastered to her chest, revealing everything, she was sure. Her linen slacks were in the same shape, molding to her legs, feeling cold and wet like an alien second skin.

"We should have stayed near the car at least," Julia griped, wiping away the steady trickle of water droplets dribbling down her cheeks. "That's what you're supposed to do when you need assistance." She tightened her grip on Maria's arm. "With the car on fire, someone is sure to spot it eventually."

Maria hushed her again.

Julia pulled her to a stop. "All right," Julia whispered. "Why do you think whoever hit us did it on purpose?"

"We were better off getting away from the car before it exploded." Maria took a deep breath and let it out slowly. "But that's not the only reason. I got a death threat before we left L.A."

Uncomprehending, Julia stared at her. "*What?*"

Maria started walking again, pulling Julia along, their shoes squishing and squelching in the mud. "A man with a distinctive Scottish brogue called me on my home phone, angry about us using Ian MacNeill's castle for the film. He said I'd live to regret it. I didn't believe it, *much…* then this happens. But it was more than that."

When Maria didn't say anything further, Julia prompted, "More than that?"

Maria gave her a hard look. "He said you didn't know what you were getting yourself into."

"Me?"

"He knew you had learned of the castle and passed the information on to me. But it was almost like he knew you. *Personally.* And he didn't want you to have anything to do with Laird MacNeill. He sounded like an ex-lover."

"I've never had a boyfriend with a Scottish accent. I don't know anyone like that."

"He said he knew your family. That if you hadn't dumped the investment advisor, he would have had to do something about it. See what I mean? It's like it's personal with him."

Julia wracked her brain, trying to come up with anyone like that, but she couldn't think of a soul. The part about him knowing about Trevor did concern her. Not that her relationship with him was secret. But how would someone in Scotland have known of it? As to her family, they didn't even go by the same last name as she did. She was Julia Wildthorn, romance author—pen name. Real name—Julia MacPherson. But no one knew that. Not even Maria.

"It's probably just some ticked-off guy who gets off on threats."

Maria cast her a disbelieving look. "You can't deny it sounds personal."

Julia thought about her grandfather and father insisting that she encourage Maria to consider Ian's castle for the film production. What if bad blood existed between her family's ancestors and this person's ancestors? And now Maria was caught in the middle of it.

"Did he say anything about owning a different castle? Maybe he wanted the business instead, and MacNeill is his fiercest competition."

"No."

Julia grimaced as another twinge of pain rippled through her ankle. She compensated by leaning more on her other foot and on Maria's arm. "What did the L.A. police say?"

"Nothing. Without a caller ID name or number, a recording of the phone call, more threats, or anything else to go on, they said they couldn't do anything about it."

Julia pulled Maria to a stop again as she heard distant footfalls. "Whoever's following us is getting closer."

"I know. That's why I'm trying to hurry up and find a town or people or something." Maria started hauling Julia along again.

"You think it's the guy who hit us?"

"Maybe not, but what if it is? What with worrying that the car was going to explode any moment, with the smoke pouring out of the engine and the smell of the leaking gasoline, and you trying to help me out the passenger's side door in a hurry because my door was jammed, we both lost everything in the car, *including* our cell phones. We have no way to call for help."

Julia patted her soaking-wet pants pockets and discovered she had four limp U.S. dollars, a handful of U.S. change, a scrunchie to tie back her hair, and... She touched the pocket of her shell, where the picture of Ian MacNeill was sitting close to her heart and the only thing still warm. She had pulled the photo out of her purse to take one surreptitious look at it, and for some reason, she'd stuck it in her shirt pocket instead of back in her purse.

In her writer's fruitful imagination, she envisioned a bond between them and that through some kind of body heat transference, the laird would know their troubles and come to rescue them. She was hopelessly romantic, which hadn't gotten her anywhere with men, but she wasn't giving up.

She glanced over her shoulder but couldn't see anything except fog and trees. "We could wander for miles and never find anyone. We should sit down and stay quiet. They'll pass us by."

"No. For one thing, it's getting dark. And for another, I have to get to Harold's meeting. And finally," Maria whispered back, "whoever is out there has been tracking us pretty damn well all along. Ever since the Scotsman shouted near the car, calling out to us."

"Was it the same voice as the man who talked to you on the phone?"

"I can't tell. The phone crackled and sputtered when the man called me in L.A., lousy reception. This guy's voice was loud and clear."

And dark and worried and sexy, Julia thought. Not at all like someone who was out to get them. The wolf again came to the forefront of Julia's thoughts. "The wolf has to be one of our kind."

Maria asked quietly, "What if he was with the guy that hit us? What if they worked in collusion?"

Maria and her conspiracy theories.

"Highly unlikely," Julia said, in an attempt at reassuring. But that didn't stop her own small, niggling worry.

She began to look for any signs of a wolf in the area, skulking around in the fog and rain.

The sudden rain shower slowed to a drizzle just as a flicker of light in the distance caught Julia's eye. "Over there," she whispered, her hopes elevating, and the two changed direction. "A building."

Distant hearty male singing drifted to them from the direction of the muted light.

"We must look adorable," Maria muttered, glancing down. Their clothes were soaked, but at least Maria was wearing her jacket, and even though she was wet, the fabric didn't cling to her the way Julia's did.

"Road," Julia said. "Dead ahead."

The rambunctious sound of men singing grew louder.
"A pub, maybe," Maria excitedly said, her voice still
hushed as she dragged Julia across the deserted road, the
music cheering them on. "We'll be safe there and can
borrow a phone and call Harold."

Welcoming brass porch lanterns glowed through
the fog, illuminating the front of Scott's Pub. The new
mixing with the old, ancient stone walls surrounded
double glass doors, back-lit from the warm wash of
lighting inside. Above the pub, six dark windows over-
looked the parking lot, and a sign read: ROOMS FOR
LEASE. A corner of the building wrapped around and
rose three stories, but it looked ghostly vacant. A sign
carved into the stone said, HIGHLAND INN.

Behind the building, trees and hills loomed tall,
dwarfing the place. Outside, three cars, a pickup, and a
van were parked, and unless tons of people had ridden
in the five vehicles, Julia assumed liquor had loosened
the singers' tongues to a good-hearted bellow. In her
romantic writer's imagination, she envisioned the place
filled with braw, kilted Highland warriors who would
save them from harm if those following them meant to
hurt them.

Maria grabbed the door and opened it, then pulled
Julia inside and shut the door. The aroma of juicy burgers grilling made Julia's stomach growl.

She needed food and water. And a towel, a shower,
and clean clothes. The place seemed like their salvation.

To keep from tracking in mud, they eased off their
muddy heels and left them out of the way on the granite
floor against the entryway wall. Then they padded in
stocking feet into a more dimly lit room, complete with

paneled bar, several tables, a dartboard on one wall, and the painting of deer on another. The singing had continued, and the men's brogue was so thick that Julia didn't understand a word of it.

A man dressed in a black polo shirt and steel-gray slacks poured drinks from behind the bar, and two others dressed the same way sang along with those sitting at the tables. Julia was disappointed not to see any kilted warriors in Scott's Pub. The six men were wearing trousers and shirts—everyday variety, nothing noteworthy for her manuscript. But they looked like a hearty lot, smiling and singing and swinging their mugs of ale.

Until a pretty blonde woman—petite and midthirties, wearing jeans and a tank top, and serving another tray of drinks to one of the tables—turned to look at Maria and Julia. The waitress's smiling mouth instantly dropped open. She nearly spilled a man's ale in his lap, and he quickly grabbed her hand to steady it.

"Sarah, lass…" But he and the other men quit singing one by one and turned to see what had startled her so.

―――⁂―――

"The women probably went inside Scott's Pub, as quiet as the place suddenly got," Ian said to his brother as they reached the road, rainwater running down their faces, their clothes soaked.

Torn between reaching the women before they found the pub and hanging back to allow them time to locate it, Ian had figured the women would feel safer with others about. He could still determine if they were all right without appearing to be a threat. He truly had no need to do other than that.

"Do you want me to walk back down the road and get our car while you check on the women then?" Duncan asked.

"Aye. Bring the car, and we'll have a whisky." Ian jogged across the road as Duncan headed back to where Ian had parked the car. They still had to reach Argent before that producer arrived, but they had plenty of time.

Ian pulled the door open, stalked inside, and saw the two drenched women seated at a table. His quarry.

They were even more appealing than he could have guessed.

One was darker-skinned, had dark hair and eyes, and looked Spanish. The other was a natural redhead with deep red-orange curls resting on her shoulders, her skin translucent ivory, and green catlike eyes that made her appear Scottish. The Spanish woman was dressed in a black suit, jacket and slacks, wet and spattered in mud. She was all curves, but the fabric didn't reveal all of her attributes like the redhead's did.

His gaze fastened on the redhead as if she might vanish in the blink of an eye. An aqua-blue, sleeveless silk shirt clung to pert breasts, her rigid nipples pressed against the fabric, her arms covered in chill bumps. He took a hell of a lot longer look than was good manners, then saw that her matching blue trousers were just as wet, just as clinging, showing a good deal of toned leg. Seeing her nearly nude body made his tighten in response.

Annoyed with himself for having such an intense reaction, he paused to consider what to do next.

Both women were sipping water and looking dismayed. The redhead saw him, her eyes widening. As if prompted, the other looked back at him, too, her eyes suddenly wary. He wondered if they were *lupus garous*. The air was still, and unless he drew really close, they wouldn't notice his scent because of the aroma of burgers grilling nearby. In truth, *he* couldn't even smell their scents in here.

"Laird MacNeill," several men said, raising mugs of ale or whisky glasses in greeting.

He acknowledged them each by name, all locals from the area, none of them *lupus garous*.

He wanted to ask the women who they were, where they were from, what they were doing here, and what had happened to them on the road, but their concerned expressions gave him the impression they feared him. He was afraid they'd bolt if he drew any nearer.

The redhead's gaze swept over him from his face downward, and he realized what a mess he was, his jaw sporting a stubble of beard, his trousers muddy. And without a rain jacket, his damp, white cotton shirt and khaki trousers stuck to him, much the way the redhead's clothes clung to her. He probably did appear a wee bit threatening.

The men glanced at the women and back at Ian. More than one raised a brow, but no one spoke. Did they think he and the women had been caught in the same wreck? Most likely it looked that way.

He pulled out a chair at a table nearby, sat, and ordered whiskys for both Duncan and himself.

"What happened?" he asked the waitress as she returned to his table with a couple of drinks, subtly motioning to the two women with his head as they leaned close to each other and whispered.

Sarah looked like she wanted to ask the same of

him. "Americans, had an accident in the fog. Lost their carry-on luggage, money, passports, cell phones, laptops, everything that was with them," she responded in a hushed voice. "They only had a few U.S. dollars to get anything to drink or eat, but we couldn't take the money. I gave them some water. Scott said to give them a meal, but they refused, saying they weren't hungry. Which I don't believe. The redhead's stomach was grumbling.

"Then the dark-haired woman used my cell phone and called someone named Howard, said they needed to file an accident report and she didn't want to miss the first meeting at Argent Castle." Sara raised her brows as if saying it was now Ian's turn to fill her in on the rest of the details.

But Ian's thoughts had focused on the scheduled meeting later today with the film producer.

Both women were sipping their water, looking at each other, quiet. They were with the film production crew? His mouth hardening, he said, "And?"

"I got the distinct impression Howard isn't coming to pick them up." Sarah waved her hand at a couple of the tables filled with men. "*Everyone* offered to drive the women to their cottage, but MacNamara warned them their wives wouldn't like it."

Ian grunted. That was for sure. "Do you know where they're headed?"

Sarah smiled. She was an American, having traveled here three years ago with a couple of girlfriends on the vacation of a lifetime — as they had called it. Sarah had fallen in love with Scott, married him, and never gone back. She tucked a gold curl behind her ear and raised her brows.

"They're staying at Baird Cottage. They wanted to

know how far it was from here." Then she turned her attention to the women and smiled.

They gave her tense smiles back, as if they were trying to make a show of it, but they still looked apprehensive.

Ian took a short draught of whisky and caught the redhead's eye. She challenged him right back, her gaze intense. Without his consent, his mouth quirked into a bit of a smile. A blush extended from her face all the way down her naked neck as she looked away. His gaze drew lower to her breasts again. Hell, if he'd had a dry shirt, he'd have offered it to her. He noted the other men were looking her way, too. That really irked him.

She glanced at him again. Something about her lowered lashes, the way her gaze fetched his, made him consciously aware of her interest in him, as though she was reconsidering her initial thoughts about him. His smile broadened. But she pulled her gaze away from him almost dismissively. He'd never been interested in a woman who fawned over him. Something about a lass who challenged him appealed so much more.

In this case, he wasn't about to fall into that quagmire. Not as much as he hated the idea of having the film production anywhere on his grounds. In his view, anyone participating in the venture was the enemy. But Ian and his pack desperately needed the money—they were in a financial mess.

The dark-haired woman glanced over her shoulder at Ian, raised her brows, and then spoke softly to the redhead. "He's the one who followed us, Julia."

Julia's voice also was hushed. "But was he trying to help us, or was he after us?"

Sarah cleared her throat to get Ian's attention and

folded her arms. "So, are you going to take them to Baird Cottage, or should MacNamara do it? He's already offered."

MacNamara had finished his beer and was watching Ian to see what he had to say about it. MacNamara's face was lined with the ages; he fished when he wasn't here drinking. But had he already had more than his fair share of beer? Ian didn't want him to drive the women in this weather if he had. Yet, taking the women in his own car was a last resort. He didn't want the Sunset Productions staff thinking he was easygoing where any of them were concerned.

Ian motioned for MacNamara to join him. The older man rose to his six-four height, smiled at the American women, and lumbered over to Ian's table. His gait was steady.

Ian nodded in Julia's and Maria's direction. "See them safe."

MacNamara bowed his head slightly and then walked back to the women's table. "Do you want me to take you to Baird Cottage?"

"Yes," Maria said, nearly jumping from her chair, clearly more than ready.

Julia rose much more slowly, and by the way she grabbed Maria's arm and then limped toward the door, Ian realized she'd hurt her ankle. His gaze slid down her body, curvy in all the right places, the silk top tucked into the clinging slacks showing off a nice arse, and nude stockings, all flecked with mud, but no shoes. He glanced back at the entryway and then noticed the two pairs of mud-coated shoes.

Maria refused to look at Ian, but Julia gave him one

last good glower as she passed him. He tilted his head to her in greeting. She narrowed her eyes and then looked away. Had she had word about his dealings with the film staff? They were *not* in his good graces. Not with all the concessions they had wanted from him and not with him having to say no repeatedly when his saying so once was more than enough for anyone he dealt with on a regular basis.

He considered Julia's height and the other woman's, too. They were too petite to be gray *lupus garous*. Were they even wolves? Or had Duncan smelled someone else?

If Julia was a *lupus garou*, he wondered if she was a red, as small as she was. She limped toward the entrance, which bothered him more than he'd like to admit. If he hadn't been trying to maintain his aloofness with the film crew, he would have swept her up in his arms and taken her to *his* car. And given her a tour of his castle and a warm welcome to Scotland, if she'd been so inclined. That was saying she wasn't a wolf. Interest in a *lupus garou* took on a whole different load of problems.

As soon as MacNamara and the American women were outside, the talk amongst the men in the pub began in earnest as they cast amused glances at Ian.

Sarah shook her head. "Didn't figure you to let her get away." She sounded disappointed and headed back to the bar.

"Thought you were going to take the bonnie lassies out your way," Scott said, bringing over a basket of potato crisps.

"They're part of the film production crew."

Scott's eyes widened. He glanced at the door. "If I'd

known that, I would have encouraged the Yanks to do business here. Think maybe the redhead is a famous actress? She looked to be Scottish and could play the part in that new film. Could be good for business."

Ian glanced toward the entryway. *Even worse.* An actress. Ian shook his head, more at himself than at Scott's question. He didn't have a clue who was famous in the movie business. He finished off Duncan's drink, paid Scott, and then rose from the chair. As soon as Duncan brought the car around, Ian planned to follow MacNamara and the women to make sure that they didn't have any more *accidents* on the way to the cottage.

In departure, Ian waved at the men, who all raised their mugs in salute and then began singing again.

Sarah accompanied Ian to the front doors. "I'd watch old MacNamara also. You never know when he might go fishing for something other than salmon or trout."

Ian knew she was teasing. MacNamara's wife had left him five years ago, and he was content not to have a nagging woman around. No, the man was a happy bachelor.

MacNamara wasn't the one who concerned him. The faint odor of gunpowder that Ian had smelled where the women's car had catapulted off the road still clung to his thoughts, and that's what worried him.

He headed out the door as Duncan drove up and cut the engine. Julia and her friend were limping in the direction of MacNamara's van. Before Duncan could get out of the car, Ian stalked after them. Forget that they were part of the film crew. He had to know—were they *lupus garous,* and what had occurred on the road?

"What happened to having a glass of whisky? And

what about the women?" Duncan asked, getting halfway out of the car.

"MacNamara was taking them to Baird Cottage. The women are part of that film production crew."

"Och." That one wee word said it all. Duncan had to know that ended any interest in the women, *lupus garous* or not. Then his brows furrowed deeply. "So where are you going in such a hurry, and what the hell happened to my glass of whisky?"

Ian didn't reply but instead pursued the women, feeling as though he was in hunting mode again.

Only this time, he'd have a word with his prey.

Chapter 3

"ARE THE TWO WOMEN WOLVES THEN?" DUNCAN ASKED Ian, his voice hushed as he hurried to join his brother while they headed for the women, Julia pronouncedly limping and clinging to Maria as they followed MacNamara to his van.

"I don't know." But Ian intended to find out.

"What *exactly* are we doing now?"

"We're taking them to their cottage."

The road that led to Argent Castle was a short distance after the turnoff for Baird Cottage, so they wouldn't be going out of their way, but the manner in which Duncan asked the question indicated he believed Ian had some other notion in mind.

An elusive smile curved Duncan's lips. "MacNamara's giving them a lift wouldn't do."

Ian didn't need his brother's humorous take on the matter. He had to know if the women were *lupus garous* and if one of them or someone else had been running through his pack's area as a wolf. If the wolf had been one of his own people, he'd take him to task. If it had been someone else, he had to know who.

But he couldn't deny that the redhead's actions and looks also had grabbed his attention, and he wasn't ready to let her go. He couldn't quit thinking about how her wet curls had looked as if she'd just taken a shower fully dressed; the way her green eyes had both glowered at him and eaten him up; how she had stiffened her spine, showing off her tantalizingly perky breasts even more; and how her lips framed a mouth meant to soften under a man's kisses. Attempting to shake loose of the image of her lush pink lips pursed at him when she had caught his gaze, he ground his teeth.

Being a human, MacNamara didn't hear Ian and his brother's silent approach, but the redhead must have sensed or heard them. She glanced over her shoulder, eyes widening when she saw Ian and Duncan closing in on them.

"I'll take the lasses to their cottage," Ian said to MacNamara. Once the words left his mouth, he thought he had sounded a little too insistent.

MacNamara turned and gave him a knowing smile, his face crinkling in amusement. "I'd best return to the pub to finish my business. 'Night, my laird, lassies, Duncan."

He didn't wait for the ladies' objections—*if* they had intended to voice any. Giving Ian a polite nod, he hurried back to the pub.

The other men would have a good-hearted chuckle when they learned Ian MacNeill had stolen MacNamara's catch for the day.

"Ladies," Ian said, bowing his head a little and motioned to his car. "I'll take you to Baird Cottage since it's on my way to Argent Castle. I'm Laird MacNeill, and this is my youngest brother, Duncan."

Both women stood still, not saying a word. Without waiting for either to respond, Ian stalked toward them and, without invitation, swung the redhead up into his arms. She gave a small cry of surprise. The other woman's mouth parted in astonishment.

"Scottish hospitality," Ian ground out, annoyed with himself for not leaving the women in MacNamara's able care but unwilling to tolerate any protest. In that instant, he smelled Julia's scent—an elusive floral fragrance that couldn't veil what she truly was. The fragrance of exotic flowers enhanced the tantalizing feminine smell of her—appealingly *all wolf*.

She was soft and curvaceous and all delectable woman, and she felt damn good against his body.

He tightened his grip on her almost imperceptibly, like a male would a female, already wanting to keep her—*in a strictly wolfish way*—and not with any thought of whether she'd be the right kind of woman for him or not. He didn't even know if the redhead was mated. *Hell*. He glanced at the other and took a deep breath, smelling the air. Maria was a wolf, too.

Both women must have realized he was a wolf in the same instant, the way they took deep breaths and their eyes widened. He smiled. His expression had to appear as predatory as he felt.

When Ian spun around and headed for the car, Duncan watched him with a darkly amused expression, but he didn't appear in the least bit surprised. Ian hoped his brother hadn't known him better than he knew himself. He had not intended to be doing this.

"Ladies," Duncan said, accompanying them.

"Sarah, the woman who was waiting tables at Scott's Pub, although she is co-owner and Scott's wife, said she thought you were with the film crew. Actresses?" Ian asked.

Duncan gave them a second look, this time his expression surprised. He wouldn't know a star if he saw one any more than Ian would.

His comment brought a smile to Maria's lips. "Hardly."

"Doing what then?"

"Assistant director—Maria Baquero. And this is my assistant, Julia—"

"Jones," Julia hastily said.

The way Maria stared at her and the fact that Julia had interrupted her boss made Ian suspicious. "Are you certain?" he asked Julia, as they reached the back passenger door.

"Why wouldn't I be?" she asked haughtily back.

"Miss Baquero seemed surprised." He studied Julia, waiting for a comeback.

Maria didn't come to Julia's defense. Which made him suspect Julia's last name wasn't Jones. Did she even work for Maria?

Eyes narrowed, Julia immediately pursed that beautiful mouth of hers and didn't say a word to refute his suspicion.

Duncan stood by the car, waiting to see about the logistics of the situation. Most likely also to see how the scene played out between Ian and Julia.

"Lass?" Ian said, waiting for a response. He wasn't used to being kept waiting, nor was he often lied to, but when she didn't answer, he shook his head. "Do you have some ID?"

"In the rental car," she said with a heavy sigh.

He thought back to the flames consuming the car. "Convenient." He deposited Julia in the backseat and said to Maria, "You can ride up front with Duncan and see the scenery." While Ian enjoyed the scenery in the backseat. The spitfire, more like it.

Duncan cast him an elusive smile, knowing that Ian rarely, *if ever*, sat in the backseat of any vehicle, and then he opened the front passenger door for Maria. She hesitated for a heartbeat and then climbed into the car, whereupon Duncan shut her door for her, and Ian closed Julia's.

"They're wolves," Duncan said to Ian, as they walked around the back side of his car, his voice low so the women wouldn't hear them.

"And they are with the film crew," Ian reminded him. He yanked open the car door, then slid inside next to Julia and closed his door.

At once, he knew this was a mistake. The backseat was too small, and he was way too close to the object of his fascination. He felt another tug of desire as soon as he felt the heat and softness of her body when his leg touched hers in the small compact car, smelled her feminine fragrance, and heard her light breathing before the engine roared to life and they were on their way.

With every intention of quashing the interest he had in her, he attempted a distraction and asked, "Where are you from?"

Maria answered, "Los Angeles."

Duncan smiled in the rearview mirror as he looked back at Ian.

"Have you been involved in making many movies?" Again, Ian asked this of Julia.

And again Maria answered. But Ian didn't listen closely to her response as she listed movie locations, movie titles, and more. She seemed to be the real deal when it came to her job and her role in this current film venture.

He asked Julia, "How badly is your ankle sprained?"

"It's fine," Julia said quickly, as if she wanted to get the focus off herself.

He didn't believe her. She didn't seem to be the kind of woman who would fake an injury to get attention. Yet he also knew sprains didn't take long to heal, not with being a *lupus garou*. In due course she *would* be fine.

"Did you sustain any injuries, Miss Baquero?" Ian asked.

"Backache, sprained wrist. Nothing that won't go away soon."

"Do you have anything for pain?" He asked because they had said they'd lost everything in the car.

"We'll be fine." Then Maria queried about the castle—when it was built and who all had lived there, and Duncan gave her a few agreed-upon details.

Ian didn't listen, as absorbed as he was in everything about Julia, the feel of her thigh pressed against his, all heat and softness, and the scent of her, sweet and feminine and tantalizingly teasing.

"Are you coming to the meeting tonight?" he asked Julia.

Julia's gaze riveted on him, her half-shuttered eyes widening, her heartbeat quickening.

"The meeting that Maria said she was coming to with some of the other film staff," he further explained when her luscious lips parted, but she didn't say anything.

"Oh, yes, of course," she belatedly answered.

Maybe she was just so tired that she wasn't registering what he was saying. Or maybe her ankle was hurting too much for her to think straight. So he asked the next thing on his mind. And *that* got a swift reaction. "Are you mated?"

Her jaw dropped. The conversation in the front seat instantly died.

Too many heartbeats passed, and he realized she might be getting the wrong impression from his query. "It's a simple question, lass." Again, he sounded gruffer than he intended. "I wondered if either of you were mated, and if so, why your mates wouldn't be here with you."

Her lips thinned a bit, and she crossed her arms at her waist. "No, neither of us is mated. And if we were, we'd still do our jobs. Our mates would not have to chaperone us."

"If you were *mine*, I wouldn't want you traipsing around a foreign country on your own. Too many *wolves* about." At the last, he gave her a hint of a smile.

To his way of thinking, the little wolf was fair game.

Ian MacNeill was a wolf. A wolf disguised as a Scottish laird. None of the peerage charts had said anything about titled lords having werewolf roots, so unless one were to encounter a *lupus garou* laird in person, it would be impossible to know if he or she was one.

Julia knew she'd get the devil of a lecture from Maria about the name *Jones*. What could she have done? She didn't want Ian to know that she was Julia Wildthorn, romance writer. And not only a romance writer, but one who wrote about werewolves. Although her stories were a mix of werewolf lore and reality, and not strictly based on their own kind. She'd be in trouble if she did that. Still, she did get some flak from *lupus garous* who didn't like that she wrote werewolf romances, period. The majority of werewolves who read her stories loved them, though. She imagined Laird Ian MacNeill would not be one of those.

Never in a million years had she considered that she'd ever meet the laird personally or that he'd be one of her kind, let alone have to give her name to him or anyone else in his clan.

If Ian knew her pen name, he might realize she wasn't here to work on the film but to write her latest story about Argent Castle and Ian and his people. Not that she wouldn't disguise the location and the people's names, but essentially, the story *would be* about the location and his people. She was certain he wouldn't want to encourage that.

What shocked her most was Ian asking if she was mated. Adding that he wondered about both of the women—and only because he thought they shouldn't be here without their mates—was a total crock. The small smile on his brother's lips confirmed that she was right in her assumption.

Maria cast a look over her seat back, her expression one of butter-him-up-or-else. Did Maria think Julia should be super-nice to the Scottish hunk whose leg was pressed indecently against hers—although she had to admit the backseat was incredibly small for his long legs and he had nowhere else to stretch them? That Julia should encourage some kind of intimacy with him just to get on his good side so Maria would have an easier time during the filming of the production? Or maybe to make amends to Maria since Julia had already caused a situation by using a fake name and catching Maria off guard?

Julia sighed, pressed her leg against Ian's a little more, and smiled at him. Her smile was faked, but his wasn't. He seemed more amused than anything. Even so, his eyes darkened fractionally.

And what eyes they were—beautiful rich brown with golden flecks of amber; intuitive, perceptive, way too observant. With the heat on in the car, the silk shell she was wearing had dried, but his gaze slid to it anyway, and she wondered if it was still as revealing as when it had been wet and clinging to her breasts. Then she thought of Ian's photo in her pocket, and she blushed.

Now she wished she'd had the photo in her pants pocket, although with sitting, she probably would have wrinkled it. Even wet, it might be ruined. That would be a disappointment. Using his picture for visual stimulation would help her to write his description as her next hero.

"What of your pack?" Ian asked Julia out of nowhere.

She waited a heartbeat, expecting, hoping that Maria would answer by filling him in on *her* pack—large, with complicated dynamics, just like a real wolf pack often was—so Julia didn't have to talk about her own. But this time Maria said nothing. With Ian running a clan and a pack, Julia imagined he had a large number of people to supervise. She figured he'd think her family insignificant, unworthy of being called a pack.

"It's just my father and grandfather and me," Julia said, brushing her hands down her wet pants legs in a nervous little gesture.

Ian frowned.

She let out her breath. This is why she hated mentioning it to anyone—well, of their wolf kind. "My mother and my paternal grandmother died when I was little. My father and his father never remated. My mother's parents died much earlier on. I had no siblings."

"I'm sorry to hear about your losses. I lost my da and grandparents some years ago. Your grandfather is the pack leader? Or has he stepped down?"

"Neither. We don't…" She cleared her throat. Others didn't understand their pack dynamics. It wasn't really a pack, in truth, but a family. They helped each other, giving advice to each other. Sometimes her father was in charge, sometimes her grandfather, and sometimes even Julia—usually when her father and grandfather were feeling under the weather and she was there to help them get well. It was their way. No jostling to be the alpha leader. Each had his or her own job to do. They were all headstrong alphas so they just lived as a family. Although she had a place of her own. "We are a family."

"Family." He stroked his chin a couple of times and then leaned back against the seat. "No pack." He said the words to himself, making her think he had come to a conclusion about her family but wasn't letting her in on it. "I'm sorry I'm taking up so much room in the backseat," Ian remarked, stretching and pressing further against her leg, muscled, hard, and hot.

She thought this time he rubbed against her because he was feeling cramped, but the heat still sizzled between them. She should have watched the scenery, gathering notes for her story, but his leg pressed against hers thoroughly distracted her. She assumed the reason he hadn't sat up front where he would have had more leg room was he was as intrigued with her as she was with him. If she'd been perfectly human, he might have taken her to his castle for a little fun, if she'd been willing.

Duncan glanced up at the rearview mirror again. Julia's cheeks were flushed with heat, and she said to Ian, attempting to pretend she wasn't enjoying his touch as much as she was, "It won't be much farther, will it?"

Ian raised his brows almost imperceptibly, a movement as barely noticeable as the smile on his lips. "Not much farther, but with the fog..." His words trailed off, and she swore Duncan took his foot off the gas and slowed down a bit more.

The brothers were in collusion, which warned her that pack ties were a real force to be reckoned with.

When Duncan parked at the cottage nestled in the woods a few minutes later, Julia sighed with relief, feeling an overwhelming need to get away from the man who could uncover her secrets. The cottage was small and cheery with a stone chimney clinging to one outside wall and a burgundy-red door inviting them in, a small window on either side of it covered in lace curtains.

Usually totally independent, Julia intended to leave Ian's car under her own power. She had to hide a smile, though, when the poor man struggled to unfold himself from the cramped backseat of the car. But then Maria stood in front of Julia's door, barricading her in and waiting for Ian to carry Julia inside the cottage.

Traitor. Julia was certain Maria was encouraging a relationship between Ian and her so that he'd be nicer about the logistics during the filming. As if Ian would agree to do anything other than what he had already approved.

She gave Maria a disgruntled look. Maria gave her a smug smile back.

Ian finally got himself out of the damnable backseat of his car, vowing never to ride in it again, even if an enticing female wolf sat back there.

"Do you have the keys to the place?" Ian asked Maria, who was blocking Julia's car door.

"We don't have any." Maria moved out of his way so Ian could get to the rear car door. "Chad, a man who runs errands for us, is bringing our suitcases and keys by. Since we're late, he might have already been here and left the door unlocked for us."

"If not, Duncan can manage it," Ian said, opening the car door for Julia.

Her lips were again compressed, luscious, rosy, annoyed. "I can walk."

"Aye, lass, but it would take too long." He gathered her in his arms and was reminded of how soft and warm and delectable the woman was. He wished the distance from the car to the cottage would have afforded a longer walk. Even so, he shortened his normally lengthy stride.

As soon as they were inside, Ian carried Julia to the sofa in the small living area. The room was also furnished with two cushioned chairs wearing green-and-blue plaid, an old oak coffee table, and a cold fireplace against one wall. The furniture was old-world and re-upholstered, a throw blanket resting on top of the sofa, but otherwise the interior of the cottage looked very much the same as when one of his cousins had lived there seventy years earlier.

Before anyone could say or do anything, partly because they all seemed to be looking to him for his say, which was the way he preferred it anyway, he said, "Duncan, take Maria to the market. They have no money, food, or transportation. She can pick up whatever they need."

"Aye," Duncan said.

Maria gave Julia a wee smile.

Ian got the impression Maria thought they might have special privileges if Julia played the game right. Julia looked worried, on the other hand. He wondered just what was going on in that pretty head of hers.

Duncan waited for Maria to leave the cottage and then shut the door. Ian's gaze slid over Julia, rumpled, hair still wet in curls, damp trousers still hugging her shapely legs, chill bumps covering her arms that were crossed tightly under her breasts, her nipples puckered against her silk sleeveless top.

She was still watching the door as if she hoped Maria would decide to return and stay. She finally said to Ian, "Thank you for bringing us here and for everything else."

He gave her a nod. He couldn't say it was his pleasure because he wanted to douse this unfathomable urge to get to know her better now. He kept telling himself he only needed to determine the essentials: who she really was, what was she doing here, and whose picture was in her pocket.

As much as he didn't want to admit it, he did wonder if Basil Sutherland, his archenemy, had anything to do with her being here. Basil was always trying some damnable way to breach Ian's castle walls and create a problem for him or his people. The cur had never tried sending an attractive female *lupus garou* before, but if that was the case, Ian was having a damnable time keeping up his guard.

Breaking loose of the despicable notion that she could be working for his enemy, Ian set about making her more comfortable and hoped to learn more of the truth about her.

He set her on the blanket on the couch. Then he slid a decorative pillow onto the coffee table and, with a gentle touch, slipped off her shoes, lifted her leg, felt her muscle tense, and rested her foot on top of the pillow.

She was watching him, a wolf's wariness reflecting in her eyes. She should be wary. He was certainly wary of her. And damn attracted, which made him doubt his own objectivity.

"An ice pack will help also." He walked into the small kitchen, found a tray of ice cubes in the freezer, and then wrapped a washcloth around a few. When he returned to the living room, Julia's eyes were closed and she was leaning against the sofa back, her breathing light, her breasts slightly rising with every breath she took.

She was beautiful and vulnerable, even available, and if his gut instincts were correct—*bad news*.

He didn't want to disturb her, but he wanted to make sure she wasn't injured all that badly. He set the bag of ice on the table, slid her trouser leg up, and reached up to pull off her stocking.

She stiffened, and he glanced at her. Her mouth had dropped open, but her eyes were shuttered and she looked sleepy. Ready for bed. Which made him think of how she would look in *his* bed.

Concerned his action had hurt her, he asked, "Are you all right, lass?"

"Yes." This time the bite was gone from her words, and she sounded more tired than anything else.

"Aye, well, I'll be sure." He slipped off her mud-spattered, sheer knee-high stocking as she tightened her leg muscle, either bracing for pain or feeling it. Then he set the stocking on the table and considered her ankle, delicate, pale, and fetching.

"Just a little redness, minimal swelling, no discoloration."

"It's been tingling the whole way here in the car. It's healing and feels just fine."

He wasn't sure she could be trusted to tell him the truth about her injury. He slipped off her other shoe and stocking and then considered her clothes, thinking how much she needed to remove them and could use his help. "Your trousers and shirt are damp, and you're shivering."

Her lips lifted a fraction. Even with such a subtle smile, she caused a spark of heat to spiral through him, and he had the most damnable urge to kiss her.

"I should have known you were a wolf," she said, whisper soft, not bluntly as he'd expected.

Unable to help himself, he chuckled.

She quickly added, "I can manage the rest—later—thank you."

He saw her as vulnerable all over again. Not calculating. Not devious. But a woman who worried about his intentions. And she should. He was definitely feeling his wolfish side. What was the matter with him anyway? She was with the film crew, and that should have been enough to deter him.

He glanced at the cold fireplace and then crossed the

floor to it. "I'll start a fire for you, and that'll warm up the place." He broke up some kindling, set it on the fireplace grate, and then lit a match.

"You could have just turned on the heater."

He shrugged. "We use the fireplaces in the castle to warm rooms. Seems less wasteful. The room will take awhile to warm up, no matter what the source of heat. Are you sure I can't help you out of your wet clothes?" He still attempted a serious expression, trying to show he strictly meant business—as in her welfare. Only he was sure it didn't come across that way.

She shook her head.

He put a log on the fire, and once it caught hold, he turned to observe her. Julia's smile was a mixture of sweet sauciness and the devil. Something about her manner appealed, despite the fact he was fighting the feeling.

The fire would warm up the small room nicely after a bit, but she was still shivering, and he thought of a way to heat her right up—in her bedroom, under the covers, naked together, kissing and caressing and hell…

"Could I get you a blanket?"

Duncan would be commenting forever about Ian's acting the nursemaid, if he could see him now. Ian was grateful his younger brother wasn't here.

Julia hesitated to respond. He took that as a yes, even though she was still considering whether to say no or not. But because of the cool cottage, her wet jeans, and the ice pack on her ankle, she couldn't hide that she was cold. "No, it won't be…"

He'd already headed for one of the rooms by the time she finished her sentence.

"…necessary."

But as soon as he walked in, he knew it wasn't her room. The blue bags sitting beside the bed didn't have her scent on them. Maria's, yes. He left the room, gave Julia a small smile as her rounded eyes watched him, and said, "Looks like the man brought your luggage, but yours must be in the other room."

Then he entered the other. Two tapestry bags sat next to the bed. He imagined her sleeping naked in the full-sized bed, the window looking out on the woods in the direction of Argent Castle. If not for the forest and the distance, he could see the cottage from one of the castle towers.

He hastily grabbed a mohair wool blanket folded at the foot of the bed and stalked back to the living area. He attempted a smile to reassure her, when he meant to interrogate her further. To put aside his foolish notion of sharing any intimacy with the little wolf.

Gently, he covered her lap with the blanket and then crouched beside her, making an effort to question her from a less intimidating height. He looked into her green eyes flecked with gold, saw the tension and unknown mysteries in them, and asked, "If I questioned Harold Washburn about a Miss Julia Jones who works for him, what would he say?"

Julia's traitorous heart was pounding as if she were running for her life while Ian crouched beside her. He *had* to have heard it and guessed she was afraid to tell the truth. Even though he attempted not to overawe her, the problem was that the man was inherently intimidating. From his darkened eyes to his husky voice, and the way his gaze shifted to the pocket of her shirt that contained his picture, she recognized both desire and a need for the truth in his expression.

What could she say? She was Julia Wildthorn, and a quick Internet search would expose her royally. Or she could say she was Julia MacPherson, and he'd know nothing about her—unless he knew something about the MacPhersons who had once inhabited Argent Castle. Either could be a disaster.

She could even say she was Iris North, the name she had given to Guthrie MacNeill when she was trying to learn if Argent Castle was a viable option for the film. Or any number of other names. She was a writer, after all. But he wouldn't believe her if she gave another alias, and he couldn't find further information on her to verify it.

Ian's brows lifted a little when she didn't respond quickly enough. She imagined that his pack and clan members probably never kept him waiting. And she'd already managed to keep him waiting several times.

Trying for nonchalant, she shrugged. "Knowing Harold, he probably won't remember who I am."

Ian seemed darkly amused. "I see." His gaze slid down her in a suggestively languorous manner, which had the effect of sending another hot flash spiraling through her already heated body. Sure, on the outside, her skin was chilled, but inside, she was way too aware of him—of his masculine scent and of the way he observed her and touched her and held her gaze. His eyes focused on hers again. "You're muddy and still shivering. I could prepare a hot bath for you."

In surprise, her lips parted. His eyes focused on her

mouth, and she quickly clamped it shut. She had never imagined a Scottish laird would prepare a woman's bath. Or act this interested in a *commoner*—of the American variety.

With a sparkle in his devilishly dark eyes, he clapped his hands on his thighs and nodded. "Then it's decided."

Before she could object, he headed for the bathroom.

Oh… my… God. If Maria thought Julia was going to willingly butter him up, her friend had another thing coming. But Julia had never suspected that she wouldn't have to do a thing to get there.

Even so, she knew this was a horrible mistake.

Giving in to circumstances that she had little control over, Julia closed her eyes and envisioned Laird Ian MacNeill—*in the historical romance she would write*—adding rose petals to her bathwater after the servants carried heated water to the wooden tub in the lady's chamber adjoining the laird's. At first, the laird had not been happy about having the lass forced on him due to a contract drawn up by his da and hers to unite the clans. But now, the notion seemed to intrigue him somewhat.

Before she could envision more of the details for her story in her mind's eye, the sofa gave a little shudder, and her eyes popped open. Ian sat next to her on the couch, his arms folded, watching her. The sofa all of a sudden seemed way too small for the two of them as his leg brushed hers in a heated caress.

"A warm bath will do you a world of good, lass. But I wondered what you'll be doing during the filming."

She loved his brogue. She could soak it up all day long as she listened to the way he rolled his *r*'s and twisted his tongue around in ways she couldn't even imagine, her gaze focused on his sensuous mouth all the while.

He touched a piece of her hair tickling her cheek and moved it behind her ear. "Lass?"

"You asked?"

He chuckled. "Either you're too tired to think straight, having been through too much in the last several hours, or…" He smiled, and the intimation was that she was too wrapped up in him to think clearly. "Water should be ready." He rose from the sofa, and without waiting for her to say she could walk, he scooped her up and headed for the bathroom.

She didn't need blankets or hot baths or anything of the sort to heat her up. His body did the trick—his hot, hard body pressing against hers, his arm securely around her waist, his hand resting beneath her breast, his other arm cupped under her legs. She was feeling incredibly warm.

"It's jet lag," she finally said, looking up at him, her head tilted back, her hair tumbling backward. "You're right. I'm exhausted, and I'm not thinking clearly." It had nothing to do with Ian being an incredibly hunky Highlander. Or that she was imagining the virile warrior wearing a kilt and a sword as he carried her into the bathroom instead of the wet clinging trousers that showed just how hot and sexy and intrigued he was with her.

He hesitated to set her down on the floor or the edge of the bathtub, staring into her eyes as if she had mesmerized him and momentarily made him forget his mission. But then he did the unexpected and set her on the marble sink countertop. She thought he meant to offer to help her further with undressing and intended to quickly decline his generous offer. Instead, he leaned his face down to meet hers and kissed her! Full on the mouth with a sensuous, hot-blooded kiss that would have knocked her stockings off if she'd still been wearing them.

She didn't even object or pull away like she should have done. What would the Scotsman think of American women if she didn't? But she couldn't, not when his lips were caressing hers in such a sexually charged way, warm and soft and needy and in control. *Very* much in control. She loved the feel of his mouth on hers, the desire sparking between them, the heat that chased away the chill.

Enjoying the feel of his masculine lips on hers, she wanted more. She wrapped her hands around his neck and parted her lips just enough to give a hint that she wanted him to deepen the kiss, but not too much to make it seem she was desperate for more. *Even if she was.*

His mouth smiled against hers as his eyes grew smokier with desire. And then he obliged. His hands shifted to her hair, stroking and grasping handfuls as he poked his tongue between her lips, drew her body closer to his, and then pressed deeply into her mouth with his tongue.

She gave as good as she got, shifting her hands from around his neck to his hips and pulling him in even closer, settling him against the heat between her legs. Felt his rigid erection against her. Rolled her tongue around his in a lover's intimate dance.

But he suddenly went very still and then groaned, pulling his mouth from hers. He wanted more. She could tell from the way his body was still pressed against hers, the way he was fighting with himself to let go, and damn if she didn't want him to keep kissing her. A wolf had never kissed her before, and she wondered if it was just Ian or if all wolves were this hot.

He gazed into her eyes, his own filled with lust, his body hard and ready for more, but he cleared his throat and said, "Welcome to Scotland, lass."

That's when she heard the car doors slam outside. He must have heard his brother and Maria drive up while she'd been concentrating too much on the kiss and everything else.

Then he moved her to the edge of the bathtub and said, "I'll leave you to your bath, unless you need any further help." He smiled and gave her the sexiest wink that a man had ever given her, and in that instant, heat suffused every pore all over again.

Before he moved away from her, she heard Duncan speaking loudly at the front door, alerting Ian, she figured, that he and Maria had returned in case Ian was too busy to hear them. Duncan probably didn't wish to incur Ian's wrath in the event the laird wasn't through with his "business" with Julia.

Ian shut the bathroom door as the front door opened.

A moment of silence followed, and Julia could imagine Duncan and Maria quickly drawing their own conclusions as to what had occurred between Ian and her in the bathroom.

Maria finally broke the silence. "Thanks so much for helping us out. We'll repay you as soon as we can get some—"

"No need," Ian said, dismissing her comment. "We'll be expecting you and your staff later." He was officious and curt, to the point, and then the front door shut, leaving Julia and Maria alone.

Julia wondered then if he felt he'd made a terrible mistake in kissing her, like she was feeling. Not that she didn't like it or hadn't wanted it to last a whole hell of a lot longer, but what had she been thinking? This was not the way to conduct her covert missions.

She rose gingerly from the edge of the tub, tested her foot on the tile floor, which felt fine, and then hurried to strip and plunge into the bath for a quick cleanup.

"Are you all right in there?" Maria asked, sounding more than curious.

"Just washing some of the mud off. Be out in a second so you can get cleaned up for your meeting."

Maria didn't budge from outside the door.

"Nothing happened," Julia assured her. Then she frowned. "Nothing happened between you and Duncan, did it?"

"Did you think either of the women was the same as the wolf we smelled near the car accident?" Duncan asked Ian as he drove them the two kilometers to Argent Castle, although the trek through the woods was closer to a kilometer.

"*You* smelled a wolf," Ian corrected. "I couldn't catch the scent of a wolf at all, not with the smoke from the burning vehicle clouding my senses. After that, the rain washed away any scent of wolf."

"You didn't know that they were wolves when you saw them in the pub?"

Ian shook his head. "You know how pungent Scott's

onion-and-garlic burgers are. The women weren't close enough for me to smell them."

Duncan's brows furrowed as he glanced at Ian. "You didn't join the women at their table?"

"They appeared afraid of me."

Duncan grunted. "Whatever for? We were trying to help them."

"We were chasing them through the woods. They didn't believe we were there to help them. Besides, they work for Sunset Productions. No matter whatever else they are, they're bad news." Although, Ian couldn't quash the urge to get to know the redhead better. After kissing her and the way she'd responded, he had an even greater desire to do so.

"That's why we took them to the cottage?" Duncan asked with a lifted brow. "Why we got them food and you drew a bath for Julia?"

"We were on our way back to Argent," Ian reminded him. "Besides, MacNamara hadn't finished his business at the pub. And the women needed food."

Duncan gave Ian a critical look. "Admit it, Ian. You drank your whisky *and* mine so we could catch up to MacNamara and take the women off his hands because you're intrigued with the redheaded lass."

With no intention of responding to his youngest brother's claim, Ian asked, "Did you think the wolf you smelled was one of these women?"

"I don't believe so. And one of our own people wouldn't have been running as a wolf, or I would have recognized the scent."

Most likely it wouldn't have been one of Ian's own people anyway, not after he had warned them not to run as wolves until the film crew was gone. If it wasn't the women and it wasn't someone from his own pack, someone else had to be trespassing on his lands again.

Only one wolf or pack came to mind. "Basil Sutherland or one of his men." The long-running feud between Sutherland's clan and Ian's had been going on for centuries, although the MacNeills hadn't encountered any recent difficulty with the Sutherlands until the previous month at the Celtic festival.

"Aye, that mess with them over the sword-fighting demonstration could have caused real trouble. He's asking for an all-out war, Ian. I keep telling you that."

"If one of Sutherland's men was trespassing, why now?"

"What if in an effort to get back at us, Sutherland or his men are targeting the women because he knew they were *lupus garous* and with the film crew and that you would take an interest in protecting them?"

Or what if Julia whatever-her-last-name-really-was served as one of Sutherland's spies—a way for him to get one of his people into Ian's castle on some devious mission?

So why did he want to take her back to the castle, lock her in his chambers, and kiss her again, only this time into telling him the truth?

Chapter 4

WITH THE JET LAG AND THE CAR ACCIDENT, JULIA WAS exhausted. But she also had a mission that wouldn't wait. She washed, carefully climbed out of the bath, again testing her foot on the floor, and found her ankle only bothered her slightly. She grabbed a towel and wrapped it around herself, too revved up for what she had to do next to lie around the cottage.

"Well, Maria? Anything going on between you and Duncan?" Julia asked again.

Maria didn't answer her, but Julia heard the kitchen sink running.

The running water set her thinking about Ian MacNeill, the bath he'd drawn, and the way he'd challenged her with his hot-blooded gaze, like the devil in a once-white, rain-soaked button-down shirt and muddy khaki trousers. That brought to mind how his wet clothes had stuck to his skin, outlining various muscle groups—legs, chest, arms—and even giving a hint of how well endowed he was. Which, of course she had noticed, taking mental notes for her new Highland story. Forget bare-assed in a kilt. The wet khakis were more than intriguing. Because of the way he'd stared at her clothes, just as revealing as his own, she hadn't felt any guilt in checking out his wares.

And that kiss? She was ready to spill all her secrets and even make some up if he'd just keep kissing her.

She was hopeless and would never make it as a secret agent. Unless kissing someone as hot as Ian was part of her cover. But she feared he'd learn the truth about her in short order then. How could she be so dumb? Lusting after the laird of the castle was definitely not in the plans.

Julia headed into the bedroom. Her tapestry floral suitcases sat on a full-sized bed clothed in a forest-green bedspread and next to a light-oak bachelor chest. A matching side table and a brass lamp sat on the other side. The walls were covered in floral flocked paper, and on one of them hung two pictures, one of a waterfall and the other, a tree-lined lake with mountains rising into the sky to meet fluffy, white clouds. Both of which she'd love to see in person.

She pushed aside the green velvetlike drapes on the room's small window and peeked out to see the piney woods. She could almost smell them through the closed window.

Unzipping her suitcase, she thought about how she had nearly stumbled over Ian's mud-caked suede boots when she and Maria had hastily left the pub. The boots had to have been his because they hadn't been there when she and Maria had first entered the pub.

Which brought her back to the way his darkened eyes had admired her. God, he was gorgeous. Even more gorgeous up close, sitting a few tables away from her. Just the hint of a smile on his lips had turned her insides to jelly. She'd forgotten her ankle, the other men in the room, the American waitress, even that Maria was warily watching her and that Ian was not the kind of man who would be interested in her—mainly because she was with the odious film crew.

Yet Julia thought he might, in that moment, have forgotten that she was with the film crew.

Despite how good he looked in rain-soaked clothes, she thought about him wearing a kilt like in the photo. Since she had to transform him into a historical Highland hero, perfect for her book, modern-day trousers wouldn't do.

He had the dark look and the aristocratic air of a titled laird—although the fact he'd left his muddy shoes outside countered his being totally arrogant—and he was in charge. She could see that in the way the other men had greeted him. Something unwritten was being observed. As if they had to watch themselves until he left. Or maybe just until she and Maria had left. She wished she could have been the proverbial fly on the wall and observed his interaction with the men after Maria and she had exited the pub.

She threw on her sleuthing clothes—a pair of olive-green jeans and a matching cashmere sweater—and then sat on her bed and braided her wet hair.

Most telling was the way MacNamara had reacted to Ian. At first, MacNamara had wanted to take her and Maria to their cottage without reservation, even saying no to the other men in a lighthearted way when they all offered with too much exuberance. But the towering Scot had seemed to need Laird Ian MacNeill's permission once he arrived. If only she could watch the way Ian interacted further with others, she'd have half her story written.

But what she hadn't counted on was for Ian to actually come up behind them, scaring the daylights out of her and sweeping her up in his arms to spirit her away

to his car and take her and Maria to their cottage. That
had her heart tripping.

He had known she was not who she said she was
as soon as she'd given that damned fake name. She'd
expected him to question her about it as soon as he sent
his brother with Maria to get groceries. But he didn't
question her further about that, which hadn't alleviated
her concern one iota. He was like a wolf with its quarry.

She couldn't believe she'd fallen asleep while Ian
had been getting the ice pack for her, either. She figured she'd use it a little longer before Maria left for her
meeting And then? Julia would be off looking for secret
entrances to the castle.

"Julia *Jones*?" Maria said, standing in her open doorway and startling Julia from her thoughts. "Why in the
world would you make up an alias?"

"You know what I write for a living." Julia sighed,
then rose from the bed, moved past Maria, and made her
way to the couch.

"I couldn't believe he'd ask if you were mated."

"He asked about both of us," Julia reminded her, as
she sat down on the sofa, propped her foot on the pillow,
and covered her ankle with the melting ice pack.

"Yeah, well he was only interested in whether *you*
are mated or not. If you're trying to keep a low profile,
it's not working. You've already got the attention of the
laird and at least one of his brothers. Really not good.
So what exactly happened between you and the laird?"

"Nothing."

Maria gave a snort of laughter. "Right. You look
guilty as hell. And here he goes and draws you a bath?
It could work well if you play your cards right. But if

you don't..." She paused. "What are you going to do while I'm seeing Harold?" The slight censure in Maria's voice warned Julia that her friend knew she would be up to something—probably something Maria wouldn't approve of.

Before Julia could respond, Maria folded her arms. "You're not going to stay at the cottage and unpack your bags, are you? Despite your ankle being sprained, I know you won't wait for my return. Like you should."

"My ankle isn't swollen, and resting it made it feel better." Julia pulled off the ice pack and considered her ankle. "No bruising. If I take it easy, it'll be fine. I want to start writing the details for the book while the castle is still quiet and not filled with the film crew. I won't be here all that long."

"You have no ulterior motive?"

Feigning innocence, Julia smiled, but her heart did a flip just the same. Julia's own guilty conscience was enough to increase her heart rate at hearing the question. She didn't want Maria to know what she was up to. What if Julia got caught? As it was, if Maria was questioned, she could honestly say she didn't know a thing about Julia's secret mission.

"Now what ulterior motive would that be, other than taking a walk around the castle to research some details for my current work in progress when nobody's about?" Julia asked.

Maria jammed her hands into the pockets of her still damp pants. "Your recommendation that we use Ian MacNeill's castle wasn't because of some more personal interest, was it?"

"Personal interest?" Julia's voice sounded a little too guilty, and she was afraid Maria would recognize that at once. Did she think Julia had some plan to snag Ian MacNeill for a mate? She hadn't even known he was a wolf. "You made it possible for me to get a chance to see the inside of a castle that is never open to the public so I can use it in my story."

If Maria really knew this had to do with Julia's family history and taking back what belonged to her family, Maria probably would not have agreed to bring her along.

Julia lifted a shoulder. "I researched it first. Then I called a Guthrie MacNeill, who handles the financial ins and outs of the family castle, lands, and businesses, and he was thrilled."

Thrilled really wasn't the way she'd describe Guthrie's enthusiasm. More guarded, thinking at first she was a nutcase, Julia assumed. And then reservedly interested, as if he had his sword out and was ready to fight if the enemy turned on him.

"Thrilled? He was pretty hard-nosed about how much they wanted, and we went back and forth with him for months. He nearly delayed the production. Guthrie said an Iris North had spoken to him and told him to get in touch with me." Maria raised a brow at Julia. "I figured he'd say a Julia Wildthorn had spoken to him. It took me aback, until I figured out you'd used an alias."

"I didn't want them hearing my 'Julia Wildthorn' name and realizing, if they discovered I was an author, that I might be trying to write about the off-limits parts of their castle, even though in my story the name and location will be masked." Hoping that would satisfy Maria's curiosity, Julia smiled broadly.

"And now he thinks you're Julia Jones. Or did you tell him the truth while I was with Duncan?"

"No, we didn't discuss it. Wildthorn is my pen name. A red name. It suits my books. Iris North was a made-up name also."

"I thought Julia Wildthorn was your real name." Maria sounded surprised.

"Everyone knows me as Julia Wildthorn. I identify with the name. It's really Julia MacPherson. But that was in the past and I never use it, ever. It's just easier that way."

"MacPherson is a Scottish name," Maria said, her tone indicating she still thought Julia was being devious about something more. "This has nothing to do with the MacNeills or their castle or anything. No old-time clan feuds, right?"

Julia bit her lip. Omission was one thing. Out-and-out lying, another. "My MacPherson family lived in the castle at one time."

Maria stared at her goggle-eyed. "Are you *serious*? So they actually *owned* it?"

"Lived there, like guests." Not really guests, though, Julia didn't think. Not from the way her grandfather sounded so cryptic. Not knowing what the situation really was, she was unable to hide her exasperation. "It's no big deal."

"You want to write about something that's more historically accurate? About your family having lived there?"

"Well, yes." In a way Julia did—it added more realism. She thought Maria was finished with the interrogation, but her friend continued to quiz her as she moved quickly about the place, looking for something. "Are you sure your family hadn't taken over the castle at some point, which I think is incredibly cool, and they truly owned it? At least for a brief time?"

"No, my family didn't own the castle." As far as Julia knew.

"What if you had some claim to it? We could move in and open the place up for tours."

Julia gave her an incredulous laugh. "Yeah, right. If my family had owned the place, they would still be running things. And probably would have to put up with a crew filming a movie here like the MacNeills. But no, it's nothing like that."

In the kitchen, Maria said, "I found the phone." Maria began speaking but not to her. "Hello, Chad? We're here. You called the police about the car? The car rental company, too? Yes, I'll talk to them tonight. You're an angel. Can you come and get me? Ten minutes? Thanks for bringing the bags by and getting the keys to the place for us. See you in a few."

Maria hung up the phone and rushed to the bathroom, peeling off her wet, muddy clothes as she went. "Something is in the castle that your family wants you to steal back. What is it, and what is its importance?"

In disbelief, Julia stared at Maria's retreating backside. "How could you have possibly known?"

"Remember the night before we left on this trip when you told me to check movie times on your computer? You were making us chicken rice soup, and you wanted to go see that Scottish time travel."

Julia had a sinking feeling she'd left something on the computer she shouldn't have. Maria had dropped in earlier than Julia had expected, so she'd forgotten what she'd been doing.

"I remember."

The shower began running. Maria hollered over the rush of water, "Your email was open to a note from your grandfather. I wouldn't have read it, but the MacNeill name and reference to his castle caught my attention. Your grandfather said he wanted you to retrieve something from within the castle. He didn't say he wanted you to ask the MacNeills for it. So I assumed he wanted you to steal it."

Julia shook her head and returned to her bedroom to get her socks and boots. "You turned off the computer so I forgot what I'd been doing before you arrived."

"You told me to turn it off because we were rushed to see the earlier showing of the movie. So what *are* you supposed to retrieve?"

"Thanks for being a friend, Maria, and for not trying to stop me from doing this." Julia felt sheepish that she hadn't trusted Maria beforehand.

The shower shut off, and Maria exited the bathroom, wearing a blue towel. "Are you kidding? You're the most interesting person I know. If you're not rappelling off a building to see how it's done for one of your books, you're learning to shoot a gun for another. Now it's searching for a hidden treasure in the MacNeill stronghold filled with brawny Scots who will thwart you in any way they can. It'll make for a great story *if* you don't get caught. Maybe even better if you do get caught. So what is it you'll be looking for, exactly?"

"It's a rosewood box engraved with the symbol of a thistle, the Celtic knot, and the name Artur MacPherson.

None of my family members were able to return to the castle after they left it in haste, from what my grandfather said. They have tried with various ruses over the years, but the place has been sealed tight with no one allowed in except the MacNeills or their kin or close friends. Before my grandfather dies, he wants me to retrieve the box and return it to the family."

At least that's what her grandfather had said. But something really worried him about that box. He'd been so adamant and just as concerned as her father that she locate it and bring it home. Why now? Why after so many years of trying to get back in and not succeeding? Why not leave it buried in the castle walls?

It was locked, he had warned her. She wasn't to break the lock. But a niggling of untruth plagued her. What was in the box that she was to risk sneaking into the castle and locating it, and then return it unopened to her grandfather?

Pandora's box came to mind.

"They left the castle in haste? This gets better and better." Maria entered Julia's bedroom. "So what's in the box? Maybe a claim to the estate?"

Julia only wished she knew. "I'm sure my grandfather or father would have said. And I'm sure once a family abandons a castle to another, if that was the case, we'd have no claim to it anyway."

Julia sat on her bed and pulled on her socks, then her boots.

"You're probably right, but... if the MacNeills have lived here since your family vacated it, wouldn't they have found the box already? Disposed of the contents, most likely?"

"It's hidden. Or at least it was." If it was valuable, the MacNeills might have hung onto it. But what worried Julia more was whether or not the box contained information that could be used against her family. So many years had passed. What information could possibly be of importance any longer?

All ready to go sleuthing, Julia collapsed on the green tweed sofa again, eager for Maria to leave so she could run off.

Wearing a more casual hot-pink wool sweater and black jeans, Maria whirled out of the bedroom and met Julia in the living area. "A secret niche? You can't be serious. If I wasn't so afraid of losing my job or had more nerve, I'd go with you. But still... I don't think you should be doing this."

"I'm just going to take a walk around. No one will see me. I'll be sure of it."

Maria didn't look convinced. "Laird MacNeill said he didn't want anyone roaming around the property without his permission. And we kind of have an in now. We don't want to ruin that."

"I'll be in the woods outside the castle, not inside." Unless Julia located the secret tunnels her grandfather had mentioned. Although he'd said the place had been too well defended in earlier years for them to try to get back in that way, and in more recent years, they hadn't been successful with a couple of quick tries to locate the tunnel entrance. A lone female might do the trick.

"Around the perimeter or within the castle—the place is off-limits unless Laird MacNeill gives us permission." Maria gave Julia a critical look. "Just because he dropped us off at the cottage, he still might not make any concessions for us. Although you can't tell me there's nothing going on between the two of you. The air practically sizzles with the way he looks at you. Don't think I didn't notice the interest you've shown him in return."

"He got me an ice pack, nothing else. Well, started the bath. Don't read anything more into it than that. He was just being nice. All right?" What Julia didn't say was how much she suspected Ian didn't trust her one bit and that was all his interest in her. Keep your friends close and your enemies closer—wasn't that the old adage?

Maria motioned to the fireplace crackling with heat. "He started a hot, little fire—probably more than the one in the fireplace. Grabbed a blanket from your bedroom. I imagine he removed your heels and stockings, and no telling what else he would have removed if you'd been agreeable. I'll bet he also carried you into the bathroom, or he wouldn't have been leaving it when we arrived."

Julia's face heated. She was not about to tell Maria that Ian had kissed her in a way that she'd remember forever. Her ex-boyfriend had never come close to setting her on fire the way Ian had.

Maria's brows rose. "He offered to remove your clothes, didn't he?" She laughed. "If we'd had any food, he probably would have fixed you something to eat."

"He's a laird. He probably doesn't know how to cook. But I'll be careful. Like a wolf in stealth mode."

Maria's dark brows rose, and her worried look returned. "You're not going as a wolf, are you?"

"No." *Not at first*. Unless Julia could locate the secret entrance easier that way. "What did you think of Duncan MacNeill?"

"He's one to watch. Quiet and lethal. As for Laird MacNeill, after Harold took one look at that photo of him, Harold summed him up in four little words, '*Bad to the bone*.'"

"Yeah." Julia thought of Ian's image in the photo and of him sitting in the pub. He'd had the same cool look as he did in the photo, his eyes hauntingly perceptive. And he appeared to be in charge, even miles from his castle. How far did his sphere of influence reach? Why didn't he have an entourage? She imagined a laird would have lots of people tagging along with him everywhere he went, trying to get on his good side, wanting favors. Maybe it didn't work that way in this day and age.

Ian looked to be around thirty or so, maybe a little older. Not old enough to be so obstinate about not wanting to film at the castle, so set in his ways and not liking change.

"Maybe we can deal with someone else." Because despite what Maria might think about Ian and her, Julia knew he was wary of her. Maybe she could make some inroads into her project by soliciting one of his lackeys, if she could make friends with someone who could get her inside the castle.

Yet her thoughts flashed back to Ian's expression, his assessing looks, and his dark eyes watching her, studying her, and perhaps attempting intimidation. She wasn't easily intimidated. But she had the feeling that sneaking around him wouldn't be an easy task.

"Don't count on it. He's the laird and in charge. Even though I spoke to Guthrie MacNeill, he was only the go-between. Ian is definitely ruling the roost. And hell, I'd say you made a pretty good start on getting his

attention anyway." Maria let out her breath and favored
her left wrist. "I know you're going to the MacNeills'
castle after I leave. Nothing I say is going to convince
you not to. You could really screw this up, you know.
If you get arrested—"

"I'll plead I was a dumb American who got separated
from the film crew on the way to the meeting and got
lost." Apparently Maria didn't have much confidence
that Julia could slip in and out of places without detection like a master thief.

Then again, attempting to sneak into the underbelly
of a castle was a new experience for Julia, so Maria's
concern wasn't totally unfounded.

"You don't think that when they drag your bones in
front of the laird of the castle, he won't figure something
else was up?"

A horn honked out front. Julia followed Maria outside and waved at Chad. He was the fetch-it guy, a surfer
type with sun-streaked blond hair. Young and thrilled to
be here, he smiled and waved back at Julia as Maria got
into the car.

As Chad backed out of the drive, Julia waved at
Maria, smiling cheerfully in an effort to assure her ev-
erything would be all right. Maria just shook her head at
Julia, full lips thinned in a grim line.

Julia had no plan to get caught during her clandestine
mission, but she wasn't about to wait around until tomorrow to try and slip inside, either.

Chapter 5

JULIA GRABBED HER KEY TO THE COTTAGE AND LOCKED the door, ready to storm Argent Castle in a surreptitious way.

Already having gotten used to being in the dry cottage, she felt the cool mist lying thickly all over the area and was reminded of the car wreck and her subsequent fear of being followed. And of being injured. Her ankle bothered her just a hint, but she shoved the notion out of her mind and walked at a quickened pace through the ancient Caledonian Forest that linked Ian MacNeill's castle and the cottage where she was staying.

The forest was like a tie to the past where time seemed to stand still. She envisioned an ancestor of Laird MacNeill, with his men wearing kilts and equipped with bows and quivers of arrows, hunting in these very woods on horseback for deer or wild boar.

Moving at a steady pace, she soon warmed up a bit. But she was getting wetter and wetter, her sweater and jeans soaking up the light, misty rain like a thirsty sponge. She'd considered wearing a jacket, but the fewer clothes the better if she was going to shape-shift. Thankfully, the boots supported her ankles and pine needles cushioned the ground, so except for a gnawing worry that she'd twist her right ankle again, it felt fine for now.

Scots pines towered overhead, the fragrance of pine sap reminding her of Christmas and hiking through northwestern California forests, and the sweet, strong scent of juniper also wafted in the cool dampness. Coming from the direction of the castle, muffled Scottish voices with their distinctive, pleasing burr garnered her attention, and she stopped walking to consider her surroundings. She imagined that the people speaking were within the castle walls, in the bailey, outer or inner, and that no one would imagine a trespasser nearing their domain.

With no known predators in the area—as far as animals that might endanger humans—and no humans wandering about, she felt safe in the woods. She was alone except for a couple of Scottish crossbills feeding on pinecone seeds, one a red male with dark wings and tail feathers, and a couple of others calling excitedly to one another and sounding like they were speaking with a Scottish accent.

The cocky trill of a crested tit added to the forest sounds, and she looked up to see the perky bird sitting on the dead stump of a pine, the feathers on his crown standing straight up like a Mohawk haircut. A golden-ringed dragonfly flittered beside her and vanished, and butterflies fluttered about.

The feeling that she was in primeval woods, transported to the long-distant past, made her imagination run free. She envisioned a clan chief's daughter dashing away from an enemy clan, seeking shelter in the castle beyond the woods, and praying she'd reach it before she was caught.

But places like this that seemed unspoiled and serene now could have harbored dangerous men throughout the ages, creating a perilous situation for any who passed through the area. Or clans who fought with one another, and if her envisioned chief's daughter had been from the enemy clan, she'd be in deadly trouble.

She patted her pocket where the script map, a hasty sketch that her grandfather had drawn from memory and given her, *had* been. She'd taken it out and left it back at the cottage, in case she was detained for trespassing and searched. What would they make of the map? Maybe that she knew where the secret entrance was and planned to break in. That's why she'd left it back at the cottage.

Only now she couldn't remember exactly where her grandfather had thought the entrance was. She stalked toward the castle walls to get her bearing but kept to the woods. At the easternmost corner tower, she would skirt around it to the eastern wall. Somewhere along there at the edge of the woods the hidden entrance was located.

Like the mob of curly, white sheep suddenly appearing before Maria and her on the road, the castle unexpectedly loomed across a moat through the screen of trees in which she now stood. Her jaw dropped. The golden sandstone castle walls and the castle inside were spectacular, overwhelming, and impressive, the very tops of the towers disappearing into the fog and giving the illusion they reached for the very heavens.

She glanced to the east, saw the round easternmost tower, and headed deeper into the woods to stay out of sight. But when she finally reached the area along the eastern wall, she could find no sign of a secret entrance. Maybe as a wolf she could locate it with her nose to the ground, smelling any traces of human wanderings or, better than that, any hint of an underground tunnel system by the cooler air seeping out of the edges of a trapdoor or the dampness within an earthen dwelling by its cavelike musty smell. The other option was locating the postern gate, or back door to the castle—the one that had been used by pedestrians or tradesmen and was located on the south side. If she could discover it, that might be an easier way to enter.

Even if she'd had a written invitation to explore every square inch of the castle—which she didn't and knew wasn't forthcoming—she felt driven to find a more covert way in. She imagined that was due to her innate sense of adventure, her family's ties to the land, and her unconquerable imagination, which dreamed up worlds of romance, mystery, suspense, and adventure.

This *was* the ultimate adventure.

Truth be told, no way was she going to get an invitation inside the castle. Beyond that, no one would give her blanket permission to search for the hidden cache her family left there centuries earlier.

With her heart beating hard from the exercise and her rush to avoid being caught if someone *was* hiking through the forest, she traversed the area, back and forth, searching, looking for any sign of something out of place, an indication that a hidden entrance into the castle was here somewhere. If she could find the secret entrance, and it was still a viable way into the tunnels underneath the moat and castle walls, she'd have a better chance at exploring the place without detection. She thought.

Listening for sounds of humans in the vicinity, she still heard none.

She sighed. Time to shape-shift because she'd never get anywhere with her search as a human. She stripped off her clothes, buried them as best she could under leaves and pine needles, welcomed the heat that pervaded every tissue as the change took place, and in a couple of heartbeats, she shifted, the motion fluid, fast, and painless.

As a human, she felt comfortable in the woods; as a wolf, even more so. Except for the worry someone might try to shoot her. But she was lower to the ground and could run faster, and with ears that could twist this way and that, unlike human ears, she could detect where sounds were coming from better. Although in her human form, she still could hear sixteen times better than a human could.

The warm coat of the wolf covered her in fur that not only kept her body heat from escaping but also had long guard hairs that kept the moist air from penetrating. Her wolf's coat was lighter because it was summer and she'd shed her winter coat already, but if she were to stay in these colder temperatures, her coat would grow thicker to accommodate the weather in Scotland.

Nose to the ground, she sniffed the area, wanting to search every square inch of land and find the secret trapdoor, if there was still one, that would lead through underground tunnels and hidden passageways into the keep. To her frustration, she'd searched for probably a good hour and a half and was almost ready to give up. Not wanting to worry Maria, Julia intended to head back to the cottage so she could accompany her and the rest of the staff to meet with the MacNeills.

But first, she wanted to do one last thing—get a look at where the postern gate was located around the rear of the castle. Was it still a viable entrance? Used still? Less fortified and not half as secure as the tower gate in front of the castle? Or was it blocked or, worse, walled up?

Running through the forest still on all four paws, she remained hidden in the shelter of the aspen and Scots pine. She had just made the turn at the southeastern tower when she saw movement on top of the curtain wall. A man had been looking out at the woods with no particular focus, as if admiring the beauty of the forest, but now he quickly shifted his gaze to her.

Ian MacNeill. He was dressed in brown trousers and an ivory polo shirt. He couldn't see her, she didn't think. Not from the height he was at. Not from the distance to the trees. Not with the forest providing a leafy canopy. Or the mist that continued to drape the area in ghostly overtones.

Yet his eyes focused directly on her, his gaze looking straight into hers as if he could see her. Not only her, though, but her eyes, as he locked onto her gaze. But he couldn't see her. She swore he couldn't. Or maybe that was wishful thinking. *Caught* in the act.

He stood so still, gazing so long at her—his lips parted as if he was surprised, every muscle in his body filling with tension, his hands clenched into fists on top of the curtain wall—that she worried he did see her. That he didn't want to scare her away, but that if he could, he'd call up the cavalry and order them to hunt her down.

She didn't dare move, just in case the movement might verify that she was here, although no matter how much she considered that he seemed to see her, she knew he couldn't. It just wasn't physically possible.

But then she reconsidered. He was a wolf. And if she could see him... *damn.*

"Ian, we got a call." A man hollered to him from a long way off, his voice dark and gruff, but Ian didn't break his eye contact with her. She thought it was Duncan's voice. "The producer and some of his staff are on their way."

Julia's breathing suspended. She had to get back, rejoin Maria, and go with her as she and some of the film staff sought audience with the man she was now eyeing. Maria would worry about her—think she'd been caught—that she was in trouble. She had to get back.

But she stood mesmerized as she stared at Ian. His dark hair fluttered in the breeze, his face sculpted in chiseled granite, his jaw taut, and the faint outline of his muscles appearing beneath the shirt that was growing damp in the wet weather. He didn't move from the spot where he was standing, eyeing her with—well, she couldn't tell. Surprise, probably. Annoyance, maybe. A wolf in these woods. *His* woods. Did he realize it was her?

"Ian! Did you hear me?" the other man shouted again.

Ian's lips turned up slightly. That faint curve of his lips did her in. He had to know it was her. "I'm here, Duncan." Ian spoke just as darkly, but his words were softer, more dangerous, and quieter, as if he was afraid he'd scare her away. And he didn't want to chase her away, she assumed. He wanted to hunt her down.

She thought he might briefly turn to acknowledge Duncan, but Ian wouldn't release her gaze, and she couldn't wait, in the event he did tell his younger brother to send hunters to locate her. Plus, she was supposed to be with the film crew who were to meet him soon. Had she taken longer in her search than she had anticipated? Maybe it had been two hours already. She bolted for where she'd left her clothes, intending to shape-shift and then head to the cottage where she hoped Maria still waited for her.

The wind in her fur, and the smell of the cold, misty air and of deer and a fox, made her take in another deep breath. Something intrinsically heavenly about the Highland woodlands appealed to the wolf side of her and to her Scottish roots. The moors, the lakes, the rivers, the waterfalls, the fields of purple heather, and the mountains. The castle, too. It was the place of romance and Highland hunks, just like Ian, who had captured her with his gaze as if he could hold her hostage there forever.

Too bad he could only be a fantasy character in her werewolf romance tales.

Before she reached her clothes, she heard something snap in the woods and stopped dead, her heart thundering as she swung her head around, listening and looking for anyone or anything that might be out here.

Movement in the trees—two men. The two men who had been at the airport. The fairer one who had taken their first rental car. The other, the dark-haired man who had been watching her with too much interest. Too much of a coincidence that they'd be here now. Too much of a coincidence that they were here together.

Were they Ian's men? Or someone else's men? Maybe whoever was responsible for Maria's car accident?

She dashed away, hoping she'd lose them before it was too late.

If Ian MacNeill hadn't seen the red wolf with his own eyes, despite the mist surrounding her and making her appear almost ghostly, he would have thought she was a figment of his own very vivid imagination. Even so, he couldn't help watching her, waiting for her to move, to prove to him she was real and not some ethereal wolf from the past. He'd seen them before. Wolves, no longer really here. Ghosts of the past. Wolves with a history. Not *lupus garous*, but real wolves.

But red wolves had never lived in the area. Grays, yes, the last killed off in the seventeenth or eighteenth century, depending on the source. Red wolves, no. He'd never even seen one before. And red *lupus garous*? Possible, although he had never met one. Was it Julia? Or someone else from the film crew?

Despite telling himself Julia was a *lupus garou* and that wasn't any big deal, he recognized that she wasn't like any female wolf he'd ever known. She fascinated him, by both her actions and her reactions to him. He'd never been so caught up in wanting to know more about a woman. A woman with secrets. With a name that wasn't her own. And with a job that wasn't truly hers?

If the wolf was the woman, her ankle was faring better. But what was she doing roaming around his lands? Out sightseeing? When he'd said in no uncertain terms that no one was allowed to. Newly turned and had to shape-shift quickly? *That* was a dangerous proposition, and she shouldn't be here in unfamiliar woods, risking detection. Or here on this job, period.

He had half a notion to locate her clothes and force her to come to him so he could advise her about his rules once more. That brought another rash of unbidden thoughts to mind. His prisoner. His.

Baird Cottage was not all that far from the castle. It would be easy for her to run as a wolf and show up on his doorstep. But she hadn't come to the front gate. She was sneaking around the eastern wall. What was she attempting to do?

"I'll be up to speak with you in a wee bit," Ian's youngest brother shouted. "They're halfway to the moat." If Duncan hadn't called out to Ian earlier about the film crew, the wolf might have hung around longer.

Not planning to personally deal with the film production staff because he had no need, Ian studied the fog sifting through the stands of aspen, silver birch, and Scots pine surrounding Argent Castle, moving like a silent predator, slipping around them in a white wispy blanket. If his clan had been at battle, the mist couldn't have been more welcome. Every muscle in his body tensed. It felt like battle, just the same.

But what he wanted more than anything was to hunt down the wolf. Her reddish coat was cinnamon in color and the underside of her muzzle a soft white. Her large, red ears had been listening in his direction, twitching as his brother had spoken, and her tail tipped in black ink had been held straight out, not moving a centimeter. The wolf was definitely a female, smaller and more slender in build than a male.

If the film crew's staff hadn't come at such a bad time, he would have signaled to Duncan to gather men to go after her while he held her gaze. But he was fairly certain she would have run if she'd heard them coming toward her in the woods. This probably wouldn't be the last time she traveled his woods in her wolf form, either. The notion of catching her at it more than appealed.

Annoyed that he couldn't shape-shift now, not with the film crew in sight, he stalked across the eastern wall walk toward the gatehouse tower on the north side of the castle.

He had thought that the sea of mist drifting into the area might keep the Americans in the village for the night, far from his castle and the cold, damp rain that threatened to spill again. Although inevitably they'd be pounding at his tower gatehouse, looking to turn the grounds into movie madness. An agreement was an agreement, no matter how much he hadn't wanted to concur with the terms.

He listened from the walk on top of the curtain wall, the whisper of a breeze carrying the tune of the haunting melody of lilting bagpipes in the distance, stirring his blood to do battle. He wondered how in the hell he could be so close to losing their ancestral home and stuck resorting to something as low as having to cast aside his pride and allow this movie-making venture.

Fighting skirmishes with his neighbors in the old days would have been easier. But the threat of losing the castle and lands due to unwise investments in Silverman's pyramid scheme? The saints preserve him and the MacNeills' kin.

Then he heard them, their footfalls in the distance on the path to the castle, clomping away, five or six, he guessed. Although when he reached the northern section of the wall walk, due to the fog and how far they still had to go to reach the castle, he couldn't see them. If they'd been wolves like him and his kin, they would have been much stealthier. But the Yanks stomped along the cobblestone road with disdain, disregarding the beauty of the quietness blanketing the land.

Then voices carried. Men's voices, one complaining bitterly, his breath short, berating the laird of the castle—*him*, Ian MacNeill—for not allowing them to drive up the kilometer-long walk from the road. And another who tried to console the first.

"The laird didn't want a horde of vehicles roaring up the path tonight, his last night before we turn the place into our movie set. You know he didn't want any of this."

"He agreed, and now he no longer has any say in the matter."

Folding his arms, Ian smiled darkly. That's why he'd made them walk.

Behind the men, a woman's voice murmured something, as if she were speaking to someone else, gently not breaking the spell of the encroaching night. It was still light out, but with the fog and the sun descending, it would be dark soon.

With a wolf's hearing, Ian could capture voices and other sounds nearly ten kilometers through the Caledonian Forest and sixteen across the moors. The woman was only about a kilometer away and speaking in a hush, talking softly to someone else, her siren's voice enchanting as it garnered his full attention. Was it Julia speaking? The whisper of a voice sounded like hers. Tantalizing, seductive, no matter what she said.

Was the wolf someone else who had shape-shifted then, if Julia was with the film crew staff now approaching the castle?

Every muscle in his body filled with tension again, but not with wanting to do battle this time. *No*, this time he leaned over the battlement, attempting to see the

vision that had such a tempting voice, like a sea nymph
who would beguilingly lure the sailors to their doom.
Soothing, like a warm balm on a troubled soul. If he
could just catch a glimpse of her, see if it was Julia, and
hear what she was saying—

"Sorry I'm late, but I saw the men from the airport.
The one who took our car and another who... well,
I don't have a good feeling about him."

"What other man? You didn't tell me about that.
What was that all about? Forget it. Tell me later what
you found," the other said, her voice having a distinctive Spanish sound to it, as pleasing to the ear as the
first one's, yet a hint of worry and annoyance laced
her words.

The woman was Maria, Ian was certain.

And the other—Julia, he thought—added, "I was—"

"It won't be so bad," Ian's brother Cearnach an-
nounced, drowning out the rest of the woman's words,
his lanky footfalls preceding him as he joined Ian on the
wall walk, high above the outer bailey.

Frustrated beyond belief, Ian tried to catch her words
again, but neither of the women spoke further. He had
been concentrating on the woman's voice with such
intensity that he hadn't even heard his brother arrive.

"*Siren*," Ian growled under his breath, realizing now
just how much the woman had swept him under her
spell. *Hell*. No woman, especially one with this film
crew, would distract him from his duty, even if she was
a wolf. Despite telling himself this, Ian had to force
himself to tear his gaze from the road, from wanting
desperately to observe the woman, to see if she was
Julia. He still envisioned that silky shirt plastered to her

breasts and the trousers clinging erotically to her legs. With irritation, he turned to face his brother.

He swore Cearnach swaggered as if pleased with the situation. His brother wore a green muscle T-shirt, navy trousers, and a well-worn pair of hiking boots. With the breeze tugging his unkempt hair and a shadow of a beard gracing his face, Cearnach looked casual and relaxed, as he usually did.

The most optimistic of his quadruplet brothers, Cearnach's name suited him—victorious or warrior from the woods. Ian believed their mother had to have known something of their personalities before they were even born through some kind of innate knowledge—all except for Ian himself. He was the gift from God. And look where that had gotten them. He assumed his mother had named him as such because he was the first born of the four brothers. She was probably relieved to birth the first of them and get the whole thing over with.

The clan, the pack, their home—all of it rested on his shoulders. No matter how many of his pack members helped to manage things, he was ultimately responsible. And he had let them down.

"Silverman," Ian growled. "True, the bastard is a thief who didn't give a damn how many people he financially ruined along the way as long as he could build his own little empire from his ill-gotten gains. Even his mate was in on the deal, pretending innocence while trying to keep as much of the money in her own pockets as possible while he disappeared. And damn that both he and his mate are gray wolves of the American variety."

The part about them being American had further soured his opinion of those with the film crew, even if they had had nothing to do with it.

"Silverman had been big in Wall Street. Reputable. Or had been for a time," Cearnach reminded Ian. "He took a lot of people in."

"Others, sure." But Ian should have overseen *their own* finances better than that.

No matter the outcome, Cearnach always found a way to see whatever folly befell them in a positive manner. "I keep telling you it's a learning experience. A way to manage our money more efficiently in the future. To be more vigilant. But more than that, it's a way to reconnect with the outside world instead of isolating our clan our pack, from everyone else."

"We socialize with the locals, Cearnach. We participate in the Highland fests, fish, and even show our cattle." Ian contented himself with keeping his pack in semi-isolation, though. Had to for those who were more newly turned. Not many clans could boast *werewolf* lineage, and those that did, kept their identities secret. He was sure the same was true the world over, or they would have learned of it.

"I know you're blaming yourself," Cearnach said, resting his forearms on the rock wall and staring out at the vista of the ancient Caledonian Forest. "But you should take Guthrie to task solely for this mischief."

Ian cast his second oldest brother a searing look.

Cearnach brushed him off with a knowing smile. "*Tch*, that is the problem. You don't blame anyone but yourself. Guthrie acts without asking any one of us if we agree with his plans in regards to our money. He is the one, and he alone, who got us into this mess. Hold *him* responsible."

Guthrie, like his name, could no more be harnessed than the wind, free to willfully roam where it would. He often had an uncanny ability to make money for the clan in unusual ways, but this time, the master deceiver had taken him in. Had his brother not learned that if it seemed too good to be true, it most likely was?

If Silverman had not vanished from the States, *Ian* would have taken *him* to task. Although their youngest brother had wanted to take this into his own hands, track the bastard down, and get their money back. Ian knew Duncan wouldn't be gentle. Not that Ian would be, either.

"The Yanks will make us solvent," Cearnach continued, cheerfully. "One took our money; another will help us to overcome."

Ian didn't think Cearnach ever sounded anything but cheerful. It was downright annoying at times. His look stern, Ian grunted and folded his arms. "They will not stay within the castle walls after nightfall."

"They have some filming to do at night, Ian. You signed the consent forms."

He had to agree, as much as he didn't want to. It was one of the concessions he'd had to make if the movie was to be filmed here. "I'm surprised they couldn't build a replica of the castle in their Hollywood." Which is just what Ian should have told them, but truth be told, the MacNeills needed the damned money.

"For this movie, the production costs can be cheaper if they film on site, so Guthrie says."

"They will not sleep inside the castle at night," Ian reiterated. He would not be swayed from this point. "Our people have to have their privacy." At least half a dozen had been turned during the latter half of the last century and couldn't control shifting during the full moon when the pull was strongest.

Cearnach nodded cheerfully.

Ian shook his head. "Are you never angry about anything, brother?"

"Aye, Ian. When Cousin Flynn took off with the bonny lass I was intrigued with many, many moons ago, I was ready to cut him in two with my sword. If Duncan had not stopped me..." Cearnach shrugged and smiled.

"Duncan was madder than you were that our cousin ran off with her over the slight. It wasn't long before you were interested in another wee lassie."

"You're right. The one that took off with Flynn was not worthy of my attentions. And the next one Flynn fell for was his undoing." Cearnach's face hardened slightly, and Ian knew his brother was thinking about Ian's handfasted bride, Ghleanna MacDonald—a human, not a wolf—and the disaster that had been, the angry words, Flynn's banishment from the clan and from the pack, and the termination of the contract with the MacDonald. Cearnach sighed deeply. "The next one was his last mistake. I always told him unmarried maids were the only ones to dally with."

Footfalls approached, and they turned to see Duncan headed their way, his expression grim. "They are here. At least the advance party. Do you want me to take care of them? You said you didn't want to be bothered."

Duncan was right. Ian didn't wish to speak with

them. He'd already ironed out the details. Now, his men could enforce them.

Although... Ian considered the woman's voice he'd heard, and he wanted to see if it was Julia's. But the way the two women had spoken to one another about some problem at the airport made him sense that something else was wrong, something that was best kept secret, and he wanted to know what that was all about. And he damn well wanted to know Julia's real name. He had half a notion to ask the director in front of her, if she was with the staff right now. Put her on the spot. See what she had to say this time.

Was everyone on the film crew a *lupus garou*? He should have thought to ask. In a way, it would make the clan's lives easier.

"See to them, Duncan. No accommodations on the premises. I don't wish to see them any more than I have to. And, Cearnach, make no concessions to any of them." He paused to let that sink in, and then he wondered what his financial genius of a brother was doing. "Where's Guthrie?"

"In his office, making calls as usual," Cearnach said. "I really would watch what he's up to now. These are desperate times. No telling what foolhardy scheme he might invest in next." Cearnach winked, appearing more amused than worried, and strolled off toward the tower stairs.

That made Ian wonder if Cearnach knew of some new folly Guthrie was endorsing. "Make sure," Ian said to Duncan, but loud enough for Cearnach to hear, "Cearnach does not speak to the Yanks in any kind of authoritative capacity."

Cearnach chuckled, not in the least bit bothered by Ian's concern or that he had said Duncan was to be responsible for Cearnach's behavior, despite Duncan being the youngest of the quads. Cearnach knew Ian trusted Cearnach completely.

Duncan gave Ian a dark smile. "Aye, these men look suntanned and pampered. All I had to do was give them a hard look as I passed the gatehouse to make my way up here, and they were quivering in their sneakers."

Ian tried not to show his amusement at the image that conjured up. "As much as I hate saying it, we need them. So just keep peace. Don't give any more concessions than I've already agreed to, and don't scare them off."

"If Flynn comes calling on them, it's not any of my doing. You know how he hates it when outlanders show up here."

"They probably wouldn't recognize a ghost if they saw one. Go, take care of them. I'll be in Guthrie's office." And making sure Guthrie didn't sign them up for any other ventures Ian didn't completely approve of beforehand.

Duncan bowed his head, whipped around, and stalked off, looking ready to do battle. Ian was blessed with brothers who, for the most part, could be trusted. However, if these had been the good old days, Ian would have a sword in hand and led Duncan in the charge.

As Ian approached the gatehouse from the wall walk, he glanced down and scanned the party of six, four men and two women. And stopped in his tracks. The brunette was the one with the sexy Spanish voice, Maria. She was standing quietly by the man who appeared to be in charge, his arms folded and foot tapping on the cobble-stone entryway, looking damned annoyed.

The other woman was Julia, the redhead, wearing a green outfit now that blended into the woods like a hunter would. But he noted the oddest thing. A leaf and a couple of pine needles clung to the back of her sweater. The only explanation he could come up with was that she'd removed her clothes, left them in the pine needles, and shape-shifted. Or was he wanting that to be the case? Wanting her to be the little red wolf who'd watched him from the woods, half challenging him, half afraid he'd seen her?

Despite telling himself he shouldn't care, beyond not wanting anyone who was not one of their kind to learn what she was, he had to know the truth.

She was taking copious notes. No one was speaking, so what was she writing down?

He noted the way the redhead looked at two of his cousins, Oran and Ethan, and the return interest they showed her. Hell, he'd told his clan that everything between his people and the Americans would be strictly business. The business they looked to be interested in wasn't what he had in mind.

And he wondered if the fact the women were *lupus garous* had anything to do with it. Which meant he had to have another word with his men as soon as possible.

And a word with Julia also, to learn exactly what she was up to.

Chapter 6

MIST NOT ONLY COATED THE FOREST AND AREA surrounding the MacNeill castle grounds in a super-natural, haunting, and breathtaking way, but also the keep itself and the outer bailey. Julia scribbled notes in her journal as she stood slightly behind Maria. She knew she'd have to come clean with Maria after they returned to the cottage concerning getting caught in her wolf form. But if she didn't shape-shift again while she was in Scotland, no harm done. No one would ever learn that she was the one who had shape-shifted as long as she didn't do it again and get caught.

No one had even raced out of the castle to hunt down the wolf. So maybe they didn't care. Or maybe the film business took all their attention right now.

At the moment, the director was tapping his foot on the ground, scowling and waiting for someone of importance to speak to him, when he was rarely kept waiting for any-thing. Two braw Highlanders watched them, arms folded and eyes narrowed, guarding the outer bailey, although as soon as they saw Maria and Julia, their mouths twitched up a bit. *Rogues*. She was certain their laird would not like it that they were flirting with the women on the film crew. The men were probably interested in them even more because she and Maria were also *lupus garous*.

Julia quickly jotted down some more notes—this time about the men of the castle and not just about the sandstone towers or the wicked-looking iron gates designed to keep the enemy out. For the first of the men, she wrote: *Redheaded male; muscular arms bulging beneath a lightweight shirt despite the chill in the air; eyes cool gray, warming a little when he spies a woman; mouth mannish, roguish, and kissable. Maybe of Norse descent. Could be a descendant of the first red werewolves.* At least for her story.

Yes, that's how she'd write the man in her historical romance.

She glanced at the other man and noted that he was now having a word in private with the redhead, whose eyes remained fixed on her. He was smiling a little more. He nodded at the other man's comment.

She ignored the blush heating her whole body and tried to concentrate on the business of describing the second man for her novel. It definitely was a lot easier to observe subjects for her stories more covertly when the objects of her note taking were unaware of what she was doing.

She wrote for the second character: *Pale yellow eyes, just as roguish; a hint of a beard; dark brown hair; tall like the redhead, just as muscled; interested, looked to be more Scottish in origin.*

In the cool dampness, Julia shivered and heard male voices up on the allure, the wall walk on top of the curtain wall. She moved away from Maria and the others to get a better view of the wall walk and made out three brawny Highlanders conversing there.

Dark-haired Duncan was scowling and looked ready to start a war. He was dressed in black, paramilitary style, as if he was an FBI agent but without the white lettering across the shirt to identify what he was. All he needed was a sword. No need even for a shield because she assumed he'd never fall back to a defensive mode as he battled his way through a fight, staying on the offensive the whole time.

In the fading light, the other was smiling and looked of good humor. His hair was fairer, a tinge of red streaking it, and an emerald-green muscle shirt showing off the right kind of muscles—not bulky but hard enough that he looked as though he got a lot of exercise. Maybe wielding a sword, although more in fun rather than in combat. He appeared relaxed, like he was listening to a bard's tale.

And the last, the one who garnered her attention the most, was Ian, the laird. He was all business and in charge, as far as she could tell from the way the others came to him to speak. He motioned for the one, then the other, to go about their business as if he was issuing orders. With a rugged face and a stern look, he was the one who caught her imagination.

The two men disappeared, while her hero remained on top of the curtain wall for a moment more and then stalked off in the opposite direction. Two more men approached him, both bowing their heads in greeting.

She sighed, pen in hand, clutching her notebook to her chest and trying to appear as though she was with those who were meeting with the MacNeills to iron out arrangements for the filming to begin.

Duncan exited the tower stairs and stalked toward them with two other muscular men flanking him as if they were medieval types ready to do battle, except that the other men were wearing black trousers and light sweaters rather than kilts and tunics. Fascinated, she watched Duncan address the director and production manager and set down the terms forcefully, while the manager nodded agreeably, if not a little shakily. The director remained stoic, as if he were a clan chief from another location and wouldn't bend to any man's rule.

"No one is allowed inside the castle before production begins. Except for the great hall, the tower prison or the dungeon, the outer bailey, the inner bailey, the stables, and the wall walk, most of the castle is off-limits to the film crew," Duncan said.

Dark and Dangerous made it clear that the private quarters wouldn't be accessible. And that's where Julia needed to be. Every deviation from the plans had to be preapproved by Ian MacNeill himself. From what Duncan MacNeill said, there would be no deviation. She figured that meant her—also.

After laying down the law, Duncan cast a glance at the party of men and then at Maria and Julia, as if punctuating his rules to each and every one of them, and measuring them to see if any would cause the clan any difficulty. His gaze briefly stopped on Maria. He frowned. Straightening her petite stature, Maria stared right back at him, not one to be intimidated. But Julia wondered why he was considering her for longer than was necessary—maybe he was interested in her after all?

Then his attention shifted to Julia, and the furrows in his brow deepened further. A shiver of warning penetrated her bones, but she held his dark gaze, trying to brush off the unwelcome feeling. He didn't like it that Ian seemed to be interested in her, she figured.

Duncan's forbidding expression didn't waver, but he returned his attention to the director, gave a stiff nod, ignored the production manager, turned, and stalked off with his men-at-arms. At least that's the way Julia considered them, like lethal bodyguards if they'd been in the States, guarding some very important person. Even though he didn't look like he needed *anyone's* protection.

She sighed. She felt at home in Scotland already, despite Duncan's attitude. Her ties to the Campbell and MacPherson clans through her father's roots, and the Fraser clan through her mother's, had stirred an interest in all things Scottish all over again. Everything about the castle felt right as far as the atmosphere, the look of the handsome Scots, and the feel of the stone fortifications with green moss clinging to them and softening their rigid look.

Now, she just had to get inside the keep and take notes about the rest of the place, find the secret niche while she was at it, and she'd be done.

As long as she didn't get caught.

After standing on the wall walk issuing orders, Laird MacNeill hadn't even bothered to come down to speak to the production manager. Not even to see her up close, which told her the way of things. Once she was here in the capacity of working with the film crew—at least that's what he'd assume—she was bad news. Was coming down here to at least meet with the director beneath his lairdship? But how long would that last once the filming began?

She imagined there wasn't any way Laird MacNeill could control everything that went on during the filming.

Would he stand on the castle wall walk, as he did now, way up above with his arms crossed over his broad chest and wearing a mighty scowl while he watched the proceedings? And if things didn't go as planned, perhaps he would motion to the archers lining the wall walk and a rain of arrows would pour down upon the movie crew.

She had too vivid an imagination.

Miscalculating the human equation, she had falsely assumed the people living here would be excited to have a film produced at their castle and would greet the director with enthusiasm and support. Where movies had been filmed at other castles, websites had proudly proclaimed the fact. Up until now, at every place the film crew had been, the Scots had been generous and friendly. She imagined there would be none of that here. In fact, Maria had said that the MacNeills didn't even have a website. After doing a little research, Julia had found that the castle had never been open to the public. Under siege and breached a few times during major strife, yes, but never *willingly* open to the public.

That made her think maybe her family had taken the castle over during a siege. Maybe then they had been overwhelmed at a later date and had to scurry out of there. Not good. If Ian learned about her Scottish roots, would he hold a grudge against her?

She glanced back at the wall walk. Ian MacNeill had stopped to watch them now and hadn't left the curtain wall as she had thought he would. At first, his attention was on the director, as if he was measuring him, the perceived enemy in his midst. His attention settled next on Julia and caught her gawking back at him. She smiled. Couldn't help herself.

Ian's masculine lips parted slightly, and she believed she'd actually surprised him with her smile. Maybe unsettled him a little.

Maria whispered, "Coming, Julia?" She glanced up to see what had gained Julia's attention. "Hmm, hot stuff. And despite what you say, I think he has a thing for you. Not to mention your interest in him." She grabbed Julia's arm. "Come on. The crew is already headed back. The Highlanders watching us look as though they want someone to entertain them tonight." She motioned to the wall walk. "Think the laird might be good for a tumble?"

Julia laughed, her thoughts running away from her again. "Yeah, really hot stuff," she murmured. And if she got too close again, she could be scalded. "But definitely not good for a tumble." In that he was a wolf, and that meant a permanent commitment.

She could just imagine what it would be like to be under the MacNeill's spell. More of his hot kisses, his hard body pressed against her, his dark, hungry look while he carried her inside the stark castle, but nothing but his heated body would fill her thoughts as she melted against him, wanting so much more.

If he hadn't been a wolf, she would have been very tempted to have a tumble with him as Maria had suggested. Just to get the feel for one of her more... sexy scenes. For the *lupus garou*, it was perfectly acceptable to have human lovers before they found their lifelong mate. But he wasn't *strictly* human, and as hot as Ian was, she should have guessed he was a wolf.

She shook her head at herself, never having had the need to act out her scenes in real life before she wrote

them, until now. It was as though the ties she had to
the ancient woods and masonry, to her deep family
roots in Scotland, Ireland, and even Wales had never
been severed when her people left the region so many
centuries ago.

With a lift to her step, she walked back through the
gatehouse where not one, but three portcullises kept
invaders out.

"I thought they only had one of these iron gates at
the entrance to a castle's outer bailey," Maria remarked,
pointing at one of the gates.

"Some did. But some, like this one, used them to trap
invaders in between gates if their enemy was unfortu-
nate to get caught that way." Julia's arms prickled as she
glanced up at the castle arch above them and pointed to
the entryway where gaps in the stone existed above the
entrance and along the length of the curtain wall.

"Machicolations, murder holes," she explained to
Maria. "The rectangular openings provided a place for the
defenders of the castle to pour boiling water down on their
enemies who were attempting to breach their defenses."

Maria shuddered. "I thought they used boiling oil."

"Hollywood's version. It would have cost too much."

Maria reached out and touched a place on one of the
stone walls where repairs had been made to the mortar.
"Can you imagine how much this place must cost to
heat? Or the upkeep on these old stone fixtures? Every
time I turn around, something's wrong with my condo.
And it's practically new. But can you imagine the ex-
penses in maintaining something this big and ancient?"

"No, not really." Julia hadn't given it much thought.
"I wonder if the MacNeills are having financial

difficulties and that's the reason they agreed to this venture, albeit reluctantly. But why wouldn't they open their doors to having bed-and-breakfast kind of affairs or wedding receptions, or both, like some of the other castles or manors are doing? Maybe this is such a short-term endeavor and not so much like a long-term invasive venture, so it seems doable."

"Yeah, that could be," Maria agreed.

That softened Julia's view of the prideful MacNeills a bit since she was having money troubles of her own with her new book delayed by writer's block.

She glanced over her shoulder and watched Duncan MacNeill walk through the gates of what probably was the innermost bailey. The inner sanctum. From there, he'd go inside the keep. She sure wished she could get inside it without anyone knowing.

Duncan walked with a regal but deadly air, and she imagined he always looked like that. His outward appearance today probably wasn't anything different from any other day, which made her wonder why he was like that. Character studies intrigued her. They were useful to draw on for her own characters in her books.

But then one of the clansmen stalked toward Duncan, spoke to him, and motioned to Julia. The warrior turned to look in her direction. His expression was dark as his gaze focused on her. Not anyone else, just Julia. Her stomach twisted into a knot.

"Lass!" he shouted at her in a commanding way. He couldn't know who she truly was or what she planned to do here. He motioned to her to come to him as he quickly ate up the ground with his lengthy stride, heading for her as if he was afraid she'd escape before he reached her.

Heart pounding, she didn't move an inch in his direction. But she didn't back away, either.

"What did you do?" Maria whispered, sounding as though she thought Julia was guilty of some crime.

"Nothing," Julia said back, her skin chilled, her spine stiff, her legs wobbly. "I didn't get anywhere earlier in my little jaunt through the woods." *They want to interrogate me about running through the woods as a wolf.*

The little party of film-crew staff had already made its way through the gatehouse and halfway across the moat. The two muscled men for whom Julia had jotted down descriptions in her notebook followed them outside as if to ensure no one was left behind and that Julia didn't leave. Both men were eyeing her and Maria with the hint of a smile. One said something to the other, which made the recipient of the dialogue grin and nod, but she assumed the first had spoken in Gaelic because she didn't understand a word of it.

"Laird MacNeill wants to see you," Duncan said to Julia as he drew close.

Her lips parted in surprise. She was dying to get inside the castle, but not like this. Secretly, elusively, not under the watchful eye of Ian MacNeill. But then she reconsidered. He probably meant to speak to her in the inner bailey or some such place. Not inside the keep at all.

"Can Maria come with me?" To her ears, she sounded surprisingly cowardly, when she wasn't normally anything of the sort.

Duncan shook his head. "He asked for you alone."

"Will you be all right?" Maria sounded worried but kind of thrilled for her, too.

"Yes. I'll be back in a little while."

"I could just hang around here and wait for you."

"It won't be necessary," Duncan said gruffly. "We'll return her home."

Maria waited for Julia to give her the go-ahead.

"I'll be back in a while." Julia's stomach was flip-flopping all over the place, and she wanted to hold onto something, not the dark warrior beside her as he led her back through the gates and then into the outer bailey, but she really could have used some support.

"What did he want to see me about?" she asked Duncan, hoping to prepare herself for any eventuality. All kinds of different scenarios were going through her mind—he'd learned who she was as a writer; he'd learned she was related to the people who had once occupied his keep—none of which he could have known. Or Ian had assumed she was the wolf running through his woods, and he was ticked off about it.

Duncan grunted. That was his only response. No flowery speech, not that she expected it of him, and no hint of what this was about. And he didn't seem happy.

A couple more men stood on another wall walk watching them, but when she shifted her attention to the one where their fearless leader had been, she found him still observing her. More than observing her. He seemed fascinated, if she might be bold enough to think that of him. She figured the reason was more because when she looked up at him, it caught his attention.

But in her developing story, he was intrigued with the bonny lass who wasn't from this part of Scotland. *Now* he wasn't as interested in running her off as he had been before he'd laid eyes on her. Despite his initial objection to his da's bride choice, he was beginning to think the arrangement might have promise.

If she could just write the scene down before she forgot it. But where was Duncan taking her if Ian was on the wall walk behind her? She didn't have a good feeling about this.

"You have a nice place here," she said, hoping to lure Duncan into any topic of conversation.

He remained silent.

"Ian's—" She meant to say Ian was on the wall walk behind them and ask then where Duncan was taking her, but the dark look Duncan gave her made her assume she'd breached some protocol. He was probably thinking she was a clueless American, which she wasn't.

But she'd been so wrapped up in fantasizing how Ian could be her hero in the story that she was practically betrothed to him already. *In the story*, that was. So not calling him "laird" was an oversight she hadn't meant as disrespect in the least.

"The laird," she rephrased, hoping to rectify her awful mistake, "is on the wall walk behind us. So where is he meeting with me?" She envisioned being taken to the dungeon. Dark, dank, smelly. Sometimes all that had existed were deep pits, and the only access was a ladder, pulled up after the prisoner was put in the hole. No windows. No fresh air. She shuddered.

Duncan glanced back at the wall walk as if he was surprised to hear that Ian was still on the curtain wall behind them. When she looked back, she found that Ian… the laird, rather, was gone.

Secret passages came to mind. Secret passages she wanted to find. Intrigue, adventure, trouble. Like

she assumed she was in. Why else would the laird want
to speak personally with her?

But as soon as she stepped into the keep, she barely
took notice of anything except one *very* important thing—
the scent of the entryway. The scent was *unmistakable*.

She'd entered a gray werewolves' den.

Chapter 7

To LEARN IF THE REDHEAD WAS THE RED WOLF WHO
had trespassed in his woods, Ian had told Duncan to
bring her to his solar. His people would be talking about
this for eons, though—allowing a bonny lass into his
solar, an outsider, someone with this film production.
He had to learn whether she was the wolf or not and, in
any event, to ensure she understood his rules. No trespassing in or around the castle and his lands. And no
shape-shifting, either.

But in truth, the woman was already garnering his
men's attention, and he wouldn't have it. They were
welcome to trysts with human females anywhere in the
world they wanted, but not here and certainly not with
any of the members of the film crew. It would be too
easy for a woman such as Julia, with her looks and her
wiles, to wiggle her way into the castle by soliciting a
secret tryst with one of his men.

Cearnach entered his solar, but Ian waved him
away. "Not now. I've other business to attend to at
the moment."

"Would it have to do with the bonny redhead Duncan
is escorting to the keep this very minute?"

"It does, and I don't need an audience."

Cearnach raised a brow. "Are you certain? She looks
to be a handful."

"Cearnach."

Cearnach folded his arms, leaned against the door frame, smiled, and watched down the hallway. "Flynn's floating around. He catches sight of her, and no telling what's going to happen. I can just imagine one bonny lass screaming her head off and running out of here like the devil is after her."

"Maybe that would be the solution."

Cearnach frowned. "What's the trouble with the lass?"

How could Ian explain what his gut instinct told him to be the truth? That he hadn't met a woman like her ever, one who turned his head and kept him riveted? One who intrigued him with a sultry smile and a challenge in her green eyes. That although she might even be from the enemy's camp, he wanted her.

But something more bothered him about her. He couldn't pinpoint just what. Maybe the secrets she wished to discuss with her friend, who didn't want her talking about them on the walk up to the castle. The smell of gunpowder near the road where their vehicle had catapulted off it. The way her friend seemed scared of him in the pub, but although Julia's eyes had widened and darkened at the sight of him, she still defied him with a confident glower. And the name of Jones. It wasn't hers. He knew it from the way Maria had looked at Julia with such a shocked expression before she'd quickly hidden her reaction.

Something made him want to get closer, to inspect Julia inside and out.

When Ian didn't answer Cearnach, he turned his attention from the hallway and looked at his older brother, one dark brow cocked. "Duncan said you were intrigued with one of the women you hunted in the woods. Now it seems what he said was true. I thought he was exaggerating a wee bit."

"Cearnach." Ian let his breath out, not about to bow to him over the issue of the woman.

A slow grin formed on Cearnach's face as he pulled away from the door frame and peered down the hallway. "From what I could see of the lass in the inner bailey, she's well worth a second look."

"She's not for the taking." Ian leaned back against his leather chair.

"If she's human…" Cearnach shrugged.

"You're not hearing what I have to say."

"I'm hearing you, Ian." But Cearnach's gaze remained focused on the hallway, and Ian didn't think his brother was taking him seriously.

But if he told his brother he *was* serious about this, it would indicate he'd already lost the battle.

Footfalls approached, a man's and a woman's.

Even though Ian had already dismissed his brother, Cearnach didn't make any move to leave until after he greeted the woman. So much for Ian being pack leader and laird over his clan. But he didn't want to make a bigger issue of it, not in front of the lassie.

Cearnach's face brightened, and he looked so damned wolfish that he was sure to send the woman running back down the hall. Forget Flynn and his ghostly appearances.

"Lass," Cearnach said, bowing low in greeting as if she were a queen. "I'm Cearnach MacNeill, the laird's next eldest brother. And if you ever need my assistance, be sure to ask. Anything, anything at all." He smiled again, the look dazzling, and Ian wanted to rid him of the grin.

Ian remained seated at his desk, waiting for Julia—if *that* was even her name—to enter the room, if Cearnach would but leave. Ian couldn't even see her since she couldn't approach the doorway yet—not with Cearnach blocking it. When his brother continued to be an obstacle, Ian cleared his throat, but about that time the woman said, "Pleased to meet you..." She paused. "Mister MacNeill."

"Too many MacNeills around here. Call me Cearnach."

"Thanks, Cearnach. I'm Julia."

Ian realized he was hanging on her words, listening to her soft cadence and waiting for her surname to see if she said it was Jones again.

When she didn't say anything further, Cearnach's brows moved up almost imperceptibly, and Ian knew he was waiting for the same thing. Either the woman didn't know any better and wasn't all that familiar with proper greetings, or she did, and she didn't want to give the false name again.

"Cearnach," Ian said, trying to hide the exasperation in his voice, but the amused look his brother gave him proved he hadn't succeeded.

Cearnach gave Ian a grand bow, which he never did to such a ridiculous extent, and said to the woman, "Laird MacNeill will see you now." Then with an eloquent sweep of his hand, Cearnach ushered her in.

Ian had never seen such a performance.

"Close the door on your way out, Cearnach," Ian said a little too harshly, as Duncan stood in the entryway, looking as though he also wanted to hear the proceedings. "Now."

Duncan gave Ian a warning look and then shut the door on his and Cearnach's departure.

Beyond the door, his brothers commented to each other in Gaelic, figuring she didn't understand them, and Ian hoped the hell she didn't.

"She's one of us," Cearnach said, his tone intrigued as he and Duncan headed down the hall. "You left out that wee detail, brother. No wonder Ian's fascinated with her."

"He wants her to mate," Duncan responded in their Highland tongue.

Even though that wasn't so, knowing what she was changed everything. Ian hadn't thought it would. She was still an American with the film crew. She was still up to something devious; he would stake his castle on that. Yet, just as Cearnach had said, she was one of them. And universally, that meant something, being a were-wolf in a world where they were vastly outnumbered.

"Take a seat, if you would," Ian said to Julia, motioning to one of the leather chairs seated in front of his desk. She stood just inside the closed door as if she was ready to make her escape.

She didn't look around at the room, no note taking now, although she still clutched her notebook and pen in her hands. She was focused on him, not moving, not speaking, looking a little pale.

"Julia?"

She quickly nodded, then unsteadily—it appeared to him—crossed the tapestry-covered floor and sat in the chair slightly farther away from the desk and closer to the door. Her back was rigid as she perched at the edge of the chair.

"I saw you in the woods... as a wolf," he said, assuming she was the red wolf he'd seen. He leaned back against his chair, putting more distance between them and trying to make her more at ease. Yet that wasn't his purpose. He wanted to warn her away from his lands, encourage her not to shift and run through his woods. It was too dangerous, particularly with the film crew here.

Her subtle, female wolf fragrance drifted to him. The scent was an aphrodisiac for a male wolf anyway, but also he noted the fresh smell of the breeze and the scent of pine and juniper from when she'd run through them, collecting the fragrances on her skin, hair, and clothes. He didn't like the feeling he was getting whenever he caught sight of her, whenever he got close to her, and whenever he was alone with her. Tantalizing, appealing, desirable.

Her eyes had grown larger, the green swallowed up by the dilating pupils.

"Julia?"

She nodded.

He frowned. She had seemed much more of a challenge before.

"Did Duncan say anything to you? Something to upset you?"

She shook her head.

"When we were in the pub, you seemed much more..." He shrugged, not sure what word to use to describe her without her taking offense.

At that, he swore he saw her almost smile. "Why did you run as a wolf?"

"Long flights, long drive, the accident. I wanted to stretch my legs."

"Yet you have no idea if hunters hunt in these

woods." When she didn't respond, he asked, "Are you newly turned? What about the rest of your film crew? Are they also *lupus garous*?"

"No."

"But your friend Maria isn't a red wolf, is she? A Mexican gray wolf?"

"Iberian."

"Hmm." He studied her for a moment more, having the daft craving to ask her to stay for dinner. But he wouldn't ask it of her, not with his kin about anyway and all the speculation that would result. More than that, he'd forbidden his clan to have any dealings on a personal basis with the film staff. So how would it look if *he* did? He'd always tried to lead by example. "What are you doing here?"

Her eyes grew big again, and for a moment, he suspected she was here for some purpose other than being with the film crew. What was she up to?

He rose from his chair then, and she looked like she was about to rise from hers, but he held up his hand to motion for her to stay. She watched him like a wary wolf, an alpha, ready to fight, not flee, not looking toward the door, her escape route. "Julia?"

"I'm…" Her chin tilted up stubbornly. "I work for Maria. She works for the producer."

"Ah. And your job is to take notes on the castle and my people?"

"For dress, um, I mean, yes, the castle and grounds, and all."

"Dress?" he asked, drawing close, half sitting against the front edge of his desk now in front of her, forcing her to look up at him. He could be intimidating when he wanted. And she seemed to need him to be, if she was going to tell him some truth of the matter.

"Not dress. Of course not. Unless you were wearing… I mean, your men were wearing kilts and the like during the time period the story is set in, but for now, just some notes about the castle and grounds."

He held out his hand. "May I see them?" He knew before he even asked that she would say no, first with her facial expression and then with her lips. Her lips fascinated him, the fullness, the way she licked them in nervousness, pursed them in annoyance, and smiled in a mischievous way.

Her eyes, green with golden flecks, although they were mostly black now, were still wide and expressive, focused on his gaze, unswerving, challenging. She didn't refuse to give him the notebook, but she didn't offer it, either.

Then he smiled, and he knew the look was pure evil. He crossed his arms, leaned forward a bit, looking down at her, and asked, "So what is your surname *really*, Julia?"

Her heart beat even harder, and he swore if she hadn't been sitting, she would have collapsed.

The name "MacPherson" screamed in her thoughts. Julia's heart had to have skipped a couple of beats.

She didn't want to lie a second time, because he had known it was a lie, but if she said Wildthorn, he could find her on so many different sites, guest blogs, and interviews, and he'd know so much more about her that she didn't want him to know. Specifically, that she wrote about werewolves, and she was sure he wouldn't

like her here writing about him and his kin and his castle.
If she said MacPherson, would he make a connection
to her family and whatever had happened in the past?
She didn't even know what had happened in the past.

She took too long to answer. *Way* too long to answer.

He was smiling now, not just a small amused smile,
but one that said he'd caught her, trapped her, and she
was in really big trouble.

"Come now, I'll learn the truth before long. What are
you doing here, and what is your name?"

She took a chance. He'd know her as Wildthorn if
he asked the director, who might not know offhand, but
somewhere there'd be a listing of her name and then
Ian would know it. The laird would never tie her into
the MacPhersons then. She took a deep breath. "Julia
Wildthorn, though what difference it makes to one as
great as yourself, I have no idea."

Impassively, he nodded. Whether he believed her
about her name or thought he was too important to be
bothered to know it, she couldn't be sure. Yet, she could
swear a trace of a smile was begging to appear both in
his eyes and on his lips.

He pulled a cell phone off his belt, and the idea
that a Scottish laird would carry around a cell phone
seemed out of odds with the notion of kilts and swords
and castles.

"Guthrie, can you join me?"

Guthrie, the financial advisor she'd spoken to.

She put the notebook on her lap and tried to quit
gripping the poor thing to death, to look less flustered
and less anxious than she felt. "I need to return to the
cottage. Maria will wonder what's taking me so long."

Doing her sleuthing in secret was the only way to go. Right now, she felt horribly exposed.

"Stay."

Her lips parted in surprise.

He didn't say anything for what seemed the longest time. Then he added, "And dine with me."

Dine with him. A small part of her was thinking fantastic thoughts. Of staying at the castle for the night. For *research*, of course. To see if she could explore the place while everyone slept. To search for the secret passages, the hidden niche where her family's box was located. It could work.

Part of her was trying to be sensible. To say no and return to the cottage. To search for the secret passages on the outside of the building and slip into the castle during the day when the filming was in progress and everything chaotic. To remind herself that these were not humans but werewolves who could hear and see her movements when others couldn't.

The more adventurous and more reckless side of her nature won out. "I'd love to."

He bowed his head a little to her, but before she could rise from her chair, someone knocked on the door. Guthrie, she suspected.

"Come," Ian said.

The door opened, and a man entered who looked similar to Ian, except that he was a redhead and wore a trim beard. He was tall like Ian, his hair shorter, his green eyes contemplative, and he wore navy trousers and a white button-down collar, businesslike. Just as she would envision an accountant. He gave her an elusive smile and then tilted his head to Ian.

"Aye, you wished to speak with me?" He was soft-spoken and seemed amused. She imagined that Cearnach and Duncan had already filled him in about her, telling him as much as they knew.

"Miss Julia Wildthorn is dining with us. Could you tell Cook?"

Guthrie's eyes widened a bit and his lips parted, and then he looked back at Julia. Unmistakably, she felt a secret communication was being imparted between the two men. "Are you a brother also?" she asked.

"Aye, Guthrie MacNeill, third eldest brother." He was a pleasant enough fellow, but he seemed a little concerned.

"Nice to meet you."

"Likewise. When did you want to eat?" Guthrie asked Ian.

"Can you have the dinner prepared in an hour?"

"An hour. I'll see what I can do." Guthrie gave Julia one last look, then bowed to Ian and hurried out of the room, shutting the door with a click.

"Is he often responsible for having dinner on the table?" she asked, suspecting from Guthrie's surprise, although he'd quickly recovered, that it was news to him. Unless… unless he suspected she was the Iris North who had talked to him about using Argent Castle for the film production. She hadn't tried to disguise her voice when she'd contacted him because she hadn't figured she'd speak to him in person, not while she was here under the guise of working with the film staff.

"Whatever I need him to be in charge of," Ian said, but she thought the meal wasn't truly part of Guthrie's jobs.

She swore something else was going on between the

brothers. "I need to call Maria and tell her I won't be back for dinner. Can I use your phone? Everything was lost in the car fire."

"Not everything, thankfully," he said solemnly. He motioned to a phone on his desk. "I'll return in a moment. Before dinner, if you'd like, we can walk in the gardens. And you can take some more notes."

"The gardens." Her heart lifted at the thought she could include them in her work, and she smiled. "I'd love to see them."

His mood appeared to lift marginally. "Aye, well I'll be back in a wee bit." Then Ian exited the room but left the door open to his office, his footfalls heading away down the hall.

As soon as he was gone, she punched in the number at the cottage. "Maria, I'm staying at the castle for dinner," Julia said to Maria quickly when she answered, before her friend could give her the third degree.

"I've never known you to act so interested in a man you've never met before, Julia. But he's a wolf, remember. You aren't thinking of taking a tumble with him just so you can stay inside the castle and see all the forbidden sites, are you?"

"Taking a tumble with him? Hmm, forbidden sites." Now that truly stirred Julia's imagination. One kilted Highlander minus his kilt, alone with her in his bedchamber. "I'm here just for dinner."

"You know the fact they're *lupus garous* explains a lot. Why they didn't want to have any filming done at the castle. Why they haven't opened the place up to other kinds of business ventures. Why Ian could track us as easily as he did in the woods after the car accident." A pause followed. "Why he's attracted to you."

But he seemed to be fighting the attraction every bit as much as Julia was with him. "He saw me in the woods in my wolf form earlier."

Maria grew silent.

"No big deal. He shouldn't have been able to see me. Wouldn't have been able to if he hadn't been one of our kind."

"All right, so if he's one of the good guys and he's a *lupus garou*, did he see anything out there that might have indicated that someone hit us on purpose when we had our accident?"

Julia had been too busy worrying about her name and what that would entail to consider the accident and whether it had been an accident or not. But Maria was right. Since Ian was a *lupus garou*, he could have smelled gunfire, if there'd been any. "I'll ask Ian."

"Ian?" Maria sounded curiously suspicious.

"Laird MacNeill." Julia had done it again, only thankfully not in front of one of his kin this time. They'd for sure think he'd given her permission. And give him an even harder time than they were already, she surmised from the amused glances passed between them and the Gaelic conversation meant for their ears only.

But if he had smelled gunfire, was Maria right about her conspiracy theory? Did another *lupus garou* clan want to harm them? Or some of Ian's own people?

Chapter 8

NOT IN HIS WILDEST DREAMS HAD IAN MACNEILL EVER considered having a tête-à-tête with a woman who was in the least bit involved with this movie-making venture. But she was considering a tumble with him? To see the forbidden sites? Hell, his people would never let him live it down.

If he was right in his assumptions, the dark-haired one wasn't a problem. She was here to do her business, and that was it. Julia was a different story. If he read her actions correctly, she was in love with the castle and his men, romanticizing what it would be like to live here. It shouldn't have mattered, but still, he'd lived long enough to recognize trouble when he saw it. Maybe he was being a little too cynical. Maybe she was just excited, and she'd do what was expected in her job and nothing more.

But something about her actions made him suspect she was one to be watched. Withholding her surname until the last, sneaking around his woods after the film crew had been told he had forbidden them to do so, and who knew what else.

Olive-green jeans that would blend well in the forest had hugged her bottom as it had swayed a little with her walk, her black boots silent on the cobblestone path as she had entered the inner bailey earlier while he'd watched from the wall walk. A slinky, form-fitting sweater of the same color had highlighted nice firm breasts, garnering more than just his notice, if he was any judge of his men's attention toward her. As wet as it was, why wasn't the lassie wearing a jacket? To show off her considerable assets, he gathered. Or was it because by wearing fewer clothes, she could shape-shift more quickly?

Silky red hair the color of burnished copper had bounced over her shoulders with every step as she'd walked farther away from his perch on the wall walk.

Once everyone had seen enough of the woman to recognize her when the film crew returned in the morning to begin setting up, Duncan could make their people aware that she needed to be watched, just in case she attempted to take an unscheduled tour of the castle on her own. He'd warned his people not to shape-shift while the film crew was on the premises, but sometimes the wolf part of the equation didn't cooperate. Not when a werewolf had too many human roots and the full moon was nearly upon them. He couldn't risk any of the humans seeing what his people could become. But she wasn't exactly human. She was one of them.

On the other hand, what if he offered for her to stay at the castle? What might he discover about the little red wolf then?

Unable to locate Duncan in the inner bailey or his usual haunts in the castle, Ian checked on Guthrie in his office to see if he'd learned anything about Miss Julia Wildthorn. He wasn't there.

The castle was too big at times. Ian had returned to the great hall when Duncan hurried to meet him.

Despite Duncan's usually dark composure, this time

there was almost a spring in his step and almost an upward curve to his lips. Had Duncan scared the director and his minions to such a degree that he had a wee bit to smile about?

Ian sat down in his favorite high-backed chair in front of the fire. "What amuses you, Duncan? I don't believe I've seen you this cheery in eons. Not unless you've been successful in a sword fight, and even then your delight in your win is shown in the most reserved manner."

Duncan sank into a chair next to Ian's. "We have a situation. Guthrie says you've put him in charge of dinner."

Ian raised his brows. "Ah, and this is what amuses you?" He wasn't worried about a *situation*, not if Duncan was pleased about it.

"Aye." Duncan's faint smile grew, only it was hard to tell what he was thinking. Not a happy smile, but more of a hunter's smile, as if he'd just found prey to make sport of.

"And?"

Duncan turned from the fire, the flames glinting off his dark eyes. "Cook took the night off. To be with MacNamara, rumor has it."

"MacNamara? Who swore off women after his wife divorced him five years ago?" Ian frowned. "She doesn't intend to turn him, does she?"

"He is just a diversion. So she says."

"Ah." Ian watched Duncan stretch out his legs.

"The truth of the matter is that Guthrie realized you needed information about the lass, and yet you've ordered him to do the cooking."

"Cooking?" Guthrie never cooked. Well, at least not since he'd ruined a few meals in the process. Ian swore his brother did it on purpose so he'd never be asked to cook.

"Aye. You put him in charge of having the dinner ready. But Cook is with MacNamara."

Realization dawning, Ian folded his arms and smiled slightly. "I wanted him to tell Cook to have dinner ready in an hour, but that he was to research who Miss Julia Wildthorn is in the meantime. Since he cannot be doing two jobs at once, and the other is of more importance, you will have Cook's job."

Duncan's smile vanished. "Me? I cook worse than Guthrie."

"Aye."

"If you're thinking to win your ladylove with a meal fit for an earl, you can forget it. We'll have whatever I can throw together that won't need any cooking." Duncan looked glum. "As to another matter, Cearnach said if you don't want the red, he's interested."

Ian shook his head. "Don't tell Cearnach the other one's a wolf, too, or he'll be giving the two of them a guided tour of the whole castle, his bedchamber first."

"Don't tell Cearnach what?" their brother asked, strolling into the great hall with two of their devoted Irish wolfhounds at his side. The brindled offspring were descendants from the earlier breed of hounds the MacNeill werewolf clan had trained to take down English armored knights in Ireland when their ancestors had first lived there.

The MacNeills were descendants of the ancient high king of Ireland, Niall of the Nine Hostages. Unlike others on the island in ancient times, the MacNeills had not used the hounds to take down wolves until they were eradicated. Instead, the hounds had done an excellent job of separating the English knights from their warhorses.

Now, the hounds served as companions. Although huge and ferocious-looking with their shaggy, wiry coats, bristly hair over their eyes, and chin whiskers, the dogs were gentle and friendly and not much good at guarding. Unless an outsider attacked one of the MacNeills or their friends.

Cearnach sat on his own chair, stretched his legs out toward the fire, and steepled his hands under his chin. "Don't tell me what?" he repeated, sounding intrigued.

"The Spanish-looking lass is one of us also. Guthrie is researching Miss Julia Wildthorn," Duncan said. He cast a look Cearnach's way. "But maybe Cearnach would get more out of her with his charming ways." He made the comment facetiously.

Cearnach smiled. "With lassies? Aye." His smile turned into a grin. "You never cease to amaze me, Ian. Here we are nearly in financial ruin, with a film crew about to breach the walls of our castle, a battle soon to ensue as to what conditions you wish met while the filming begins, and you are concerned about a couple of lassies?" He nodded sagely. "You fear one of us will forget our loyalties?"

Instead of the silly grin Cearnach often wore, his smile slipped, and he put on an air of being circumspect. In another man, Ian might have fallen for the ruse. But not with Cearnach. "The MacNeills never forget their loyalties to the clan." Cearnach slapped his thighs and swore softly under his breath. He waggled his brows. "Just which of us will win the lasses over is yet to be seen."

"They are not staying," Ian warned. "I intend to ensure they are only with the film crew and have no other agenda."

"What other agenda would that be?" Cearnach asked, still not sounding truly serious. "They are Yanks, not from our enemy's clan here, correct?"

"We have no idea why they are truly here. Why would *lupus garous* work for humans in such a capacity? Risky business to be sure. And that's what I'm bound to find out."

Duncan said, "But Maria truly seemed to be with the film crew. The other? The redhead? She has the look of a Highland lass, no doubt about it. But if you wish for me to check into Maria's background, I will."

"Do so," Ian said, "since Guthrie is already checking into the other."

Duncan motioned to Cearnach. "Since he has nothing better to do, shall he be Cook?"

Usually when Ian gave them a task, they were more than happy to carry it out. Even if they had to make a meal, it was no big deal. Was it that they didn't want to show how poorly they could cook in front of the female red?

Cearnach frowned at Duncan. "Where's Cook?"

"Cearnach, you have the job. Dinner in an hour." Not wishing to discuss dinner with his brothers further, Ian changed the subject. "Earlier today, Guthrie was about to sign a deal to have a gift shop in the great hall after the film is released to sell Highland paraphernalia from the movie. I emphatically said no."

Duncan snorted. "Like a *Jurassic Park* gift shop. Only this time selling action figures in the form of brawny Highlanders wearing kilts, replica swords, and all manner of Scots' relics, no doubt."

"I have an old sword or two I wouldn't mind selling off if the price was right," Cearnach offered.

Ignoring him, Ian asked, "Has Guthrie talked to either of you about serving as extras in the movie? To fight in some of the battle scenes?"

Duncan looked at Cearnach. Cearnach reached down to pet Anlan, but as soon as he did, Dillon raised his head to be petted also. Both his brothers were acting suspiciously enough that Ian assumed the worst. "You did."

Duncan shrugged. "Most of the men of our staff have signed up. We mock fight all the time. Why not show off the skill of our swordsmanship, something we have done since we were mere lads, unlike the whelps in the film who have been given a few lessons to get by in the movie?"

Ian shook his head.

"We're getting paid for it, Ian," Cearnach said. "You might want to join in on the fun also and earn a little pocket change on the side. Although as an earl, you should be the star of the film. I can see it now, though. They'd match you up with the hero of the film, and you'd give him a real fight, none of this fancy, choreographed showmanship like they do in the movies. The women would fall in love with the true Scotsman, and you would be an overnight success. If *lupus garou* females knew that's what you were, they'd be climbing our walls to get to you."

Duncan smiled a little. Ian furrowed his brow, envisioning crazed women attempting to slip through the

gatehouse to ravish him. Which again made him think of
Julia. And with her, the thought appealed.

His brothers were observing him, smiling, as if they
knew just what he'd been thinking.

"Extras," Ian said, rising from his chair. Both hounds
raised their heads and watched him. "At least Guthrie's
got enough sense not to sign up to be one." His brothers
cast each other looks, and Ian frowned. "He said he's not
going to be an extra."

"He was the one who approached the film crew about
us all serving as extras. Although they call us background performers," Cearnach said proudly. "All we're
going to do is fight our own people, like we would do
normally, only we get paid for it this time. And we could
use the money. The big-name actors will be fighting
each other. But no, technically, Guthrie isn't perform-
ing. He's the one who got us all involved."

"You won't be fighting your own battles like you
normally would do, Cearnach. I'm sure they'll have
you fight the way they want the scenes filmed. Hell,
next you'll tell me that if they want a couple of wolves
to attack the clansmen, you'll be volunteering to
perform in that capacity." Ian gave them both a disgruntled look.

Duncan cast him an elusive smile. Cearnach laughed.
"If we could get away with it, and we earned good
money..." He let his words trail off.

"I'll see you both later." Ian patted his leg, and both
hounds stood, stretched, and hurried to join him as he
headed for his solar to see what Miss Julia Wildthorn
was up to now.

"I imagine our laird would not mind if the redheaded

lass wished to storm the castle walls to get to him," Cearnach said, but fortunately Duncan kept his counsel.

Although when Ian cast a glance over his shoulder to give Cearnach a quelling look, his brothers were grinning their fool heads off.

"Which of us will get to keep the fair damsels, Duncan?" Cearnach asked.

Neither, Ian thought to himself. He already had enough trouble running the castle without having an American of the red wolf variety or an American Iberian gray stirring up new difficulties.

He'd hoped he could get close to his office and overhear more of Julia's conversation with Maria, as much as he was intrigued by her comments about having a tumble with him. But with the dogs tromping together behind him like a couple of horses and the floorboards creaking in one spot, there was no chance at that.

When he reached the solar, he thought her expression seemed animated and content. Julia looked like she belonged there. If he hadn't heard her strange expressions and American accent, she could have been Scottish. But that wasn't what was making him feel strangely at odds when he entered his solar.

She was sitting in his chair, which no one—not even his brothers—ever sat in, warming his seat and bringing to mind the thought of her sitting in his lap. His loins tightening, he decided then on taking a more secluded walk with her.

"Ready for our walk?" Ian asked Julia, startling her from speaking to her friend over the phone in his office. He was surprised that she hadn't anticipated his appearance, but she seemed to be listening intently to whatever her friend was saying and turned abruptly to see him.

The dogs came into the room with him and stood by his side. Her brows rose to see them, and he took a seat on one of the guest chairs, which oddly made him feel as though he'd given up the castle. He realized then just how important his chair was. The unofficial seat of power, the place where his da had sat and his da before him—not on that particular chair, but an earlier one— giving counsel, advising on war, settling disputes among his people. And now, an American, a female red wolf, was sitting in that seat.

He told himself it was foolish. That it meant nothing. Yet the situation reminded him of something that had occurred in their past. But he couldn't recall what exactly; he'd have to ask his Aunt Agnes, the repository for all their history.

"Have to go, Maria," Julia finally said. "See you later."

"Tonight, right?" Maria asked loudly, as if she was afraid Julia had already pulled the phone away from her ear and was going to hang up before her friend knew the answer. Because of that, Ian heard her words.

"Of course. See you later." Julia signed off and rose from the chair. "The gardens, right?" She came around the desk and began petting Dillon, then Anlan. "Irish wolfhounds. What an odd choice of dog for *lupus garous* to have."

He hadn't even considered she might be afraid of the dogs. Not everyone loved them like his family did. So he was glad to see her approach them with confidence like an alpha would, and with obvious interest in them, the way she smiled at them and continued to stroke their heads as they vied for more of her attention. Hell, not only were his men and he besotted with the lass, but his dogs now, too.

"The one with the darker face is Dillon. The other is Anlan. They love us whether we're in our wolf forms or as humans. They wouldn't bite the hand that feeds them." He watched the way she smiled at the dogs, a genuinely affectionate smile.

With the way they seemed to hit it off, he had another idea. "They need to run. Would you mind if I took you to the falls? Instead of the gardens?" He felt devious for asking the question. Sure, the dogs needed to run, and the gardens wouldn't do. But anyone could have taken the dogs out while he walked with Julia in the gardens. He wanted to get her alone, away from his people, just the two of them. He needed some answers. Sometimes the castle seemed too large to locate anyone, but at other times, like now, it seemed too small for real privacy.

Her expression brightened. "Falls? Oh, I'd love to see them."

But then recalling the way she'd been limping earlier, he reconsidered. "Your ankle is no longer hurting? The falls are quite a distance from here."

"No, my boots are giving me enough support. I'll be fine. The car accident and tromping over the rocky ground in heels caused all the trouble."

He wanted to take hold of her arm, wanted to walk with her through the castle to see if she leaned against him at all. Her enthusiasm made him have no doubt as to her sincerity about desiring to see the falls. Whether her ankle was up to the hike was what concerned him now.

"We could wait until tomorrow." Although he didn't want to.

She smiled dazzlingly up at him. "No, no, I'm just fine. A walk to the falls with someone who knows the lay of the land will be fun."

The implication that anyone who could act as guide would do deflated his ego a bit.

In silence, they walked down the two flights of stairs and then through the great room where Cearnach, Duncan, and *now* Guthrie lounged. Each gave him a furtive smile. He wondered what was going on with dinner. And he wondered why Duncan wasn't researching anything he could about the Iberian wolf. And more than anything, what Guthrie might have learned about Julia Wildthorn.

Smiling, Guthrie said, "I have some news for you, Ian." He glanced at Julia.

Ian bet the news was about the little red wolf. "You can tell me the news later." Although he was dying to know what his brother had learned since he seemed in such good spirits. "We're going to the falls. Be back before dinner."

"The falls," Cearnach said, raising his brows, as if he knew just where this was leading. "About dinner, now that Guthrie is finished with his assigned task... and since you gave him the order initially about fixing—"

"Aye, well, seeing as the three of you have nothing better to do, make it a family affair." Ian smiled a wee bit and then he guided Julia toward the entryway, dogs in tow.

His brothers spoke in Gaelic to one another. "They'll never make it back here in time for dinner," Duncan said lightly. "It won't matter how badly we cook."

"She'll be staying the night and be here for breakfast," Cearnach warned. "If Cook isn't here before then, and I doubt she will be, we'll have the daunting task before us once again."

Guthrie had the last word before Ian and Julia were outside. "He doesn't know what he's getting himself into."

Chapter 9

GUTHRIE'S COMMENT ABOUT JULIA WARNED IAN THAT something about her would surprise him. He was already thinking along those lines anyway, but now his curiosity was elevated another notch. Usually, he was cautious, but Julia made him want to take risks he normally wouldn't take. Maybe that was because she had been running through his woods as a wolf, very risky business, and he wanted to prove to her he was just as daring.

Life had grown dull of late. The same sword-fighting routines with his people. The same visits to the local tavern, to the Highland games, to his usual fishing haunts. No more wars or clan fights or political intrigue that involved his people. Aye, life had become dull. Until Silverman stole their investments and a red female walked into his life.

As soon as they were beyond the castle walls and walking through the woods in the dark, although with their wolves' vision they could still see well enough, Ian slipped his arm around Julia's to offer support and to judge if she faltered because of her ankle. He surmised she was not the kind of woman who would give up on an adventure, even if it killed her. Maybe because she'd been running around his lands after being injured earlier and, before that, had been fleeing from what she thought had been a pursuer.

The dogs stayed nearby, exploring, sniffing the ground, and looking for rabbits, but they didn't stray far.

"Why did you and Maria rush off after the accident? I called out to you to see if you were all right," he said, wanting to know if she had really been scared of them and intending to make amends.

"We thought whoever hit our car might have done so on purpose."

Ian pulled Julia to a stop. "Say again?" He'd assumed they had just thought he and Duncan were bad news, maybe drunken, but he'd never considered that the other vehicle might have hit them on purpose.

"Maria told me that because of choosing your castle over any others, a man with a Scottish brogue called her and said she'd live to regret it as soon as she arrived here. I assumed it was an idle threat. But she thought the tires were shot out. I believed they just blew when the tires hit the rocks. It makes the same noise. I know, because it happened to me once."

Ian began walking again, more slowly this time. "I thought I smelled the faint odor of gun smoke."

"Oh." She looked a little pale.

"Did you?"

"Not where we were when the car hit the stone wall. We didn't go back up to the road."

Ian nodded, figuring that if they had come up to the road, he and Duncan would have run into the lasses. "So you thought Duncan and I were after you in a bad way?"

"Yes. At least Maria did."

Pondering the way she said the words, Ian didn't respond for several minutes. Was she a better judge of character? Or something else? "But *you* didn't worry about us?"

"I… well, you had called out to us, and I thought you truly wanted to help. I mean, your…" She looked up at him. First, her gaze latched onto his, and then she looked at his mouth. "Your voice sounded so…" She cleared her throat.

"So?"

She gave a wee shrug, looking away, her face blushing with color.

"So?" he asked again, wanting to know what she'd thought of his voice that made the color blossom on her cheeks and extend down her throat. Were her breasts blushing as well?

"Nice," she said.

Nice. But he didn't think that's the word she would have described his voice. Not the way she'd acted so embarrassed.

"Then again, I didn't really think anyone had hit us on purpose, either. A gray wolf ran in front of the car, and Maria slammed on her brakes. Right after that, the vehicle hit us. It was foggy and the guy was traveling faster than we were. I figured he knew the lay of the land so he was familiar with the roads, much more so than we were."

What she said all sounded reasonable, except for the one thing she'd mentioned. The wolf. "A wolf?" he asked testily.

"I thought it might have been a…" She hesitated to say and then rubbed her arms. "I thought I saw him earlier, running parallel to the road." She took a deep breath. "Maria tends to watch movies where everyone's in on some kind of a conspiracy, so she thought the wolf was in league with the other driver."

Ian wrapped his arm around Julia's shoulders and pulled her close. "You're shivering, lass." He worried she was scared that someone might come after her again. But he didn't like the notion someone had threatened Maria and then the car accident had occurred. That he'd smelled gunfire. And then there was the wolf. A gray wolf. Not one of his own. A trespasser. What if Maria's assumption had been right? What if the wolf had been in league with the driver of the vehicle? What if they had been part of Basil Sutherland's clan?

"It's a little chilly out tonight," Julia said.

"Do you want to go back?" He hoped not. In fact, he realized how much he was enjoying a walk in the woods with her—away from his brothers, his cousins, and the rest of the pack, away from her girlfriend Maria, even. And not just that they were alone. He enjoyed being with her when he hadn't been with a woman on a quiet hike on his beloved land ever.

"No. If I keep walking, I'll warm up," she assured him, and snuggled a little closer.

He smiled, tightened his hand around her shoulder, and gave a light squeeze. Warming her up was just the notion he had in mind. But still, the idea that someone wished the women harm preyed on his thoughts. "Has Maria had any other calls?"

"No. Although her phone was lost in the car fire."

"I'll have my brothers check into it when we return. Were you included in the threat?"

Ian's hand rubbed Julia's shoulder, the heat of his body pressing closer to her side. She knew he was just trying to keep her warm, but he felt good, protective, perfect for the hero in her story, but more than that. He was causing her hormones to tumble wildly into uncharted dimensions. She didn't want to think about the man who had called Maria or his threats. Just about what Ian was doing to her, triggering her sexual drive. "Yes, after a fact."

His dark brows knit together. "After a fact?"

She shrugged, trying to concentrate on his fingers tightening on her shoulder in a shielding way, not wanting to discuss this since she didn't have firsthand knowledge. "He mentioned me as an afterthought." She wasn't about to tell Ian the guy had warned her away from the laird, that he acted as though they had known each other personally, or anything about the ex-boyfriend. Although *lupus garous* could have human sexual partners, that didn't mean another wolf wanted to hear about it.

Ian pondered her response for a while, his hand gliding over her shoulder and down her arm in such an affectionate manner that she felt she could melt into the pine needles blanketing the ground, pulling him with her and stripping him of his clothes so she could see the muscles she'd had a glimpse of earlier in the pub when he was soaked to the skin. And run her hand over them, memorizing the hot feel of his skin, the—

"Does Maria have any idea who the disgruntled Scot might have been?"

Here Julia was thinking about sex, and Ian was just concerned about the call Maria had gotten. Julia sighed and snuggled deeper against Ian's hard body. "No."

HEART OF THE HIGHLAND WOLF 129

His arm tightened around her shoulder, and her heartbeat sped up. She hated that she could see anything romantic coming from him touching her. He was a Scottish laird, and she was an American nobody. He was a gray, and she was a red. He probably knew Gaelic, Scottish, and English, maybe other languages, and she knew American English and that was it.

And why she was even thinking about anything like that, she hadn't a clue. He was *not* interested in her! Except to keep her warm because she was shivering. For heaven sakes! As for the threats to Maria and her, he was laird here and probably didn't like anyone with the production being threatened because he was making money off it.

Yet she reminded herself that the way he was making her feel with his touching her was perfect for her story. The Scottish laird was now warming up to taking her as his bride, although he'd mentioned a handfasting, instead of an actual marriage, to get to know her for a year. Like an engagement period with sex. If she produced an heir, he'd marry her. If she didn't in a year and a day, they could call it quits.

She harrumphed.

"Hmm?" Ian said, quietly walking beside her, his hand caressing her shoulder and alternately squeezing her against him from time to time.

Her face heating, she glanced up at him, not having thought he would hear her. He was looking ahead, the dogs having disappeared for a few minutes, now returning again, making sure Ian was still with them, and then loping off.

She might as well get in a little research while she

was at it. "So about the custom of handfasting, do you still do that?"

His face darkened a little, and for a few minutes he didn't say anything. She wondered what would cause him to be annoyed about the topic. Then he finally said, "Sort of a trial marriage. The Scottish Marriage Act did away with recognizing handfasting in 1939. But then in 1977, the Marriage Act allowed for handfasting again, but now it's legalized."

"What about your parents?"

Again, he hesitated for too long—at least she felt as though it was for too long, as if he didn't wish to speak of it.

"We normally don't marry, not unless the one marrying has a title, like my parents did. Do your people?" He frowned a little, looking somewhat surprised.

Her mouth dropped slightly. She caught herself and snapped her mouth shut, then shook her head. "No, you're right. We don't marry. Just…"

Mate. For life. But all of a sudden it seemed like too personal a discussion.

Thankfully, Ian took up the slack. "The mating was prearranged as many for those who have titles are. But my parents soon fell in love anyway after they were married in the kirk. The exception…" He stopped speaking as if he thought better of mentioning it.

"The exception?"

"If the werewolf was mated to a human. Then some acknowledgment would have to be made of the arrangement—either a handfasting or a church ceremony. Otherwise, humans who are just looking for a roll in the heather wouldn't need such a commitment.

To carry on a title, a commitment would have to be made."

She shouldn't have been so nosy, but she was a royal, which meant no human roots for eons, and she wondered if one of his closer ancestors had been human. It wasn't a bad thing; it just made it more difficult for the wolves to remain in their human form during the full moon, and they couldn't shape-shift at all during the new moon when they would remain as a human the whole time.

"Are you a blue blood?" he asked.

"A royal?"

"Not a titled lass, if you are from America."

"No, that's what we call *lupus garous* who have very few human genes in their recent history."

"Aye. Blue blood."

"I'm a royal." Blue blood sounded too much like a titled person to her. The term "royal" just seemed more suitable, maybe because that's how her family had always referred to themselves and because the States didn't recognize titled lairds and the like. But the funny thing was that she referred to royals as blue bloods in her stories, attempting to disguise the werewolf truths somewhat. Had she subconsciously picked up the term from her grandfather when she was a child?

"Royal sounds titled, to my way of thinking." He smiled at her, and she got the impression he understood her reluctance to use his term for the same reason.

"So, are you? A blue blood?" she asked.

"Aye."

"But you were thinking about a human in your line. A marriage commitment. Weren't you?"

He let out his breath in an exasperated way. "Aye."

All of a sudden, she got the very distinct impression that *Ian* was the one who had married a human. She didn't know why that bothered her. Maybe a shortage of female werewolves also existed in the United Kingdom. She had no right to judge him, and it *really* wasn't any of her business. So why did the next words out of her mouth contradict that? "What happened?"

She could have bitten off her tongue after the words slipped out.

"You're very intuitive."

A compliment, but no explanation.

They walked on and she felt her ankle beginning to bother her, which added to the annoyance of wanting to know more about the woman Ian had married. But it could have been very long ago, and the woman might even be dead by now. If he'd changed her, she'd have to be a werewolf, and he'd still be mated to her. For life. He wouldn't be holding Julia this close if he had a mate, though.

"We handfasted, but we didn't make it to the end of the year," he finally admitted. His voice was gruff, annoyed.

The sinking feeling that the woman had died came to mind. Suddenly Julia wanted to change the topic if it made him so uncomfortable, yet she was also dying to know what had happened to the woman.

"She was titled and had lands and money," he said, distractedly.

"You weren't marrying her for love?" she asked, surprised. When he looked down at her, his mouth twitching, barely hiding the faintest of smiles, she could have kicked herself.

"When it comes to power and money and titles,

lass, sometimes they're all that matter. Besides, in the Highlands, my da couldn't locate another werewolf lassie for me to mate." He shrugged, although his nonchalant attitude seemed contrived. "I needed an heir, and her da and mine came to an agreement, so she seemed the right choice."

"You changed her?"

He shook his head. "It wouldn't have worked out. She didn't even like our Irish wolfhounds. Complained they slobbered, shed fur all over our tapestries, and took more of my attention than she did. Spoilt, she didn't even like the relationship I had with my kin. She wished to be the center of my attention. I had a pack to run, a clan."

"So you ended the relationship?"

"I might have stuck it out for longer, for my da and her da's sake. But when I caught her with my cousin Flynn, and not in a way befitting the woman who was handfasted to me, I'd had enough."

Julia didn't even want to know what he might have done to his relation. But her curiosity was piqued. Where did he catch the woman and his cousin? She envisioned Ian stalking out to his stables, dogs at his side, wanting to take an early-morning ride and catching his bride-to-be with his cousin, both naked, rolling in the hay.

Then she considered the story she wanted to write. She'd have her hero and heroine start out with a handfasting, at the hero's request, but shortly afterward, he'd decide he couldn't live without her and wanted to wed her in the kirk. Julia wouldn't include the cousin, or maybe she would as an interesting side character who was often in the barn dallying with the lasses.

But then again, if *lupus garous* didn't marry here in

Scotland, just like they didn't in the States… No, he'd
be titled, so that was the reason for the marriage. And
maybe, the hero was a *lupus garou* and the heroine was
not. Maybe that was what was bothering her story hero
to such an extent about marrying the woman. He would
have to go along with the lawful ceremony to satisfy her
family and other human types, but then ultimately, he'd
have to turn her. What if she objected? Not everyone
could handle such a feat. Some went mad. Sure. That
could work.

Yet as they continued to walk to the falls, she kept
pondering where Ian had caught his cousin and his
handfasted bride in the throes of passion, and tried to
envision how Ian would have handled it. And was dying
to ask him the truth. But she was certain it was an un-
pleasant memory, even if it had been a very long time
ago, and this time she kept her mouth shut.

They walked forever, it seemed, and although she
was thoroughly enjoying being in the woods with the
hero of her story, the dogs running around excited and
happy, her ankle was beginning to bother her more. But
she was afraid to say anything and spoil the hike. She
kept envisioning that the falls were just a few feet away,
since the sound of the rushing water had been growing closer forever. She tried not to lean against Ian, to
give away that her ankle was hurting. She would rest
the remainder of the night once she retired to bed at the
cottage, but she so wanted to do this.

Turning back now would be like climbing the
Himalayas only to be stopped near the summit and
forced to go all the way back down without reaching the
peak. A deeper reason was the fear of being a failure in

her own estimation and, worse, showing the Scotsman she wasn't hardy enough to make it.

The roar of the falls was deafening to her *lupus garou*'s ears, and she walked more quickly to get to the spot.

Ian chuckled. "Not anxious, are we?"

"Oh, yes." But she couldn't tell him how much so.

By the time they reached the falls, and she saw the water cascading over rocks, creating white foam, and the rowan trees laden with bright red berries leaning over the stream, Julia was hot. And spellbound by the beauty of the area. She sat down next to the water and began removing her boots.

"The water's cold, lass." To her surprise, Ian crouched in front of her and helped remove her boots.

Before she knew what he was up to, he gently peeled the sock from her right foot, making her feel as though he wanted to strip off the rest of her clothes and make wild passionate love to her. Instead, he lifted her foot, considered both ankles, and *tched*. "It's swelling."

She realized then that he wasn't considering wild abandoned sex but just checking to see if she'd hurt her ankle further. So much for red-hot kilted lovers. And for a little red American wolf who had only one thing in mind. But his concern for her endeared him to her.

She sighed. "It's swelling just a little. The cold water will do it good."

But now, the way he looked at her, his eyes smoky and dark, he gave her the impression he wasn't as unaware of her as she thought he had been. Then he pulled off her other sock with such a gentle touch that his tender action made her think again of him undressing her the rest of the way.

She couldn't help it. If he didn't keep looking at her with such keen interest while his thumb stroked her good ankle, she wouldn't be having this problem! Yet the way their gazes collided and froze, she couldn't help but believe he was thinking along the same lines as she was.

His gaze slid to her lips. He looked like he wanted to kiss her. And she wanted to kiss him back. She licked her lips, anticipating, wanting. She knew it would mean nothing more than a little wolf intimacy. Nothing long-term, no commitment to anything further, and she was willing, if he was.

But he seemed hesitant. Probably because she was American and with the film production staff—or so he thought. His gaze searched her eyes as if looking for an invitation. But he was still crouched at her feet too far away for her to make a move quickly in his direction, to grab hold and kiss him, not when her ankle hurt. He had to make the first move.

"Are you sure you want to stand in the water? To press weight on your ankle then?" he asked, and God, his voice was husky and sexy and more erotic than any man's voice she'd ever heard. If he did voice-overs for films, he'd have the women swooning in the aisles.

Idiot, she said to herself. *He doesn't want me like I want him.* She held out her hands to allow him to pull her up. "Yes. The cold water will be like an ice pack and help the swelling go down."

"Aye." He hesitated to take her hands, though, as if he thought it might not be a good idea for her to stand in the swiftly moving water when she was partly incapacitated.

But she knew she could do it. At least she was bound

and determined to try. When he didn't take her hands quickly enough, she placed them on either side of her and pressed against the earth. Which sent a ripple of pain into her ankle, and she moaned a little.

He quickly moved in close to her and leaned down to lift her at the waist, but as soon as he did, she wrapped her arms around his neck, and again their gazes met. She lifted her face to his and kissed him.

His mouth was hard and firm and still. For a moment, she thought he didn't want her. That she'd attempted to seduce a laird, for heaven sakes, when they probably were used to doing the seducing on their own terms with whom they wanted. That's when she again noticed how cloudy with lust his eyes were. How his hands had stilled on her waist. How his lips had remained noncommittal.

She wasn't the kind of woman who forced herself on an unwilling man, ever. Yet by the way he looked at her and the virile smell of him, she knew he was just holding back. And that made her want even more for him to acknowledge the craving he had for her just like she had for him.

She swept her lips over his mouth, kept her arms locked around his neck, closed her eyes, and savored the feel and smell of him. Piney woods, manly, wolfish, delicious. She concentrated on his mouth and licked the seams, her heart pounding, his beating at a faster pace. She felt the gradual change in him, the way his lips took on a life of their own, sweeping across hers very much the way she had his, tongue teasing her lips open and pressuring her to give herself to him.

Luring, hard, wanting.

But he wasn't gentle like she'd been. He angled his mouth over hers and kissed her lips with passion and strength and determination. It was as if he'd been holding back because he couldn't control the primal need once it was released. And she welcomed it. Welcomed what his kissing did to her. Fed into desire so strong, her body melting with shivers of pleasure, that she wanted him like a wolf wanted a mate. She couldn't have him in that way. But she could still satisfy some of the pent-up urge as she kissed him back with the same desperate desire, like a woman who'd been without a man for way too long.

He rubbed his cheek against hers, first on one side, then the other, his stubble lightly abrasive, but she didn't care. She yearned to have more of him, more of his heated kisses, the way his mouth molded to hers, claiming her for his own; the way his lips swept gently and roughly across hers, willing her into submission.

His tongue licked the seam of her mouth, and then when he found her opening to him, he entered, his breath heavy, his body hardening, his hands tightening on her shoulders. She savored the velvet warmth of his tongue, the stroking heat, the simulation of what he would do if he could thrust into her as her mate. She moaned with the thought, tangling her tongue in a gypsy dance, tightened her arms around his neck, claiming his mouth, *him*, if only for the moment.

Hungry, greedy for his touch, she encouraged his deepening kiss, his hands hard on her shoulders, holding her as if he never wanted to let go. Her hands were on his waist, clinging to the fortress of a man, hard and hot and sexy.

But before she was through, before she was ready

to end the kiss, she felt his body tense slightly, felt his mouth pulling away a hint. No! She wanted more. Much, much more.

His breath heavy, he broke from the kiss, smiled tightly, and pulled her from the ground, careful not to let her foot touch the soil. "Your ankle?"

Chapter 10

JULIA BIT BACK HER SEXUAL FRUSTRATION.

It almost seemed comical, as if she had forgotten her mission to see the falls in a kiss that had sent her soaring to the moon and falling back to earth again in a matter of seconds at the edge of the stream. But it wasn't over. She could feel it in the way Ian's body was hard with desire and her nipples were firm and her breasts swollen, the way she ached deeply for fulfillment, the way she wanted him to keep on kissing her until they were too exhausted to do anything else. But he was putting on the brakes, showing her that he did have some control when she seemed to have lost all sense of hers.

She tried to quash the irritation with herself that she'd let her emotions get the better of her, when she never usually did. Not with men. Not like this.

Silent, he kept an arm around her waist and held on tight as she stepped gingerly into the icy water. The rocks were slippery, but Ian's strong grip kept her on her feet. The dogs raced in and out of the water, snapping at the spray and running about them in excited circles. She almost envied them—the fact they were dogs and didn't care whether they were Irish or American or English or Scottish. That titles and land and power didn't mean anything to them. But dogs mated with any other dog, and that didn't agree with her. No, wolves had it right as far as choosing a mate for life.

"They like it here," she said as Ian wrapped his arms around her, pulling her back against his chest tightly so she could see the falls while the water iced her swollen ankle. But more than anything, her attention remained riveted on his touch. She couldn't help it. He was too damned sexy.

"One of their favorite places to run," he said, his voice low and gravelly, appealing and hot.

His arm moved higher under her breasts. The cold of the water seemed to fade away. With her eyes closed, she concentrated on the feel of him pressed against her back. He was fully aroused, and she recalled the way his wet trousers had clung to him in the pub. He was really well hung.

He leaned down and nuzzled her neck with his whiskery cheek. She melted like a stiff rag dipped in water. He said something in Gaelic, a whisper against her ear that sent tingles of anticipation zipping through her system. Love words? Curses? She didn't know.

And didn't care.

His mouth nibbled her ear while his hand slid over a breast. Sweet heaven, she was already getting wet, and it had nothing to do with standing ankle deep in the water or the light spray from the waterfall.

With her back to his chest, she was at a disadvantage. No way to kiss him or hold him close. She was at his mercy. A new experience for her. She wanted him, wanted to kiss him, to bare her skin to him, to feel him thrusting deep inside of her, to satisfy the deep-seated ache that was growing with his simple touches. Yet for their kind, there was no way to go that far without becoming committed to each other for life. And there was no way that was happening.

She did the only thing a hot-blooded female could do when backed up against a hard-bodied hunk who was stirring up her hormones to firestorm proportions—rub up against him. Give him a little back.

He groaned. Then his hand tightened on her breast, his tongue licking her neck, and his free hand moved down her thighs, then between her legs, and cupped her tight against him. She stilled.

She'd awakened the Highland wolf.

The pleasurable feeling of his touch, the way he showed her how much he wanted her, increased the unbearable ache between her thighs. She pushed her back harder against his rigid staff, and his fingers rubbed between her legs, pressing the jeans fabric and her silk panties between her feminine folds.

She moved, wanted to be free of her clothes, to feel him thrusting inside of her, deep, rigid, free, and feral. He breathed so hard, his heart pounding, hers beating just as fiercely, as he continued to stroke her that the roar of the falls seemed to fade into the distance. She'd never experienced anything as erotic as this when she was still wearing every stitch of clothes, minus her shoes and socks.

"Bonny lass," Ian whispered in her ear, his voice husky and sensuous with its Scottish burr.

She spread her legs, hoping she wouldn't push against him too hard and make him lose his balance on the slippery rocks. But he seemed surefooted and, like the castle itself, steadfast and immovable.

Except for his hands, which were doing sweet things to her body. First, his fingers pressed erotically against the fabric between her legs. And then, his free hand slipped under her sweater until he'd reached her bra and tugged it down, exposing her breast to the underside of the soft cashmere sweater.

Again, he spoke in Gaelic, and she managed a weak smile between clenched teeth as she rode the rising tidal wave of pleasure, his fingers rolling the nipple between them while he continued to stroke her. The roar of the falls in front of them drowned out her heavy moans.

"Are you talking dirty to me?" she murmured, so breathlessly that she didn't think he could hear her.

He chuckled and nipped her ear, but he continued to press to his advantage, his fingers shifting from between her legs and beginning to work on her zipper. The fastener slid downward, and he jerked her jeans past her hips as if impatient to get on with business. But he left her panties in place until his fingers pushed the panel aside at the crotch so he could access her eager wetness.

If he hadn't been half holding her up, she would have sunk into the churning water at her feet. But his arm tightened under her breasts and his other hand plied her with hard, urgent strokes, dipping inside and then slipping out to stroke her some more.

She could barely breathe now, could barely stand as his member strained against his trousers and pressed hard against her back. She felt the end coming, so close, so very, very close that she could almost taste the beauty of the rising climax, the need so great she could hardly stand the sweet ecstasy, desperate for release.

Like the beauty and power of the falls, she felt the climax shooting through her, a heavenly exquisite release like no other. She melted in pure satiated exhilaration in his arms. Limp and without body, she didn't think she could make it back to the bank of the burn, much less to the castle. Ripples of climax filled her with a wondrous sensation, and she savored every moment.

He helped tug her clothes back in place and fastened her zipper.

As if he knew she was unable to make it to the bank on her own, he lifted her in his arms and carried her back. "I believe we might be late for dinner," he said, with a half smile that garnered a smile from her own lips. Dinner could wait an eternity.

Ian had never been with a woman so utterly sexually responsive. Ghleanna had been so unreservedly cold to him that he had barely believed it when he'd caught Flynn with her, both bare-arsed in the woods, doing a hell of a lot more than kissing. He'd banished Flynn from the clan, returned his not so bonny bride-to-be to her da, and sworn never again to fall into that trap with another human female, no matter how titled or wealthy she was. But Julia was a sexy wolf siren.

Ian let out his breath as he carried her to the woods. He hadn't planned on letting things get out of hand, just on taking the dogs for a walk and asking her about the car accident. He knew from the glint in Guthrie's eye that his brother had discovered something interesting about Miss Julia Wildthorn. And he wanted to learn what it was as soon as he could. They certainly didn't need any further trouble in the clan.

In the meantime, he hadn't meant to give in to the strong-willed fascination he had for the lass. Yet alone in the wilderness and seeing the way she had enjoyed the hike—despite the pain her ankle must have been giving her, as evidenced by the swelling—and the excitement she'd exhibited about witnessing the falls, he felt like a youthful lad all over again, perceiving everything in a thrilling new way. She moved him in ways no one else had ever done.

He laid her down on the pine needle and leafy cushioned forest floor and considered her flushed face, her eyes and mouth faintly smiling, more in blissful satisfaction than amusement. The lass was bonny and desirable, and as much as he hated to admit it, he'd been unable to help wanting her from the moment he'd started tracking her down in the woods earlier, his prey, his claim, and later when he'd seen her in the pub. Thinking she was human had made all the difference in the world.

A wolf—that was another story. But once they'd reached the falls, and she'd sat down and begun removing her shoes…

That was it. He didn't want to stop there. With the utmost control, he'd managed not to kiss her, knowing she wanted him to as much as he desired kissing her back. But he also knew it would go much further than that if he gave into temptation.

He'd wanted to see her ankle, knowing it was hurting by the way she leaned into him and the way her breath caught when she took a step on several occasions, but he didn't trust her to tell him the truth. The problem was that once he'd removed her sock, he hadn't wanted to end it there. The longing in her eyes told him she hadn't wanted him to, either. Then the kiss happened, and again, he'd struggled with controlling the outcome. Tried to keep from giving in to desire so strong that he didn't believe he could suppress it once they'd started down that rocky road.

So he had done the next best thing he could, abruptly cutting off the kiss and carrying her into the water, hoping to chill both their desires. But *losing all restraint*, he had brought her to climax. Hell, he'd really thought he had everything under control.

At least he had left her clothed for the most part, but that hadn't stopped his craving for her and certainly her delicious response to his touch hadn't curbed his appetite for her, either.

He thought to lie with her in the woods, allowing her some time to rest her ankle and so that his arousal would have time to settle down, but as soon as he lay down and then pulled her into his arms and pillowed her head against his chest, she began stroking his erection through his trousers.

Losh. He'd never had anyone bring him to near completion when he was still wearing his clothes. With her hand on his trousers, she stroked him through the fabric, and he fisted his hand in her hair. He groaned with ravenous need, felt her silky hair in his tight grip, and saw through a lust-filled haze that her green eyes watched him, judging the way her touch made him feel and using that to guide her. But then she unfastened his zipper and slid her fingers down his rigid length through the boxer shorts, found the fly opening, and exposed him to the cool air. Her touch was enough to make him lose any reasonable thought.

Her hand continued to work its magic, except now, skin to skin, every stroke, every heated touch, firm and steady and determined, made him silently beg for more. She slipped her leg over his thigh as if opening herself up to him again, which brought unbidden notions to mind—of peeling off her trousers and her panties, and getting on with the business of pleasuring her all over again. But then she kissed his mouth, pressing her tongue between his lips, and he moaned with feral hunger. He released her hair, slid his hand down her back, and cupped her arse, wanting to do more as her hand continued to firmly stroke him.

Until he couldn't hold back any longer. He closed his eyes to savor the sensation, a tidal wave of need rushing through him, before the most earth-shattering release shook him to the core.

Cursing in Gaelic under his breath, he pulled Julia into his arms and kissed her hard against the mouth. She responded with a faint moan, her mouth desirous, yielding and softening against his. He wanted to hold her and kiss her and take her for his own—a woman he didn't know, who had only wanted him in the heat of the moment but couldn't possibly be interested in anything further than a little wolf intimacy.

"I'll return," he said, his voice husky and strained as he gently laid her back against the ground. "Stay here." He couldn't help making comparisons between the little red wolf and his betrothed. Was it the wolf in Julia that had made her respond so willingly to him?

But then again he was reminded of how Ghleanna had responded to his cousin's sexual overtures just as amorously. Too many years had passed to stew over that; nonetheless, he still couldn't help feeling Flynn's death was due to his own anger over the incident.

Yet, Ian couldn't explain the craving he had for Julia,

either. He'd felt obligated to please Ghleanna. He also wanted to please Julia, but only because he found so much pleasure in her company, not because he saw it as an obligation.

At the water's edge, he cleaned up and then returned to Julia who was lying on her back, her eyes closed, her arms wrapped around her waist, shivering slightly but bonny indeed. He still intended for her to rest her ankle before the long trek back. Lying down beside her, he pulled her into his arms, and she snuggled against him, willing, enticing—and damn if he didn't want her all over again.

Their fur wet, the dogs curled up nearby, waiting for him to give the word that they would be returning home. But he didn't want to return home. Not when he had the little red wolf in his arms like this.

Hell, forget just dining with him. She was staying the night.

Julia loved resting against the braw Scotsman, his arms wrapped around her, his breathing steady, his body hard and warm and protective. The air grew chillier, yet she wouldn't give up cuddling with Ian in the woods like this for anything while listening to the melodic rush of the falls, the breeze stirring the pine needles, and the sound of Ian's blood pumping through his heart. Not until he said it was time to go.

She wanted the moment to last forever. To envision it for her book. To sleep with him in her dreams after she returned to the cottage she was sharing with Maria.

She sighed, not wanting to return to the castle and have to face Ian's brothers, who would most likely tease him mercilessly about his walk with her in the woods when she was gone. Or maybe they would be careful with what they said to him since he was laird. That made her want to know more about his relationship with his brothers. *For her story*. Having never had any siblings, she thought it would be good to take a few notes concerning their rapport with one another.

She closed her eyes. She'd had unconsummated sex with a Highland laird. His brothers probably all knew what Ian had on his mind. She'd been hopeful he wanted a little afternoon delight, even if it was early evening, but she hadn't really believed he'd go very far. Some wolves would not, not unless they planned on taking the other for their mate.

She let out her breath. After tonight, she could never go back to feeling the same way toward Ian or his kin. They were real people, not just names in an email or a disembodied voice on the phone or a lifeless representation of someone in a photo. How could she sneak around the castle trying to locate her family's box behind the MacNeills' backs?

She couldn't. She'd just have to call her grandfather and tell him she couldn't do it.

Ian's hand finally caressed her hair, and he leaned down and kissed her head. "You're shivering, lass. Are you ready for dinner?"

"Hmm. I imagine everyone's eaten already." Then she groaned. "They wouldn't have waited for your return, would they have?"

"No. They know better."

That made her again wonder if they knew what he'd planned with her. On the other hand, he *had* tried to resist—and probably would have, if she hadn't pushed the issue.

He rose from the ground, inspected her foot, frowned, and then pulled on her left sock and shoe on her foot, but not her right. She thought she'd be fine, but he shook his head and handed her the other shoe and sock. "Hold onto these."

"What? You can't carry me all the way back to the castle." She felt awful. Just to see the falls, she'd put him in this predicament.

"Here," Ian said. "Climb onto my back."

"Ride piggyback?" she asked, horrified. "Help me on with my sock and boot. I can manage."

"You're not walking all the way to the castle, lass. Do you think I can't handle it?"

"No. It's just that I'm heavy and—"

"Heavy? As heavy as a pillow of goose down. Climb on." He leaned over for her.

She hesitated. "It's a long way back. If I'd realized how far it was and that my ankle would be giving me fits, I would never have come here." She slipped on her sock so her foot wouldn't be so cold.

He gave her a dark smile, lifted her boot from her hands, and tied the laces around his belt loop in front. "I wouldn't have missed it for the world. We have four choices. You can ride on my shoulders, on my back, in my arms, or be tossed over one shoulder. Any will work for me. Your choice. But walking isn't one of them."

Her lips curved up a hint. He sounded like a Highland barbarian who was totally in charge. Not a laird, though. She would expect a laird to give the task to one of his clansmen. But then, they were quite alone. Would he have handed her over to one of his men if one had been available?

Exasperated with herself all over again for having to do this to him, she let out her breath. "All right. Which will be easiest for you?"

"Easiest?" His light growl sounded like she'd just stomped his manhood into the ground.

She backpedaled. *Alpha male.* "Which would be most comfortable for you?"

"Climb onto my back, lass."

She harrumphed. "If you throw out your back, I warned you."

He chuckled and hoisted her onto his back, grabbed her legs as she hung her arms loosely about his shoulders, and started walking. She really hated to do this to him, but with her legs wrapped around him, her head against his shoulder, his hands grasping the underside of her thighs, she was feeling sexy and interested all over again.

But it wouldn't be the same once they returned to the castle and Ian was back to being in charge and serious when it came to dealing with her. She was still with the film crew, as far as he knew, except instead of searching for the family treasure in secret, now all she had left to do was write her story.

She just hoped her grandfather wouldn't be too upset with her when she called to tell him that the mission he had sent her on was a washout. But the worry kept nagging at her that the matter was too serious not to make the effort.

—◆—

No matter how late Ian and Julia arrived at Argent, he knew his brothers would be waiting up to see what had become of him. And of Julia. He could have driven her back to her cottage and saved her the embarrassment. But he'd promised her dinner, and in any event, he didn't want her to return to Baird Cottage.

Because Julia appeared to be Scottish, he imagined she had roots here. That made him wonder about her ancestors and the freedom her family must have enjoyed by leaving Scotland, traipsing through the wilderness, and settling the new lands on the North American continent. No call for titled nobility. No need to make appearances with strictly human types like they had to do in Scotland. Titles meant social obligations.

Although he and his *lupus garou* family had wanted to keep their land and titles so that they could continue to do what they needed for their pack, the social part of the deal had been hard to stomach at times. The social events were mostly attended by humans, and when he and his family went to such affairs, they always felt out of place and longed to return to the isolation of their woodland estate. Also, titled lords were expected to take wives of suitable breeding. But few Highland werewolf clans had existed, and fewer still that Ian and his family were not at odds with.

So he'd chosen a human, a viscount's daughter, not of werewolf lineage, and although they didn't suit, he'd hoped her social graces would help him to overcome his abhorrence of attending social functions while keeping his werewolf genes secret. But her constant sniping at his ineptness in the social graces had turned him cold even in the bedchamber. He shook his head at his negative thoughts and turned his attention to the woman clinging to his back, his current dilemma.

"I can walk now," Julia said when they were still in the woods but nearing the castle. He knew she shouldn't walk, but she was afraid of being seen while he carried her on his back.

The playful intimacy between them appealed, especially since he couldn't remember a time when he'd felt this way with a woman.

The dogs explored a little distance from them but returned quickly as he'd taught them.

"Either I carry you in my arms or on my back, lass. Shoulders, if you prefer. But you're not walking a step in any direction on your own. By tomorrow, your ankle should be healed. But tonight, you've transportation."

He loved the feel of her legs wrapped around his body, opening herself to him, her breasts pressed against his back, the feel of her soft thighs in his hands, and her arms around his shoulders, hugging him, the jostling as he walked making her rub against him. Already, he was hard and wanting her all over again.

"I can hold your arm and…" She let her words trail off as she tried to look around him.

He strode into view of the castle, the dogs raising their heads and sniffing the air. Julia wiggled to be free, but he tightened his hold on her. "If I drop you, you may sprain something else, lass."

"All right, all right. Let me down, and I'll…" She didn't say anything further as two of his cousins, Oran and Ethan, waved a greeting, both grinning at them at the main gate.

As soon as Ian carried her inside, the men closed the gates, and he knew what the topic of conversation would be for weeks.

"Ian... I... oh, come on, let me down," she said, sounding exasperated with him.

"I gave you the terms of the agreement." He continued to stalk toward the keep as the dogs ran alongside them.

When they reached the inner bailey, Julia tried again. "We're almost there."

He didn't reply. He was used to giving orders, used to his people obeying them. One little red wolf was not going to change his mind, no matter how much she cajoled.

When he reached the front door of the keep, she said, "All right, now you *have* to put me down so you can at least open—"

The door swung open, and Guthrie greeted Ian with a guarded smile. Ian knew Oran had to have called ahead to let his brothers know he was coming. "Your dinner is being warmed as we speak," Guthrie said.

"Thank you, Guthrie." Ian carried Julia into the keep.

"Ian," she whispered.

"Aye, lass?"

"I will get you back for this."

He chuckled and carried her through the great hall where Cearnach and Duncan were standing next to the fireplace, watching she and Ian and looking a wee bit surprised, their gazes shifting to her boot tied to his belt and then to her bootless foot.

He said in greeting, "Brothers." Then he continued to the kitchen and deposited Julia on a chair. "Now, you were saying?"

Chapter 11

JULIA WAS WORRIED NOW THAT IAN WOULD TALK TO his brother Guthrie and learn just who she was, as she assumed that was the secret communiqué passed between Ian and him. Nonetheless, she observed that the kitchen was a state-of-the-art affair as Ian set her in a high-backed chair at a long table. It looked to seat servants, unlike the ones they'd passed in a dining hall.

Several long, dark tables were situated in the dining hall, and each had at least twenty chairs that looked fit for a king, all high backed with seats and backs wearing a rich forest-green brocade. The walls were covered with paintings of local scenery featuring picturesque mountains, tranquil lochs, fields of purple heather and yellow gorse, and the ancient forest. And the floor wore beautifully woven Turkish rugs.

But in the kitchen, the long, light-oak table seated twelve, and she now sat at the head of the table. In here, everything was practical—racks where stainless-steel serving ladles and the like hung, and pots, too, in a rack over a large, freestanding counter. All the counters were granite. And unbelievably, three fridges, two dishwashers, and three ovens filled the kitchen. Plus a microwave.

Thankfully, Ian didn't seem to be in a rush to learn who she was—as far as her being a werewolf romance author. She smelled something, she couldn't tell what, heating in the microwave, as well as the faint aroma of pizza. One of the ovens had been used, and the heat from it had warmed the kitchen to a degree. Fluorescent fixtures flooded the room with light, and leaves fluttered in the breeze on a tree outside a large kitchen window overlooking the garden. She really did want to see the garden and take notes for her story.

Ian pulled a serving dish out of the microwave and considered it for a few minutes, frowning at whatever it was. Then he crossed the floor to the stainless-steel sink and set the serving dish in it. Afterward, he went to the freezer portion of one of the fridges and pulled out a packaged pizza. "My brothers tried too hard. Is pepperoni pizza all right with you?"

"Won't they be disappointed we didn't eat what they made?"

He leaned down under the sink, pulled out a trash bin, and then plucked out a couple of discarded pizza boxes and showed them to her. "That's what *they* ate." He shoved the trash back under the sink and then motioned to the serving dish. "I swear they try really hard to make something inedible so that when Cook is unavailable, I don't make them prepare the meal."

She chuckled. At that moment, she wished she had brothers like that. Who were funny and sweet, but who would be protective, too.

After unwrapping the pizza, he shoved it in the oven and then went to the freezer and pulled out a bag of ice.

"I didn't think you drank anything with ice in it."

"Only when we have American guests. But this," he said, wrapping some of the cubes in a towel, "is for your ankle."

"I wouldn't have thought you'd have American guests here very often."

He raised his brows at her slightly. "I haven't met any that I would consider inviting over for tea."

She assumed that being a *lupus garou*, he wouldn't invite *anyone* over, beyond his kin, who wasn't on his short list of friends. Unless he had to because he was a laird.

He scooted her chair around so that he could move another over and then elevated her foot on the seat. After wrapping her ankle with the makeshift ice compress, he glanced up. "Comfortable?"

"Yes, thanks." As comfortable as she could be with the way the darned ankle was throbbing. But she wouldn't have missed the falls for anything, nor the wild intimacy she had shared with Ian.

"The pizza will be ready in a few minutes. Can I get you something to drink? A wee bit o' Scotch, lass? Or wine?"

"A cup of hot tea?"

"Aye." He boiled some water and then made her a mug of tea and handed it to her. His fingers strayed to a red curl grazing her cheek. "I need to speak with my brothers and have them check into a matter."

"The man who threatened Maria?"

His gaze was steady and concerned. "Aye. If you don't need anything further for the moment…"

"Do you have a spare cell phone? I'd like to call Maria and tell her that I'm still here and that after we finish dinner, I'll be back."

"Call your friend," Ian said, "but tell her you are staying the night."

Just like that, he was giving her another order.

She was amused, rather than annoyed, and actually, as long as she had a spare room to stay in, the whole scenario might work out well, she thought. She might be able to take a peek around while everyone was sleeping. But she was afraid he planned to keep her cloistered in his own chamber.

Maybe he didn't intend that, though. It might be too difficult to explain his actions to his kin. It was one thing to have a human female for companionship but entirely another considering that she was a wolf.

Or would he change his mind once he learned what she did for a living and what she was doing here now?

—⁓—

When Ian had told her to stay, Julia's eyes had widened. She didn't say anything for a moment, and he thought she was weighing the situation—his pack's reaction, her friend's response. Then Julia cleared her throat and ran her hand up and down her mug of tea, reminding him of how she'd brought him to release earlier. He felt his loins tighten.

"You're a wolf," she finally said.

He smiled, unable to help himself. It amused him to hear her say so, although he thought she was more concerned about the fact he was a *lupus garou* and she was, too, and what that meant between them.

He shrugged as if her staying meant nothing to him one way or another. Just a friendly suggestion. She wouldn't have to return to the cottage. He wouldn't have to take her. Seemed the best thing to do under the circumstances.

Her hand kept sliding over that damn mug, and his groin tightened further.

"I don't have a change of clothes," she finally said.

He glanced down at her soft wool sweater and green trousers, the smooth bra hidden under the sweater that he'd managed to pull away from a breast, the scrap of silk between her legs that had yielded to his touch, envisioning how much he wanted to see her out of all of it.

"Either Duncan can drop by your cottage and grab a bag for you, or we can find something here for you to wear. It's up to you." He thought she was really considering staying with him. Or maybe he was just damned hopeful. But it was her choice.

He shouldn't have wanted it. Not when she was part of the film crew and he hadn't wanted any of them in the sleeping quarters. But she wasn't exactly one of them. And that was another reason he shouldn't have wanted her to stay, considering that she was a sexy, enticing female wolf.

Still, he hadn't learned what she was up to, another good point for having her stay.

He reached across the table and took hold of the hand that had been manhandling the mug, wanting to show her how much her actions had already affected him. Instead, he raised her fingers to his mouth and kissed them.

"Stay with me." He meant it to be a command, but it sounded like he desperately wanted her to agree.

"Why?"

She couldn't have surprised him more. He quickly tried to come up with a good reason. The true reasons — he craved having her close; he wanted to know her secrets — weren't what he wished to reveal.

"I thought you might like to experience a night in a castle."

"Ah."

He thought from the impish expression on her face that she didn't believe him.

"All right. For the night then," she agreed.

As much as he didn't want to let on how much this pleased him, he squeezed her hand in acknowledgment. Their gazes momentarily locked, and then he said, "I must speak with my brothers."

"I'll watch the pizza."

"You sit, stay. I'll be right back." He didn't want her leaving the chair for anything.

When Ian left Julia, he assumed his brothers would still be gathered in the great room, seated about the fire in their usual chairs and doing what they normally did if they hadn't already retired for the night. But he knew they wouldn't be. As soon as they saw that he had returned, all attention would be upon him, and the questions about the woman would begin in earnest.

Green eyes narrowed in concentration, Guthrie was reading through a sheath of papers that looked to be something to do with their finances. He stroked his trim red beard for a second, the only one of the brothers who wore one, and then he flipped to another page. He was more studious than any of his brothers, serious and dedicated to the pack finances. And he'd taken this whole financial mess they were in to heart. Ian had been careful not to admonish Guthrie for it, after he had gotten over the initial shock. Instead, he insisted he was at fault for not overseeing matters more. When it came to numbers, though, Guthrie normally knew what he was doing.

Cearnach was whittling away at yet another traditional Scottish handle fashioned out of rosewood for a dirk, although he was now designing the Celtic knot with its interlacing strands over the entire surface. Ian wondered just how many his brother could sell before the market was saturated with his handmade daggers.

Duncan was sharpening his two-handed claymore, and Ian mused that at least two of his brothers looked to be preparing for battle. The wolfhounds trotted beside Ian, their nails clicking on the floor, and all eyes shifted to watch Ian cross the room to join them.

His brothers all raised brows and waited for him to speak. He sat down on his comfortable recliner and said, "Maria, Julia's companion, believed the accident was no accident." He explained the gray wolf sighting and the phone call Maria had received. From their dark expressions, his brothers looked ready to do someone bodily injury.

"They could have been killed," Duncan said.

"Aye, and that's why I want him or, if there are more of them in on this, all of them found." Ian gave Guthrie his attention and waited for his news about Julia Wildthorn.

"She's a romance writer." Guthrie's eyes sparkled with mirth. "She's all over the Web. Author photos, interviews, blogs, you name it." Before Ian could wrap his mind around that, Guthrie added, "A werewolf romance writer, as in she writes about werewolves."

"Hell," Ian said. Of a million different scenarios he could have come up with, that was not even close to being one of them.

No one said anything for a moment, and then Cearnach smiled. "I'd say we have a houseguest." He shrugged. "Someone has to change her mind about what

she writes. Might as well be you, since you're the most
persuasive of any of us, Ian. At least, I'm sure, in regard
to the lassie."

And then it dawned on Ian. That was probably why the
little red wolf had been taking such copious notes concerning the castle and the surrounding lands. Hell, would
she write about him? His people? Not in his lifetime.

More than ever, he wanted to see that notebook of
hers. A werewolf romance author?

"Because of our money difficulties, I was thinking…
since she is everywhere on the Internet, why not exploit
the fact we have a famous author staying with us?"
Guthrie said.

"Is she famous?" Ian asked, surprised as hell.
Werewolves didn't need the attention.

"Well, no, but she is all over the Internet."

"And that helps us how? We're not advertising our
castle so that tons of guests can stay here. We've already had the discussion about opening the place up as
a bed-and-breakfast. No museum tours. No gift shops.
No wedding showers or baby showers or any other kind
of parties."

"Flynn would be upset," Duncan agreed. "He'd throw
a fit and do his ghostly bit and have visitors running for
the exits."

Ian saw the expression on Guthrie's face, deep in cal-
culated thought. "No ghost shows," Ian further clarified.

But he was considering another possibility. Was the
woman as intrigued with him as he was with her, or
was it all a ploy? The enthusiastic trip to the falls. All
that had happened between them once she'd arrived.
He kept telling himself that what they'd shared meant

nothing but a much needed release to quell the growing intrigue they had for each other. But even so, the notion she would use him for her book-writing venture soured his stomach.

"All of this is on the Internet, you say?" Ian asked Guthrie.

"Aye. Just put in her name on any of the more popular search engines, and there it is, page after page. A couple of her books were even made into films," Guthrie said.

"Films." Ian eyed Guthrie with suspicion. "The movie Sunset Productions is filming here isn't about Highland *werewolves*, is it?"

"No, it's strictly a fictional historical piece."

"You're sure?"

"Aye. I've seen the script. The Highlanders are precisely that. No wolves among them."

But that didn't mean the red wolf sitting in the kitchen wasn't writing her own version, featuring Ian and his kin, that *would* be made into a film.

"One other thing, Ian. I recognized her voice when she spoke in your solar. She's the woman who first conferred with me about using the castle for the film production. She used a different name. Iris North."

Ian ground his teeth. "Is Julia Wildthorn her pen name then?"

"I couldn't find anything about an Iris North. That may have been an assumed name as well."

Hell. "All right. Learn everything you can about the man who called Maria and threatened her, the truck that hit their car, and the gray wolf that's roaming our lands." Ian rose and headed for the stairs.

"You've left Julia alone in the kitchen?" Cearnach

asked. The unspoken question was: shouldn't one of them see to her? Maybe watch her?

But she wouldn't be going anywhere. Not with her ankle bothering her so.

"Aye. I'll be right back." After he checked out the woman on the Internet, whatever her name truly was. "She'll be fine until then." As in, leave her alone. He didn't want his brothers romanticizing about her like he'd done, and he didn't want her writing them into her next story, either.

—⁓—

Julia waited while the minutes ticked by for what seemed like hours. The oven had beeped after fifteen minutes, letting her know that the pizza was done. She'd pulled the pizza out and turned off the stove, but when Ian still didn't return after a good forty-five minutes more, she assumed the worst. Guthrie *had* been given the task of learning about her, not cooking the meal, and he had found out all about her books and told Ian—and just as she had suspected, Ian didn't like it.

She sighed. Forget spending the night in the castle. She was beat, and it was time to return to the cottage and regroup.

The great hall where she'd seen Ian's brothers gathered earlier was quiet, and if she hadn't known better, she would have suspected they all had forgotten about her and had retired for the evening. But more likely Ian was checking her out on the Internet and reading all about her. And his brothers were waiting on his return to learn what his take on the matter would be.

She knew how distracting the Internet could be and

how time passed quickly when she was wrapped up in her research. She visualized him frowning and scanning and clicking on more and more links to find out all he could about her. Imagine his surprise if he found the interview she had done with *Love Romance Passion* and the catchy title: *Get into Bed with Julia Wildthorn (An Author Interview)*.

Oh, yeah, that would be a real eye-catcher. She was certain he'd love that. *Not*.

The damage was already done. She sighed deeply. She probably should have told him her name was MacPherson. How bad would that have been?

Bad—if she was from an enemy clan.

Not expecting any help from Ian's brothers, as they'd be loyal to the laird and not an American troublemaker like herself, she let herself out through the kitchen door, which exited into the gardens. Dahlias, sweet spicy-smelling begonias, hydrangeas, wild orchids, and sweetly fragrant thistles, all in pinks and salmon colors, vied for attention in the expansive garden but also crowded around the cobblestone walkway she hoped would lead to the inner bailey.

She limped along a path as quickly as she could manage. When she came to a small wooden gate, she pushed through and closed it again.

Her ankle was hurting, although she knew it would get better if she could stay off it for the rest of the evening. Finally, she managed to make her way through the smaller inner bailey. Halfway across the outer bailey, she thought she might even make her escape. But then the redheaded man she'd written about at the gatehouse, and who had seen Ian carrying her piggyback later, approached her from one of the outer buildings. A stable, she thought, as she believed she heard a soft nicker coming from there.

"Where ye off to, lass?" He looked suspicious and big... make that *very big*, now that she was up close to him.

She motioned toward the gatehouse, not wanting this man's interference but unable to do anything about it. "I'm headed back to the cottage."

He glanced in the direction of the keep and then looked at her skeptically. "No one is taking ye back?"

"I wanted to walk."

"Laird MacNeill had to carry ye because of yer... injury." He motioned to her ankle. He narrowed his eyes at her. "They don't know you've gone."

"Oh, they know. Is the gate unlocked?" She limped toward the gatehouse before he answered.

"Wait here."

She'd heard that one before. *Wait here*, Ian had said in so many words. *He'd be back*. Only this time she figured whoever the redheaded guy was, he'd get some action. She could imagine him rushing into the keep to tell on her—and all of Ian's brothers running to intercept her. Or at least, that would be the story she'd write. Ian would be stubbornly refusing to come for her, his bonny betrothed. He had discovered some secret about her and no longer wanted her, again.

What would be the secret that the heroine would be hiding?

She pondered the answer to that question as she continued to limp toward the gatehouse. A man exited the rounded tower to the left and crossed his arms in defensive mode. He was the other man she'd written about, who also had witnessed her inelegant ride on Ian's back.

"Is the gate locked?" she asked, even though she knew it had to be. She couldn't decide whether to smile sweetly or be very businesslike. She doubted anything she did would encourage him to unlock the gate. Not without him first hearing what Ian wanted.

"We're awaiting word from his lairdship," the man said, brows raised and patting a cell phone on his belt. Even though he was trying to look all businesslike himself, a faint smile curved his lips.

She folded her arms. "I'm an American citizen. And you have to let me out."

"American citizen, is it? Ye've no passport from what I've heard tell."

The car, the fire. She didn't have a passport. Why hadn't she thought of that? Could they arrest her for it?

"You don't have any right to keep me here against my will. Let me out, *now*."

A car's engine rumbled to life in the inner bailey.

The man's smile grew. "Seems you have your ride after all."

She knew it wouldn't be Ian, and although she told herself that was best for all concerned, she was disappointed. She liked Ian and his brothers, and these men also, truth be told. But the fact was that she was a romance author who wrote about werewolves. She was certain she'd hit rock bottom in Ian's estimation of her.

Sure enough, when the car drove up, she saw that Guthrie was driving. The guard hurried to open the passenger door for her, not waiting to see if that was what was going on or not.

"Your ride," Guthrie called out to her when she didn't move to enter the car.

"She's hurting," the guard said.

Guthrie exited the driver's side, but when he did, she started to limp toward the car. She wasn't about to be carried again. She didn't get far, however, before Guthrie lifted her up in his arms and placed her in the passenger's seat. "If you'll get the gate, we'll be off," he said to the guard.

The other man bowed his head slightly to Guthrie and then opened the gate while Guthrie climbed into the driver's seat. "So, you're a romance writer."

Which is how all the trouble began. She didn't respond.

"I take it your *pen name* is Julia Wildthorn."

Uh-oh. She gave Guthrie a sideways glance, and although he kept his focus on the road that crossed the moat, she knew he was sensing her reaction. She didn't say anything. Best to leave things as they were. In one lump of a mess.

But Guthrie wasn't leaving it alone. "Iris North, is it?"

———— ⁓ ————

When Ian's cousin Oran came to him with the news that Julia was limping toward the gatehouse, planning to walk home, Ian couldn't believe it. Well he could, as far as her determination was concerned. But he hadn't left her alone all *that* long. He glanced at the computer screen. It had been over an hour since he had left her. Hell.

"Tell Guthrie to take her home," he had said abruptly,

and then when his cousin had marched smartly out of his
solar, Ian had gone to the kitchen, expecting a burned-up
pizza or, at the very least, a slice of it gone.

But she'd taken it out and left it sitting on the stove
top. Now it was cold and hard, just like the pit of his
stomach. He wasn't about to chase after her, though.
He'd already done enough damage in failing to follow
his rulings concerning his people associating with anyone on the film crew by taking the woman for a walk
and then allowing the heat of the moment to get out of
hand with her.

"She had to have gone out the kitchen door," Cearnach
said, joining him and looking a little apologetic. "Or we
would have seen her and stopped her."

"She's trouble," Ian said, hating that she'd left and
that he'd resolved the issue the way in which he had
done. But how could he tell his people to act in one way
and then do what he wished? It didn't matter that he was
the laird. He led by what he hoped was the *right* example.

"Aye, that she is, Ian. The kind of trouble *I* wouldn't
mind having. I'll see you in the morning, unless you
need me for anything else," Cearnach said.

"See you in the morning." Ian wrapped up the pizza
and stuck it in the fridge. Knowing his brothers, one of
them would heat it up for breakfast. No sense in letting
it go to waste.

But he only had an appetite for the red wolf. No
matter what she wrote about or who she truly was. He
wanted *her*.

Chapter 12

"WHAT HAPPENED TO YOU?" MARIA ASKED, HER EYES wide, her voice surprised as she came out of her bedroom while Guthrie carried Julia into the cottage.

"I took too much of a walk," Julia said to her. To Guthrie, she said, "You can set me on the couch. Thanks so much for giving me a lift home." She was certain the fact that she didn't say anything about whether she was truly Iris North or not hadn't gone unnoticed. But she figured she didn't owe one of Ian's brothers any explanation, and he hadn't pressed the issue.

"*Ladies*." Guthrie smiled at Julia, appearing somewhat amused, and then he hurried out of the cottage as if he might get in trouble if he lingered too long.

Maria locked the door. "So what *did* happen?"

Julia sighed. "Nothing. I took too long a walk and my ankle is swollen."

"I'll get you an ice pack." Maria hurried into the kitchen. "I thought you were just having dinner."

"Ian took me for a walk."

"Ian?"

"Laird MacNeill."

"Ah." Maria banged around in the freezer. "A long walk? Where?"

"To the falls. It was beautiful." Julia sighed and closed her eyes, wrapping her arms around herself like Ian had done. Until his fingers had slipped her bra down and his other hand had worked its way into her panties.

"I thought you might be staying the night, as late as it was getting."

"No." Julia let out her breath again. "He knows I write romances. Werewolf romances. If he or anyone else had been interested in me, finding that out was the end of that. Besides, I'm not here for that."

"The secret niche and the box hidden in it," Maria said, returning with an ice pack. "Any leads on that?"

"No, but he's having his brothers check into who might have called you and about the accident. So maybe something good will come of it anyway. Do you realize we have no passports now?"

Maria sat down on the couch beside her. "Yes. Harold's trying to make arrangements for us to get the paperwork to file for some."

"Did the police say anything about the car accident?"

"They want to talk to you. What are you going to do about tomorrow when we start setting up for the filming to begin?"

"I'll be there." Julia rose from the couch, and Maria hurried to help her to her bedroom. "But for now, I'm going to sleep."

Her expression worried, Maria watched Julia as she climbed into bed, placed the ice pack over her ankle, and then pulled the covers over herself. Julia tried not to wince when even the covers hurt her foot.

"You don't have to go with me in the morning," Maria said.

"I do. I need to write this book, and I need to..."

Well, Julia wanted to get her grandfather's permission to ask Ian to look for the box. "I need to sleep. I'll be fine, Maria. How are your wrist and your back?"

Maria gave her a disgruntled look. "Unlike you, I know when to rest. I'm doing great. Sleep well." She padded back to her own bedroom, and when the bed next door creaked, Julia closed her eyes to sleep.

But she couldn't sleep after all. Her ankle throbbed for a couple of hours, and she couldn't quit thinking about the box and whatever was contained within. Or about Ian and his kin, and how she really wanted to ask his permission if she could look for it. Might as well keep this strictly on a business basis.

Her eyes and mind tired, she climbed out of bed. She limped into the kitchen to speak on the phone there and turned on the light. Not having her mobile cell phone was the pits. Figuring she should make up another ice pack, she grabbed the dish towel and filled it with ice cubes. Then she glanced out the window at the dark night, punched in her grandfather's number, and hoped the hour was decent for him. Her brain was too foggy to figure out the time-zone differences.

She sat down at the small kitchen table and propped her foot up on another chair, laid the ice pack over her ankle, and listened as the phone rang and rang and rang. She hated how her grandfather refused to get an answering machine. Hanging up the phone, she thought about writing a little on her story, but then the phone jingled and she jumped. She grabbed the phone and said, "Hello, Grandfather?"

But it wasn't her grandfather's voice.

"Hello, Julia MacPherson, daughter of Dermott

MacPherson, granddaughter of Findlay MacPherson, great-granddaughter of Conaire MacPherson. Shall I go on?"

On hearing the cold Scottish brogue, she felt a chill snake down her spine. Instantly, she wondered if this was the man who had called Maria in L.A. The man who had threatened her. How or why he knew so much about Julia made her heart quicken with concern.

"How do you know it wasn't Maria answering the phone?" She hastily glanced at the kitchen window, no curtains, the woods dark, and another chill of concern flooded her veins. He was watching the cottage.

"I know all."

He had to have seen her turn on the light, probably even tried to call her, but she was trying to get hold of her grandfather. She moved into the living room where the lace curtains wouldn't hide her, either. Not from a *lupus garou*'s eyes. If he was a *lupus garou*. The wolf in the fog came to mind.

"Who is this?"

"You're mine, lass."

Ignoring his comment and trying not to let him know how much his call had unnerved her, she said, "The film is taking place, whether you like it or not."

"Do you know what this is all about?" he asked, his voice soft and deadly.

All at once she had the sickening feeling this wasn't about the filming at the castle.

If he'd been angry or shouting, she could have handled it better. But she had to agree with Maria. The man sounded dangerous. "Ian MacNeill got the contract for his castle instead of yours," she said slowly.

"*Ian* MacNeill is it now, love?"

Hell, she'd made the slip again. "Laird Ian MacNeill," she corrected.

"No matter. He's a Scottish laird because he owns a plot of land."

A castle, she wanted to say. Not just a plot of land. And he had to be something, a baron or an earl or something, didn't he?

"Anyone can buy a title and call themselves a laird nowadays. Just do a Google search if you don't believe me, lass. You will find all kinds of sites that sell land in Scotland so that women can become ladies and men can become lairds. The title means little."

She didn't want to believe him. Yet she did. Doing a search would be easy, if her laptop hadn't gone up in smoke with the car, and then she could see if what he said was true. Unless he knew she couldn't do a search. Sure, because he probably knew all about the accident. Had caused it even.

"Do you know what's in the box, love?"

Her heart dropped. The box. He knew that it existed. Why would he know about the box? Dread bunched in the pit of her stomach. Did he know what was in it?

"What box?" she asked, attempting to sound genuinely confused, not rattled.

He didn't say anything. She collapsed on the sofa and put her foot up on the pillow still sitting on the coffee table. "Hello? What box?"

"Ah, love, you try a man's patience. Laird MacNeill won't allow you to explore the castle at your will."

"What do you think is in this box that you believe exists?"

"Why, love, you don't want to know." The phone clicked dead.

The blood pounded in her ears as her heart continued to race. She took a deep settling breath. Maria had been right. The man sounded serious about this. The only way she could fight back was by knowing the truth. She quickly punched in her grandfather's number again.

To her relief, she heard her grandfather's voice. "Hello?"

Julia blurted out without preamble, "Someone knows about the box. About me. He warned me not to look for it. But I can't anyway, Grandfather. Not unless I'm allowed to ask Laird Ian MacNeill's permission. I can't do this."

She heard her grandfather's breathing on the phone so she knew he was still there, but otherwise silence filled the airway.

"Grandfather?"

"You can't ask his permission," he finally said, his voice gruffly stern.

"What's in the box? Why would this man be threatening me?"

Again prolonged silence.

"Are you still there?"

"It's a betrothal contract. For the Lady MacPherson to mate with the Sutherland, and failing that, the first female direct descendant born to Conaire MacPherson to the current laird of Argent Castle."

Julia knew there had to have been at least a half a dozen or more female descendants of Conaire MacPherson through the years. But if Lady MacPherson had mated with a Sutherland, was Julia one of them?

That was an awful thought because she would now be Ian's enemy. But if the first one had not satisfied the agreement, had one of her kin mated a MacNeill since they had ruled the castle for some time?

She suddenly felt sick to her stomach, thinking of how Ian had touched her so intimately. In a voice that was barely audible, she said, "Ian MacNeill isn't distantly related to me, is he?"

As if he hadn't heard her, her grandfather said, "*You* are the first female descendant in a long line of male descendants."

With her lips parted, she stared at the table and leaned back hard against the couch, not believing that could be true. Trying to remember any talk of females born on her paternal side of the family, she came up blank.

"The contract would have been drawn up so long ago that no one in this day and age should have to honor such an agreement. The contract *can't* be valid today." If her grandfather was saying what she thought he was saying, she was Ian MacNeill's betrothed.

"You know our ways," her grandfather said. "*Lupus garous* live long lives. We honor our commitments."

"So…" She cleared her suddenly very dry throat. "So I'm supposed to be betrothed to Ian MacNeill?"

"The current laird of Argent Castle. As long as he's the laird, then yes."

"Then if we're to honor this contract, why are you having me locate it in secret?"

"I meant to destroy it, Julia."

She frowned. "But you said we honor our commitments."

"So many years have passed, and we have had no females in the family tree for all that time, so the later generations seem to have forgotten the contract. I assumed no one would know of it, but if someone locates it, then we'll have to agree to the terms. I don't want you tied down to someone that you don't care for, Julia."

Something was being left unsaid. Her grandfather had been too concerned about this. "Why now?"

"I can only assume he learned of the document recently. Whoever it is has been blackmailing your father and me. He doesn't want the agreement found. He doesn't have a copy. The only one that exists is in that box. Conaire meant to take the box when he left the castle, but he didn't have enough time. Getting his family out safely was his primary focus. So now, once I destroy the contract, it's done."

That sent a chill rocketing up her spine. "But who would…" She stopped to think of the men she'd met: Ian, his brothers, the couple of men standing guard, a handful of others who acted as bodyguards or had spoken to Ian on the curtain wall. How many were part of Ian's pack, his clan? Then there were the two men she had seen in the woods. The same ones she'd seen at the airport.

"Ian's family is short on money," she said under her breath. What if that was the reason one of them was blackmailing her family?

She barely breathed. Her family had done well, but they hadn't made enough money to keep a blackmailer in riches. "So this man believes you sent me to try and get the contract."

"You haven't gone by the name 'MacPherson' since you were little. I didn't think he'd connect you to the family."

"Okay, so is he someone in Laird MacNeill's clan?

Assuming the guy is a werewolf. But what would his reason be? The MacNeills are having some major financial problems, or I'm sure they wouldn't have agreed to filming the movie here. Not being *lupus garous*. What if the laird himself, or one of the men on his behalf, was attempting to blackmail you because of their financial woes?" Julia asked.

"I don't know who it could be."

"He has to have gotten wind of it somehow. What if one of Ian's brothers didn't want the laird to mate with an American so the title could go to one of the brother's offspring?" Then she reconsidered what the man had said about Ian's title. "Can you do a search for me on the Internet?"

"Let me turn on the computer. What are you looking for, Julia?"

"If you can buy a title in Scotland. The man said that Laird MacNeill had the title because he owned land. That anyone can be titled if they purchase land."

While she waited for her grandfather's computer to boot up, she tapped her fingers on the sofa. "If there is a marriage agreement, would that information have been written down in family journals?"

"Undoubtedly."

"In ours?"

"Your grandmother destroyed ours when you were born."

Julia swallowed hard. "Is that why you insisted I change my name to a red name when I was little? To Julia Wildthorn?"

"In hopes that our past would never catch up with us, yes."

"Julia isn't a Gaelic name. I looked it up. It means young in Latin, youthful in French."

"You're named after your great-grandmother who was French from Selencourt."

She let out her breath in frustration. "What if I walk up to Laird MacNeill's castle door and demand he mate me—*because* I am his betrothed?"

Ian would laugh her off the grounds. That would be the end of the blackmailer's hold over them. Even if Ian was behind it.

"No, Julia." Before she could ask him why it wouldn't work, he said, "When Argent Castle was besieged, we were running out of food, and then when sappers undermined the west wall, we had no choice but to give in."

"The castle was *ours*?" Her mouth gaped in surprise, and she couldn't let go of her disbelief. "Are you certain?"

"Yes. Conaire MacPherson agreed to give his only daughter in marriage. But he couldn't give his only daughter up to the usurper. Several of our kin escaped and eventually fled to Prince Edward Island."

"But if the MacNeills haven't found the box before this, it may never be found. And whoever is blackmailing us will not have a leg to stand on. Even if Ian's family did locate it, Ian wouldn't force me to mate him based on some contract made centuries ago." Not when she was an American—and a werewolf writer on top of that.

"If not you, then a subsequent laird and a daughter born to you, or a granddaughter, would be liable under the same contract. Do you want to risk that?"

"Maybe the MacNeills don't even know or don't care. Things have changed since those early years."

Her grandfather didn't say anything, and knowing

her grandfather, she envisioned him pacing. But then he said, "About the titles, you're right. If you own some land, about any amount will do, you can claim yourself a laird... or lady."

"Oh, brother. But since he has a castle, he seems more lordlike. What if he doesn't want me? This Laird Ian MacNeill? Then the contract would be null and void. Right?"

Silence.

"Grandfather?" She had a sinking feeling about this.

"Both are bound by the contract. If Ian mated someone else, you or your next female heir would be the next laird's mate."

"So if I were already mated..."

"If you had a female child, *she* could be mated to the current laird when she turned of age."

Julia ground her teeth. "Why didn't you or Dad ever tell me about this?"

"We thought we could destroy the contract before you ever knew about it."

"The castle *had* been ours." She was truly amazed to think her family had at one time lived in the massive stone castle. Not just lived there but owned it.

"Since the time of William of Normandy's rise to power, yes. Although it was built on a Roman site and was timber after that."

And now impenetrable stone. Ian might not think much of her as a werewolf romance writer, but *her* family, not his, had once owned Argent Castle, and *the MacNeills* were the usurpers.

"It's a contract, Julia. We need to destroy the cursed thing and be done with it."

"All right. I'll... I'll try to find it, and I'll destroy it as soon as I do. I don't want to get caught red-handed trying to return to the States with it, though."

Her grandfather remained quiet.

"If they catch me with it, the game is over. I should destroy it immediately."

"Don't open the box. Just bring it here *to me*. 'Night, Julia. Stay safe." And then he disconnected.

She stared at the dead phone, not knowing what to think. *Don't open the box.* Was there something more to the story that her grandfather wasn't telling her?

Feeling wrung out and irritable, she hung up the phone. Her ankle tingled and annoyed her, so she knew it was healing. But with what she'd learned about the MacNeills of the past and the one who was blackmailing her grand-father and father now, she couldn't sleep. The castle had been *her* family's! That meant the kitchen where she'd sat and the great hall that Ian had carried her through. Ian's office most likely would have been that of the laird of her clan, and her own people would have been there, not his.

She considered how horrible it had to have been for her great-grandfather as the MacPhersons tried to keep the MacNeills from entering the castle grounds. How the family must have felt about being forced to give up a daughter to the invading force. And then having to flee their own home.

Well, if Julia had anything to do about it, she would find that box, destroy that document, and set her fam-ily free from an obligation they should never have been forced to agree to. Unfortunately, she couldn't do any-thing about returning the castle to the rightful owners — the MacPhersons.

Notepad in hand, she tried to think of the way she was going to write her story to get her mind off her ankle and Ian while she gave her sprain some more time to mend. But all she could think of was how lighthearted Ian had seemed in the woods, walking with the dogs, walking with her. And then how hungry he had been for her at the falls, desirous, craving, and needy—for her. No man had ever wanted her like that. Not in a feral way. But then again, she'd never had a wolf interested in her before.

She reminded herself that *he* wasn't the one who had laid siege to her family's castle, either. That had been an ancestor of his.

She ground her teeth, forced herself to focus, and began to write her story.

It wasn't about Highland hunks. She was too angry with them for having taken her family's ancestral lands and castle, and forcing her great-grandfather to make a contract that would have tied them to the MacNeills through an unwanted betrothal. And now one of them was blackmailing her family? No way could she make them heroes in her book. She let out her breath hard and began to pen her story.

Spurs clanking, sidearm holstered, Ian MacNeill grabbed hold of the mulish horse's reins and looked up at the woman who rode the animal and was just as stubborn as the blasted horse. "Here in Texas, ma'am, we don't cotton to horse thieves, so why don't you just come on down from there, and we'll have us a little talk before you get yourself into any further trouble."

Another two hours passed as Julia wrote ten more pages of her new adventure—a cowboy story set in Texas that featured a transplanted Scotsman. Lots of them had ended up in Texas, so it wouldn't be a far stretch. Only he'd wear chaps instead of a kilt. She sighed. She really did like the idea of kilts. But leather chaps, now they also had appeal. She'd change his name later, but she gleaned some satisfaction from turning Laird MacNeill into a cowboy.

She stretched her fingers and toes, tensing in anticipation of pain, but her ankle felt well enough again. She rose from the couch intent on getting some sleep while the dark still cloaked the area.

Despite what she knew now about the contract in the box, she was sure this trip was just what she needed to break through her stubborn writer's block. She'd tried everything that usually worked: cleaning her condo—which always sorely needed it between writing the last book and starting a new one—watching a movie, reading a book, taking a walk, gardening on her small patio, even digging out some earlier manuscripts that she'd never sent off and revising them. But this time, nothing had worked. Then when she'd mentioned to her father the trouble Maria's producer was having in locating a castle in Scotland to film the movie, her father had let her in on the family secret.

A Highland secret of old. Perfect to include in her story, but with different names and a different location to protect the innocent and the guilty.

But now, everything had changed. A blackmailer was involved, and he may even have had something to do with their car accident, although she hadn't wanted to worry her grandfather about it.

What if she wrote about the secret documents in a box hidden in a castle, and even though the documents could be something different in her story, what if the black-mailer let Ian know that Julia had verified the existence of such a box in a Scottish castle—now *his* Scottish castle—through her fictional writing and claimed that was too much of a coincidence?

So she was writing her cowboy story instead. No secret boxes. Or… maybe there could be one, and the damsel in distress was fleeing Ian's ranch after unsuc-cessfully attempting to locate the hidden cache—a title to the ranch. *Her* ranch. That would work.

With a smile on her lips, Julia fell asleep for a while. The dark still blanketed the cottage and would for an-other couple of hours. Maria wouldn't be getting up until it was light. Before then, it would be time for Julia's next big adventure. She would be just like the warring clan trying to find a weak spot in the enemy's defenses.

Only this time the castle was hers. And the enemy was truly the MacNeills. Or at least one of them—the blackmailer—and maybe more.

By the time she had awakened and dressed for her clandestine activities, her ankle felt much better, but it was still stiff and tingling. She was afraid that if she walked too much, the ankle would start to bother her again. If she could just slip into the castle and find the box, she'd be done with her mission and could lie around the cottage for another day just letting her ankle heal up sufficiently.

As quietly as she could, she slipped out of the cottage, locked the door, and hurried through the forest toward the castle, hoping whoever was blackmailing her family hadn't been watching the place when she left. But it had been hours, and she assumed he'd never figure her to run off like this. Yet she kept a wary watch for anyone who might follow her.

The breeze ruffled the branches of nearby trees, birds tittering back and forth, as she strained to hear over her own footfalls and thought she heard something snap. A dead branch. Or something. She froze. Whirled around. Peered into the forest. Saw nothing, no one. She was alone.

Her step more hurried, she resumed her hike and finally managed to reach the easternmost tower. She skirted around it to the eastern wall and noted no one on the curtain wall, making her feel safe to go about her sleuthing business. She sat on the damp ground to untie her boots, intending to shape-shift. After removing the one, she set it aside and heard an almost inaudible clunk as the boot touched the ground. With her wolf hearing, she thought it sounded like her boot had hit something that was metal, not rock. She scooted over to feel what had made the noise. Her hands moved over the rusty iron, and her heart nearly quit beating. Was it a door? Or just a discarded piece of scrap metal?

Whatever it was, it had been buried for some time and left undisturbed. Maybe for years. She swept away the leaves and accumulated dirt, and smiled. Her grandfather had been right. Or at least this appeared to be what he had described. But the trapdoor was secured with an ancient and corroded lock.

She pulled out her second set of standard *lupus garou* lock picks, the first having been lost in the car fire. But she wasn't sure the picks would work on something this old. Then she laughed at herself. She hadn't brought the sketch map of the place, but she carried lock picks with her? Yeah, if anyone had caught and searched her, they wouldn't have suspected a thing.

Something in her peripheral vision caught her eye, and she turned to look. Just a pine branch swaying in the breeze. She stared at the location for what seemed like forever. Nothing moved except the tree branches swaying in a waving dance.

With her attention back on the door, she inserted a pick in the lock and jiggled and twisted until it creaked open. She felt that the whole of the castle and the surrounding area would have heard the noise, but perhaps it was just her enhanced wolf hearing that made her feel so self-conscious.

With her heart beating in excitement and trepidation, she pulled the lock free and set it on the ground. She sat and slipped her boot back on, tied it, and then stood and tried to lift the metal door, the brutal rust-caked metal harsh against her bare skin. The door didn't budge. Stuck. Damn it.

Disappointment slid through her. She wished she could have carried a crowbar with her. If she'd still had the rental car, it would have had a crowbar.

She pulled her sweater sleeves down, covered her hands with them, and tried again. A little give. Her spirits lifted. She crouched lower, putting her legs and back into it while trying not to hurt herself, and attempted to lift it again. It moved.

She grinned. She could do this. With her muscles straining, she tried again. It moved more. She let out her breath. She needed a big can of WD-40. She felt like she was in the *Wizard of Oz* and had to use a can of oil on the Tin Man, or in her case, the rusty trapdoor. Although a hefty-sized crowbar would work even better.

Her muscles were exhausted, her green sweater wearing rust stains, and her hands raw from the metal digging into them, but she wasn't about to give up. Not when she was this close to getting inside.

With the last bit of reserve strength she could muster, she pulled up on the metal, which gave the most pitifully horrible screech before she was able to flip the door onto its back on the ground. Her skin sweating with exertion and anxiety, she quickly buried the door with leaves and dirt, but if anyone came to look in the woods, they'd find the open hole into the abyss. She could crouch beside the opening forever to ensure no one heard her making noise, or she could figure that no one would hear her since no one was about, most likely because they all were dead to the world, asleep inside the thick walls of the castle. She might as well enter the tunnel now.

She gave one last look at the woods, the hair on the nape of her neck prickling with unease. Not from the worry of exploring the tunnels, but because of the feeling that something watched her from the woods. But she saw nothing except for trees and more trees. If one of Ian's people watched her, he didn't sound the alarm. It had to be nothing. Just her imagination getting the best of her.

Steeling her back, she started down a rickety ladder into the abyss.

Chapter 13

STANDING ATOP THE CURTAIN WALL, IAN MACNEILL watched the road that led over the moat to the gatehouse and that would be filled with Yanks before he knew it. But there was only one he wished to see. Werewolf-romance author Julia Wildthorn. He'd read every interview and felt he'd gotten to know far more about her than he knew about some of his own distant cousins—from her favorite coffee-flavored ice cream topped with hot chocolate fudge sauce to bathing in lavender bubbles in candlelight.

Hell, and the whole world knew it, too.

For now, he tried to enjoy the peace and quiet of the forest and his holdings before the battle of wills began with the film crew. He tried again to put out of his mind the lass who was so soft and curvy and hot and willing. All night, he'd thought about her, and no matter how much he tried *not* to think about her, he wanted to share the pizza with her like he'd planned, and more.

Hell, he should have tracked her down and brought her back to the castle, instead of sending Guthrie to return her to her cottage. But it had irked him that she had left without word to him, and a small part of him had warned that she was here only as a writer and not interested in him for more than anything but using him. In the heat of the moment, he'd told his cousin to relay the message to Guthrie to take her home.

Now, he concentrated on the darkness, knowing the Americans wouldn't show up until it was light, but still, he almost hoped he'd see the defiant little red wolf running across his lands again. This time, he'd chase her down, wolf to wolf.

Until he heard something in the woods in the direction of the east wall.

Something faint. Metallic. Something unnatural.

The first thing that came to mind was the secret tunnel entrance, but it hadn't been used in over... a couple of centuries, he thought. Probably longer than that.

He stalked toward the easternmost tower. Maybe a red deer had stumbled across it or a pine marten had scurried over the trapdoor. But it sounded more like...

The door creaked. *Hell.* He quickened his pace. Duncan saw him from the bailey below, although Ian hadn't a clue why his brother was up this early. Unless Duncan was anxious about the film crew arriving and wanted to be prepared. His brother watched Ian, knowing something was the matter, but Duncan was farther from the wall and down below, so he might not have heard the sound. When Ian navigated through the gate tower, he heard the trapdoor creaking even more. Someone had gained entrance. Then a bang. The door had been dropped on its back.

Damnation. As soon as Ian exited the tower, he sprinted along the east wall walk, his warrior brother racing to the curtain wall from down below and looking for direction from him. But Ian concentrated on catching the culprit at his task. The man probably wouldn't realize that Ian and his people could hear noises within the castle walls because no one but the clan knew they had a wolf's distinctive hearing. Beyond that, he and his people normally would be sleeping. Within the thick walls of the castle, they most likely wouldn't have heard more than a muffled distant, ghostly sound.

He reached the spot where he could see the entryway to the secret tunnels at the periphery of the woods. No one was there, but whoever it was had cleverly covered the trapdoor. The entryway was still open; it wouldn't have been all that visible unless anyone had been looking for it. Ian hadn't had to deal with the enemy breaching his walls for a very long time.

Time for the hunt. He motioned to his brother, indicating the trapdoor in the woods, and then waved that he was coming down. Ian wouldn't shout his intentions and alert the intruder that they knew he'd broken in. In that case, he'd probably escape. Best to catch him at his task, discover his plan, and show him how foolish his endeavor had been.

By the time Ian reached the inner bailey, Duncan had already enlisted the support of Cearnach, who grinned as if they were going into battle and were sure to win. Guthrie had even torn himself away from getting an early start on reviewing the financial mess they were in to see what was going on. No matter what other interests the brothers had, the instinct to hunt overrode most.

Several of their clansmen also stood by, buttoning shirts and tucking them into trousers, eagerly awaiting orders.

"We enter the tunnels through the trapdoor," Ian said. He held up his hand before Duncan could object. "We could spend hours searching all the tunnels and never come close to finding the culprit. But if we go to the tunnel where he entered, we can follow his scent."

To two of their cousins, Ian said, "Secure the trap-door once we've descended into the tunnel." To two other men, he added, "Watch from the wall walk. If he leaves the tunnel while we're trying to reach it, give us a shout out, and we'll track him down in the woods."

"Could be just someone out for a walk that stumbled upon the trapdoor, got curious, and—" Cearnach said, as Ian and his brothers headed for the main gate.

"Carried something to break the lock?" Ian asked, giving his brother a shake of his head. "Seems calculating, to my way of thinking." Ian finally noticed that Duncan was wearing his sword. "Prepared for any eventuality?"

"Aye. If he's willing to break into a fortress like ours, maybe he's armed."

"Maybe Flynn will scare the devil out of him," Guthrie said, sounding amused. "You know how he doesn't like strangers. If Flynn even realizes someone is roaming about underneath the castle who hasn't been invited, he'll greet him."

Duncan pulled his sword out of its scabbard at his back. "Flynn can't do anything to him unless the man is afraid of ghosts. But this…" He thrust the sharpened blade at an unseen enemy. "…this will put the fear of God in a man."

"Unless he's armed, don't use your weapon, Duncan," Ian said dryly, his blood hot with annoyance that anyone would attempt to break into their ancestral home. Yet he was concerned that someone might get hurt—not the idiot running around in the bowels of the underside of the castle, but his brothers who would stand by his side in any battle.

The culprit who had breached their defenses would soon learn how much wrath Ian could bring upon him.

—◆◆◆—

Even though it was dark in the underground tunnel leading to the castle, darker still on the walls where torches once scorched the rock with flickering flames, Julia could see with her wolf's vision. She hurried down a rickety ladder that creaked and shuddered and bent with every step. She imagined the ladder rungs breaking, leaving her stuck down there and trying to figure out a way to sneak out of the castle from the inside. But if that happened, she'd first try to locate her family's box hidden in the wall somewhere on the third floor of the keep where the family's quarters were.

She'd barely reached the fourth rung when the rotting wood cracked with a snap. Heart in her throat, she half slipped, half fell as she tightened her hold on the rails, slivers of wood embedding themselves in the palms of her hands and fingers. She attempted to reach the next rung without falling to the rock floor below and breaking her neck or a leg. Legs would heal after a while; necks wouldn't.

But she hit the next rung so hard that it snapped, too. Stifling a strangled cry, she grabbed the ladder rails with all her strength, despite the slivers of wood digging into her hands and feeling like stinging nettles, and tried to keep from falling farther. Her arm muscles shaking, she managed to stop her fall, half sliding over the next rung and then finally managing to land on the one below without too much of a jolt.

Barely breathing, she navigated ten more. But when she reached the third from the bottom, it split in two with a nerve-racking crack. She fell too fast and broke the next rung—and missed the final one altogether. She dropped none too gracefully to the rock floor, jarring herself as she landed on her hands and knees with a hard whack. Pain radiated through her knees, making her realize just how little padding kneecaps had. Smacking her already splinter-filled hands against the rock floor added further insult to injury.

A stealthy cat she was not.

But at least with her faster ability to recuperate, she'd overcome her minor aches and pains more quickly than if she wasn't a werewolf. And she hadn't landed on her right foot, risking injuring her ankle further.

She glanced back at the ladder, her gaze rising until she stared at the open hole above. Now that it was missing several rungs, she wasn't sure she could navigate it back to the surface. No sense in worrying about that right at this moment, though.

Turning her attention to the tunnel before her, she got to her feet, her knees and hands still hurting. If she couldn't make it back up the ladder, hopefully once the film crew was on site, she could slip inside the castle and into the noise and confusion outside before anyone caught her.

Of course, the crew wouldn't be setting up until later this morning, and she would have to hide until then. Which could be easy enough if the castle was half empty while Ian and his people monitored the film crew outside. Or she could remain down here. But that was a worst-case scenario. She had no intention of getting stuck in the cold, dark bowels of the castle for hours.

The tunnel was narrow and the ceilings low, with water dripping into puddles and moss covering most of the walls. In some places, she had to crouch. She'd envisioned tall ceilings, maybe with smooth tile walls. Nothing this rugged or primitive. Or confining, damp, cold, and smelling of earth. Buried alive came to mind.

With all the work she'd done trying to get the door open, she'd gotten hot and sweaty. Now she was even damper than before and colder, despite the pure adrenaline rushing through her bloodstream and goading her on. She shivered.

She'd expected that the tunnel would lead straight to where she needed to be. But when she'd walked for some time and come to three different tunnels that branched out like a chicken foot from the first, she stared into the dark, trying to decide which might be the right one.

The longer she attempted to deduce the right one, the longer it would take to discover if she was correct in her assumption. She headed toward the one to the right.

Muffled voices in the keep way above her made her pause, but she couldn't make out the words. They wouldn't be able to hear her moving quietly along the wet, rough floor where she had stumbled a few times because of the unevenness and slippery, rocky ground, but she'd held her tongue in case a louder sound could travel through the ceiling of the tunnel into the lower part of the castle.

A misty light loomed deeper in the tunnel, and she halted, her heartbeat speeding up. But the light blinked out. A shudder slipped through her. She'd hoped to get the contract, return to the film crew, and take notes for her book—without anyone being the wiser—and then return to California at the end of two weeks' time. Although the men in her story were now cowboys and the castle was a ranch where nearby underground caves stored food, and outlaws and Indians had once hid out—like in Salado, Texas, a place she'd researched once for a possible story.

But finding her way around under the castle was going to be a lot more difficult than she had thought. Her grandfather had made it sound as though it would be no trouble at all, a straight shot to the upper floor. Locating the chamber and the hidden niche might be harder. Had it been so long ago that he had forgotten? Or was there another entrance that she should have taken? Oh, hell, her grandfather hadn't even been born when the MacPhersons left the castle. He must have been going on recollections from what his parents had told him.

She groaned. So much for being a super-sleuth.

Suddenly, footfalls walked behind her, headed in her direction, and she attempted to keep her rising panic from overwhelming her. She hurried as fast as she could. No place to hide. No alcove, just a narrow path where she had to squeeze through in some places. The foot-steps sounded odd though, a strange steady rhythm as if made on a movie set, surreal.

Then she came to an opening where the tunnel split into two. She began to take the one to the right. Then halted. If she continued to take the rightmost path, she could find her way back, she reasoned. If she'd been in her wolf form, her footpads would have left a scent she could follow. But in her human form, unless she had bread crumbs to leave and no rats were gobbling them up behind her, her memory would have to suffice.

As soon as she walked forward through the rightmost tunnel, she again saw the light. The footfalls had died

behind her. But they'd been in the same tunnel she'd
been in. Had someone been following her, listening to
her progress, and then when she stopped, he did also?

A wedge of panic stuck in her belly. What if the
blackmailer had followed her?

For an instant, she wanted to continue on through
the rightmost tunnel, to seek the light and find a way
out. But the dark tunnel heading in the other direction
beckoned her to go that way and remain hidden in the
comforting blackness.

She glanced back over her shoulder, realizing that
despite hearing the footfalls, she hadn't seen any light
coming from that direction. It still remained eerily silent, as if someone was waiting for her decision. But any
lupus garou could still see her in the dark, just as she
could see any of them.

The light ahead moved toward her, footfalls accompanying it, and that decided it for her. She hurried toward
the leftmost tunnel, tripped on a bit of rock jutting out of
the floor, and fell. She cried out, furious with herself as
soon as she did, expecting the man with the light to rush
forth and grab her, or the one who'd been following her
from behind to do the same. But she'd hit her shin hard,
bruised it, and torn her jeans, and from the way her skin
was burning, she must have torn her skin, too.

Footfalls from much farther away ran down the tunnel she was in, real footsteps, men's long strides, heavy
and determined. She was in real trouble now.

A cold hand grasped her arm, and she gasped. No one
was there, no one visible. But she felt the pressure of the
hand on her skin as if it were real. A ghost?

Not seeing him, or something that looked ghostly,

made her feel as though she was imagining the whole thing. But she didn't imagine the cold, tight grip on her arm or the way the area surrounding her had turned from chilly to icy, her hard breathing coming out in little puffs of frosted air.

Trying not to panic further, she allowed the strange force to help her to her feet. She could barely walk, her shin shrieking with pain, and she couldn't set her right foot down flat against the floor because it hurt so much. The unseen force guided her as she limped into the dark tunnel and up a long flight of stairs carved out of stone. He wasn't gentle. Instead, like a caveman with his catch, he pulled her up and up, hurrying her until she reached a trapdoor above her. The cold hand receded and the ghostly entity was gone, she thought.

She reached up to push the trapdoor open, but when she applied pressure, it didn't budge. Stuck on the stairs, afraid to return to the tunnel and try another way for fear she'd run into the men who were searching for her, she hesitated, looking down into the abyss. The men's foot-steps were still distant but growing closer every second, their footfalls echoing off the walls, making it sound like a legion was after her.

The trapdoor suddenly swung open above her, and in pain, she scrambled through the opening. The trapdoor dropped back in place, and a rod slid through a notch to keep anyone from reentering that way.

The ghost had rescued her.

"Where should I go now?" she whispered, hoping he'd aid her further, although she still was having a hard time believing a ghost existed and felt foolish for trying to speak to one. She glanced around the room, spying two doors. One probably led into a hallway, and the other, maybe into a bathroom.

The ghost didn't respond, and she couldn't see any sign of him. Maybe he didn't have any other plan in mind and no way to help her out now.

She quickly scanned the room. A king-sized bed took center stage against one wall and was clothed in forest-green velvet from the bedcover to the pleated skirt. Dark green curtains draped down from the top rails as if to keep out the cold drafts or give the occupants privacy. The bed was taller than most, and she thought she glimpsed a copper pot underneath. Surely they had bathrooms in the castle.

A chest sat against one wall, wooden pegs situated above for hanging clothes. A fireplace on the opposite wall had kindling and logs in place, but it looked like they'd been sitting there for a very long time. No ashes remained from a recent fire, and the hearth was perfectly clean.

She limped quickly to the door in front of her, but the lock suddenly clicked. She twisted the door handle, but it was locked from the outside. Her heartbeat accelerated. The ghost was locking her in?

She fished in her pocket for her lock picks, but they weren't there. What had happened to them? Had she dropped them in the tunnel when she fell? Her skin prickled with fresh anxiety.

She quickly scanned the room again. Another door. To a bathroom, maybe. Or a closet?

Maria would be furious with her when she learned that Ian MacNeill's people had caught Julia inside the castle. But still, she hadn't any plans to get caught just yet.

The trapdoor behind her shuddered. She jumped, stepped painfully back against the door that she presumed led to the hallway in the castle, and groaned.

At the tunnel door, a man growled, "Hell, how did she find her way up here?"

"*Ian*," she said under her breath, barely breathing.

"She's bleeding, Ian. Maybe Flynn came to her rescue?" Cearnach said, his voice tight.

Blood? She couldn't have left that much behind for them to have taken notice. Although her shin did feel wet and cold and burned with a vengeance. And they were wolves.

"He doesn't help strangers, and certainly not intruders, Cearnach."

They had to be talking about the man or ghost or whatever it was that helped her into the room.

"But she's a female red," Duncan said. "He probably wants her for his own."

She took her first deep breath, sampling the smells in the room. She smelled Ian's faint scent in here.

"Damn it, Flynn, unlock this door!" Ian said. The trapdoor shook, but it didn't open.

Cearnach laughed. "He's aided her escape. If I know him, he's led her out of the castle by now. If he can't have her, you can't."

The tunnel door shuddered again. "We can't even call our men to search the castle since the phone reception is nonexistent down here," Ian said. "Come on. We'll have to go up through one of the other tunnels."

"Which will take us to the other side of the castle, Ian," Cearnach said. "You know which room he led her to, don't you? Think Flynn is trying to tell you something?"

She thought the room was too feminine to be a man's. The tapestries on the walls were of women sewing on benches while Irish wolfhounds slept at their feet in tones of greens and golds and reds, and floral rugs covered the floor, picking up the colors of the wall tapestries. All appeared to be feminine in design. The room's two paintings—one of the nearby waterfalls with rowan berries hanging over the water, and the other of a loch where a red deer sipped from the water—also made her believe the occupant was a woman.

But then she thought back to what Cearnach had said. She didn't think a ghost would have something in mind other than rescuing her from the MacNeills. Unless he meant to play tricks on them.

"Maybe he didn't aid her escape," Duncan said.

"What do you mean?" Ian asked, gruffly. The trapdoor gave another hard rattle, and she thought the men might break through.

"Maybe he's locked her in the chamber."

Cearnach chuckled. "He might have. Maybe we won't have to send out the clan to track her down after all. Maybe you can just keep her."

Keep her? The contract came to mind.

She swallowed, her throat parched. She could imagine being locked away in the dungeon once they reached her and no one being able to find her while Ian tried to learn why she had broken into their castle. If she gave in and told them why she was here, they'd search for the hidden box. And then do what?

The Scots had the reputation for being wonderful hosts. From what Maria had said about Ian and his not wanting to open his castle up to any strangers, maybe he didn't believe in Scottish hospitality. *Lupus garous* lived by their own rules.

The men tromped down the stairs, and Julia felt even more panicked as she tried the door again. She called out softly, "Flynn? If you're in here, please let me out." *Before it's too late*. She tried to sound commanding, but she was afraid she sounded a lot more like she was pleading.

The door remained locked. She considered the other door to the room, hoping this one was a way out and not a door to a bathroom, which it probably was.

If it was the story she was writing, the door would lead to an escape route. Too bad she couldn't write herself out of this scene. With a pronounced limp, she rushed to the door and twisted the handle, which opened the door easily.

And she discovered another bedchamber. She sniffed the air. Male, gray wolf. Laird Ian MacNeill's familiar and very appealing, sexy scent. She looked at the large bed dressed in black that dominated the room. *His bedchamber*. But it had a door that most likely led to the hallway, and she hurried to the door and twisted.

Locked.

Chapter 14

IF FLYNN WASN'T ALREADY DEAD, IAN WOULD HAVE strangled him. He didn't believe Flynn wanted to give the wolf to him, not when Flynn had loved women, even Ian's betrothed, so much—actually, too much, in that case. If Flynn had wanted to give Julia to Ian, why lock the trapdoor? To keep her from escaping?

No, he wanted some concession, Ian was fairly certain. Forgiveness for his earlier crime, maybe.

"You know him better than any of us, Cearnach. What game is he playing now?" Ian asked, stalking back through the tunnel.

"Going outside again probably would have been quicker," Duncan mused.

"I had our men secure the trapdoor from the outside in case the intruder tried to slip out that way. Hell, if Flynn locks us down here, I swear I'll have him exorcised. Do you hear that, Flynn?"

"It's hard to believe he wants you to have the wolf, but he did lead her to your lady's chamber and not the study or the great hall. You know how he is. No matter how hard it is to figure him out sometimes, he always has a good reason for doing what he does," Cearnach said.

Ian gave Cearnach a dark look. "Except when it comes to women. His loyalty is a bit skewed."

"Aye, but he's had nearly two hundred years to

change his ways, and this past year he has really made a concerted effort to leave the women alone."

"Only because they don't like his ghostly appearances and run shrieking from his presence."

It took them another fifteen minutes to reach the next tunnel, which would exit through the kitchen. Ian yanked at the trapdoor. "Locked." He growled. "I will kill him. We'll split up forces. Once one of us gets through, we can help the others." He banged on the trapdoor a couple of times, partly in frustration and partly in case someone was in the kitchen and could hear them, but it was too early for that.

"Which way are you going?" Cearnach asked as Ian headed back toward the trapdoor where Julia had entered.

Ian grunted.

Duncan cast him an elusive smile. "He's going to try to sweet-talk the woman into opening up. Maybe Cearnach should try. You will probably scare the wee lass half to death after the way she left here in haste last night."

His brothers laughed and headed off down the tunnel to try their luck at other trapdoor exits.

As much as Ian hated to admit it, Cearnach probably would have better luck convincing Julia to open up at this point. But Ian was dying to learn what she would say about what she had been up to this time.

Ian hadn't gone far down the tunnel when he thought he heard the muted sound of pots and pans clanging in the kitchen through the trapdoor. His brothers had already made haste down the tunnel in the opposite direction, but Ian hurried back down the tunnel and then up the stairs to the trapdoor and banged hard.

A woman squeaked.

Hell, probably gave whoever it was a near heart attack. "It's me, Ian," he quickly called out.

"Ian?" a voice called back, sounding unsure.

"Unlatch the trapdoor, lassie," he said, trying for more of a coaxing tone of voice.

"Ian?" she said again.

It sounded like his cousin Heather, but even he had a difficult time recognizing her voice through the stone and metal.

"Aye, aye, open the trapdoor."

"What are you doing down there?"

She wasn't making a move toward the door, and she still sounded skeptical.

"Heather? Go fetch one of your brothers. They'll tell you we were chasing an intruder through the tunnels and Flynn locked us down here."

"Flynn? Oh, aye, the rat."

At least Heather had had her fair share of dealings with their ghostly cousin so she knew exactly what Ian spoke of.

A bolt slid aside, and he shoved at the trapdoor. It gave, and a wave of relief washed over him as he hurried up into the kitchen. Shouting down below, he hollered, "Cearnach, the trapdoor to the kitchen is open!"

And then he bolted for his chamber, praying that Flynn had indeed locked the lass in and hadn't aided her escape. But Ian planned to track her down, no matter where she might have managed to slip off to—and would learn just what Julia had in mind to do.

~~~

Julia sat on the edge of Ian's bed, suddenly more tired than she'd ever been. Her ankle hurt; her leg burned where she'd cut it on the rock; she was locked in Ian's bedchamber; and unless she could weave a whopper of a lie that anyone might believe, she soon would be flayed alive. Trespassing, breaking and entering—never mind that the MacNeills had stolen the castle from her family in the first place—and intent to steal—even if she was retrieving something that belonged to her family originally—would be the first of the charges. Breaking the ladder rungs could be added as destroying personal property.

The rush of boots hurrying toward the door, then slowing, growing even slower, and then stopping right beyond the door made her throat go dusty dry. Her heart was beating so hard that she thought it would soon take off. Her palms were sweaty and her skin chilled. She didn't think he'd have her arrested. Not when she was one of them and putting a werewolf in a jail could have dire consequences if she couldn't control her shape-shifting.

But even if she managed to get out of this mess and wanted to return home pronto, she had no passport, no credit cards, and not enough cash to do anything. She wasn't one to give up, but right now, she felt like she was in her great-grandfather's shoes—under the enemy's thumb without another plan to fall back on.

The handle turned, but the door didn't open. Locked. She stiffened, held her breath, and sat very still.

Then a metal key poked inside the lock and twisted. A click sounded, and the door was shoved open. Standing in the doorway, one red-faced Laird Ian MacNeill quickly scanned the room for her. His eyes widened a little when he saw her sitting on the edge of his bed.

Ian MacNeill. By ye ol' legal contract, her betrothed mate.

She managed a small smile. "You offered for me to stay overnight." Even though daylight was dawning and it was a little late for an overnight affair. She patted the bed. "Is this the room you had in mind?"

———————

Ian stared at the breathless vixen sitting on the edge of his mattress, looking pale, scared, and dwarfed by the size of his massive bed. Her heart was pounding hard, her red curls windswept, her lips parted slightly. She was beautiful and dangerous and his undoing. A maiden in distress with something to hide.

The thumping of boots headed toward Ian's bed-chamber alerted him that his brothers, most likely, and others were on their way.

"You've hurt yourself, lass," he said quietly, looking her over and seeing the rip in her jeans on the lower part of the left leg and the blood on the fabric. He stepped through the doorway and said into the hallway as Cearnach led part of the pack—his brothers and two cousins—toward him, "She's here and fine. Ready yourselves for the film production staff's arrival."

Cearnach waited for further word, most likely wanting to know just what Ian intended to do about Julia and what kind of shape she was in.

"The crew will be here soon. Have your breakfast, and I'll see you later," Ian said. *Much later*, he wanted to add.

Cearnach looked at Ian's door, although he was too far from the room to see inside. "She was bleeding."

"Aye."

"Do you want me to send Heather up with bandages?"

Ian shook his head. "I'll take care of it."

Cearnach gave him a stiff nod and then turned and motioned Duncan and Guthrie and their cousins to go back the way they had come. Everyone looked reluctant to be dismissed without further word.

In Gaelic, Guthrie asked Cearnach, knowing damn well Ian could hear him, "He's not too angry with her, is he?"

"He's in love, can't you see?" Cearnach said lightly and laughed.

Love. Hell, Ian was in perpetual lust when it came to the little red wolf. He closed the door and locked it. Julia's eyes darkened. Otherwise, she schooled her expression, but her back was as stiff as his breakfast table. He didn't want any interruptions, and the only way to ensure that was to lock the world out.

"So you wished to stay the night after all," Ian said, giving her a rough-edged smile and stalking toward her in a much too predatory way. Two could play at whatever game she had in mind.

He hadn't been able to sleep because of her. The lingering scent of her, the feel of her soft curves in his hands, her silky hair, the sound of her voice breathless with desire, and her soft moans in the throes of passion while they had been at the falls had remained in his thoughts. Making it impossible to sleep.

He'd never craved having a woman as much as he did Miss Julia Wildthorn. After the disastrous attempt at fitting into society and handfasting with a titled human woman, he'd stuck to commitment-less trysts with human females. But Julia was something else. She was desire personified.

She was the enemy, sneaking into his castle with who knew what kind of agenda, and he had the unbiddable urge to conquer her, to keep her, to bring her to heel like one of his Irish wolfhounds. But he didn't think she'd be the least bit trainable, and the challenge intrigued him.

Her hand clenched the bedcover, her eyes widening and darkening further.

"I regret having left you alone for so long last night that you decided to return to the cottage because of my neglect." He reached her and towered over her, intimidating.

She stared at his crotch, and he felt the stirrings of yearning all over again. Hell, he was supposed to be a battle-hardened earl, clan chief, and pack leader, and the woman was winning the skirmish without a fight.

He crouched at her feet and then untied the boot on her right foot, being careful not to hurt her and worrying that she'd put too much strain on her ankle again. When he pulled off her sock, he saw that the ankle was indeed swollen. He *tched*. Then he worked on her other boot and sock. "I suppose you changed your mind and wished you had stayed the night at the castle after all. For the unique experience."

He tried to maintain an aloof air befitting an earl and a pack leader. But his voice was too raw with need, and he was certain she could recognize what she was doing to him.

Her other hand tightened in her lap in a small fist. Her heart beat rapidly. His gaze rose to meet hers. She looked like she was resigned to her fate, willing to do anything to get herself out of this predicament. He had ideas about that, certainly.

He wanted to ask her how she'd found the secret tunnel entrance, which he presumed she had already known about. He wanted to ask why she'd known about it and why she'd sneaked in that way. But instead, he stood and rested his hands on her shoulders, and then gently encouraged her to lie back against the mattress, her legs still dangling over the bed. "You no doubt discovered the gate to the castle was locked, and unable to gain access that way, you located another entrance. Although I'm wondering why you would not have called me. I would have come and let you in."

"My cell phone was burned up in the car accident. And if I'd had one and called you, you would have sent one of your men to open the gate. *You* wouldn't have come to get me."

He smiled at her last comment. "Aye, I would have. To save you the scrutiny that my men would have given you, had you returned to me in the middle of the night." He towered over her, watching her eyes, large and now nearly black, one hand clenched in a fist on her stomach, the other still clinging to the cover.

"So you sought another way in and fortunately managed to locate the trapdoor." He didn't bother to mention that it had been buried for a couple of centuries or more and that her finding it had been either fortuitous indeed or due to the directions given to her. Which made him wonder if one of his men had confided in her, or if someone else, his enemy maybe, had learned of it and had paid her to enter in that manner. But for what purpose?

"Fortunately for you, you had some assistance in

finding the right tunnel to the room adjoining mine, or you could have been wandering around in the cold, damp passages for a very long time." He leaned over and unfastened the button on her trousers and then pulled down the zipper.

She barely breathed, yet she didn't resist. "A ghost," she whispered.

"Aye. Flynn. My cousin. The one who'd had his way with my handfasted bride. Dallied with one too many married lassies after that, and an angry husband made him pay for it. He didn't frighten you?"

"I saw a… light up ahead. And heard unnatural footsteps behind me. But they didn't… sound right somehow, like they were produced on a movie set, unnatural."

Ian smiled a little. "That's Flynn. He usually attempts to terrify, not rescue, an intruder. Wonder what he was thinking?"

Gently, he tugged her trousers down her hips and lower, trying not to scrape the fabric against her bloodied shin. He laid the trousers on the floor and said, "Stay."

She stared up at him, a wee smile on her lips. "I wouldn't run around the castle without my pants on."

He gave an almost inaudible snort back. "Not with your ankle giving you pain again." He went into the bathroom and gathered up bandages, a wet cloth, and a hand towel, and returned to her.

"You're not too mad about what I write?" she asked, her words spoken softly. She sounded as though she was afraid to hear his answer.

What difference would it make what he thought about her writing? Was that the real reason she had taken off last night, not because he'd rudely neglected her?

Surprised that was the issue she'd bring up and not the one about the fact she'd been running through their tunnels, he paused to consider her sincerity. She truly looked like she had to know the truth. He couldn't deny that the thought she wrote about werewolves bothered him. Although he'd warned himself that he'd reserve judgment until after he'd read some of what she'd written. Maybe her stories were like the tales of werewolves of old. Hideous, monstrous beasts and nothing more.

He took another tack. "Guthrie says you're famous. Could be good for business to say you stayed here for a time." He crouched in front of her and dabbed at her bloody shin. His gaze strayed to her panties—a red lace thong. Trying to concentrate on cleaning her cut and not on how beautiful her slim legs were or how easy it would be to slip off the thong—or how he wanted to remove her sweater and bra, too—he wiped carefully around her injury.

"Hardly," she laughed tightly, wincing.

"I'd beg to differ. You've been interviewed all over the place." His gaze returned to hers. "Lavender baths, Celtic music, and candlelight to get you in the mood for writing your scenes?"

Her lips parted slightly. Kissable full lips begging for his touch.

"You mentioned on a personal blog that you had writer's block. Is that why you're here?" He taped a bandage over her shin, smoothing down the edges to keep it in place. He had to know—was she writing about his people in this new story of hers? Was she writing about him? And if so, was he just one of the characters in her book and nothing more?

"I had writer's block, yes," she said, pursing those beautiful lips, her eyes narrowed a little.

"But no longer?" He scooped her up and resituated her on the mattress so that her head rested on his pillow. Then he tucked another pillow under her right foot and covered her with a lightweight cashmere throw.

"Nope. The writer's block is all gone."

He detected a hint of a smile in her expression and in her tone of voice. But he did not find it amusing that she would write about them—not as werewolves. "Is that so? What is your next story about then?"

Again, the flicker of a smile, but she attempted to remain serious. "Cowboys in Texas."

He stared at her uncomprehending. "Cowboys?" he finally said. He didn't believe it. He folded his arms. "On your blog, you said you loved everything Scottish. That you intended to write about Highlanders of old. That you had family roots in Scotland."

The hint of a smile faded from her expression. For a moment, she didn't say anything. Trying to come up with another story? She was a storyteller all right.

"You must have spent half the night reading everything there was to read about me," she finally said.

"I've never known a published author before. I was curious." More than curious. "So why come to Scotland to write about Texas cowboys? You didn't say anything on your blog about wanting to write about them."

She shrugged. "A good friend of mine was writing about hunky Wyoming cowboys. And another, about Texas Rangers—you know, the good guys with the white hats? I just... well, changed my mind. Writer's prerogative."

"I see." But he still didn't believe her. "Do you have your notebook with you?"

She sighed. "No. I guess in my hurry to return here, I forgot all about it."

"Hmm," he said, thinking she looked dreamy-eyed and huggable. But if she could steal into his castle without a bit of remorse, he'd have one of his brothers look for her notebook in the cottage where she was staying and find out just what it was she was writing. As soon as her friend was on the premises during the shoot and Julia was incarcerated in his bedchamber, he'd send somebody. "Any other aches or pains you want me to look after before I get some ice for your ankle?"

She raised her hands and showed him her palms. They were rust-stained and red in places where slivers had entered the skin. He swore under his breath and looked over her hands, rubbing gently where her soft skin was unmarred. He shook his head. "I'll get the ice and a pair of tweezers and be right back." When he reached the door, he said, "Stay, Julia. I don't want you injuring yourself any more than you have already. The cost of personal liability insurance is enough as it is in this place."

She gave him another small smile, and he thought how tired she appeared. The truth of the matter was that he was damned tired also. Taking a wolfish nap with her certainly appealed, after he took care of her injuries. After that? She was his houseguest for as long as it took for him to learn the whole truth about her.

He left her, not wanting to, but not trusting her entirely so he locked the door. This time when he told her to stay, he intended to hurry and return to her, and he didn't intend for her to slip away.

When he reached the kitchen, every chair but his own at the table was filled with his brothers and cousins. They all stopped eating as half-empty dishes of porridge, black pudding, square sausages, eggs, tattie scones, and haggis littered the table.

His cousin Heather smiled brightly at him, dark hair pulled back in a ponytail, dark eyes flashing with excitement. "My brother Oran said the author Julia Wildthorn was the one you were chasing in the tunnels. Was it really her? Was she researching the castle for another one of her books? I've read all of them. Where is she? Can I meet her?"

He frowned. "You have her books?"

"Aye, is she writing one about *you* this time?"

He glanced at his brothers, who cast him bigheaded smirks and then continued to eat their breakfast in silence. He wondered again whether Julia was using him and his kin to write her current novel. Cowboys, his arse.

"Heather, can you get me an ice pack?" He avoided the issue of her meeting with Julia just yet and began searching through a drawer of stuff—containing everything from pliers to staples and pens. When he had a moment alone with Heather, he'd ask to see the books she had of Julia's.

"What are you looking for?" Cearnach asked.

"Tweezers."

No one said anything right away, and he was certain they were all either trying to remember where a pair were or to figure out why he would need them.

Cearnach said, "In the blue bathroom. I'll get them."

Duncan forked up a bite of sausage. "She wasn't too disturbed to see Flynn, was she?"

"No." Ian took the ice bag Heather handed to him.

"Did she tell you why she sneaked into the secret tunnels?" Guthrie asked.

"I believe the more important question is—how does she know about the secret tunnels? An American? A red wolf? Never lived in Scotland before?" *Unless she had lived in Scotland before.* As many years as their kind lived, she could very well have resided in Scotland for a number of years earlier in her life.

Guthrie set his coffee mug down. "She's a writer. A published author. What if Julia Wildthorn isn't her real name? What if it's a pen name, and she's truly a Highland—"

"MacPherson," their Aunt Agnes said, sweeping into the kitchen, her silver hair coiled up in a bun, her gray eyes surveying the crowd at the table before she sat down in Ian's vacant chair and motioned to Heather to bring her a plate of food, which would consist of fruit, fruit, and more fruit.

"You're back from your trip to London so soon?" Ian asked, astounded. "Where's Mum?"

"Still there." She waved a dismissive hand as if London wasn't her favorite place to be, although he knew better. "Guthrie called me and said we had a little red wolf in the house. I had to see for myself."

He wondered if her interest was something more than that. She'd said often enough that he had to mate and produce some offspring who would inherit the title. And she hadn't wanted to be here while the filming was in progress. He wondered just what Guthrie had told her that would have influenced her to return home.

"What made you think she could be a MacPherson?"

Ian asked, as Cearnach returned to the kitchen with the tweezers.

Aunt Agnes waved a piece of honeydew melon at him. "Some portraits of the MacPherson family are stored in one of the tower rooms. This Julia Wildthorn? She reminds me of them. When Guthrie informed me we had a famous author here and showed me a picture of her on the Internet… well, the lass looks so much like the MacPherson woman in the portrait that I'd swear she was one of them."

Ian was suddenly suspicious. "Why would we have portraits of the MacPhersons in one of the tower rooms?"

"I'm not sure," she said vaguely. "But I can look into the family journals and see if I can learn anything. Or you could ask her directly."

He didn't like where this was going. "Cearnach? I need to speak to you for a moment."

Cearnach rose from his chair and quickly followed Ian into the great room. "What did you need me to do?"

"I want you to run by Baird Cottage when the place is vacated, as soon as Julia's friend Maria is here doing her job."

"And?"

"Locate that notebook of Julia's. I want to know what she's been writing in it."

"Her new story?"

"Or anything else that might clue us in about her. And grab her bags so she has a change of clothes. I also want to know about those paintings in the tower," Ian said.

"So she's staying with us then." Cearnach folded his arms. "I'll get the journal. As to the paintings, except for seeing with my own eyes if the woman favors them, Aunt Agnes will be the one with all the historical knowledge."

"I have to know what's going on with the lass."

"Is she all right, Ian?" Cearnach asked again.

"As long as she stays put, she'll be fine. I'll see you later."

"I'll make sure everyone's in place for when the film crew gets here."

"I'm counting on it." Ian headed for the stairs and then turned slowly. "Have Guthrie do a search for anything on a Julia *MacPherson*."

"Will do."

Then Ian headed up the stairs, although he heard Guthrie ask Aunt Agnes in the kitchen, "Who were the MacPhersons to us?"

This was just what Ian was dying to know.

If his family had portraits of them stored in the tower room, the MacPhersons must have at one time lived in this castle. And if Miss Julia Wildthorn was a MacPherson, not giving him her true name, had she something more to hide?

Family history had never much interested him. The present, the future, keeping the clan afloat, hunting with a bow, and wielding his sword in mock battles— he laughed at himself over that. He did kind of live in the past—because of their long lives and because some of the activities he'd loved to do in his youth were still his favorite pastimes. But it was *his* past. Not that of his ancestors. Still, if Julia had some tie to his family's past, that definitely made his family history much more interesting.

He rubbed his chin, realizing that if he didn't shave

soon, he'd be as whiskered as Guthrie. Ian stalked up the stairs, wondering why in the world the MacPhersons' portraits would have been in their castle. Had the MacPhersons pledged loyalty to his father or grandfather or great-grandfather before him? But only those who had money and importance could have afforded or would have wished to have portraits made of themselves.

So who were the MacPhersons?

Chapter 15

IAN TOOK WAY LONGER TO RETURN TO HIS BEDCHAMBER than Julia had thought he would, and although she meant to remain awake, staying up most of the night, all the exercise she'd gotten from running through the woods and walking to the falls earlier, and the jet lag from traveling finally caught up with her. Somehow she managed to climb under Ian's goose-down comforter to snuggle against his soft mattress and even softer pillow. While enjoying his heavenly manly scent surrounding her, she fell asleep.

It wasn't until she heard a whispered "*MacPherson*" next to her ear and felt strong arms pulling her against a hard, hot body, that she became aware Ian had joined her in bed. Her hands touched a bare chest, and her bare leg slipped against his. Had she even heard him say the name MacPherson? Or had it just been a dream?

Figuring there would be time enough to deal with the trouble she was bound to be in once she was more awake, she snuggled against him, mindful of her torn-up shin and sprained ankle. She thought she heard him roughly groan as she moved her leg up on top of his to keep it from hurting, and then the dawning day blinked out.

—◆—

While Ian and Julia stayed in his chamber above, Cearnach couldn't help speculating about what was going on between the two. He'd never seen his older brother so taken with a woman, and he was hopeful that this time Ian had found his match. And that she wouldn't upset him like Ghleanna had done. *The witch.*

In the meantime, while Duncan and several others monitored the film crew, Guthrie continued to look into who might have threatened the women and attempted to find anything about a Julia MacPherson, and Cearnach headed off Maria who stalked toward the castle entrance, her look grim, determined, and battle ready. But now that Maria had arrived at the castle, Cearnach had another mission in mind. Locate Julia's journal. First, though, he had to deal with her friend.

As upset as Maria appeared, he thought she was going to try to walk right through him. "Maria Baquero?" he asked, holding a hand up to stop her or grab her, whichever he needed to do to keep her from storming the castle.

"Is she here?" she asked brusquely, but worry threaded her words.

He smiled. "Aye." Although he hadn't had word from Ian as to what he was supposed to say to the lass if she'd arrived looking for Julia. He folded his arms. "She's with Ian."

Maria folded her arms, mirroring his stance, a scowl on her face. "I'm not speaking to one of Laird MacNeill's people. I want to see *Julia.*"

That put him in his place. Cearnach bowed his head a little. "I'm Laird MacNeill's next eldest brother, Cearnach MacNeill, and in his stead, I run things. His Lairdship does not wish to be disturbed. You'll have to come back later. Or better yet, as soon as he is free, he can speak with you while you're working here today."

"My business is with Julia, not with Laird MacNeill."

"Laird MacNeill has business with Miss Wildthorn. Or... is it *MacPherson*?"

Maria's mouth dropped open, and she stared at him. "What?"

He assumed then that she didn't know what Julia's real name was. Or that she did know and was surprised to learn the MacNeills knew the truth, even though they hadn't been certain. But it didn't hurt to try and learn the facts from Julia's friend while Ian was with Julia. He doubted the two of them were talking much right now.

"I don't know what you mean," Maria said, too indignantly.

"No matter." Cearnach smiled. "Would you like me to pass a message along to... her?" he said, not sure what to call Julia now. Was she even named Julia?

"What happened? Why is she here?" Maria asked, her voice low and threatening.

"His lairdship had asked if she wished to spend the night. She returned to the cottage for a while and then came back here."

Maria looked a little pale. Had the lass known Julia was going to try and sneak into the castle? He suspected so. "She might be free around suppertime. But as I said, as soon as she's available, I'll let her know you want to see her."

They eyed each other with wariness. Maria wasn't budging, and he wasn't, either. He'd have to give the word for someone to keep an eye on her for the rest of the day. He didn't want her sneaking into the castle and causing an uproar like Julia had already done.

Then thinking of the man who'd called her with a threat, Cearnach hoped to show he wasn't the enemy. "Have you received any more threats, lass?"

She shook her head. "I think Julia may be right. That the caller did so because he was pissed off, but that since he couldn't change things, he's given up." Her teeth gnawed on her lower lip. "Except for the business with the car."

"We're still looking into it. If we get any leads, we'll let you know. All right then?" he asked.

When she didn't make a move to back off, he motioned for Duncan, who was watching nearby as the scene played out. "Duncan?"

His brother stalked across the inner bailey to join him, eyeing Maria in an intimidating way.

"You know Maria, Julia's friend. If we get word from the lass that she's available to see her…" Cearnach let his words trail off. "I have other urgent business to attend to." His and Duncan's gazes met. Duncan got the message. Ian needed Cearnach to take care of some other business, and Miss Maria Baquero was Duncan's charge until Cearnach returned.

"See you in a short while, Cearnach."

"Aye, be back shortly." Very shortly. While Cearnach was in charge, he didn't want anything to go wrong in his absence.

―᷍᷍―

Julia stirred, her leg resting over Ian's thigh, her hand on his belly, her warm breath fanning his chest hair. He hoped to get some answers from her now, although the way she was touching him made him want something else entirely.

"Are you awake, lass?" he asked quietly, not wanting to rouse her if she was still not fully awake. While she'd been dead to the world, he'd managed to remove the slivers from her hands, and he hoped her fingers and palms would be healed by now.

"Hmm," she said, dreamily, stretching her fingers against his skin.

He ran his hand over her sweater-covered back, the cashmere as soft as she was. "What were you really doing in the tunnels?"

She didn't say anything. She was awake, but she seemed intent on avoiding the issue.

"My Aunt Agnes says you look very much like one of the MacPhersons. She's positive you're one of them." He wasn't about to mention the portraits in the tower room yet, hoping she'd tell him the truth on her own. But if Julia denied being a MacPherson, he'd show them to her. He wanted to get a look at them himself first, though, to see if there really was a resemblance.

Julia's fingers stilled. The soft touch had been driving him to distraction, but now he wished she was still plying her gentle strokes across his chest. She barely breathed and lay quietly, not saying a word. He suspected then she *was* a MacPherson. But what was her family to the MacNeills?

"Is Julia your real name? Or do you have another alias for your given name also?"

She gave him an annoyed look. "Julia. And if you must know, I go by Wildthorn. If you'll look for any documents on me, my driver's license, passport—"

"None of which you probably have now due to the accident."

She paused. "Well, yes, but if you saw them or had access to my records, you would see I go by Julia Wildthorn."

"But you were born a MacPherson."

"Yes," she said so softly that he almost didn't hear her.

So what did that mean to him? Nothing. He still didn't have a clue as to what the MacPhersons were to his family. And without something more to go on, he didn't believe he could get her to tell him the truth. They were at an impasse again.

"My Aunt Agnes is the family historian, and she's cut her trip short to London to return here and research the family journals—all because of you. I have to say I was much surprised. She never shortens her vacation when she's visiting her favorite place to shop. And what with the mess the film crew is making of the castle, she hadn't planned to return until it was all over."

Since she hadn't allowed Guthrie to handle her own investments, Aunt Agnes hadn't gotten into the financial straits they had. She could still enjoy a vacation away from the castle for a very long time without straining her finances.

Julia swallowed hard.

That got a response. "You might as well tell me what's on your mind, lass."

She didn't say anything for a long time. He knew from the way her heart was beating way too fast that she was thinking about what she was going to say to him.

He let out his breath, about to try yet another tack,

when her fingers lightly caressed his chest again. "I'll tell you what I know if you promise me something."

"It depends on what it is." He wasn't about to give in to the lass without knowing what this was all about. He twisted one of her curls around his fingers, his gaze on hers.

She seemed to ponder that notion and then finally said, "You don't love me."

He was so surprised at her comment that he just stared at her.

She gave a little shrug. "I'm a romance writer."

"*Ah.*" That explained it.

"No, *listen.* In the olden days, men and women married for lots of reasons—because they had to, because it was convenient, for financial reasons or status, maybe because they loved each other. None of that matters. All that is important is that we live today, now, in the present, and the past isn't crucial in the scheme of things."

Her voice had taken on an almost desperate quality, still soft, still sexy, but she seemed afraid.

"Aye," he agreed, yet he thought even that concession might be a little premature, depending on where this dialogue was going. "For the most part," he countered, just to give himself some leeway if he needed it.

"Not for the *most part.* It's as it should be. People should marry for love."

"Even in this day and age, people marry for reasons other than love."

Her fingers went very still again.

"For the sake of argument," and because he damn well wanted to hear where this was going, he said, "all right, so the man and woman marry for love and...?"

"Not the man and woman. Us."

He raised his brows.

"I mean, you don't love me, and well, I don't know you at all, and so..." She shrugged again.

He fought laughing. But she sounded serious, which put a damper on what he thought should have been funny. "All right, so I don't love you," although lust was definitely part of the problem, he thought, because even now he wanted her. He tried to think with his other head and continued, "and you don't love me and...?"

"Well, if there was an agreement that said you had to mate me and I had to mate you, there would be no reason to do so. Because we don't love each other."

"A betrothal agreement?" He frowned and gave a gentle tug on her curl. Her believing in relationships that had all to do with love had to be a by-product of writing romance novels, but the notion of a betrothal agreement between them made him wonder what was truly going on. "What if, for the sake of argument, I did love you?"

Her eyes grew big. "Well, you don't. You already said you don't. And since we have no other reason to mate, then that's that."

She wasn't making any sense, so he thought he'd go about it another way to attempt to get at the crux of the matter. "Let me tell you the way it is. You were aware of the location of the secret entrance."

She let out her breath, and the heat of it stroked his chest. Hell, he was already halfway aroused. He was ready to forget the interrogation, assume she had wanted to return to him and the gate had been locked, forget that she had known where the tunnel was and had sneaked in for some other nefarious purpose, and get on with more pleasurable business.

"I dropped my boot on the metal door and heard a clunk."

His hand settled on her shoulder and then he caressed it. "All right, but you were looking for the secret passage, and don't deny it."

She lowered her gaze to his chest and teased a nipple with her fingertip.

He stifled a groan. "Why were you looking for the secret entrance?"

"It seems rather obvious. To get inside."

"You were already inside the castle earlier in the evening. You could have stayed the night at my invitation. Why use the tunnels?" The thought that kept coming to mind was that she meant some misdeed, that she was the enemy, and in any other situation, he would have fought that enemy before giving in. But her sweet, torturous touch gave him other notions, and he was ready to yield to the sensation and forget whatever reason she had tried to slip into the castle unnoticed. Was that her ploy? If so, he'd met his match in battle.

She sighed. "I had the notion I could describe it for my story."

That part of her story he believed. "You're writing about cowboys, remember?" Which he didn't accept as true one wee bit.

"*Okay*, I'm sure if your Aunt Agnes is going to go through the journals recounting your family's history, you'll find out eventually. The God's honest truth is that your family stole the castle from mine. So," she said, poking a finger at his chest, "if it weren't for the

MacNeills, *I* would be living here, not you. And it would be at *my* invitation that you could stay with me in *my* bedchamber, not the other way around. *But* the coverings on the bed would be a pretty pale blue, not this dark."

His mouth gaped. He couldn't believe what he was hearing, particularly since the lass seemed so sincere. Argent Castle had been her family's? Positively ludicrous.

Ian looked momentarily stunned. Julia couldn't describe it any other way. As he pulled away slightly from her, he looked as though he wanted to leave her this moment and prove it wasn't true, or maybe that it was wishful thinking on her part.

Then a slow grin appeared. "Is that so, lass?"

He didn't believe her? Just like that?

"Okay, fine. We owned the castle. You laid siege to it, and then my great-grandfather, Conaire MacPherson, had to capitulate. He had to agree to the MacNeill's terms to give up his daughter to mate with whomever the current laird was."

Ian frowned. "None of this is true. No MacPherson has ever mated with a MacNeill in my family line. That would only have been a couple of generations back, and *that* I would have remembered."

"You're right. No MacPherson, at least from our clan, mated with yours. They escaped. And since then, we've only had male offspring."

He raised his brows.

"Well, except for me, of course."

"You're the first?"

"Yes." She waited to see his reaction.

He was looking down, contemplating her words, and

not saying anything. Then he looked at her. "So you would be..."

"Your mate. According to the contract."

He smiled. "I see. So that's where the issue of love comes in." He gave her an amused frown. "Who put you up to this?"

Her own frown was not amused. "No one *put me up to this*. But I'm glad that you don't believe in it. Once I find the contract, my grandfather wants to destroy it, and that will be the end of that."

"Everything on my land is mine. I'm afraid if a box was left here, it is mine as well. If we're able to secure it, I'll inspect the contents and make a decision as to whether it will go to your grandfather or not." He sounded like he was humoring her.

Maybe he thought she knew of a chest hidden in the walls that contained a wealth of treasure, and she planned to steal it but pretended instead the box contained a betrothal agreement. Now how stupid would that be? He'd inspect the contents for certain anyway.

"So your grandfather sent you to find the box and destroy the documents so you don't have to mate me."

"Right."

"Hmm. I don't believe this. You know why I don't believe this?"

"No, but I suspect you're going to tell me."

"The knowledge would have been passed down from generation to generation. I would have been told that I was to be mated to a MacPherson, if that were the case."

She shrugged. "Good. Then like I said, you don't have to worry about the contents of the box."

He shook his head.

She let out her breath hard. "Someone has been blackmailing my grandfather." She watched Ian's face darken, waiting for him to take in the new information, to see if he thought it was as amusing as the last.

But he didn't say anything.

"Whoever it is knows about the contract and told my grandfather he has to pay if he doesn't want me to have to mate the current laird of Argent Castle."

"When did this occur?"

Now he sounded like he believed her. Or maybe he was still humoring her. "Recently."

"How recently?"

"I don't know. I didn't ask. But it had to be recent."

He reached over her, his hot body pressing lightly against hers. He plucked something off his bedside table and then handed his cell phone to her. "Call him."

She hesitated. She was certain her grandfather wouldn't like it that she had told Ian about the contract when he'd told her not to. But she hadn't had much choice. After punching in her grandfather's number, she listened to the phone ring and ring and ring. She wondered then if he wouldn't answer because the caller ID might say Ian MacNeill.

But then her grandfather picked up the phone and said, "Hello?" His voice sounded suspicious and businesslike.

"Grandfather, I need to know when—"

Ian slipped the phone from her fingers and leaned back against the bed, pulling her tight against his hard muscular frame and holding her hostage. She would have melted against him, loving the feel of him, except for one thing—fear of what her grandfather was thinking right this very minute—and that made her stiffen with apprehension.

"Hello, Mr. MacPherson? This is Laird MacNeill. I understand someone's been blackmailing you." With a smug smile, he glanced down at Julia and swept his fingers down her bare butt, the string of a lacy thong she was wearing making her feel exposed and sexy although she was trying to concentrate on what was being said.

She frowned at Ian, figuring her grandfather would really be angry with her for telling the truth.

The smile slipped from Ian's face and he said, "Hello? Mr. MacPherson?"

She could hear the dial tone. Her grandfather had hung up on the laird of Argent Castle.

Ian stared at the phone for a minute before he realized Julia's grandfather had indeed hung up on him. Hell. He tossed the phone aside on the mattress and then ran his hands down Julia's back and reached down to cup her soft arse. He loved her choice of panties. "Do you know where this box is hidden, lass?"

"Somewhere on the floors where the bedchambers are."

"Aye, well, before we go looking for this secret niche, had you anything else in mind?" He hoped that the way she'd been touching him, she had, and not just to get his mind off questioning her about sneaking into the castle.

She rubbed her thigh against his, and he slipped his hand down to pull her thigh higher, spreading her legs farther apart. She moved her mouth to his nipple and licked, and that was all the answer he needed.

Chapter 16

IT WAS INSANITY, IAN KNEW, BUT THE SWEET TORTURE was too much to resist as he squeezed Julia's arse, the thong she wore riding high and exposing her lovely globes, while she caressed his nipple with her tongue. He groaned with need and slid her sweater up her back, snagged her bra, and struggled to unfasten it. No matter how much he'd tried to deny it in the beginning, the chemistry between them sizzled.

To think *if* all the lass had said was true, which he didn't believe for a moment, Julia was his for the taking. Betrothed to him. *His.*

Even though the situation would be similar to that in the past—instead of his da's choice of mate for Ian, it would have been his great-uncle's—Ian didn't feel the circumstances were that alike. For one, Julia was a wolf. And there was no way he could deny his attraction for her any more than she could deny hers for him. For another, she didn't seem to despise his kin like Ghleanna had done, nor did Julia act in any way like he was a social outcast as his former bride-to-be had.

Still, he and Julia were worlds apart in many ways. She was a werewolf romance writer from America, and hell, he didn't even know if her interest in him had only to do with finding the elusive box and writing the background for her novel.

Cowboys, right.

Before he could unfasten her bra, she slipped her warm fingers into the open fly of his boxers and touched him. That made him struggle faster with the clasp on her bra, cursing in Gaelic under his breath when he couldn't unhook the fastener, to which she softly chuckled.

Pressing breasts still covered in the soft sweater against his chest, she reached back to unhook the bra. When it was free, he pulled the sweater over her head, the bra going the way of the sweater, somewhere on the floor.

Sunlight poured into the chamber through two narrow windows, and Ian assumed the supper hour was nearly upon them. He pressed Julia gently against the mattress and took his fill of her, her red curls splayed upon his black cotton-covered pillow, her green eyes filled with heat. Her lips parted, and her tongue slipped out to wet them, inviting him in, her breasts full, the nipples rosy and fully extended, welcoming. Now all she wore was the red lace thong and nothing else. Except for the bandage on her shin.

He ran his hands on either side of the bandage, softly, gently, feeling her muscle tense. He kissed her knee above the injury. "How is it?"

"Tingling. Tickling. Healing."

"Your ankle?" he asked, trailing a kiss down her leg until he reached her ankle and examined it. The swelling had abated again.

"It's fine."

"No more walking or running on it today. Tomorrow, it should be well healed."

"I want to search for the box."

"Forget it," he said, gruffly. "If we look, I'm sure

we'll find a copy of the contract in the vault. One way to outwit the blackmailer—I'll just make you mine."

Her lips parted, but he didn't wait for her to object. Right at this moment, if he didn't have to worry about anything else, he wanted to brand her as his own, like a cowboy would. Let her write that in her story. He wanted to claim her so that no other man could ever do so.

With that damning thought in mind, he captured her mouth and silenced any objection she might have made. But she quickly matched his fiery display of affection, tonguing him in return, her hands sweeping down his back and then slipping under the waistband of his boxers. Her fingers dug into his arse, squeezing and tracing, making his blood feverish with desire. He yanked the boxers off and tossed them on the floor with the rest of their clothes.

His mouth was on hers again, his hand fully on her breast, weighing the feel of it, the soft voluptuous handful as the rigid peak poked at his palm. Her eyes were half shuttered with desire, her breathing hard as she kept up with his searing kisses. He wanted her. He wanted all of her. Yet he told himself it was just sexual frenzy that they were caught up in and nothing more. But he knew better. He'd never had anyone like this, never craved a woman like he did her. Never had lost sleep over a woman before.

He slipped off the scrap of lace she wore and tossed it aside. Grasping one knee, he pushed her apart for him, her short, red curly thatch just as tantalizing as the rest of her. Plunging his fingers into her delicious heat, he drove as deep as he could and then began to stroke her swollen nub. She arched against his fingers, her soft moans nearly undoing him. And then she reached around to touch the length of him, but he groaned his refusal. He couldn't allow her to touch him, not until he'd had his way with her. He'd never last.

Lifting one leg over his hip, opening her wider to him, he continued to ply her with his strokes, his mouth silencing her cry as she came with his fingers deep inside of her and measuring the hard internal shudders. For a moment, her breath came quickly, and then she reached up to give him his due. But he still wanted to be inside her, thrusting into her tight sheath, slick and hot with pleasure.

He was so close to climaxing, just from the way her tongue had probed his mouth and lips and tongue, the way her hands had taken charge of his erection, and the sweet, sexy smell of her that he couldn't extend the eroticism a minute more. With her deftly firm strokes, she brought him to a desperate fevered pitch. And he came, the bliss of her touch turning his world into an explosion of gratification. Sinking down next to her, he pulled her against his body, her own—soft, supple, and boneless.

They'd be late for the meal, *again*.

After unlocking Baird Cottage with his lock picks, Cearnach strode inside to search for Julia's journal but stopped dead just inside the entryway.

He sniffed the air and listened for any sign of anyone in the place, although he had assumed no one would be here but the two women, and both were at Argent Castle. But other than smelling the scent of the women and that of Duncan and Ian's presence here earlier, he caught a whiff of someone else.

If he ventured a guess, and he didn't like where this was heading, their staunchest enemy, Basil Sutherland, had been here. Cearnach hurried into the first bedroom, where the bed was neatly made, but the fragrance was Maria's. Then he checked out the other bedroom. The bedcovers were half crumpled on the bed and half hanging on the floor, and when he drew closer, he smelled both Julia's scent and Basil's on the sheets. Worse, the musky smell of sex. *Hell*.

He knew Ian was taken with the little red wolf, and this would kill him.

Considering how Ian had reacted after Flynn had met with Ian's betrothed in the woods and had his way with her based on their mutual consent, Cearnach didn't even want to see the black mood Ian would be in once he learned of this new deception over a woman he cared about.

Cearnach lifted Julia's journal from her bedside chest, and then feeling sick about this whole mess, he hurried back to Argent Castle. He checked on the progress of the filming of the movie, which, as he was afraid it would be, was noisy, the castle grounds overrun with humans, and enough to make him want to join his mum in London to get away from it all.

When he glanced up at Ian's chamber, he took a long, deep breath. How could he break the news to Ian about Julia and Basil without shattering Ian's world again— despite the fact Ian always claimed he'd been better off without his betrothed? Cearnach knew better. Since then, Ian had lived with ponderous regret over having

sent their cousin away and feeling responsible for getting him killed.

With his teeth set, Cearnach stalked toward the castle,
only to be stopped when Duncan waylaid him. "You
found the lass's journal?"

"Aye. Was Maria any trouble?"

"Some. Guthrie's watching her." Duncan frowned at
Cearnach and folded his arms. "You seem troubled."

Cearnach dismissed his concern. "I can see why Ian
didn't want this production here. What a mess."

Duncan nodded. "Is something else the matter?
I don't think I've seen you this worried since Flynn got
himself into trouble with Ian."

Cearnach didn't say anything. The problem was that
no matter the situation, he was always able to make
light of it. Not that time. No matter how many years had
passed, he could never see that disaster in a lighthearted
way. "If nothing's the matter, I'll see you in a bit."

Duncan said, "Aye."

But Cearnach knew from the dark arch of Duncan's
brows that his brother didn't believe nothing was the
matter.

Trying to learn anything useful about the woman who
was still with Ian in his chamber, Cearnach settled in
Ian's solar to read all that Julia had written, not sure
what he'd learn and hoping he wouldn't find anything
damning. Any more so than he'd already found. But
something was saving a place in the journal, and he
opened to that page. A picture of Ian wearing his kilt
stared back at him. It looked to be taken at the Celtic
fest. Turning it over, Cearnach didn't find anything
on the back. Hell. What was the lass up to? Ian never

allowed his picture to be taken. And it made Cearnach believe she had to have confederates working with her. Ian would be sick about this.

In the journal, she had described Cearnach as carefree and happy-go-lucky, but she hadn't seen him when Ian left him in charge. Business came first, fun and pleasure second. He had thought he was just like Ian in that regard, until now. Ian seemed to be dabbling in both business and pleasure at the same time with the lass when he normally was much more serious. Had to be as pack leader and clan chief.

Supper had come, and the brothers and their cousins had eaten, and still Ian and Julia had not emerged from Ian's bedchamber even to partake in the meal. After what he'd discovered at the cottage, Cearnach knew nothing good could come of this.

He returned to the solar and picked up where he'd left off, flipping to another page in the journal. Not only had she done an excellent job of writing about him, but she'd captured Duncan's warrior instincts, Guthrie's studiousness, and the layout of the castle, as well as some of their cousins' gruff appearances and roaming eye for the lassies. She had only praise for the MacNeill clan, which surprised him. Was it a ploy, though? In case they found her journal?

He read through the beginning of Julie's American Western story, where Ian MacNeill featured prominently and the heroine was already stealing a horse, which made him wonder if she intended to steal something from them. Something of importance.

From both the notes she had written about Ian, her hero in the Highland historical romance she had started and then seemed to set aside, and now in the cowboy story, she was in love with him. Maybe only on paper, but he obviously was her hero, the one who would capture the heroine's heart if they could ever be on the same side of the law. A made-up tale for sure, if she was in a conspiracy with Basil Sutherland. And no matter how much Cearnach didn't want to believe it, he couldn't see it any other way.

Duncan stalked into the solar and looked at Cearnach sitting on the settee against the wall, journal in hand. "Are they still in his bedchamber?" Duncan asked quietly.

Cearnach gave a slight bow of his head and then rose, crossed the floor, and placed the journal in the top right-hand drawer of Ian's desk.

"Does she say much of anything?" Duncan asked.

"Aye. She portrays all of us. *In a good light*," Cearnach added, not about to reveal what he'd discovered at the cottage to anyone but Ian. "So what's going on with the film crew?"

"They want everyone who signed up as background performers to show up to wardrobe first thing in the morning so we can be fitted for costuming. And then?" Duncan smiled darkly. "We're to learn how to swing a claymore properly."

"Weel, do they want us to do the teaching?"

Duncan laughed. "If Ian got wind of it, he'd be out there leading the whole bunch in training. An armorer is supposed to hand out swords tomorrow."

"My claymore will be the one I got as a lad. With the sword having the proper balance and weight, I can manage anyone."

"The director won't like it."

Cearnach snorted. "The director doesn't have to like it. As to costuming? I'll be wearing my own plaid."

"Aye, same here." Duncan motioned with his shoulder in the direction of Ian's bedchamber, the door shut tight. "Is it serious?"

"What? The relationship? Or what she's up to?" Cearnach tried to keep the bite out of his words.

Duncan's brows pinched together as they headed down the hall to the stairs. "I didn't think anything, or should I say *anyone,* would distract him from the film crew's business while they were here. Appears that a little red wolf has done the trick. Do you think he is still interrogating her?"

Cearnach shook his head. "What do you think?"

"I think he's working awfully hard at it, and if he doesn't get the truth soon, they'll miss out on dinner also. Maria Baquero isn't going away, though."

"I'll speak with her again," Cearnach said. "I've heard some ugly rumors I need to find out the truth about."

"What's that, brother?"

"Basil Sutherland and his men have been added to the roster of fighting men for a couple of battle scenes. The scripted battles will surely take a turn for the worse, and Ian will be sorely vexed once he learns of the situation."

Ian would kill Basil, Cearnach thought, if he learned Julia was playing Ian for a fool while working with their enemy.

"Och. Well, wait until after he's eaten." Duncan glanced at Ian's chamber as they passed it by. "Or maybe after he emerges from his chamber. He should be in good form by then, don't you think?"

Once Ian learned the truth about Julia? Cearnach truly didn't want to be the bearer of ill tidings—*again*.

Ian appreciated his brothers' thoughtfulness in keeping their voices down as they passed his bedchamber. He assumed Cearnach had found Julia's journal. Now, he had to solicit his kin's help in locating the secret niche in the region of the living quarters, if such a thing still existed, and learn what it really contained. A betrothal contract? He didn't believe so. Something valuable, he assumed.

Julia had fallen asleep again. He dressed and then left her naked and buried under his covers in his bedchamber while he summoned his aunt to the solar. He assumed she would know something about the MacPhersons, more than what she'd mentioned earlier in the kitchen about their portraits being in one of the tower rooms.

After she arrived at his solar, he started with the questioning at once before Julia became aware he'd left her alone. "What connection do we have with any red wolves by the name of MacPherson?"

"I've been looking into the records, but... well, no one told me the woman was a red wolf and not a gray." She looked down at her lap and thought about it for several minutes. But when she looked up at Ian, he could tell from her expression that she didn't recall anyone like that.

"I'll keep looking through the records, though. I meant to have someone type them up and save them on a computer." She waved a hand dismissively at Ian.

She had never been interested in computers. "But you know what a chore that will be, and no one in the family has been interested in doing the work."

"If you discover anything, will you tell me?"

"Aye, of course." She frowned at him. "You know she writes about werewolves? Do you know what the stories are about?"

"Heather reads them. She said she has a whole collection of them."

Aunt Agnes wrinkled her nose. "They are not literary in the least." She shuddered. "Books about sex, that's what they are."

"Guthrie has asked Heather to get one of her books for him to look at."

"*I'll* take a look at it. Unless it has to do with financial reports, he doesn't read."

Ian couldn't help smiling a little. His aunt was of the opinion that unless the book was nonfiction, it wasn't worth reading. So the thought she would want to *peruse* a romance novel filled with sex amused him. "Cearnach said he would read it."

Agnes gave a snort of laughter. "Cearnach doesn't read, unless it has to do with how to carve a new handle for a dirk."

"Duncan said he would."

Agnes stared at Ian in disbelief. "A romance novel? You can't be serious."

Very serious. In fact, Ian had the feeling that all his brothers planned to flip through the books, looking for anything that might catch their interest.

"Do you recall anything about a red family who was named MacPherson? You must have some idea."

Aunt Agnes eyed him warily. "Seems to me you've been interrogating the lass all morning and half the afternoon. Surely you've made some headway with her."

Ian leaned back in his chair. "She says I'm betrothed to her."

His aunt didn't react one wee bit. She didn't laugh at him or look shocked. She didn't show any expression that would reveal she'd even heard him.

Then her face split into a grin. "It's about time. If there's nothing further, I'll be on my way to see what I can learn about the lass. Do tell your mother about this latest betrothal. I'm sure she'll be pleased with the news." And then before he could respond, his aunt hurried out of the solar.

He assumed she hadn't heard of this contract, either, or maybe she had but had never seen it. Without locating it, they really had nothing to go by.

He'd fully intended to return to Julia in his chamber when Cearnach knocked on his door frame. Which was, in and of itself, not something he usually did. Ian leaned back in his chair, considered Cearnach's dark expression, and knew something dreadful had to have happened.

"Come. What's the problem, Cearnach?"

Cearnach closed the door.

Now Ian *knew* the problem had to be dire.

Ian waited, although the suspense was killing him. But he could tell Cearnach did not want to be the messenger. And the last time he looked this worried was when he'd had to tell Ian about Flynn's transgressions with Ian's betrothed.

"Flynn and Ghleanna are the past, Cearnach. Nothing could be that bad. Now, what is the news?"

Cearnach sat in a chair in front of Ian's desk and shifted uncomfortably. "I think your telling Flynn you'd exorcise him when he locked us in the tunnels hurt his feelings. I haven't seen him about bothering anyone of late."

That was what this was about? Ian knew Cearnach and Flynn had been best of friends, and telling Ian about their cousin's affair with Ian's betrothed had probably been the most difficult thing Cearnach had ever done, but hell, their cousin had deserved worse treatment than he'd received. Ian frowned. "He knows I wouldn't get rid of my own kin."

Cearnach cleared his throat, the inference being that Ian had indeed sent Flynn away from clan and family.

"Aye, well, he had lain with my betrothed, Cearnach. Was I to keep him here and pretend it did not matter to me? How could I have led the clan, the pack, if my own kin would steal my betrothed right under my nose and I did nothing about it?"

"Aye, and a cold fish she was."

Ian stared glumly at the window.

"He saved you from a fate worse than death."

Ian looked at his brother.

"He was… is still our kin. Whether he planned to or not, he gave you the freedom to mate whomever you please, as long as the woman is truly the right one for you."

"Are you referring to Julia?"

Cearnach's eyes darkened and narrowed. "You know *nothing* about the lass, Ian. If it were me, I'd tread lightly where she's concerned."

Surprised, Ian stared at his brother. Cearnach sounded

truly angry, when he was barely ever angry. "What has happened?" Ian asked in a gentler tone.

"You don't know her, Ian." His brows furrowed deeper. "She could be sleeping with the enemy for all we are aware."

Ian had considered that Julia might be in the enemy's camp and that could be the reason for her trying to sneak into the castle. But sleeping with his enemy—

He studied Cearnach's grim expression. "Speak freely." Although Ian didn't want to hear what Cearnach had to say if he truly had uncovered evidence Julia was in the enemy's camp—or worse, in bed with his enemy.

Cearnach's jaw was clenched, but he said nothing. He swallowed hard and rose from the chair, crossed the floor, and looked out the window. "Just be careful."

He turned and looked at Ian, his eyes misty with tears. Just like when he'd learned Flynn had died at the hands of an angry husband. "Be careful," he said again. Then he quit the room, and Ian felt the joy he had known when he was in Julia's arms wither.

What had she done?

Chapter 17

WHEN JULIA WOKE FROM HER LONG SLEEP, IAN ROSE from the chair nearby where he'd been watching her. He couldn't quash the concern he had that she might be in collusion with the Sutherlands, to what end, he didn't know, though. Yet, damn his bloody soul, he couldn't help wanting her anyway. "Are you hungry, lass?"

"Hmm," she said, stretching in the bed, the covers barely covering her breasts.

He wanted to look away, not see how enticing the siren was while the words of warning his brother had given him still tugged at his conscience. "What do you know of the Sutherlands?"

She took a deep breath, peaceful, not in the least bit worried. Either she was a consummate actress along with being a great storyteller, or she hadn't been part of a plot with his enemy after all.

"Basil Sutherland," he added, studying her.

She shook her head. "I don't know any Basil Sutherland. No Sutherlands, either." She suddenly pulled the covers higher and sat up. "Maria! She'll wonder what became of me."

Purposefully changing the subject? "She was told you're with me."

Julia rolled her eyes. "I'm sure that went over well."

"She wanted to see you. Once you're dressed..." Ian clenched his teeth. He wanted this business resolved with the Sutherlands. "How did you know where the secret entrance was?"

"I told you." She sounded taken aback. "My grandfather told me. But I couldn't find it, and then I just happened to hit it with my boot and realized the trapdoor was there."

"Why didn't you tell me about this betrothal contract in the beginning?"

"At first I didn't know about it. Then when I told my grandfather I wanted to ask your permission to locate the hidden box, he said I couldn't. He said... if you were mated, or I was, the next female in my line would be betrothed to the next laird of Argent Castle." She attempted a smile. "I told him I would tell you about the betrothal contract, and you'd end this nonsense now. No more problems with a blackmailer. You'd just say, 'No way in hell,' to that, and that would be the end of the difficulty."

He raised his brows a little. Did she think he really found her that objectionable? "Because I don't love you."

"Well, sure, and because I don't have a title..." She paused.

"Hmm?"

She continued, "I'm American. And a werewolf romance author."

"I haven't read your books. Maybe they would interest me."

"I doubt it."

He leaned back in the chair. "Have you had visitors to the cottage?"

She frowned at him. "You... and your brother. I was here most of the night or in the woods or the tunnel or... why?"

"Cearnach dropped by the cottage to get your bags so you'd have a change of clothes since your trousers were ruined in the tunnel and your sweater was wet." Although Cearnach hadn't told Ian what he'd found in the cottage when he had picked up Julia's bags and her notebook, Ian assumed he'd smelled a Sutherland's scent in the place.

"And?"

Ian shrugged. "A Sutherland had stopped by."

"I don't know any…" She paused. "Maybe he talked to Maria?"

Ian had considered it, but Cearnach's words of warning—she was sleeping with the enemy—made him think otherwise. "No, Julia."

She chewed on her lower lip, and then her eyes widened. "Maria's okay, isn't she?"

Her change of topic threw him.

"Maria's here, working on the film."

Julia's whole body was tense now, and her gaze searched the room. "My bags. Where are my bags?"

"What's going on, Julia?"

"Someone called me last night when I was trying to reach my grandfather to ask his permission to tell you that I needed to search for the box. I couldn't get hold of him at first. As soon as I hung up the phone, it rang, and when I picked it up, thinking my grandfather had called me back, it was *him*—the blackmailer."

"The blackmailer." No matter that Ian meant to sound like he believed her, he was having a hard time relying on anything that came out of that beautiful mouth of hers now.

"Yes." She spied one of her bags in the corner of the room and, without wasting another moment, climbed out of bed in all her naked beauty and crossed the room to her bag. "His voice was cold, threateningly so. And I realized then," she said, tugging on a sweater, no bra this time, "why Maria thought he was dangerous and not just some flake." She jerked on a pair of jeans, no panties.

He frowned. "Where are you going in such a rush?"

"I've got to speak with Maria. Warn her he knows where we're staying. That he called last night. I don't think he's after her. He's after me. He said he didn't want me to find the contract. He's blackmailing my grandfather. Aren't you listening to me? I told you about it this morning. Or most of it. But she can't stay at the cottage any longer. If he's out to get me, he could use her to come after me. Don't you see? She'll have to stay at Harold's rental with the rest of the film crew. Well, I will, too."

Ian didn't want her to stay with Harold, or anyone else, for that matter. No matter how crazy it seemed, given Cearnach's warning about Julia, he wanted her here with him. Whether it was because he thought he might be able to keep her from doing whatever Sutherland wanted, or because he truly thought she might be in danger, he couldn't decide.

She grabbed a pair of socks and sat down on the bed. "He knew it was me answering the phone, Ian. He knew before I said anything. He was watching the cottage when he spoke with me." Her eyes widened as she looked up at him.

"Omigod, he didn't pick our lock and let himself in while we've been gone, did he?" She shook her head and yanked on her socks. "I've got to talk to Maria. Ask if someone came to see her last night while I was running through the woods... um, and tunnels at your place."

"Between the time you were with me and by the time you ended up in the tunnels, you had been at your place for a number of hours."

"Sure, sleeping some. I wrote in my journal. And I had the two phone calls. What else...?" Her eyes narrowed. "What is this all about?"

"I'm not certain. Cearnach wouldn't tell me. Perhaps we should take a ride over to your place and check it out?"

She hurried to slip on her boots and frowned. "Fine. I'm ready. But I have to warn Maria about the blackmailer."

If anything, she was consistent about this story. But he didn't think Cearnach was wrong, either.

He led her into the hallway, down the stairs to the great hall, and then outside where he walked her through the inner bailey to the outer one. When he saw the director talking to some of his people near the stables, Ian took hold of Julia's arm and led her toward them. "Come on."

"What... what are we doing?"

"Maria's nowhere around," he said, motioning to the outer bailey. "You can talk to her when you get back."

"Yeah, but—"

He motioned to one of his cousins as he came out to greet him. "Saddle Rogue."

"Aye," Oran said, and hurried into the stable.

Julia rubbed her arms and chewed on her bottom lip. "I've never ridden a horse before. Well, except for a trail horse, and they're ornery as all get-out. Not in the least bit obedient. One was a stubborn old nag that tried to

rub me off on every tree we passed. I love them, but...
from a distance."

He smiled at her. He couldn't help it. "And you're
writing a cowboy story? Don't they have horses?"

She frowned at him. "Sure, but the heroine doesn't
have to have a horse."

"Unless she steals one."

She just stared at him, her lips parted, kissable. God,
how he wanted to kiss them. Then she narrowed her
eyes. "When Cearnach picked up my bags, he wouldn't
have also lifted my journal, would he have?"

"You wanted to write. How could you without your
notebook?"

She glowered at him. "Don't you know it's wrong to
read someone's private journal?"

"My name was in it. Seemed acceptable to read
what you'd written about me." Although he hadn't
stopped there.

She opened her mouth to speak, but when she saw
Rogue, she didn't say a word, just gawked and shivered.
"That's not a horse. It's as tall as your castle."

He chuckled, mounted the horse, and then reached
down offering his hand and, with a grip on her arm,
swung her around the back of him. "Hold on, lass."

She quickly wrapped her arms around Ian's waist,
and the feel of her breasts pressed tight against his
back, the snug feel of her arms around him, her head
resting against him, felt damn good. He galloped in
the direction of the gatehouse, hoping to hell Cearnach
was wrong.

Everyone on the film crew and Ian's own men paused
what they were doing to stare at Ian and Julia riding

toward them. Their mouths gaped, while Duncan and Cearnach frowned at him.

"That's Laird MacNeill," one of the members of the film crew said. "He owns the castle and lands around. Too bad he wasn't wearing a kilt and we could get a shot of him."

Ian wasn't about to be in any blasted movie.

∗∗∗

Heart thumping, Julia held on to Ian for dear life while the horse pounded the pavement with a monstrous gait. Most likely Ian was sick of the shambles the film crew was making of his castle and wanted to get away. She'd agree with him there.

At this point, he probably wanted to take a ride to the cottage at a more leisurely pace, well, if he'd slow the horse down, rather than drive her to the cottage in his car.

She admired the way he handled the beast, as if he had grown up riding a horse. And he probably had. Afraid for dear life that she'd fall off the horse's rump, she tightened her hold on Ian, his stomach firm and his thighs taut, hard, and hot. Loving the feel of him any-time she had the chance to hold onto him, she realized just how addictive he was.

But this horse was way too big, way too wild-looking, and galloping way too fast. Kind of like his rider.

Wolf whistles and cheers went up around the castle grounds. With her whole body burning with embarrass-ment, not to mention Ian's touch as she pressed her body close to his, and fearing she might just bounce off the horse's rump at any moment, she noted that everyone with the film crew who had witnessed the event was grinning. If Maria learned of it, she would definitely give Julia even more of a hard time later tonight after they were through filming for the day.

But once they were beyond the gatehouse, Ian slowed the horse to a trot, and they headed in a much more un-hurried manner toward Baird Cottage as if he wanted to prolong the contact between them. *Or* delay the arrival at the cottage and whatever was bothering him about it. She didn't have a good feeling about that, although she tried to tell herself everything would be okay.

She slid up and down against Ian's back while the horse's gait slowed, the friction making her hot for Ian all over again. And she thought about her story, trying to put to good use all the sensory details she was gathering.

The hero had rescued the heroine from the enemy clan. She was too exhausted to take another step, while the enemy was in hot pursuit. The hero held her tight as he rode hard back into the outer bailey, his body scorch-ing and solid, the smell of him all male, of the piney woods and the fresh clean air and the leather saddle.

As Julia clung to Ian, she wished he was wearing that loose-fitting tunic with the kilt that she'd seen him wear in the photo. She couldn't help it. Her cowboy story had morphed back into the Highland story again.

She was grateful he wasn't riding fast right now. Slow and easy was much more to her liking so she could enjoy their physical closeness more. She loved the way Ian smelled, all man and wolf, wild and untamable, his free arm hugging hers. She would never mind riding a horse if she got to travel with Ian like this.

Yes, he was just perfect for her story. Too bad she couldn't get him to act out all her scenes so she could write them without any effort.

"Are you all right, lass?" he asked, breaking into her dream world.

His thick burr tantalized her, adding to her love of all things Scottish. She imagined him stripping off his plaid and then her curling up in his arms at night in a cavernous bed, surrounded with furs and—

"Julia?"

She didn't want the fantasy to stop. She sighed. "I've changed my mind about horses."

"What's that?"

She snuggled her head against his back and tightened her arms around his waist. "I rather like riding like this."

"I'll have to teach you to love to ride on your own."

That sounded a lot like he meant for her to stay. Yet something about his demeanor earlier had said something was wrong at the cottage, that it had to do with her and some man named Sutherland, and that it was a really bad something.

She was afraid to discover what it was.

When they arrived at the cottage, Ian helped Julia dismount and then swung off the horse and tethered him to a nearby tree. Julia fought rubbing her arms, chilled from the uncertainty of what she'd find in the cottage.

All wolves were great observers. They considered their surroundings, sniffing at the air to analyze scents from foe or prey or friend. They watched and listened and were wary and curious at the same time. But instead of using all his enhanced senses on the cottage, Julia noted Ian was watching her. It made her uncomfortable, as if he was observing her reaction, seeing if she had something to hide, when for once, damn it, she didn't.

She kept thinking he'd open the door, and there lying on the floor would be the body of a dead man. With a knife in his chest, with her fingerprints all over it. At least Ian acted as though they were entering a murder scene and she'd done the murdering.

Her hands ice cold, she took hold of Ian's hand, and he looked a little surprised. She was afraid he'd pull away, and he did, but only after he gave her fingers a small reassuring squeeze. It wasn't enough. He didn't trust her. She knew that for sure now.

She was on her own.

She walked into the living area and raised her nose and sampled the air. The smell of an unfamiliar gray lingered. "A gray wolf," she said. "I don't recognize his scent." She moved into the kitchen, but before she could take a strong whiff of the air in there, the phone rang and she gave a startled cry. "Sorry." As she grabbed the phone, her first thought was that her grandfather was calling to give her hell for telling Ian about the contract.

"Hello, love. I see you've brought the laird himself with you today. Are you going to tell him we're lovers now?" the familiar Scottish voice said, soft with a menacing threat.

Her skin already felt like ice, but now it prickled with fresh goose bumps. Her knees felt weak, and her heart picked up its pace. "What have you done, you bast—"

She didn't get the rest of the words out. Ian moved swiftly to take the phone from her hand as she slumped onto a chair, feeling light-headed and nauseous.

"She's so bonny, my laird. So very sweet. Is she as sweet with you?" His voice was hard, and then the phone went dead.

Ian's face turned dark as he set the phone down in its cradle.

"It's him. The man who called last night, Ian. He's watching the cottage. He has to be."

"Stay here." Then Ian stalked off toward her bedroom, and she didn't even *want* to know what he'd find in there.

――――ᴡ――――

Ian would recognize Basil's scent and voice anywhere. The bastard had definitely left his sperm on Julia's sheets. Although her scent was also on the sheets, Ian didn't smell her musky fragrance, and so he didn't believe she'd been with the madman when he'd come. Ian would stake his life that after she and Maria had left the cottage, the bastard had ejaculated in her bed, claiming her in his sick way.

Ian ran his hands through his hair. *Hell. Cearnach.* His brother had about given him a stroke over believing Julia was Sutherland's lover. But none of her actions had revealed any dishonesty in that area. And when she'd answered the phone, she had turned so paper white and was so near to collapse that there wasn't any way that she could have faked her fear.

Ian called his brother. "Cearnach, find Maria and tell her not to leave the castle grounds. She's either moving in with Harold's people or with us. But she's not to return to Baird Cottage alone."

Cearnach didn't say anything.

"She's not in the wrong, brother. She's all right."

"Julia?" Cearnach finally asked, his voice apprehensive.

"Aye. The sick bastard just called here. Guess who the blackmailer is?"

"Blackmailer?"

"Aye. Hasn't Aunt Agnes told you yet? I'm betrothed to Julia MacPherson. We just have to locate the contract hidden in the walls of the castle. But Basil Sutherland's been trying to blackmail Julia's family over it."

Silence.

"You there, Cearnach?"

"Aye."

"You don't sound happy for me."

"You're sure about the lass?" Cearnach still sounded glum.

"I'm certain. He's watching the place. It's Basil Sutherland. Julia's staying with us. We're returning now. Everything all right there?"

"Aye."

Cearnach didn't sound as though everything was all right there. Hell, now what was wrong?

"We'll see you shortly."

"Aye, Ian. That's good news." Cearnach sounded more like his cheerful self now.

"You can tell me the other bad news when I arrive," Ian said, knowing Cearnach better than that, and cut the connection.

He stalked back into the kitchen where Julia was still

sitting at the table, only now she was drinking a glass of water, still pale as death. "Are you all right, Julia?"

"What did he do in there?" she asked, her voice small.

"Nothing that matters. It looks like Cearnach already got your bags. I didn't see anything else of yours in there. I've already called him so he'll be talking to Maria and making sure she doesn't come back here alone."

"Ian, tell me. What did he do in there?" Julia asked again, her green eyes staring up into his, willing him to tell her the truth.

He pulled her from the chair and gently kissed her lips. "He soiled your sheets."

"As in…" Her eyes widened. "Cearnach thought… thought this man and I had… oh, Ian, I've never seen him in my life." Tears misted her eyes, her expression saying he couldn't have thought that ill of her.

Her disconsolate voice and expression struck a deep chord. "He's a sick bastard. We've been fighting each other for centuries. We'll fight for centuries more." If Ian didn't kill him first. Ian rubbed her back with a touch that was both possessive and tender, wanting to return her to the safety of his castle where no one like Basil Sutherland could ever reach her. Then he swore under his breath and drew her into his arms and held her tight. "Forgive me, Julia, for thinking anything ill of you."

The box and its contents held no real interest for him. Julia was all he cared about. When he thought she couldn't be his, that she was another man's woman, he'd felt his whole world crumble. And he realized then how this wasn't anything like what had happened with Ghleanna's deceit. He hadn't cared about her. Hadn't loved her.

He looked down at Julia, her face lifted up to him, her eyes gazing at his mouth, now grim, his brow furrowed.

And then she kissed him. The kiss was sweet and unassuming and sealed a promise. If he read it right, there was no one else in her life. She could be his. And damned if he didn't want her. He kissed her lightly back, but he wanted to return her to the castle forthwith, not wanting to do anything here with her after what had already happened.

"We've missed supper. We'll return to the castle and eat, and then we'll look for that box." Still feeling bad about what he'd suspected had happened between Sutherland and her, even though he had been trying damned hard not to jump to conclusions, he tried to cheer her with another hug and a smile.

She seemed reserved, and then he wondered if she was still worried about Sutherland and his bullying. She had every right to be. But he didn't believe the bastard would do anything now. Not if he hadn't already.

Ian led her outside, vowing to put a stop to Basil Sutherland's games one last time.

Her heart still in her throat, Julia felt the change in Ian's demeanor. He was loving toward her again, his hand around her waist, possessive, caring, wanting. She had no doubt the notion he had that she had been with this Sutherland had pained Ian. And she didn't blame him for believing the worst of it, because under the circumstances it would have looked pretty damning.

Yet Ian seemed a little preoccupied, worried maybe, and she wondered if it had to do with Sutherland being close by, so she didn't say anything and followed Ian's lead. They weren't far from the castle, only about a

mile away if they cut through the trees, and as fast as
the horse moved, they'd be there in no time. Yet, she
couldn't help feeling a little cold, a little anxious, a
little scared.

Ian locked the cottage, untethered Rogue, and then
mounted him and pulled Julia up behind himself. He
tightened her arms around him. "Hold on tight, lass.
We'll be at the castle in a few minutes."

Again, she felt the tension in Ian's body. It wasn't
directed at her, she didn't think, But Ian seemed to
have some concern about Sutherland and where he was
at present.

She glanced around the forest but didn't see any sign of
anyone. She lifted her nose and sampled the air, but only
smelled Ian's delightful scent, the horse, oiled leather, the
piney woods, and a hint of rain in the atmosphere.

Even so, she kept a wary watch for any movement.
If the man would cause their car wreck, what else was
he capable of?

As soon as Rogue cantered through the forest, the
quickest route to the castle, Ian sensed his horse tensing,
nervous, and shying away from shadows. Ian sat taller,
studying the trees.

Julia tightened her arms further around him and whispered, "I smell a wolf. No," she said, squeezing harder,
sounding scared, "two wolves."

Ian pulled his phone from his belt, but four wolves
dashed toward them, materializing out of the pines.
Rogue shied, whinnied, and suddenly reared. Julia
screamed and slid off the horse's rump, landing hard on
the ground with a thud. Ian's heart dropped when he lost
Julia. Snarling, the wolves went after Rogue.

Ian jumped off the horse, slapped him on the rump, and hollered, "Home!"

The horse bolted for the castle.

Seeing that Julia was unharmed, Ian searched for the blasted phone he'd dropped. As soon as he located it in the pine needles and leaves, he went for it. A wolf crept closer, ears flattening back, mouth snarling, showing off the extent of his wicked canines. None of the wolves here was Basil. *Damn him.*

Giving up on the phone, Ian began ripping off his clothes. Julia scrambled for the phone, managed to jerk it up, flipped it open, and punched a button.

"Help! We're in the woods. Four wolves attacking."

The wolf pounced on Julia, knocking her flat on her back. She screamed.

Ian's heart nearly stopped.

His people would have heard her scream. They'd see the horse galloping riderless back into the outer bailey. Someone had to have gotten her phone message. They'd send help. But for now?

They were on their own.

Filled with rage, Ian shape-shifted as fast as possible and faced down the wolf that had knocked Julia onto her back. He didn't want her to shape-shift and attempt to fight any of the wolves, not with being a smaller red against the heavier gray males.

Snarling and growling, the other three drew closer to join their buddy, all wrinkling their noses and looking ferocious. Shouts from the castle were already reaching Ian. In part, the shouts were to gather the men, but in part it was a way to let the wolves know Ian's pack was on its way, so the other wolves should leave before there was bloodshed.

Ian was intent on watching the wolves for the smallest twitch of a muscle to indicate they were readying to lunge, so he heard, rather than saw, Julia yanking off her clothes. Hell. But he couldn't take his eyes off the wolves. Damned if they turned their attention on her, though.

He charged the closest wolf, and with his teeth bared, Ian grabbed for his neck. The wolf yelped and tried to dodge away from Ian's sharp teeth. But Ian was too fast, too determined, and too damned angry. No wolf of the Sutherland clan attacked his soon-to-be-mate or trespassed on his land without paying for the transgression.

His neck bleeding, the wolf finally jerked free. He ran a short distance away, head bowed, panting, ears flat. The other three stood their ground. Until they heard shouts in the woods and something like the sound of horses galloping toward them. Ian knew his men had unleashed the wolfhounds.

At the feel of the earth trembling and the dogs barking and his men shouting to locate Ian and Julia, the wolves backed off and then turned and vanished into the foliage. Ian nudged Julia with his nose, comforting her in their wolf way.

"Hell," Cearnach said, riding Rogue back to the scene of the fight. "I hope you took a good chunk out of Basil again." He leapt down from the horse and eyed Julia.

She growled at him, and he smiled back.

"Glad to see you're all right, too, lass."

It appeared Julia wasn't about to let Cearnach get by without an apology. Ian didn't blame her.

Not willing to shape-shift again in the event some of the film crew had followed his men here, Ian nudged

Julia to run with him. At any other time, they'd have had no trouble returning to the castle in their wolf forms. But now that it was overrun with humans?

Hell, Ian was relegated to shape-shifting out here, which could prove disastrous, or going in the back door as if he was a servant.

He trotted alongside Julia through the woods as Cearnach gathered their clothes, remounted the horse, and then followed with the wolfhounds and several of their men. For safety's sake.

Ian glanced back at the woods with one thought: Basil Sutherland would pay.

Chapter 18

HERE'S WHERE THE POSTERN GATE IS LOCATED, JULIA
thought, after wondering earlier how easy it would have
been to sneak in this way. Two burly Highland guards
were posted at the entryway, and she realized she couldn't
have slipped in sight unseen, if she'd tried before.

Adrenaline still ran high through her veins, as she and
Ian dashed inside the castle walls as wolves, their tails
like bushy flags, their gait strong and hurried. Cearnach
led the way on horseback, making sure none of the film
crew was about to see Julia and Ian running onto the
castle grounds as wolves. Still in human form, more of
Ian's men were sprinting to catch up as they protected
Julia and Ian from the rear in the event Sutherland's men
tried anything more.

Back home, she'd never had trouble with werewolf
packs. None had lived near them. It made her realize just
how peaceful life with her family had been with just a
grandfather and father. Her family was an oddity, really.
But they had raised her that way after her mother and
the rest of her grandparents had perished. Julia didn't
have any siblings, and with no pack or pack fights or
squabbles over territory, she really had been rather iso-
lated from the usual pack dynamics.

Although instinctually she knew what to do.

Ian hadn't wanted her to shift, but he had to realize
she would have fought the wolves if necessary, and that

as a wolf she'd have had a better chance at aiding him against other wolves than as a human. That she wouldn't have let him fend for himself.

Even though she'd never fought any wolves before, the instinct was inborn to protect her own pack, and with a strange realization, she became aware that she'd readily adopted Ian and his pack.

She and Ian darted through the garden and ended up at the kitchen's back door. A woman's face appeared in the window of the door, her eyes widening, and she quickly jerked the door open and let them inside. She was pretty, a taller female like the grays were, with dark hair like Ian's and dark inquisitive eyes. Her studied gaze shifted from Ian to Julia.

She was about Julia's age and smiled brightly at her. She greeted Ian, and then she said to Julia, "I'm Heather MacNeill, the laird's cousin, and you must be the famous author. I've got every one of your books. Will you autograph them for me? After you've shape-shifted, of course." She grinned again.

Maria burst through the kitchen door, tugging away from a red-faced Duncan, her own cheeks flushed with color. "Where is—" She stopped, fixed her gaze on Julia, and took a ragged breath. "Oh, Julia, the whole place went crazy when Cearnach got your call. We heard your screams, and the horse tore into the courtyard like a crazed animal. And... and Harold *fired* you." She glared at Duncan, wagging an accusing finger at him. "*He* told Harold you'd trespassed on the property last night. And Harold went and fired you."

Julia's wolf's gaze turned to consider Duncan and his expression, expecting he'd show a little remorse.

She should have known better. Instead, he folded his arms and gave her a hint of a smile.

She had expected Maria to fuss at her about disappearing in the middle of the night and being unable to visit with her to reassure her for hours today, but Harold didn't even know what she was doing on the "job." So why would he fire her?

"Guthrie had been watching me all morning after Duncan put him in charge of me. And that was after Cearnach made Duncan responsible for watching me." At this comment, Maria sounded more than annoyed. "Then Harold came over to speak with me, you know, in that loud, booming voice he has that is set on one volume—high—asking where you were.

"Someone on the film crew must have known you were in the castle. Duncan overheard Harold asking me about you because he was so loud. Although, come to think of it, he would probably have heard anyway because of his wolf's hearing."

Maria glared at Duncan and then spoke again to Julia. "Harold wanted to know why you were cavorting with Laird MacNeill and getting special treatment when you have a job to do. I waffled about what your job is, and he wasn't convinced." Maria clenched her fists and then folded her arms. "Harold ordered me to fire you, and you're to be banned from the castle while the filming is going on."

Astounded, Julia finally realized what this was all about. *Harold was jealous.* But the part about Harold banning her from the castle made her smile. She could just imagine what Ian would have to say about that. She glanced at him. He gave her a wolf's smile back.

"He's the director. He calls the shots. He's used to being treated like he's somebody important. So when one of his flunkies gets the royal treatment instead, he wants to know why." Maria took a breath. "Not that you're one of his flunkies, Julia. I swear Duncan purposely told on you to get you fired."

Surprised that Duncan would do this to her, Julia glanced at him to see his reaction. He gave a dark smile and shrugged. "You did, lass."

"Yeah but you didn't have to tell Howard," Maria said, her words venomous.

"He wanted to know why she wasn't doing her job and was instead riding a horse with Laird MacNeill. I didn't tell the director she stayed in the laird's chamber for most of the day." He smiled even more evilly, Julia thought.

Julia straightened her tail, raised her head, and glowered at him. Just his dark clothes and persona warned her that Duncan could be dangerous, but she hadn't thought he'd have it in for her. Then again, he wasn't there to coddle people like her, either. Did he not like that Ian was paying attention to her? Or was he just worried that she was real trouble and he wanted to nip her devious ploy in the bud? Had to be, if he spoke up accusing her of something so low. Even if it was all true.

Ian nuzzled her cheek and then licked her, as if assuring her everything was fine. But it wasn't. She'd come here with the film crew. She didn't have a passport, money, an ID, anything. And she'd thought she'd be staying with the rest of the film crew at the other mansion. Now that wasn't happening. Which meant she had to rely on Ian's generosity, because Duncan and Cearnach still appeared to be viewing her in a dim light.

Cearnach entered the kitchen, carrying Julia's and Ian's clothes. Apparently overhearing something of the conversation, he gave Duncan a brief nod and said, "You did what was right." He handed the bundle of clothes to Heather. "Take it to Ian's bedchamber, will you, lass?"

Just like Ian's brothers, Heather didn't seem concerned about the mess Julia was in, either. Ian's cousin nodded and hurried out of the kitchen.

Cearnach sounded serious, not annoyed but rather pleased with his younger brother's actions. She wasn't happy with Cearnach, either, after he let it be known to Ian that he believed she was Sutherland's lover.

Ian shook his head and nudged Julia to join him.

But she paused long enough to nuzzle Maria's leg and hand to thank her for her concern. Maria dropped down to give her a hug, clasping her arms soundly around Julia's neck, and rubbing her cheek against Julia's furry one.

"You scared me half to death. Cearnach said I have to move in with Harold and his people or into the castle with Laird MacNeill and his clan. But since Howard's jealous you're getting special treatment while Laird MacNeill won't let him into the castle, I'll stay with the film crew. Otherwise, my head will be next on the chopping block. You didn't tell me the bastard that threatened us in L.A. called you last night, though. We'll talk later, okay?"

Julia nodded, needing to talk to Maria about the blackmailer, the betrothal contract, and everything. This time, she trotted alongside Ian and headed with him through the great hall. She couldn't believe Howard had fired her! She didn't even work for him. And then to say she was banned from the castle and grounds?

But she couldn't get over that Duncan had gotten her fired. She was sure the fact she'd been staying with Ian hadn't helped. But did Duncan really despise her that much? She truly did like Ian's brothers, despite themselves. She guessed it was because they had Ian's best interests at heart and didn't want him hurt. That made her realize just how special they were. To Ian, at least.

She glanced at Ian as they headed up the stairs, shoulder to shoulder. He licked her cheek. Thank God, they'd been close to the castle. What if the wolves had followed them to the falls and had attacked them there? They'd have been so far from the castle that the cell phone might not have reached Ian's people.

She shuddered. Then a horrible notion occurred to her. What if Sutherland or his men *had* been watching them there while Ian had been stroking her into ecstasy?

She groaned.

Heather smiled in the hallway outside Ian's chamber and said, "I left your clothes on the dresser."

Ian dipped his head to acknowledge her comment but then hurried Julia along. She had a feeling he was perturbed with her, probably because she'd shape-shifted when he hadn't wanted her to do so in front of Sutherland's wolves.

And sure enough, as soon as they were in the room, and Heather had closed the door for them, Ian shifted and, in all his naked glory, frowned at her. "I didn't want you taking the risk of shape-shifting and fighting Sutherlands' wolves."

She summoned the urge to shift, and when she stood before him ready to disagree with his logic, his eyes instantly took in her nudity, and he didn't say anything for a moment. Then his hands covered her shoulders, and he took a deep breath and pressed his forehead lightly against hers. "I could have lost you."

She thought he sounded different. That their relationship had changed. Her hands slipped around his back at the waist, and she raised her chin to dispute his faulty logic, but Ian brushed his firm, warm lips against hers and said, "You are mine."

Had she missed the "I love you and want you for a mate forever and *ever*" declaration somewhere along the line when she wasn't paying attention?

She frowned a little. "As in? This sounds awfully permanent. What if there is no betrothal agreement? What if this was all an elaborate ruse for me to meet you and garner your interest?"

His eyes widened a bit, and he appeared surprised to hear her say so. "Was it?"

She shrugged. "I have only my grandfather's word, and normally that's enough, but I'm beginning to wonder—"

"But it's not of your doing." He was frowning now.

"No. Where are we going?"

"You know where we're going," Ian said, caressing her shoulders with the pads of his thumbs.

"I don't mean that. Where is this relationship going?"

"I told you. You are mine."

Julia ran a finger down his chest. "Hmm, does that mean you intend to mate me?" Which she assumed was where this was leading.

"Aye."

"And what about love?"

"My parents learned to love each other in due time."

"Ian, I'm a romance writer for a reason. I don't write about people falling in love just because I love romances. I write it because I believe in it. I would never mate someone who is not in love with me and me with him."

His mouth curved up a bit.

"I'm serious about this."

"Aye, lass. And I told you how it worked for my parents. If it was good enough for them, it's good enough for me."

She sighed deeply. "Then you will have to find someone else to be your mate because it isn't good enough for me."

Ian's frown deepened. "Why are you being so difficult about this? I want you, and you want me. You can't deny it, lass. Ever since we first met, even before that, you wanted me."

"To use for a description in my novel."

He shook his head. "If I was in a legion of kilted warriors, would you not pick me out of the whole lot to be your hero?"

She smiled and kissed his chest. "I admit you stand out among men and I see only you."

"Aye. See, that is the right of it."

"And me? If I was at a huge social function filled with elegant ladies, would you have even noticed me?"

"Aye, mud splatters and all, lass. Clinging wet garments showing all your womanly curves, and the glowers you gave me that first day at the pub. Had there been a thousand women, I would have had eyes only for you."

She laughed. "Oh, yeah, you and every other male in the place. I looked close to naked."

He grinned. "That's the way I like you."

She rolled her eyes.

He lowered his head to kiss her. He was as gentle with her as if she was the most exquisite and delicate object of his desire, and if he wasn't careful, he'd lose her. Yet she could see the more forceful side of his nature wanting to take control—the laird, the clan chief, the alpha pack leader who would have his way. She felt it in the way his hands tightened on her shoulders, the way his thumbs continued to stroke her, insistent and possessive.

She was drawn to his strength and his pride, the way he took care of his people, the way he took care of her.

In that instant, she realized just how much she wanted him, to belong with a pack, to be part of his family, and the question begged to be answered. Had her grandfather set her up? Had he known what she hadn't realized herself, that she needed more than just her grandfather and father in her life, more than flitting relationships like she'd had with her former boyfriend? A wolf who could share her dreams and offer her new ones? A pack and all that went along with being part of one? The time to reconnect with her Scottish roots?

Ian's hands slid down her arms in a soothing touch, his darkened gaze on her face, waiting for her response. If she said one last time that she couldn't commit to him unless he loved her, truly said he loved her, would he shun her?

But she was certain he loved her, even if he couldn't say so. She couldn't stand the idea of returning home without him. And the wonderful thing about her chosen career? She could live anywhere and dream up romantic worlds wherever she made her home.

"All right," she said, meaning to sound firm and resolute, but her words came out breathy instead.

A small flicker of a smile lightened his dark, worried expression. Then he slanted his mouth over hers and kissed her, caressing his lips against hers, pressing harder. Her fingers clung to his waist. He parted her lips with his tongue as his hands gripped her arms right above the elbow.

He groaned a sexy, husky sound that made her shiver with sweet realization. He desperately wanted her like she wanted him.

His hands shifted to her waist, roaming lower to her hips, his fingertips lightly touching her buttocks. She mimicked his actions, and his mouth curved upward against hers. "Siren," he rasped out.

His hands encircled her flesh and squeezed, and she did the same to him, felt his hard buttocks, when hers were so much softer, less firm.

He moaned with sensual approval and pulled her up tight against his hardening body. Her breasts swelled, her nipples tingled, and her woman's inner core throbbed with excruciatingly desperate need.

But she wouldn't beg him to finish her off despite feeling she'd die in sweet anticipation. She wouldn't rush their joining like she was dying to do. She could tell by his controlled and rigid expression that he attempted to take this slow and easy even if it killed him.

He cupped her buttocks and lifted until she wrapped her legs around him, opening herself to him before he carried her to the bed.

Then she was on her back, and he was between her legs. He separated her legs with his probing fingers, his thumbs stroking her nub, his mouth on hers again, sizzling, caressing, insistent.

Her blood was so hot that she felt feverish, her heart pounding as if she were running with the wolf, her body slick and wet and aching for completion.

His lips possessed hers completely, his tilted slightly for better access, his tongue pressing into her mouth, sweet, warm, and erotic. Her tongue teased his back, her hands sliding from his waist to cup the back of his head, to glory in the feel of his mouth on hers. He was attuned to her as she was to him. As if they were meant to be from the beginning of time. He felt right. *They* felt right. *This* felt *so* right.

His fingers plied wickedly pleasurable strokes between her thighs, and she couldn't hold off the impending climax. The sensation lifted her higher and higher to a point of no return when he pushed his fingers between her swollen cleft, and the climax struck with a tidal wave of bliss. Without waiting for her to descend back to earth, he prodded her with his thick erection and nudged her entrance, pushing gently inside. Stretching her, he allowed her to accommodate his size until he was deeply entrenched.

Then he began to pull out slowly, his burning, hooded gaze on hers, watching her reaction. She raised her knees, allowing him deeper access, and he took advantage, thrusting—plundering her, pleasuring her, possessing her.

She arched against him, feeling the heat, the pressure, the tension and hardness, the love—yes, even if he couldn't say it—the love between them growing, expanding, and morphing into something decadent, delicious, and even dutiful.

She shuddered as another climax hit her.

"Julia," he said, his voice a hiss, a groan, a declaration.

He dipped his head and took her mouth, his hard, taut body sinking against hers, his hands gripping her face, his eyes closed as he kissed her deeply and thoroughly. Then he lifted his mouth away from hers and gave her a quirky kind of smile. "I will have to learn to cook if we keep missing the regular mealtimes. Unless you know how to cook."

She raised her arms and folded her hands beneath her neck. "Ah, now the truth comes out. You wanted me for afternoon delight and to cook your meals when you miss them."

He gave her one of his roguish grins and leaned down to suckle a breast. "How could I have found such a canny wolf right in my very own backyard?"

"I *knew* there were strings attached." But then she gave into the erotic feel of his tongue and heated breath on her nipple and groaned. "We may just have to starve, my Highland hero." She wrapped her legs around his, her heels bumping against his buttocks at the juncture of his thighs.

And he growled with a sound that made her think he'd lost the battle. Sex or food?

Sex, she surmised as his fingers worked miracles on her nipple and his mouth did wondrous fluttery things to the other. Before she knew it, he was bringing her to climax all over again, and then somehow, she managed to slip a leg between his, and rest her head against his chest, while he wrapped his arms around her. And slept. *Briefly*.

—–∿∿∿—–

Losh, the lass made him lose all self-control with the way her engaging body was flushed and willing and offered to him like the ultimate sexual feast. Even now as he woke from a long nap, he wanted her as if she'd awakened some primal need in him that had never seen the light of day before.

He tried not to think of what his brothers would say as he missed yet another pack meal. At this rate, he'd have to hire another cook just to provide room service. In ye old days, the laird could have his meals served in his bedchamber anytime he wished. But he had never subscribed to having the kitchen staff overworked in that manner to satisfy some selfish whim. One mealtime, three times a day. For everyone. If anyone wanted a snack at some other time during the day, they were welcome to fix it themselves.

But he was rethinking his position. If nothing else, he couldn't have Julia missing all her meals. He sighed. The trouble was that spontaneity was half the pleasure of having sex with her, and trying to regulate it to coincide with mealtimes wasn't going to happen.

He looked into her sleeping face, a glow still there from their bouts of making love. He should let her be, let her sleep, but she was just too damned enticing. And very willing, her insatiable urges just as compelling as his own.

He turned her hips away from him, her back still flat against the mattress, her breasts exposed, her face turned away in the same direction as her hips. Then he pushed her upper leg higher and touched her between her legs from the back. He pressed into her silky wet sheath with his fingers, and she stirred, moaned, and moved her leg higher, prompting him to continue, her mouth curving up, although her eyes remained shut.

She was tired but willing, giving him permission to proceed, to take his pleasure in her ripe folds again. He penetrated her tight, slippery sheath with his stiffened erection and pumped against her bare, rounded arse, the feel of her soft buttocks pounding against his groin and quickening his desire. She stirred with a humming sound of pleasure as his hands slipped around her, claiming her sensual nub, stroking, and caressing. Her moans budded with her arousal, her feminine sweets swelling and growing more sensitive to his touch. By the way she moved against him, he knew the stimulating sensation was making her crave completion, and she ground against him wanting it, wanting him. God, she was beautiful and sexy and his.

"Ah, Ian," she said on a breathless groan.

And he came again, her body milking him, hot and shuddering around his arousal with a tight grip. "Julia," he muttered into her hair, his hand on her breast, feeling the swollen mound in the palm of his hand, the nipple erect and mouthwatering. Mine, he wanted to say, but instead he gathered her up in his arms and held on tight, the words not needed.

But in the back of his mind, he knew that trouble was brewing—Sutherland was bound to cause more difficulties soon. And now it wasn't just Ian and his people he was targeting, but also Ian's mate.

Chapter 19

J‌ULIA SMILED TO SEE I‌AN SLEEPING SOUNDLY BESIDE her in his bed and sighed. If she didn't get out of bed, she'd be here forever, she figured, between his unappeasable hunger and her own.

Trying not to jiggle the mattress, she slipped off it and headed for her bag, grabbed a change of clothes, and then stalked into the bathroom to shower and dress. She had to speak to Maria about all that had gone on, and she supposed she should tell her she was now a mated wolf, if her friend hadn't already guessed where this had been heading.

Thankfully, when Julia left the bathroom, Ian was still dead to the world. She hurried out of the bedchamber before he could catch her, stop her, and change her mind. Which, given the way she felt toward him, would not be difficult for him to do.

As she walked down the stairs, she could hear the noisy business of the film crew doing what they had to do in the inner bailey while she smelled the delightful aroma of baked bread and sausages wafting through the place. Her stomach grumbled. She'd have to look for Maria, *after* she got a bite to eat. If Ian caught her, no telling when she'd get to eat again.

When she reached the great hall, Cearnach was seated in the sitting area, carving on a dagger handle. His attention quickly shifted to her, and she froze. She wasn't afraid of him, but she felt like an intruder all of a sudden. And the business of his thinking she'd been Sutherland's lover still grated on her, no matter that she tried to tell herself it didn't matter.

She'd noted before that he was always cheerful, but not now. While she saw him carving his handle, he'd been thoughtful. But now that he was watching her, he frowned, and then looked past her to the stairs. She turned that way, expecting Ian to have caught up to her already, half figuring he'd drag her back upstairs before she had a chance to eat or speak with Maria.

"He's still alive, lass, isn't he?" Cearnach asked.

Julia envisioned centuries earlier when a woman who didn't want to be married to a horrible man might poison him to rid herself of the nuisance. Cearnach waited for her answer, no smile on his lips. He couldn't be serious.

Then his lips curved up slightly, and he waved his dagger at her. "My brothers say I have an odd sense of humor at times. Don't mind me, lass. In time, you'll get used to it."

Did he think she was going to be a permanent fixture here? She hadn't even discussed with Ian what she had to do—writers' conferences, speaking engagements, book signings. In fact, next year, she planned to have a big book signing at Powell's in Portland, Oregon, for her new book, *Taming the Highland Wolf*.

Then she smiled. Maybe Ian would come with her and wear a kilt. A braw Highland warrior would surely boost sales, *if* the women buying the books weren't too taken by the Highlander and forget what they were there for.

She nodded at Cearnach, realizing she hadn't responded to his comment.

"Heather's baking bread, if you're hungry. You must be, the way Ian has sequestered you away in his bedchamber and not allowed you a morsel of food. Go. He'll be down here as soon as he discovers you've slipped away from him."

"How would you know—"

Cearnach's smile broadened. "Weel, lass, if I were him and you were mine, you would not be down here talking to my next eldest brother."

"Thanks." She strode across the great hall, rushing to get to the kitchen, her face feeling as though she'd been sitting in the sun too long.

He chuckled. Then the carving renewed.

When Julia reached the kitchen, Heather beamed at her, tucking a dark curl behind her ear, and then motioned to the stove top where sausage, eggs, and potatoes were cooking in skillets. "Miss Wildthorn, do you want something to eat? Cearnach said if you ever got away from Ian, we'd better feed you or you'll perish from lack of food."

Julia smiled. "Yes, anything really. And please, call me Julia." She noted that a stack of her books were sitting on one end of the kitchen table.

Heather set a plate on the table filled with eggs, potatoes, sausage, and a slice of bread. "Eat whatever you like. The hounds will devour what you don't like." She motioned to the books. "I brought them for you to autograph." She grinned. "I have to tell you, Ian's brothers have all been sneaking peeks at the contents. I caught Cearnach trying to slip one into the front of his shirt.

I told him he's welcome to read the books, but I wanted you to autograph them first."

"Cearnach?"

"Oh, aye. He teased, saying he was just trying to rile me, but I caught him sharing one of the racier scenes from one of the books with Duncan—you know, the one where the heroine tied up the hero with a long silk scarf—and both were grinning. They might say they're not interested in romance, but they're not fooling me."

Heather pulled up a chair next to Julia and said in a low voice so Cearnach might not catch wind of it, "They've got a casting call for background performers. Since you're no longer working with the film crew, would you like to join me in applying for the job? They need six fair maidens." She folded her arms and sighed deeply. "Ian probably would say no, but if we both go, maybe it'll be all right."

Julia finished the slice of bread. "Everything is delicious. Thanks so much, Heather."

"Oh, my pleasure. So... what do you think? Want to try out for a part?"

Julia didn't think Ian would like it if she tried out for a part, either, but just because she'd mated with him didn't mean she was giving up her rights as an individual. It meant, though, that she'd better hurry up. She quickly finished the meal, even though she would have preferred to savor everything more slowly. Then she rose from the table, smiled broadly at Heather, and said, "Let's hurry before Ian wakes and learns of it."

Afterward, she wouldn't have any qualms telling him like it was. She just didn't want to be stopped in the beginning, figuring she might crumple under the pressure.

Not that she was the crumpling type, but she figured Ian could be quite persuasive.

Heather jumped up from the table and headed for the door to the gardens. "This way," she whispered conspiratorially. Out loud, she said, "Want to see the gardens, Julia?"

"Oh, yes, I'd love to," Julia said, playing along.

"If Cearnach learns what we intend to do," Heather whispered, "*he'll* try to stop us so Ian has time to get here and change our minds. None of Ian's brothers will even let me go outside while all the Americans are about. But since I'm in your company, I'm safe."

Safe. Right. Just like Maria had been safe with Julia in the car. And if Heather had been with her in the woods when the wolves had confronted Ian and her, she'd have been in just as much trouble. But within the confines of the castle grounds, Heather *would* be safe.

It didn't take long for Julia and Heather to meet with the man responsible for hiring and secure their bit parts, Heather because she was Scottish and looked perfect for the role, and Julia because she looked Scottish and luckily didn't have to speak, which would have revealed she was as American as peanut butter.

"Are you all right with going back to the keep on your own?" Julia asked, not wanting Heather to get into trouble for that also. "I need to speak to my friend Maria about some things."

"Oh, aye. I'm to look over some gowns, but I have just the thing to wear that I wore in the old days—lots more authentic than Hollywood costumes." Heather was so excited about the prospect of playing a background role in the film that the feeling was contagious.

Julia just hoped Ian wouldn't say no to the deal—in Heather's case. In Julia's, he'd better not.

"Heather!" Guthrie called out, stalking in her direction.

Julia whipped around, her heart pounding. But Ian wasn't with them. Guthrie's dark look warned her that he was not happy with either of them.

Heather folded her arms. "Oh, bother. I've been found out. I have an escort back to the keep, it appears."

Guthrie gave Julia a harsh look. Yep, she was the instigator in getting Heather in trouble. She raised her brows at him.

Guthrie said to Heather, "You're not supposed to be out here. Isn't that what Ian said? What happened to Cearnach? He was supposed to be watching you, and waiting for Ian to..." Guthrie looked back at Julia. "Where's Ian?"

As if she and Ian were joined at the hip now. "I would imagine he's still sleeping. Or showering or eating." She shrugged. "I don't keep his schedule." She thought to tell Guthrie she didn't poison him, either, but she was afraid that might be taken wrong so she clamped her lips tight.

"Where are you going?" Guthrie asked her.

"To speak to Maria. Is that all right with you?" Julia asked, her voice annoyed.

Guthrie snorted. "Ian's going to be sorely vexed when he learns who have been hired on as extras."

"Who?" Heather and Julia asked at the same time, and Julia wondered how he'd learned so quickly that she and Heather were going to be in the film.

"Sutherland and several of his men."

When Julia found Maria, she was looking glum as she gave orders to someone on the staff until she saw Julia approach and quickly dismissed the man she was speaking to.

"Oh, Julia, what's going on with you and Laird MacNeill? I figured they had you locked in the dungeon or something." Maria raised her brows. "Actually locked in the laird's bedchamber. What's going on? Anything I should know that I haven't already guessed?"

"I've told Ian everything—my name, about the secret niche, the betrothal contract."

"Whoa, wait a minute. Betrothal contract?"

"I called my grandfather last night and didn't have time to mention it to you—"

"Because you were breaking into the castle?"

"I found the secret tunnels. I got caught. One of their cousins, a ghost named Flynn, locked me in the lady's chambers adjoining Ian's."

"Ohmigod, an honest-to-goodness ghost?"

"Yeah."

"I want to meet this ghost. But back up a bit. So you were locked in the laird's chambers and…?"

"Things got a little out of hand." Julia smiled, not about to mention what had happened at the falls earlier.

"You're mated."

"Not then, but now, yes."

Maria let her breath out hard. "Okay, I figured that was where this was going as soon as you fell in love with his photo, and then when he saw you and couldn't keep his eyes off you at the pub."

"I was nearly naked."

"Yeah, well, when he saw you on the castle grounds

and wanted to speak with you personally and then you didn't come home for so long, I knew that was it. So what's the deal about this betrothal contract?"

"According to my grandfather, the contract says I'm betrothed to the laird of Argent Castle."

"Ohmigod, Julia, you can't be serious."

"I am. So Ian's going to have everyone search for the box, and then once we find it, we'll destroy the document."

"What? You're already mated to him."

Julia shrugged. "We don't need any agreement. Not when we are what we are."

"Well, I hate to be the bearer of bad news, but Harold is still mad about you getting all these special privileges."

"Great. Now what?"

"He wants you to pay for your trip out here and for the lodging at the cottage. We can't get out of the contract on the place, even though I'm not staying by myself there now. I'm just lucky he didn't can me, too. I don't have money coming in from the sale of books like you do."

"My credit card is maxed out."

"How?"

Julia let her breath out in a huff. "Trevor convinced me to invest in several ventures that turned out to be way too risky. He needed some cash flow and promised to pay me back with interest."

Maria's eyes narrowed. "You didn't tell me all this before, Julia. Why did you keep it a secret?"

"You'd have told me not to do it."

"You're so right. But I'm truly sorry. What about your father or grandfather?"

"I'm on my own. They both counseled me about

giving Trevor any money. Told me that if Trevor's hunches didn't pan out, it was my loss, and they wouldn't bail me out. I don't blame them, really. It was my mistake. But I really liked the guy."

"Yeah, until he took what he made on the business and left you high and dry. No promises to repay you, right?"

Julia shook her head. "He just vacated his apartment without leaving any word. For two months, I thought he would contact me, that he felt badly that he'd lost my money, but that once he was working a steady job again, he'd contact me. I didn't expect him to pay me back right away. I guess a part of me didn't believe he would ever pay me back, but not because he didn't want to. Just because he couldn't afford to.

"But then... well, I figured he wasn't going to call and had no intention of ever paying me back. He sold his investments at a loss, but he still received some money from them, and even if he wasn't making much money, he could have sent me something as a token payment."

"He also could have let you know where he planned to go before he even left."

"Yeah, you're right. It wasn't like I was going to go after him to drag the money out of him."

"You shouldn't have messed with a human."

"He liked what I wrote. I can't say that about the wolfish guys I've met. Although from what their cousin Heather said, Ian's brothers kind of liked what I've written. Would Ian, though?" Julia shrugged.

"What about Laird MacNeill? Would he pay off your debt?"

"I'm pretty sure they're in debt up to their eyeballs

already. And that's why they've agreed to filming here. I wouldn't think of passing on my debt to them. Maybe what I earn from being a fair maiden in the movie will pay for my flight and lodging. I won't be getting any royalties for my books for several months."

Maria's mouth dropped. "Has Laird MacNeill agreed to allow you to play a part in the movie?"

Julia laughed. "Are you kidding? But it's not for him to decide."

"Well, we have a tiny bit of a problem."

"What's that?"

"Guthrie told me Basil Sutherland and his men are their sworn enemies, and they'll be fighting in a couple of battle scenes. He also said that his men are the ones who attacked Laird MacNeill and you in the woods. The situation could become dangerous."

"Basil Sutherland is the one who called and threatened you in L.A., and he's been blackmailing my grandfather and father about the betrothal agreement. So he really can't be trusted. But I need the money," Julia said. "Not only that, I *want* to take part. Participating will help me write my book." She motioned to the trailer where she was to select a gown for the movie. "I've got to get a costume. We'll talk later."

"Better hurry. As soon as Guthrie enters the keep, you know he'll let the laird know you're out here. And then? You'll be back in that bedchamber of his." Maria grinned. "Not that it would be a bad place to be, I'm sure."

Julia groaned and then turned and hurried toward the trailer, excited about this new venture she was bound for and not about to be thwarted—by Ian or his enemy.

—◦◦—

Finding Julia missing from his bed, Ian sighed, figuring she'd had to escape him just so she could eat a meal and take a break. He took a shower and dressed and then headed down the stairs.

"Ian, we have a problem," Guthrie said, stalking into the great hall. "Cearnach asked me to bring you the news because he's dealing with another issue right now."

"What is the problem now?"

"You said to make sure that none of Basil Sutherland's people were hired as extras. But somehow, they managed to get hired anyway. Maria said they needed more men. Basil and thirty of his men showed up at the gates today, ready to do serious battle."

Ian stalked down the stairs and headed for the entryway, but he paused to see a portrait on the floor, leaning against the wall, that looked as though it was an old-time portrait in oil of Julia.

Guthrie chased after him. "The painting's from the tower room. Good likeness, isn't it?"

Ian shook his head. "If I had seen that before, I would have really wondered what was going on. She looks like a reincarnation of the woman." He stalked again toward the door.

"Maria showed me the contract you agreed to. They can hire whoever they need in order to have enough actors to film the movie."

"Can't they digitally create the masses or whatever it is they do?" Ian growled. "Basil and his men will not fight ours."

"The director is ecstatic. The men all have their own

costumes, and their garments are old enough to look authentic. They wore the costumes today to convince the man who was hiring the background performers to choose them."

"They *are* authentic."

"Aye. But it saves the director money. He doesn't want us using our own swords, though. Too lethal-looking."

"That's because they *are* lethal."

"Aye, and he said they're so heavy to wield that we'll use the lightweight movie props."

Ian cast Guthrie a dark look.

Guthrie shrugged. "He liked that they looked authentic. But he's concerned about injuries."

"If the MacNeills fight Sutherland's men, they'll use their own swords, and we won't go into battle with toy ones."

Guthrie smiled a little. "You'll join us?" He handed him some paperwork.

Ian read over the script of a couple of scenes and found a contract for him to sign to take part in the movie—and he grunted. "I don't know how you could get us into this mess, but what kind of a clan chief would I be if I didn't lead our people against the Sutherlands?"

"I'm fighting also," Guthrie said with pride.

Ian gave him a tight nod.

"The director said if you'd appear in the film, he'd give you some special roles. But there's one other thing…"

The way Guthrie said the words made Ian give him a wary look as they exited the keep and stormed across the inner bailey. "What else is wrong now?"

Guthrie cleared his throat. "Since Julia was fired as Maria's assistant…"

"Which she wasn't anyway," Ian reminded him.

"Aye, well, the director had need of six fair maidens, and she signed up to—"

Ian stopped abruptly and glowered at Guthrie. "Julia will *not* be one of them."

"She and Heather—"

"Not Heather, either."

"Heather will obey you since you're the clan chief, but I doubt Julia will."

"Where is she?"

"She went to speak with Maria."

Duncan hurried to greet them and motioned to a metal trailer. "Julia's in that contraption changing, from what I've been told."

"Aye." Ian stalked off to talk to Maria, who was busily speaking with someone on the film crew. As soon as she saw Ian headed for her, she cut off her speech with the other man, dismissed him, faced Ian, and plastered on a fine smile.

"Basil Sutherland and his men won't be part of this fight scene or any other," Ian said, closing in on her.

"But your contract clearly states that we can hire them. I'm sorry. It's all legally binding."

"You're not sorry. But if we have a bunch of dead men—"

Her smile faded. In a low voice, she said, "I understand your concern, Laird MacNeill. But my hands are tied on this issue. If I'd known beforehand, I might have been able to stop Roger from hiring the men. But it's done. Unless we can prove cause that they shouldn't be on the set—criminal records, drunkenness, refusal to listen to direction—something that would allow us to release them from the contract, we can't do anything about it. And besides, that's why everyone has to use the sword props."

Ian shook his head. "Where's Harold Washburn?"

"He's directing a scene in the forest. He can't be interrupted. Did Guthrie tell you he wants you to play some special roles in the film?"

"Aye." And Ian would, only to ensure that Sutherland's men were kept in their place. *Saints preserve us.* He'd never planned to show his face in film. But then again, maybe no one would watch the bloody thing in the U.K. "I don't want Julia in the movie."

"She's selecting a dress." Maria waved at the trailer. "Neither she nor Heather will be in the film."

"Since Heather is your cousin and part of your clan, I suppose the poor woman doesn't have any recourse."

Ian lifted a brow to hear Maria's choice of words.

"But Julia already told me she wants to take part in this. For research."

"For a cowboy story set in Texas?"

Maria's eyes widened. "What? She's writing a Scottish werewolf story."

"She's no longer writing a story about Highlanders." At least that was the story she was sticking to, but he truly didn't believe it.

"Oh. Well, she never said anything to me about that. Writers do change their minds. She's over there selecting a dress. But, Laird MacNeill, if she wants to do this, let her. You know she won't appreciate it if you make a big scene over this."

Without commenting, he stalked off to the trailer, intending to change the lass's mind. Now with Basil Sutherland and his men involved, Ian didn't want any of them getting close to her. He yanked open a door and walked inside. Two women were pulling long dresses on, while Julia was standing in a pale blue thong and a matching bra, her back to him.

"Here," a woman said, handing a predominantly red-and-green plaid tartan with a stripe of yellow to Julia. "Put this on."

Hell, anyone could walk into the trailer and see her half naked like that. He stared at the colors of the plaid. *Cameron*. She wasn't wearing that plaid, either. Not that he had anything against the Cameron clan, just that it was not *his* tartan.

The woman brushed past Julia and said, "Sir, you don't belong in here. You need to leave this instant."

Julia turned, the skirt pulled against her chest as she saw Ian. Her eyes widened, but then her lips curved up a little. Seductive minx.

His gaze switched to the scrawny blond guy who was putting up one of the women's hair. So why was this man in the same room with the half-dressed women? At least with *one* half-dressed woman. *His* half-dressed woman.

"Out," Ian growled. He pointed to the man. No human male was going to see his mate in such a state of undress.

The man gave Ian the once-over, smiled apprecia-tively, and said, "Nice bod." Then he hurried outside with an exaggerated swing to his hips.

"The rest of you, out," Ian commanded.

The woman who had initially told Ian to leave said, "Who do you think you are, ordering everyone about?"

But the two women wearing the long skirts grabbed their shoes, smiled at Ian, and hurried outside.

"He's Laird Ian MacNeill who owns the castle and the

lands we're using for the picture," Julia said, frowning at him. "I'm sure he just wants to wish me well in private."

"Well, make it quick," the woman snapped. "We have to get ready to film this scene soon. And the director won't be pleased with the delay." She stomped outside and slammed the door.

Ian closed the distance between them and pulled the plaid from her arms and tossed it on a table. "I don't want you—"

Julia wrapped her arms around his neck and kissed his mouth, silencing his objection. "Ian, I have no money after losing my ID and purse and all in the car fire. And I want to do this."

"To write your cowboy book?" he asked, his fingers caressing her naked arse.

She smiled. "I've changed my mind." She slipped her hands down to his arse and squeezed. "You haven't once worn your kilt. And if you're in the movie, I could get to see you up close and personal."

"I'll be fighting a couple of battles to ensure the Sutherlands don't hurt my men. No women are allowed in the scene. At best," he said, wrapping his arms around her back and holding her tight against his body, "you'd only see me from a distance anyway."

She smiled. "If you're taking the job, one of the maids gets to kiss you before you go into battle in one of the scenes, the man who hired me said, and again after you finish with the scene. The director said that normally he'd reserve such a scene for the star of the film, but since you're the laird, if you're willing to take part, he thought it might help sales. Although if you don't do a good job at it, the scene might be cut. And no way am

I allowing any other woman to kiss you. Besides, we can make it look genuine."

"Ah, Julia, we're using real swords, and my staunchest enemy and his kin will be in the battle."

She stiffened. "I know. Maria tried to stop them after Guthrie told her the situation, but the contract clearly states you don't have a leg to stand on in this. As to another matter, please don't tell Heather she can't participate. She has her heart set on it. She says nothing ever happens here that's fun and exciting any longer. That's why she attended the university in Texas. She'll remember this forever."

"Like with you, I don't want her to get into any confrontations with Basil or his men."

"She only has a part screaming and running away from the battle. Nothing else. Your brothers can make sure none of Basil's men get near her. Then she's in the castle and safe."

"And who's going to protect you?"

"You, of course."

Outside the trailer, he heard Guthrie speaking. "Hell, who's going to tell Ian about the training?"

Duncan responded, "Cearnach, you're the next eldest brother. It's your job."

Ian frowned and handed Julia her clothes. "Get dressed. We'll find you something else to wear."

Once Julia was wearing her jeans and a sweater, Ian opened the door and stepped outside to see his three brothers waiting for him, arms folded, brows raised.

"We have swordsmanship training scheduled for this afternoon," Cearnach said. "Shall you lead us in practice?" He smiled.

Chapter 20

LATER THAT AFTERNOON, THE OUTER BAILEY WAS quiet as a fight instructor prepared to teach the background performers some techniques of sword fighting. Arms crossed over his chest, Ian stood with his brothers and the rest of the males in his pack who planned to participate, while standing tall and proud, his hair nearly black, his countenance just as dark, Basil Sutherland stood across the way with his men. Everyone looked somewhat amused as they watched the instructor prepare to speak.

Although Ian hadn't wanted Julia to be here when Basil was also here, she was watching from the wall walk, notepad in hand and pen poised, scribbling notes. Basil glanced up to see what had caught Ian's interest, observed Julia for longer than necessary, and then he cast Ian a wry smile.

Damn the man.

The fight director showed them the stance to take and the thrusts they could make, and then had another man on the staff demonstrate with him. Slash, thrust, block, parry. Clang, clang, clang.

"No one will be an expert, of course. But you only need to know how to choreograph the fight scenes. No sword flourishes. They are a waste of energy and can get you killed in combat." After showing several moves and ways to counter attacks, how to take a punch and fall properly, and how to roll and kick when the sword wasn't enough, the instructor finally asked, "Who wishes to demonstrate with me next?"

Everyone, even Basil and his men, looked at Ian.

The instructor smiled, bowed his head a little, and invited Ian over with, "My laird?"

The director was watching him, judging him, Ian was sure, to see if he could play the part well enough.

Ian walked over, drew his sword from behind his back, and took a battle stance. The fight director looked at the sword. "It's real." He glanced at the weapons master. "Get him another sword."

Ian shook his head. "I'll fight with my own, if it's all the same to you. As good as you are, you won't have to worry."

A few snickers erupted from his men.

The weapons master approached with a sword in hand, ignoring Ian's comment, as the fight director tilted his head slightly to Ian. "You're right." He motioned to the weapons master that the sword prop would not be necessary. "Let us begin. You first." There was a significant pause, and then he added, "My laird."

Ian only wanted to show that he and his men did not need to learn any swordsmanship techniques and to eliminate any more training sessions they'd otherwise have to suffer. They trained all the time on their own and needed no supervision from a fight instructor who had never fought a real battle. Not like his own men and Basil's had done.

Everyone was quiet as Ian bowed his head a little to the fight director and then moved forward with such ferocity that the instructor was taken aback. His eyes widening, he whipped his sword around to block Ian's and fell back several steps as Ian continued to advance on him.

Did he think Ian soft because he was a laird? Or did he think Ian had too big a head because he *was* the laird, that his own people would kowtow to him, that he truly didn't know how to fight, and the instructor would show him what a real fighter could do?

Ian's mouth curved up a wee bit. He would not suffer the arrogance of the man, especially when the overconfident whelp thought Ian was the one being arrogant.

He heard Cearnach say quietly to his brothers, "He has the right of it, eh, brothers? The fight director can take some lessons from Ian. Let *him* learn from a master."

Not that Ian was always on top of a situation. With Basil and some of his men, he truly had a fight on his hands. But with the fight instructor, aye, he was good, but he hadn't the centuries of experience in real fighting. And from the looks of it, he'd never come up against a man who knew what he was doing when wielding a sword.

It didn't take long for the instructor to hold up a hand in truce. His heart was pounding and his breathing was hard. The man was sorely rattled. "I see you know what you're doing with a sword." To the rest of the men gathered, he said, "Let's pair up, and we'll practice."

Ian's brothers slapped him on the back and then paired up with their own people as Basil's men did likewise.

The director approached Ian as he stood aside, watching Basil's men and not trusting them.

"Good showmanship," Harold said. "I've never seen Barker caught off guard like that. The man was really sweating." He watched the rest of the men and shook his head. "Hell, looks to me like Barker can go on home now. We've already got a cast of warriors. Good show."

"No more practice then?" Ian asked, his gaze alighting on Julia as she feverishly took notes. With the wind tousling her fiery hair about her shoulders and the sun attempting to brush away the clouds, its golden rays streaming down upon the stone walls and Julia, she looked like a winsome fae creature standing on his wall walk—who needed a good tumble, and he was ready to return her to his chamber at once.

Harold said, "Waste of time to have any more sword-practice sessions."

The sun shone more boldly like a brilliant golden sphere coming to claim the castle, and everyone stopped what they were doing to look up.

Harold glanced heavenward.

Then several of the men sheathed their swords and began pulling off their shirts.

"What...?" Harold said.

"No more practice." Ian stalked off as his men bared their chests to the sun.

Julia rushed down the tower steps to meet Ian in the bailey. "What's going on?"

"Worshipping the sun. This may be the only chance they get. And once we use up our quota of sunny days for the year, that's it."

She chuckled. "And what about you?" She slipped her hand inside his shirt and ran her fingers over his chest.

God, her touch was like heaven. He wrapped his arm

around her waist and headed for the inner bailey. "I'd rather worship you."

She smiled. "You say the nicest things, and I have to tell you that you were brilliant when you fought the instructor," she said on a sigh.

"Aye."

"And you're always so humble about it."

He grinned at her.

"I think you embarrassed the instructor, though."

"If he can't deal with it, he shouldn't be teaching sword fighting to battle-hardened warriors." He glanced at her journal. "Get some good notes for your Texas cowboys? I thought they only used guns."

"I might change my mind again."

He scooped her up in his arms and quickened his pace. "I'll change it for you."

The smile she gave him said she was ready.

"I have something to show you," Ian said. Her raised brows made him think she believed he wanted to show her something naughty. He laughed.

She blushed beautifully, and he kissed her nose. "I would love to know what you're thinking."

But when he walked her inside the keep, he carried her to where the portrait leaned beside the wall. He would swear it was a portrait of Julia, wearing a dress of silks of an earlier age, an *arisaid* of the MacPherson plaid wrapped around her. The portrait had to have been painted long before Julia was born. It looked just like her, though, with the same fascinating green eyes, the same ivory skin, and the same red hair.

Mutely, Julia stared at the portrait. Then she whispered, "Who is she?"

"Fiona MacPherson," Aunt Agnes said, coming from the direction of the kitchen, her gray eyes switching from the portrait to Julia to Ian. "See why I knew she was a MacPherson? She looks just like her."

He put Julia down, but her knees gave a little, and he held her arm. "This is my Aunt Agnes."

"The family historian," Julia said. "I'm pleased to meet you."

"Hmm, are you now? What might I discover as I sort through the family journals?"

Julia's spine stiffened regally. "That at one time, the castle was *mine*."

For a fraction of a moment, his aunt just stared at her. Then her lips curved up a wee bit. "Do tell. Weel, we shall see, won't we?"

Then his aunt swept out of the room toward the stairs.

Ian shook his head and led Julia to the kitchen. "I had no idea you had it in you. I don't believe I've ever seen anyone cut my aunt down that quickly."

Julia smiled up at him. "I might not be able to fight with a sword, but give me words," she said and swept her pen in the air as if she was writing, "and I can stand my ground."

"Ah, and as soon as I have some time, I intend to read these books of yours to see if your pen is as mighty as a sword."

Before they reached the kitchen, he heard Heather whispering near the garden door leading into the kitchen, "I'll meet you tonight after everyone's retired for the evening."

Ian's blood heated, and he stalked off to see just who his cousin intended to meet in secret after dark.

Julia sighed. Ian hadn't caught who the man was who had been speaking to Heather. She gave a name, John Smith. An American. Human. With the film crew.

And Ian was furious. He stalked out of the kitchen and through the gardens and went to speak with Maria before she left, to locate this John Smith, and to tell him in no uncertain terms what would become of him if he even dared to see Heather again.

Heather was upset, rubbing her arms and staring out the kitchen window at the gardens. "I went to college in Texas because I needed to get away from Ian and his brothers and my own brothers who watch me like the wolves they are. And so what did Ian do? He sent one of my brothers with me, and when he wasn't around, either Ian's brothers or my other two brothers would pop in and watch over me. Not once was I able to slip away to date an American." She let out her breath in heavy exasperation and then appealed to Julia with darkened eyes. "Can't you speak to Ian?"

Julia shook her head. "Not about this. You're his responsibility. I'm sorry, Heather."

"Was your pack the same way?" Heather shook her head. "It can't have been since you came here alone and didn't have anyone to watch over you."

"My pack is... *different*. It's just my grandfather and father and me." She realized then that she hadn't even told her father and grandfather what had happened between Ian and her—that they were now mated—and hoped that they wouldn't be too upset with her over it.

"What would you do if you were in my place?"

Julia smiled. "Well, it would depend. If I really like the guy..." She shrugged. "But I'm not giving you any advice."

Heather smiled and then nodded. "Thank you." Then she opened the kitchen door and hurried into the gardens.

Uh-oh.

Julia saw a cell phone lying on the kitchen counter and hoped Ian, or whoever owned it, wouldn't mind her calling her grandfather. She punched in his number. The phone rang and rang and rang. She took a deep breath. Her grandfather would undoubtedly figure it was one of the MacNeills again—because of the caller ID—and not want to talk to him. But not only that, he was probably still mad at her for telling Ian the truth about the betrothal contract.

She disconnected the phone. Why couldn't her grandfather have an answering machine?

She glanced around the kitchen, realized she was totally alone, and thought about the secret niche. Ian planned to have his men look for it. She was part of the family now. Why couldn't she look for it in the meantime while he was busy trying to scare off a potential bad boy who wanted to see Heather?

Her skin prickling with tension, she stalked across the great hall, glanced at the portrait that looked eerily like her, and then headed up the stairs until she reached the third floor. These were the family's bedchambers. But where would her family have hidden the box? Where would her family have stayed? In all of the rooms. The castle had been theirs.

She peered into the first of the rooms. She smelled mostly Guthrie's scent and then slipped inside. The bed curtains and bed coverings were done in navy blue, the walls covered in paintings of the ocean and sailing ships. The room contained a dark wood chest, a wardrobe container, and bedside tables, but the secret niche would undoubtedly be in the walls somewhere. A stack of financial reports sat next to Guthrie's bed. Poor guy to have to read that stuff before he tried to sleep. She peered behind paintings and tried to see at the rear of the wardrobe chest and the tall headboard at the head of the bed. Unless the niche was at the back of the wardrobe chest, she didn't think it was here.

Next, she found Cearnach's room. Every wall was covered with swords and dirks and shields and made her think of an armory. All he needed was a stand of armor to make the room complete. She examined every inch of wall that she could reach, except where large, bulky pieces of furniture blocked her view.

She really thought this was going to be easier to find. She should have known better. If it had been that simple, Ian's people would have learned of it long ago.

She discovered a woman's room next and thought she might have found Aunt Agnes's chamber, but the fragrance was not hers or Heather's, although it reminded Julia that Agnes had gone in this direction earlier and probably was in her room. On the dresser stood photos of Ian and his brothers, Heather, and three men that Julia assumed were Heather's brothers.

Maybe this was Ian's mother's room. The furniture was less massive, the legs curved in the Queen Anne style and easier to see around, the bed drapes and coverlets pale green, and pictures of heather and floral gardens filled the walls. But no sign of a hidden niche.

Disappointed, and afraid Ian would catch her at any moment, she found Duncan's bedchamber. She'd expected dark, black, like Ian's room. But instead, his bed was covered in forest green and everything was big. Big dresser, big bed, big shelf unit, big wardrobe container. Big. Massive. Like the castle itself. And the paintings on the walls? Hunting scenes. Men, Irish wolfhounds, horses, and wolves, but hunting what?

She quickly checked the walls in the room, really not wanting to get caught in...

Footsteps headed her way. Her heart nearly beat out of her chest. Two doors, one to the hallway and one to who knew where. But then she wondered if he had a trapdoor like the one in Ian's lady's chamber. She quickly searched under the rugs and found one.

She reconsidered. She wasn't looking for anything but the secret niche. Who would blame her? It wasn't like she was trying to steal from Duncan or anything. The footfalls grew closer. But then again, she should have asked to search his room. She flipped up the carpet, pulled up the trapdoor, slipped inside, and realized she couldn't put the carpet back in place. Too late. She was down in the stairwell, and the footfalls were nearly here. She closed the trapdoor and hurried down the steps. *Dumb, dumb, dumb.* But then she had a thought. What if the secret niche was in the tunnels?

Ian hadn't found any sign of a John Smith, and Maria had already left with the rest of the film crew for the night, and the gates were locked. On his way back to the keep, he got a call from Duncan. "Yeah?"

"You haven't told us if the lassie is your mate yet, brother."

"Aye, she is."

"Weel, then, your mate is down in the tunnels again. This time, she slipped through the trapdoor in my chamber."

"What—"

"I followed her scent. She'd been to every room until she came to mine, and then I discovered the carpet pulled aside. When I opened the trapdoor, I could smell her faint fragrance inside the stairwell. She's down there but not in sight. I didn't want to go after her until I warned you. No mobile phone reception down there, and I didn't want you to worry when you discovered she'd vanished."

"She'll lose her way."

"Aye."

"Hell." Ian was still sorely vexed about Heather, but he'd hoped to settle in with Julia after they shared a meal. "I'll be there in a few minutes."

"She's looking for the box."

"Aye. I gathered as much."

"Do you want me to get hold of everyone?"

"Aye, our brothers and cousins. Was Heather with her?"

"No."

"Did you see her?"

"No, Ian. She's not anywhere about."

Ian swore. "All right. I'm almost to the keep." How could he have only two women to keep track of, and he'd lost both of them? Once this business with the film production was over, he'd have his people focus on looking for the box. Was Julia worried about what was in the box? Afraid he'd see what it contained? Was she hiding something more? Hell.

He was stalking through the kitchen door when the mobile phone on the table began to ring. It was Heather's, and he wondered if the guy she was supposed to rendezvous with was trying to call her. He yanked up the phone and gruffly said, "Who is this?"

That's when he saw the caller ID. *Findlay MacPherson.* Julia's grandfather? Ian opened his mouth to identify himself when the caller hung up.

~~~

Ian would probably be annoyed with her anyway, so Julia put on her adventurer's hat—so to speak—and began to explore the walls, looking for any indication that there was a cutout in the stones anywhere down here. She figured that in due time she'd be able to locate the trapdoor to the lady's chamber that she had gone through before, although probably before long, Ian would come after her. But until then, she was looking for the secret hiding place.

Still, as she considered how rugged the walls were, she didn't think the niche would be down here. She should have asked her grandfather. She shook her head at herself. He had said it was on the third floor. She glanced back in the direction of the stairwell to Duncan's chamber. Where would the niche have been? The laird's chamber? The lady's? Someplace else that would not be as obvious? But she hadn't even checked the laird's or lady's chambers.

That decided, she was heading in what she thought was the direction of the lady's chamber's trapdoor when she heard what sounded like horses running through the tunnels. Ghosts?

She turned and saw the wolfhounds, Anlan and Dillon, stop suddenly, sniff the air, and study her. Then they both barked, letting everyone know where she was. Having done their duty, they ran the rest of the way to her and butted her with their heads, poking her with their noses in greeting. She smiled and petted their heads.

"Lead me to your master," she said, figuring Ian or his brothers couldn't be far behind. And she might as well get this over with.

When Julia had joined Ian and his brothers in the tunnels, he had been dark and sullen. His attitude continued through dinner and even after they retired to bed, and she wasn't sure what was bothering him so. But he wasn't talking about it, and she gave up asking.

The next morning at the kitchen table during breakfast, his brothers watched her and Heather, their gazes returning to Ian and waiting for him to speak, but when Julia had had enough and rose to leave the table, Ian caught her wrist.

She raised her brows. "We have the filming in the woods today. I'm getting dressed." She waited for him to release her, ready to twist away from him like she'd learned in a self-defense class she'd taken to get some of her scenes right for a story once, if he didn't let go soon. His gaze met hers, cool and concerned. Maybe it was just the fact that Basil would be with his men at the filming today, and Ian was worried about her and Heather.

She smiled and leaned down to kiss his cheek, and for a minute, she thought his black mood would disappear, that he would gather her up, return her to his chamber, and then ravish her before they took part in the film. Instead, he released her. "Everyone ready?" he asked.

A chorus of "ayes" filled the kitchen, and then everyone got up from the table and began clearing the food and empty plates away. All but Julia, who caught Heather's eye. She looked in awe of the American red wolf.

Julia sighed and headed out of the kitchen. If Ian didn't lighten up, it wasn't going to look very convincing that she was totally in love with him when she had to kiss him during the filming. Even though she was.

She'd even considered being a no-show, as annoyed as she was over Ian's mood, except she needed the money and she wasn't one to neglect her obligations. She thought of searching instead for the box while everyone else was preoccupied, and at this rate, wouldn't Ian be happier if she wasn't anywhere near where Basil or his men were? The truth of the matter was that she wanted to watch the action, not only for her book, but because she worried about Ian or his men fighting Basil and his. The thought anyone could get hurt while she was unaware of it as she did her sleuthing work in the castle bothered her too much.

She regarded the blue gown and MacNeill plaid *arisaid* she'd wear, and the chemise that was underneath the gown. All of the garments covered her up so much, that she wondered how Ian could even find her appealing. In research for another story, she'd learned that dampening petticoats and chemises had the effect of making them transparent while they clung to women's legs and other parts of their bodies. It was a way to give suitors a little bit of a risqué show, which was sure to garner their intrigue.

Although in the present day, women wore so much less that even that would probably not be noteworthy. Still, she wore no stays or panties, and the thought of getting Ian's attention while she wore the garments appealed. So she soaked the chemise. She was afraid that if she only dampened it, the garment would dry out before they finished filming the scene and he'd never notice.

But after she added the gown and the plaid *arisaid* over that, she felt buried in all the fabrics anyway. Oh well, she'd given it her best shot.

She slipped down the backstairs that led to the servants' quarters, wanting to avoid Ian and the rest of his family, just in case Ian decided she shouldn't be in the film today, and then she headed outside into the inner bailey. Maria waved at her, and Julia headed straight for her.

"Julia, Guthrie called me last night and was quite incensed that some guy named John Smith, who's supposed to be with the film crew, was trying to pick up Heather and meet with her in the dark of the night. There isn't any man named John Smith on the crew, nor in the film cast. I've checked the rosters. I told Guthrie this, but I'm not sure he believes me. The thing of it is, it sounds like an alias. Unless she can point out who he is, I haven't a clue. Can you let Ian know?" Maria's gaze lowered to Julia's bodice, and she smiled just a hint. "Trying to get Ian's attention?"

"I'll tell Ian." Then Julia shrugged. "I feel buried in

fabrics. I'm sure that I look frumpy and indistinguishable from anyone else out here."

"Well, I'd say you'll get his notice all right."

Heather joined them, smiling and dressed in her blue-and-green MacNeill plaid mantle and coffee-colored gown. "Are you ready?" she asked Julia. Her eyes sparkled with excitement, then her gaze shifted to Julia's bodice, and she grinned broadly. "Oh, Ian will have a hard time concentrating on fighting if he sees you've dampened your chemise."

"It's not all that revealing," Julia objected. At least she didn't think so.

"Oh, aye, it'll catch his attention."

At least Heather was perfectly happy today, even if everyone else wore dark moods. "We've got to go." Julia looped her arm around Heather's and headed for the bridge across the moat.

"Have a good time," Maria called after them. "I'm working on another scene. Have fun!"

Julia waved back.

"I heard you were in the tunnels again last night. That you searched Ian's brothers' rooms, and even their mother's, looking for the secret box," Heather said.

Julia sighed. "Yeah. I was alone and I thought maybe I'd get lucky. But it didn't work out that way, and now Ian's not very happy with me."

"He's worried. About the filming today, about the guy I tried to see last night, and concerned you might have hurt yourself in the tunnels again. He has a lot on his shoulders. Even with the money problems we're having, he worries about all of the pack and keeping us together and not losing the castle." Heather squeezed

Julia's arm and smiled. "But he'll be fine once the filming is done."

Great. That could take weeks. Then again, she figured this was like the way Maria acted when she didn't want anyone helping her through her concerns. And that Julia wasn't buying when it came to her mate.

But for now, she saw Basil Sutherland—and he was the same man she'd seen in the airport watching her, his gaze taking in the whole of her appearance, his men standing with him, their looks just as dark and leering. Maybe dampening her gown hadn't been such a good idea after all.

Chapter 21

WITH GOOD WEATHER UPON THEM AND CAMERAS IN place, everyone began taking their positions for the filming of the battle scene in the woods.

Ian cast a wary glance around, identifying where Basil Sutherland and his men were situated. He saw Julia and Heather nearby with two of Heather's brothers watching her and Duncan sticking close to Julia. Four other maidens with smiles on their faces but wringing their hands were still huddled with his mate and his cousin.

Nearby, Basil stood tall and broad-shouldered with a fierce scowl to match his size. What Ian didn't like most about the bastard was the way he looked the "fair maidens" over with too much interest, his gaze quickly settling on Julia.

Someone directed the four other maidens to where they needed to be. Heather gave Julia a hug and then tore off to her own spot of woods with her brothers in tow before the filming of the scene began.

Only Julia remained within his visual range, which he'd made sure would be the situation and the only way he had agreed to allow her to remain in the film.

Julia smiled at Ian and looked to be in her element, the MacNeill plaid suiting her. Tendrils of red curls fluttered across her cheeks on the breezy day, a light mist draping the woods before the sun burned it away.

He envisioned her wearing a slip of a lace bra and a skimpy thong or being naked, and the brief thought flitting across his mind of how much he'd like to lift her gown while he wore his kilt and show the lass a bit of Highland loving. But then he stared at her bodice, the way the fabric looked so sheer across her breasts, her blue gown just high enough to cover her nipples, and he frowned.

Hell. He was ready to grab her up and carry her straight back to his bedchamber.

He knew she was disappointed in his brooding silence this morning. He couldn't help it. He couldn't stop worrying about what was in that damnable box and that she wanted to find it without his people knowing about it. And he didn't want her out here while Basil looked her over as if she was his next meal. Right now, she looked like a delectable offering.

Heather, too, had irked him, and he felt as though Julia was leading his cousin astray with her unconventional ways since she hadn't lived by pack rules in her own family.

Not hearing the director's call to begin the fight, Ian's brain was so muddled with the thought of Julia and what he wanted to do with that sweet body wrapped in the plaid of his clan that he realized, as a brawny American Scotsman attacked him, that the battle had begun.

The braw fictional Highland laird star of the film, John Duvall, clashed with his nemesis nearby as the cameras began rolling. But Ian feared it wouldn't take long for the real fight to begin with his own archenemy and the disaster that could follow.

Guthrie and Cearnach moved in with Duncan to stay

near Julia now, making sure that not one of Basil's men could approach her. Heather's brothers were watching over her. The other four fair maidens were human women from the village, and Ian assumed neither Basil nor his men would bother them.

It didn't matter that Ian was to fight a towering Scotsman standing near the star of the film in an effort to protect "his laird." Basil Sutherland remained Ian's focus, his true enemy currently battling with a human actor as if he were taking a stroll in Edinburgh, just like their handlers had taught them—thrust, parry, swing, make it look good and real, but don't hurt anyone. Choreographed nonsense. Ian and his people had all listened with feigned interest until he'd fought the instructor himself.

All agreed that when it came to fighting the battle, it would be accomplished in their own way.

With claymore swinging, Ian quickly attacked the towering human Scotsman, who in his panic to avoid the fury of Ian's sword, tripped over his own feet and fell on his back with a whomp!

That was not part of the planned scene, but the director didn't yell, "Cut!" And Ian did a mock final stab into the man's chest. The actor looked so surprised that Ian winked at him and said in Gaelic, "Die, mon, so I can fight the real threat."

Not possibly understanding Gaelic, the man seemed to catch Ian's drift. He clutched his chest, shuddered, and died.

Ian looked around for Basil. Catching his eye, Basil smirked at Ian as he continued to leisurely battle another human actor.

The star of the picture glanced at the man Ian had just laid to rest, lifted his chin a bit as if in acknowledgment that Ian had done well, and then fought another human actor.

John Duvall didn't do a bad job with his choreographed skills, although the man was using a lightweight sword, as Ian engaged one of his own men, finding much more sport this way. At least his own man knew how to fight. Basil's men appeared to be doing the same, disengaging from the director's men and fighting their own instead, which was easy enough to do.

As in Ian's own camp, Basil's men consisted of families loyal to him who were not direct descendants of the Sutherland clan. Their plaids were different but muddied to appear as though the men had been living in other than ideal conditions for the past few weeks, and no one could tell they were fighting their own clansmen since they were just the background performers, a blur of swords and men.

Basil seemed to have the same thought in mind or was following Ian's lead, as if he realized a fight between Ian and his men and the Sutherlands would cause the director to stop the film. At least for now.

Without having to fight real actors, Ian threw his heart and soul into battling his distant cousin, but before long, the man had morphed into five, his men preferring better odds by ganging up on him. Five to one was a little much, but once Ian had whittled it down to three, he was more in his element.

At some point, he thought he heard the director yell, "Cut!" Ian couldn't be certain. Distractions on the battlefield had to be ignored. One last man to cut down, his redheaded cousin and one of Heather's brothers, Oran, who had been ogling Julia with too much interest when she'd first arrived at his castle gates. Sweat poured down Oran's brow.

"You were to be protecting your sister," Ian said in Gaelic.

"Aye." Oran swung his sword again at Ian's, the resounding metal clanking through the woods. Otherwise, a quiet stillness had settled everywhere.

"Then why are you fighting me?"

"Heather wished me to."

Ian raised a brow and struck another metal-clanging blow.

Oran fell back but quickly regrouped. "She wanted you to show off your skills in front of your ladylove." He grinned. "I told her there was no need. So she said I might catch one of the fair maidens' interest for the night instead."

Ian shook his head. "Unless the fair maidens take pity on a man who's flat on his back..." With that, Ian swung his weapon so hard when it struck Oran's sword that his cousin's sailed through the air, hit a tree with a thwack, and landed on the ground with a thud. Using fancy footwork, Ian shifted his leg quickly behind Oran's, gave a shove against his cousin's shoulder with his free hand, and once the astounded Oran lay on his back, Ian thrust his sword at his cousin's belly in a mock kill.

Still speaking in their native tongue, Ian growled, "Die!"

On order, a faint smile appeared on Oran's lips, and he said in a hoarse whisper, "I shall win at least one lady's favor tonight, I'm thinking. I thank ye, my laird."

Then he closed his eyes, his hands falling away from his waist, and died.

"Cut!" the director seemed to yell again. Hadn't Ian already heard the director call that before?

Resounding clapping filled the woods.

"The guy's good," someone said near the director.

"The *guy* is a *laird*," Duncan said sharply.

John Duvall gave Ian a thumbs-up. "You ever want a job in the film business, you've got it." He headed off for his trailer.

Julia dashed through the woods toward Ian, and he sheathed his sword and stalked in her direction. The plaid *arisaid* had been belted at her waist and wrapped loosely over her head like a hood to cover her beautiful red curls but then it fell away. With her racing footfalls, she was stunning, her breasts bouncing against the dark blue gown scooped low and the chemise covering the rest of her bodice, which upon careful inspection again, still looked awfully sheer.

Hell, woman. Not only wasn't she wearing any bra, but it appeared as though she'd dampened her chemise, which made it as transparent as if she wore virtually nothing at all, showing off the bountiful swell of her breasts. The dark blue gown rose high enough to conceal the color of her nipples, but it didn't hide the way the crowning glory of those twin peaks pressed against the fabric.

No matter how much he wanted to see where that damnable Basil Sutherland was now and what he was doing, Ian couldn't pull his focus away from his mate. She reached Ian and grabbed him in a full body embrace, jumping his bones literally as she wrapped her legs around his hips. The heat of her supple body seared him as her maneuver pushed her skirts back, revealing her hose-covered calves now locked behind him as she crossed her ankles and straddled him in way too much of a sensuous manner.

His arms quickly encircled her, hugging her even tighter against his body and rousing him further. She tilted her face up to him, smiling luminously, and he lowered his head and kissed her. He only meant to give her a light brush on the mouth in greeting, to show his appreciation for Julia being Julia, but the kiss soon transformed into a passionate melding of lips and tongues. By their own volition, his hands cupped her arse and held her tighter against his groin.

At first, silence filled the air, and then several chuckles erupted, drawing his attention.

"Should have gotten *that* scene on tape," someone said. "The audience would love it."

"Yeah, but the focus is supposed to be on the stars of the film. Not two Scottish unknowns."

Julia stiffened in Ian's arms and pulled away slightly, her mouth leaving his, and he assumed she was going to make a retort. He could just imagine her saying she was not Scottish born but American, and she wasn't unknown. She was a werewolf romance writer with fans all over the world.

But he didn't want anyone else to know about that. He covered her mouth with another kiss, while still holding the voluptuous woman, and carried her back to the walk across the moat.

"My hero," Julia said, between tonguing his mouth with relish and tightening her legs around his waist.

"'Tis good then that we won this battle today and the castle is safe," he said, smiling, feeling much lighter-hearted now that they'd gotten through one battle scene without any difficulty between his men and Sutherland's, and that Julia and Heather were both safe.

"Oh, aye, Ian," she said, attempting to mimic his brogue, and he loved her effort. "'Tis time we are eating?"

"Afterward," he promised, his hands squeezing her arse buried under the layers of cloth, which made him glad that women no longer wore so many articles of clothing. "You wear no stays, lady." He said it in a teasing manner as if lightly scolding her for being so wanton.

She smiled brightly.

"Are you still wearing those skimpy scraps of lace I love so much?"

Her face flushed. "Are you wearing anything under your kilt?"

"You are without?" he asked, feeling higher to see if he could recognize a piece of fabric at her hips. He was already hard and wanting as her body rubbed against his while he walked.

"Only if you are without."

"Traditional dress requires wearing the kilt and nothing underneath. While my brothers and cousins and I served in the Scottish Highland Regiments, we went commando. Although at Highland games and for dancers who perform high kicks and pipe bands who participate in high-stepping marches, participants often do wear undergarments as it's required, lass. Breezy weather can be a wee bit of a problem also." He shrugged. "Our long tunics or shirts protect us from chafing wool so we need not wear anything else while we participate in sword-fighting demonstrations."

"From what I've heard, it's a personal choice."

"Aye. During all-male gatherings, we often don't bother. With women present? Depends on the women." He smiled.

"You are *so* bad."

He chuckled and pressed his head against her breast. "Your chemise is damp, lass."

"In the old days, women did whatever they could to catch the men's eyes. To hell with restrictive fashions. About that betrothal contract, though…" Julia demurred as Ian tightened his hands on her arse.

"Hmm, lass?"

"Maybe we don't have to find it."

"Oh, we have to find it all right."

She sighed.

He kissed her lips. "Just for historical reference." And for whatever else was hidden in the box.

Her gaze met his. He gave a dark smile. "Whether you were mine, lass, or no', once your da and mine contracted for us to be betrothed, it was taken out of our hands."

"My father had nothing to do with this. Nor your father, either."

He shook his head. "In *your story* where I'm your hero."

She frowned. "How would you know—"

"Stands to reason you would view me in that way." He reached the inner bailey, thinking his castle was too damned far from the woods.

She sighed. "Are you feeling better than you were this morning, Ian?"

He didn't want to tell her how worried he'd been that something could go wrong in the fight scene today. Or that he still had his doubts about the box's contents, or that he couldn't help being concerned that Heather would sneak off with the human and get herself into some real trouble. He didn't reply.

When he entered the keep, he quickened his pace as he made his way to the stairs and his chamber. After they reached it, he shut the door with his hip, stalked across the floor, and set her on his bed, with every intention of cleaning up before he ravished the delectable lass.

"I will join you in a moment after I wash up," he said, removing his sword and setting it on the dresser.

"But... I don't want to wait." Seeing Ian in his sexy kilt had made Julia hot and bothered the whole day, between getting everything in place for the shoot and then shooting the picture. And wearing no undergarments underneath her layers of clothing, plus with dampening her chemise so it felt like she barely wore anything beneath the gown, she felt sexy and wanton and had envisioned ravishing the Highlander once he'd finished fighting his enemy.

She leaned back against the mattress and touched the brooch securing the *arisaid* at her bodice, but after trying to unfasten it, she found she couldn't free it.

As he watched her, an almost imperceptible smile tugged at Ian's mouth.

She frowned and tried to unlace the ties at the sides of the gown, instead, but couldn't see what she was doing.

"Ye need a lady's maid, aye, lass?" He moved in closer to her, his gaze dark and speculative. He leaned down to remove the brooch at her bodice, his fingers touching her breasts and making her whole body heat with anticipation.

How could his simple touch turn her into a burning inferno?

His darkened eyes focused on her as he pulled the brooch loose and then set the pin on the side table.

"No, Ian, I only need you." The fact of the matter was that she'd been very capable when she'd dressed earlier. But now under Ian's hot gaze, she couldn't seem to unfasten anything.

She ran her hands up his thighs under his kilt, brushing her thumbs upward and feeling his hard muscles tighten. Heat reflected in his eyes, desire flaring, the craving for her revealed in his predatory gaze.

His voice thick with need, he said, "You know, lass, the danger you're asking for?"

"With Sutherland?" She stroked Ian's thighs in a seductive way. "Or with you?"

"Julia." That simple declaration told her he wasn't giving her up for anything. And she knew he loved her, even if he still didn't say the words.

His hands felt solid on her shoulders, gently pushing her back. But as he leaned forward, she moved her fingers underneath his kilt and between his legs, soundly cupping him. She felt the fullness and hardness and incredible length of him. Heard the intake of his breath and the groan, and then he briefly closed his eyes. The thought of taking a shower forgotten, he opened his eyes, quickly removed the belt at her waist, and tossed it aside. How easy it was to change his mind, and she loved that he craved her so willingly that he could be swayed in that way.

She wanted him to untie her laces at the sides of her gown, but instead, he leaned over and cupped her breasts beneath the smock and chemise and fondled them in a loving way. He pushed the gown lower, exposing her nipples, which were only screened by the sheer, damp chemise. His thumb stroked over a nipple, grazing it, and making it grow and tingle and stir her craving for completion even more. His gaze focused on hers, glazed with lust. Then he ran his hand down her waist, so lightly it tickled her ribs.

She reached down to grab his kilt and push it up, to get this show on the road, but he thwarted her, roughly tugging at her laces to untie her gown. She slipped her fingers inside his open tunic, felt his muscles tense beneath her touch, and wanted him naked and joined with her.

He tugged the blue gown off and then worked on the smock and her hose and garters, until all that was left was the paper-thin chemise. He took stock of her, his eyes roaming all the way down the clinging fabric from her breasts to her ankles.

His heated gaze made her feel sexy and vulnerable and desired.

He ran his large capable hand over the soft fabric draping her legs and then, with his strong fingers molding to her calf, pushed the fabric upward. His voice raspy with need, he said, "This reminds me of when I first saw you."

When she was soaking wet at the tavern. Only she hadn't been quite this naked. And she'd felt his ravenous gaze then, too, only she'd been considering his wet clothes in the same interested manner.

He lowered his head and kissed her mouth as her hands caressed his hard muscled chest. She was having a difficult time concentrating on anything but the way he pulled up her gown, slowly, his hand brushing a sensuous stroke up her thigh. Every touch was loving and sexy, and she was thankful his dark mood had dissipated.

She tugged at his shirt to pull it free from his plaid, but it was too long. He yanked off his belt, and then his plaid and stood only in his long tunic, his legs bare, his look feral. She was reminded of the Scots of ancient times, how she was in a castle that was several centuries old and was living the fantasy with the Highlander of her dreams.

Then he hauled her chemise over her head and dropped it to the floor, and she gave a little pull upward on his tunic, which made him smile and wrench the fabric over his head. He was beautiful, every square inch of muscled man, the dark hair on his chest trailing down. And her gaze settled on the hefty size of him, primed just for her.

Fully naked now, she reached up, wanting to pull him down to join her, to fill the ache that was making her crave having him deep inside her.

But despite her being in a rush to make love, maddeningly, he seemed to be in no hurry whatsoever.

Ian stared at the beauty before him: the flush of her skin—which amused him because it seemed no matter how many times he made love to her, she wore that innocent blush whenever he viewed her—her darkened nipples tight and kissable, her fiery red hair splayed across his pillow, and the red thatch of curls between her legs, dewy with eagerness. He knew she was impatient to make love, but he wanted a moment to enjoy her naked splendor before that happened.

Then he pushed her knees apart with one leg, spreading her open so his fingers could plunge into the wet slickness between her folds. And she arched her leg pinned between his, pressing into his arousal. His control slipping, his touch greedy, he rubbed her in a lascivious manner. She responded with a sweet, sexy moan. He loved her, lusted for her, wanted her forever and knew she was the one he had needed to make him whole.

He kissed her breast, rubbed his whiskery cheek against the nipple, and licked and sucked and paid homage to one and then the other as his fingers continued to stroke her lower. She ran her hands through his hair, her heartbeat quickening, her body arching, restless and yearning, pushing to have him work her faster, and then she cried out his name in a sexually charged way. She sank against the mattress, her body quivering with orgasm, her mouth curved a little in a smile.

Taking advantage of her readiness, he stroked her silky thighs and then parted them farther so he could enter her. With a thrust, he slipped inside and claimed her again.

The lass's rocking against him, her hands gripping his backside, and the way she raised her knees for deeper penetration created a feverish hunger so great that he felt it would consume him until his passion exploded. He collapsed, satiated and drowning in fulfillment. He moved aside and lay on his back. Then he pulled her against him, loving the way her leg slipped between his, straddling him, claiming him.

Dinner would again be late as they slept first and then renewed their lovemaking.

Until he heard his mum's voice wrought with irritation as her quick footfalls drew toward his chamber.

She wasn't due to return until after the movie was finished. What was she doing home now?

"Where is he? What do you mean he's too busy to see me, Cearnach? I'm his mum! And I've returned to put a stop to this madness!"

Chapter 22

FOR MODESTY SAKE, IAN PULLED A COVER OVER JULIA
and himself before his mother broke into the bedchamber. With brows raised, Julia tilted her lips up to his,
offering herself to him. He kissed her smiling mouth,
while his mum's tirade to Cearnach continued as they
approached Ian's chamber.

If she barged into his bedchamber, which she was not
prone to do, he would deal with it. But he was not leaving the bed just yet, and again he kissed Julia's willing
mouth as his fingers combed through her silky red locks.
She didn't seem to mind that his mum was nearly at his
room in full-fledged battle mode and pressed her mouth
against his with as much enthusiasm.

"He is the laird," Cearnach reasoned with their
mother. "It's his decision, and I think it best if you at
least knocked—"

"*What* is he doing abed at this hour?" she railed. Then
she shoved the door open.

Ian broke free of kissing Julia, turned to see his mum,
and raised his brows. "You wished a word with me, my
mother?" His voice was cold.

His mother's mouth gaped, but she quickly folded
her arms, narrowed her eyes, and scowled, looking
from Julia to Ian, while Cearnach standing slightly behind her appeared apologetic, grimacing as he offered
a wee shrug.

She motioned to Julia. "*What* is *this*?"

He thought Julia was the reason for his mum's tirade. But apparently something else had angered her. He now suspected she didn't even realize that Julia was a wolf, thinking her just a human here for a little sexual pleasure. He wasn't surprised no one had told his mother about Julia, though. When his mother was in one of her unreasonable snits, it was impossible to get a word in edgewise. She was used to being the grand dame of the clan and the pack after his father died and Ian had still not taken a mate. But now Julia had the position of the lady of the manor, and his mother would have to step aside. He hadn't considered that part of the scenario.

"This is Julia Wildthorn, *my mate*. But I'm sure the introductions could have waited for a more... *suitable* time."

His mum's mouth gaped again, and she glanced with a glower at Cearnach, who shrugged once more. "*Why* didn't *you*..." She paused and turned back to Ian, her face livid. "I want a word with you *at once*."

Ian cast her the barest of smiles. She might think she could dictate to him like she had done with their da, but Ian was just like his sire, and he would do what he thought best for the clan and the pack.

"Later," he said, his voice bordering on terse now, and he swept his hand down Julia's back in a gentle caress, hoping his mother wasn't upsetting her.

His mum opened her mouth to speak, her eyes still narrowed in contempt. Then her gaze shifted to Julia, her expression hardening even further, and she whipped around and stalked out of the room.

Cearnach bowed his head a little in apology and then shut the door.

Down the hall, his mother harangued Cearnach as their footfalls headed for the stairs. "Why didn't you tell me Ian had taken a mate? And *who* is she?"

Julia sighed softly, stroking Ian's nipple with her finger. "I take it she's not pleased about something. And... I don't think I've made the best first impression on her."

He let out his breath. "I hadn't thought of how this might affect my mum, although she wasn't to return until month's end. By then, I would have sent word to her. Seems something else caught her ear. Maybe something to do with the film. The fact Basil and his men have gained entrance to the castle during the filming, Heather's participation, even our clansmen taking part in the film, perhaps. No telling what has gotten my mum's knickers in a twist."

He continued to stroke Julia's back while she curled her fingers in his chest hair. When she didn't say anything, he asked, "Are you all right, lass?"

"My family's very small, Ian." She looked up at him with tears in her eyes. "I love your brothers, and your cousins, too. I've met some of your other kin and clansmen and clanswomen, and I love how much they're dedicated to you and how kind they've been to me. I love being here and feel as though I'm home. But you have to know it bothers me that your mother doesn't seem to like me. And your aunt..."

"My aunt is my father's sister, and she will show you every respect. My mum, as well. Give them time. They'll come around." And then he kissed Julia, a long lingering kiss that meant she had a pack, a clan, and an even larger family, and she was loved.

But the nagging worry that Basil would soon cause

real trouble was at the back of Ian's mind. In the morning, the filming of a battle in the inner bailey was scheduled. Keeping Julia and his clansmen out of harm's way
was his driving concern for now.

The next morning, Julia felt uneasy as Ian led her down-
stairs to breakfast. She worried his mother would make
a scene at the meal, but she was hopeful that his mother
wouldn't even show up. And that made Julia feel even
worse. She hadn't expected Ian's mother to replace her
own, but she had hoped they'd get along.

There she was, seated at the main dining table along
with Aunt Agnes, the two older women waiting for Ian
to join them like a couple of wolves anticipating their
quarry. But both barely spared her a glance. His mother's red-gold curls were streaked with gray and piled on
top of her head in an elegant coif, while her green eyes
remained sharp and observant. She wore a black sweater
and slacks and looked like she was in mourning as she
cast Ian a scornful look. Aunt Agnes was wearing a pale
blue sweater and slacks, which looked good on her, and
she smiled a little at Ian.

His brothers and cousins milled around the kitchen,
talking to each other about the upcoming scene, while
Cook and a couple of other clanswomen worked on the
morning meal.

"I will teach your brothers to cook," Julia said, feeling the weight of his aunt's and mother's gazes return
to her as she walked past them. "Then if Cook has other
plans, they can fix meals fit for—"

"An earl and his lady," Ian said, kissing her cheek

and pulling out a chair for her. "I think that an admirable notion."

His mother glowered at Julia. She didn't bother to see his aunt's reaction to their comments. Upon hearing Ian and Julia's conversation, everyone crowded into the dining room, offering greetings and small smiles, and then took their seats.

Half were dressed in kilts and tunics, ready for the start of the mock battle, and Julia envisioned the dining hall being part of the old world when the clan met to break their fast. Half were still wearing civilian clothes and would change after breakfast, which made her think of time travelers from the future who had landed in the middle of a seventeenth-century scene.

Everyone politely waited for Ian to say or do something.

He handed a platter of brown bread to Julia. She set a slice down on her plate and then passed the loaf to Heather.

"We took the castle from the Sutherlands," Agnes said, without waiting for anyone else to speak, as the dishes of eggs and sausages made their rounds.

Astonished, Julia looked up from the bread she was buttering. Agnes's focus was on Ian.

"Argent Castle," his aunt clarified, speaking to Ian.

He straightened. "Aye. My great-grandfather fought them and ousted them from the castle. That I'm well aware of, Aunt. Basil Sutherland reminds me every chance he gets."

Julia stared at Agnes in disbelief. Her grandfather said the MacPhersons had owned the castle. Was he mistaken? She didn't believe so.

"Do you know why our family fought the Sutherlands in the first place?" Agnes asked.

"Territorial disputes, as far as I'm aware."

So Ian hadn't believed that Julia's family had owned the castle. All this time, he'd been humoring her?

"Before this happened, your great-grandfather's son, your grandfather, was to mate a MacPherson," Agnes said, her gaze drifting to Julia and then back to Ian.

Ian sat back in his chair. Julia closed her gaping mouth. But she wasn't the only one who appeared surprised. Forkfuls of food hung suspended in air, open mouths ready to take a bite and then stopping while the news hit them.

"I discovered it in some of the family journals. The union was meant to tie the clans together, to unite them against the Sutherlands," Agnes continued.

"An alliance," Julia whispered.

"Aye," Agnes said, giving her a sharp nod.

"With the MacPhersons?" Ian's voice was rife with disbelief.

"Aye. But the Sutherlands didn't want this union. They stormed Argent Castle before this was to occur in a month's—"

Ian held up his hand to stop her. "The MacNeills stormed Argent, you mean."

"No. The MacPhersons owned the castle."

Julia's grandfather had been right. She felt a wave of relief that he hadn't been wrong and that she hadn't told Ian anything but the truth.

Ian frowned. "I don't understand."

"Before our people arrived at Argent, Sutherland had already taken the castle after weeks of laying siege to it. We, the MacNeill clan and the families who owed us allegiance, seized the castle from Sutherland. But the MacPhersons? They had completely vanished. Some said they had escaped through secret passageways. Others, that they had been murdered for attempting to align with the MacNeills. No one ever discovered their whereabouts. It was said Sutherland had forced the MacPherson to agree to give his lovely daughter in betrothal to the laird of Argent Castle instead of the MacNeill."

"But there were no females born to the MacPhersons," Julia inserted.

"Oh, aye, there was. The woman in the oil painting. Fiona MacPherson. She was to be Ian's grandfather's mate. If anything were to stop that mating, the contract would be valid for a subsequent mating between a MacNeill laird and a MacPherson lady. We wished the ties between the clans."

Julia cleared her throat and all attention focused on her. "But my grandfather said the contract was between the laird of Argent Castle and a MacPherson lady."

"Aye. That contract was drawn up by the Sutherlands. Being so arrogant that they could see no other clan ever taking hold of Argent, they believed stating that the mating would be between a laird of the castle and a female MacPherson offspring would be sufficient."

Ian smiled, lifted Julia's hand to his lips, and kissed it. "Except the MacNeills became the lairds and the contract would have been what the MacPhersons and MacNeills had intended in the first place. The old Sutherland outfoxed himself."

Agnes gave a coy smile. "Seems you became the

beneficiary of the contracted agreement instead of your grandfather."

But his mother did not smile. "I wished to speak with you last night."

"Aye." Ian didn't say anything more, and his mother's face blushed with indignation.

"You shouldn't be in this film. Your da would be turning in his grave. As for the Sutherlands, they should never have gained entry to the grounds. And..." His mother gave Julia a glower. "...you should have told me you planned to mate some Yank. And a werewolf romance writer?" She gave an annoyed *tch* under her breath.

Before Ian could respond, his redheaded cousin Oran hurried into the dining room from the great hall. "The director is threatening to fire the whole lot of us if we don't take our places at once."

"The nerve of the man," Ian's mother said. "I will give him a piece of my mind." She rose from her chair but waited for Ian to agree with her.

He gave her a wave of his hand. "By all means." Then he turned to Julia. "Ready to don your gown?" He gave her a lascivious wink.

His expression said that if they went up to the bedchamber together, they'd never make it to the inner bailey for the filming of the scene.

Come to think of it, that would have suited her fine, if she had not known that Ian had to make sure his people remained safe with the threat of Basil and his men on the premises.

Within the hour, everyone involved in the film had taken their places. But it took many hours to get the scene right, and then when the actual filming began for the final take, Basil Sutherland didn't take long to move from where he was supposed to be fighting human actors to challenge Ian instead. Sutherland and he performed in the background while the camera's focus was primarily on the stars, but whether in practice or fighting a real battle, Ian concentrated on the man and the sword before him. His brothers and Heather's were watching the women while they battled nearby. But this was the fight Ian had darkly anticipated.

"You can't have her. She was meant to be mine!" Sutherland's whole body was filled with tension, tenser than was safe, as he swung his sword at Ian. Sutherland's breathing was heavy and his dark eyes narrowed with hatred, his patience shredded by all the retakes while filming the scene that had taken until nearly evening.

Ian blocked the blow with a hefty clunk. "You're a bloody fool, Sutherland. You tried to kill her on the road and—"

"Kill her? I disabled the car and meant to rescue her, but then I saw your bloody headlights approaching and drove off. They weren't supposed to run into the dyke."

Ian thrust his sword at Basil, but the man rallied with a hefty block. A deafening clang resounded.

"Julia's mine," Ian said, his voice low and controlled, his muscles loose, his breathing regulated. He thrust again at Sutherland's breast, keeping his feet spread a shoulder width apart for better balance. He glided across the pavement, planting the soles of his feet on the ground as much as he could to maintain equilibrium, and kept up the frontal attack.

Sutherland fell back again, his face red, his hands clenched tightly on the hilt of his sword. "The contract states otherwise, and you know it."

Ian faltered. The tip of Ian's sword dipped just enough that Basil took advantage. With a wicked thrust, Basil stabbed at Ian's chest, but Ian jumped back and swung his sword to counter the momentum of Basil's weapon. Sweeping it aside, Ian felt the tip of Basil's blade slashing across his shirt, cutting it, slicing his skin, and drawing blood. *Hell.*

Retaliating, Ian swung his sword so hard that when it hit Basil's, the jolt went up Ian's arm. Basil's haughty grin slid from his face.

"What do you know of the contract?" Ian growled, thinking of how Sutherland's people had invaded the MacPhersons' holdings and taken them hostage before his grandfather could claim his mate. Although if he had, Ian wouldn't be in the position he was now with Julia.

Both Ian and Basil kept their postures straight, their chests facing forward to maximize the ability to simply twist away from a dangerous strike.

"You can't be daft as all that. You besieged her castle. Vanquished us. The contract drawn up between Sutherland and the MacPherson clans stated Fiona MacPherson would be my grandfather's mate. That if the mating was not a success, another MacPherson lass was promised to the laird. Since that union never occurred, Julia is mine." Basil's face was twisted, red, his eyes narrowed in confrontation, and even his breathing was reedy.

"Yours?" Elbows close to his body, sword poised, Ian lunged at Basil, not about to be thrown off guard again. "If that were so, how come it's taken you so long to realize this?"

"I only just discovered my great-grandfather's journal."

Basil blocked Ian's blow with a frantic sweep of his sword. A clang of metal rang out across the inner bailey.

"The contract states the MacPhersons and MacNeills would be united through a mating before the Sutherlands seized Argent Castle," Ian said. Although he didn't need any contract to say Julia was his.

"Did your da or anyone else tell you that a MacPherson would be yours?"

No. And that had bothered Ian, although Oran's arrival in the dining hall had made him forget to question Aunt Agnes about that. Why wouldn't his family have made him aware of a contract such as this? At the very least, he would have searched for the lass and resolved the issue. If all parties had agreed, he would have destroyed the contract himself with her family and his as witnesses. Unless his family had believed the MacPhersons had all died.

"You know what I say is true," Basil said, winded as he fell back from Ian's thrust, the blade nicking Basil's shoulder. Blood tinged his garment. He cursed in Gaelic.

"The contract would no longer have been enforceable," Ian countered, although among the *lupus garous* it would have been. Their long-standing traditions made it so.

"Ah, MacNeill, you don't believe that. You have taken my promised mate when she belongs to me. Your kin had taken my castle before this. How much more can a man endure?" Basil usually kept cool in a sword fight, but his stance was off, his forehead beaded with sweat.

"The lass's family owned the castle before you," Ian said.

"They were weak and needed a protector. We came to their aid," Sutherland said, finally getting a second wind.

Ian gave a dark laugh. Basil responded with a thrust of his sword, but Ian quickly countered and knocked it aside.

"You're a good storyteller, Sutherland. They may have needed a protector, but only from *your* kin." Throwing his weight into the swing, Ian caught Basil's sword so hard that the blow ripped the sword clean from his hands and sent it sailing through the air.

Ian noted then how quiet the bailey was. No shouts or clanging of swords from the other men. No sound other than Basil's heavy breathing. The man dove for his sword.

Ian slammed into him, knocking him down, and Basil fell hard on his back against the pavement. His head hit with a dull thud. His eyes swimming with tears, he looked dazed.

Running footfalls caught Ian's attention, and he turned to see a pale-faced Julia racing toward him. Before he could sheathe his sword, she wrapped her arms around his body and held on tight, her mouth kissing his chest, her hands gripping him for dear life.

"Ian," Julia murmured against his chest and with his sword flat against her back, he kissed her lips and felt the heat of her pressed against his body, her soft breasts and her hair tickling his skin where his shirt hung open.

The world stood still in that instant, everything fading

into the background. Vaguely, he was aware that Basil's men cursed him in a steady stream of Gaelic, variations on the theme of whoreson, as they hauled the dazed Sutherland out of the inner bailey.

"Cut!" the director called, from what sounded like a million miles away.

"You won," Julia whispered through her tears.

Ian hadn't won. The conflict between Basil and him was like a pot of stew, simmering, heating, and bubbling into a rage, then cooling down and simmering again until the next time. In the past, that hadn't mattered. Sutherland wanted the castle back, but he couldn't lay siege to it in this day and age. Now he wanted Julia, too. But he damn well couldn't have her, either.

Ian swept Julia up into his arms as cheers in Gaelic, whoops, and hollers rent the air. He stalked toward the castle with his bundle of soft, warm woman.

When he entered the keep, the place was quiet since everyone was still outside wrapping up business. His brothers and the others would watch the film crew and would not leave the inner or outer bailey until everyone who didn't belong was let out for the night and the gates shut and locked.

He carried her through the great hall to the stairs.

The sound of running feet behind him didn't make him slow his pace. He recognized the footfalls. *Maria's.*

"Laird MacNeill," she called out.

"Talk to her," Julia said, her sparkling green eyes beseeching him.

"We have other business to attend to," he said under his breath.

She made a face at him. "Oh, right, and it's not like

you're subtle about it, Ian. I mean, everyone here today knows just where you're taking me."

His mouth curved up marginally, although he still couldn't rid himself of Basil's haunting words. That Julia was his, not Ian's. "Everyone needs to know you are mine."

"As if anyone would be that clueless."

Maria dove in front of Ian, but he quickly sidestepped the lass. "Not now, Miss Baquero."

"Laird MacNeill, Howard wanted me to tell you that you were brilliant," Maria said, running beside him.

"Aye, he has the right of it."

Julia shook her head. "Did he also mention how humble Ian is?"

Maria smiled and then continued, "You don't have much of a part at the final feast, but he wants to give you a bigger role. He wants you to kill off your archenemy on screen."

Ian raised his brow at Maria.

"Not for real, of course. Will you agree?"

"I don't want Basil or his men inside the castle. My men and Harold's actors will be there."

"We've discussed this before. They're contracted as background performers, and without just cause to let them go—"

"Maria," Julia said, "you know the animosity that exists between the two clans and how dangerous that powder-keg combination can be."

"That's what Howard loves about it. It looks so real. No one could act the way Ian and his men do when fighting against Sutherland and his men. Harold swore he was watching a real battle in the bailey just now."

"Which he was," Julia reminded her.

Ian headed for the stairs with Julia still clasped tightly in his arms.

"Please agree to do this small last part, Laird MacNeill," Maria tried again. "He wants you to sit at the head table with John Duvall while Julia is sitting at one of the lower tables. Then Basil makes a move on Julia and—"

"No," Ian ground out. "Julia will take no part in any of this."

"He's offering a lot of money. He wants you both in this scene."

Without answering her, Ian stalked up the stairs.

"If the price is right, we can do it," Julia said, smiling up at Ian. "He can pay for my flight here, the cost of the lodging, and wages for the scene."

"Who is the laird of Argent?" he asked Julia gruffly.

She smiled wickedly. "Oh you are, my laird. Settle the matter between you and Sutherland once and for all."

"It'll never be settled," he said darkly.

"I'll tell Howard you're agreeable." Maria hurried back the way she came.

"Besides," Julia said, smiling up at him in way too willful a manner, "I'm the lady of the castle, and you would be remiss in not remembering that. Particularly when it used to be *my* castle."

"Then I will have to prove again to you who is laird." And with that declaration, Ian carried his bonny mate into his bedchamber with every intention of making the world kneel at her feet as she did for him.

Chapter 23

FOR DAYS, WHILE THE FILMING CONTINUED ON SCENES involving the cast of main characters only, Cearnach and several of the MacNeill clansmen ensured that the director accessed only those locations already agreed upon. In the meantime, Julia, Ian, and his remaining brothers; a few cousins, including Heather; and even Aunt Agnes searched the castle for the secret niche where the MacPhersons had hidden the box. Aunt Agnes was sure she knew where the cache was hidden on numerous occasions and, when proven wrong, excitedly explained where she thought it might be next.

When they were still unsuccessful, Julia seemed so disappointed that Ian took her back to the falls, except this time, riding horses with the dogs in tow and an escort, as if they were living in the past and the enemy clan was all around them. And it had become so once Basil and his men had signed up as background performers and come after Ian and Julia in their wolf forms near Baird Cottage.

Her feet bare, her jeans rolled up and showing off her slender calves, Julia sat on the edge of a boulder and took in deep breaths to sample the fresh air and the cold moving water, her face tilted up to the sun, her eyes closed. Her red hair was loose and fluttering in the breeze, while light blue jeans and a pale blue sweater outlined her shapely curves. She was stunning, as much a part of the picturesque scene as the frothy water rushing across moss-covered boulders and trees shading the fringes.

Ian thought he'd never look at the falls in the same way again—as just part of the landscape with nothing to make him stop and enjoy them on a partly sunny summer day. He'd always equate the falls with Julia now, and the way she had made him take pleasure in the scenery and realize just how blessed he was with her in his life. Julia was the one who made all the difference in the world to him.

He removed his boots and socks, and then sat behind her on the rock, pulling her between his legs, his arms wrapped around her, his chin resting on the top of her head, his knees boxing her in. Her back melted against his chest, relaxed and at peace.

He wanted to find the box as much as he knew she did. He was curious about its contents and why her grandfather was so adamant that no one should see them. But all that *really* mattered was that Julia and he had found each other. "You know, lass, you are a treasure to me."

"Hmm," she said, snuggling closer. "If you're trying to make me feel better about not finding the box, you are. Coming here and being with you like this..." She sighed. "I wonder what it would have been like in earlier times."

"Much like it is now," Ian said. "The rocks, the water, the trees. We would have had the horses, a guard, and the dogs with us just like today. Will you write that in your story?"

She caressed his knee. "I will, but only in a fictional way. I need to talk to you about something else, though."

"Aye." He kissed her head, hoping the *something else* wasn't too grave an issue. "What is troubling you then?"

"I have a book signing scheduled for Powell's in Portland, Oregon, and other appearances I must make for a couple of new releases."

He frowned. "More 'Getting into Bed with Julia Wildthorn' interviews? Can you not at least disguise your author picture some?"

She chuckled. "Wildthorn is a pen name, and I won't be using the MacNeill name, which would scandalize your mother."

"I believe she is coming to terms with what you do." He leaned over and kissed Julia's soft cheek.

"Oh? She hasn't spoken to me once. At least your Aunt Agnes is helping us look for the box. She's funny. Her face lights up so when she has another thought of where it could be, and off we are on another wild-goose chase."

"Aunt Agnes has read your books. Every one of them. And she even had Duncan rent a video of *Romancing the Wolf* and then watched it with several of our people in the pool room."

"When?"

Julia sounded so surprised that he smiled and kissed her cheek again, and then hugged her tighter. "When you and I were abovestairs making love."

"That really pins down the time." She sighed. "So what did everyone think of it?"

"Aunt Agnes was livid that the heroine ended up with a human for her mate, when your story showed that she was mated to the alpha leader of the pack."

"That's Hollywood for you. They thought that

humans would appreciate it more if the heroine fell in love with the human and he didn't try to kill her. It's a human thing, I'm sure."

"But it was not *your* story."

"Yes, but to get a story into movie format, sometimes authors have to give in a bit. Your mother didn't watch the movie?"

He chuckled. "Unless it's BBC, Mum doesn't watch the telly. Aunt Agnes wanted to know if you could change your name to MacNeill on your books to honor us."

"Hmm, I'm sure that would really go over well with your mother."

"You only have to be concerned with how I feel about it."

Julia looked back at him. "So how do you feel about it?"

"Whatever makes you happy, love. About these book commitments you have, can you just do them online?"

"No."

Her bluntness amused him. "Then *I* will have to accompany you."

She smiled, her look so pleased that he was glad to oblige. "Would you?"

"No mate of mine is running around the world by herself. Didn't I mention this when we first met? That there are too many wolves about?"

"Oh, Ian, I would love for you to…" She paused, and then her eyes widened. "You could wear your kilt."

"I *only* wear it for special occasions."

"Oh yes, this would be special. The women would fall all over themselves to see you in a kilt."

"I would not want women hurting themselves to see me in a kilt, although I believe you exaggerate a wee bit."

"Believe me, I don't exaggerate. One look at you in your plaid, and you'll have them swooning in the aisles."

That made him recall his brother's comment that women would be climbing the gates to get to him. "You are not worried about the attention I might draw?"

"Only if the women are so wrapped up in you that they forget to buy my books."

"I'm not good with talking to outsiders, Julia. I may not make the best of impressions. I may scare them all off."

She smiled. "Lay on the brogue, and they won't know what you're saying, but they'll love every word of it."

"Or I could speak Gaelic."

"Ah, my wild Highlander, not even I will know what you'll be saying then."

He kissed her ear and whispered in it, "Then you will have to learn, my bonny lass."

"If you teach me," she said, kissing his mouth back, "I'm sure I'll be a fast learner."

After another hour of enjoying the falls, Ian led Julia to his horse and lifted her onto the saddle in front of him, while Duncan, Guthrie, and the two cousins escorting them looked on.

They'd only begun to canter back to the holding, when Guthrie said, "Will you need any other Highlanders to accompany you to America, lass?"

Duncan nodded. "I'm sure I could clear my schedule to see to your safety also."

"Wearing kilts?" she asked brightly.

Ian shook his head.

⌒⌒⌒

The last day of shooting had come, the day to film the final feast where the hero of the movie would vanquish the villain forever. To Ian's surprise, his mother had become more worried about Julia's safety than he would have thought possible.

Wringing her hands, his mother caught him in his solar after trying unsuccessfully earlier—several times—to get him to change his mind about Julia being at the feast. "Ian, you really can't allow this. You are armed with a sword. Julia has nothing to protect her."

"She has me."

His mother frowned. "You will be too far from the table where she's to sit. I've seen the arrangements and talked to that damnable director, who merely smiles at me as if I've lost my senses, but he can't possibly understand the animosity the Sutherlands and MacNeills share. You must reconsider."

"I've already agreed to the scene, although I've made some modifications. Duncan and Cearnach will be sitting near her. They won't let any harm come to her."

"I've said all along this is folly. Do you know why I named you Ian?"

"Because you were so relieved to have the first of us birthed?"

She frowned at him. "Be serious, Ian. You were my firstborn, the one who would take over the clan and pack when your da was no longer able to lead. You are truly a gift from God, the one who has led this pack through prosperity and crises too numerous to mention. Everyone looks up to you, even during this madness that we've had to participate in to keep our castle solvent.

You *must* make other allowances. Julia is too important to the pack to lose now."

To the pack. His mother still couldn't say that Julia was important to her. Despite Julia's conceding that it didn't matter, he knew deep down it did. "We'll be fine, truly. Have no concern." Ian was apprehensive enough for both of them as it was without worrying about his mother's interference.

Shortly thereafter, he took his seat at the head table, nearer to the end, which, considering he was the real laird of the castle, should have irritated him, but didn't. The hero of the film and his antagonist would play out their roles in the final scene while they sat at the center of the table. Ian's focus was on Basil, seated at one of the lower tables across from where Julia was sitting with Heather. He was too close, and Ian didn't like it. His men were sitting near the two women, but the way Basil kept leering at Julia was for real, not acting in the least.

If Julia hadn't insisted that they play out the scene to earn some extra money and have Howard pay off her plane fare and lodging expense, Ian would never have gone along with it.

"You say you wish to know of my relationship with the lady," the laird actor was saying to his nemesis. "You, Baron, would be well advised to deal with your own problems and leave us well enough alone in the Highlands."

The baron growled, "I will know if the lady is to be your wife."

"She is the cousin of my greatest ally. So, aye, she will be my wife."

The baron jumped up swiftly, the laird actor's guards rushed forth, and Basil was on cue to try and grab Julia in the ensuing skirmish between the laird actor and his enemy. At once, the hall was filled with chaos. Basil's men leapt from their positions to fight Ian's, and Basil fought Duncan before Ian could get to him. But the bastard jumped onto one of the benches, which hadn't been part of the planned scene, leapt to the table where Julia had been sitting, and then lunged for her. Basil's own man swung a sword at Duncan, keeping him occupied so he couldn't follow Basil. Cearnach was likewise engaged with one of Sutherland's men.

Julia dashed out of Basil's immediate path, but Sutherland clansmen on either side of the fray hemmed her in, and she couldn't get far enough away.

Ian's plans to keep her safe were failing.

Basil seized her arm. She grabbed a mug off the table and tried to hit him up the side of his head, but he blocked her blow with his sword arm, knocking the mug from her grasp. Ian cursed in Gaelic, shoving actors and Basil's men out of his way, while trying to get to Julia.

"Julia!" he shouted.

"Ian!" She sounded desperate and afraid, her eyes wild as she struggled against Basil's iron grip.

Basil tugged her through the fighting men, attempting to get her out of the hall. In the script, he was to die, but Ian assumed Basil had never had any intention of dying. It appeared now that he'd only agreed to the bit of playacting to make a move on Julia while everything was so chaotic.

To add to the horror, Ian's mother appeared, wearing a dark blue gown with the MacNeill plaid *arisaid* fastened over it as she waved a *sgian dubh*, forcing men to move out of her way. *Hell*. Now he also had to rescue his mum.

But the clansmen on both sides moved out of her path as they continued to fight. As one of Basil's sub-leaders raised a sword to Ian, his mother reached Julia and shoved the black knife into her hand.

Basil was still trying to pull Julia against him as she struggled against his confinement. And then, she twisted her arm down and under and, with the maneuver, managed to free herself. When Basil looked at the *sgian dubh* she fended him off with, he merely sneered at her. "You would have to threaten me with something a little more imposing, lassie."

He struck at her blade, and she dropped it from the impact with a gasp. He grabbed her arm when she was still too stunned to respond.

Knocking the man to the floor that he'd been fighting, Ian rushed to Julia's defense. "Release her at once, Sutherland." Ian planted himself between Basil and the entryway. "You won't leave here with her." He had to remind himself that he couldn't kill the bastard. That this had to look real for the movie, although at this point, he didn't care what was going on with regards to the shooting of the film.

Then the bastard struck at Ian's sword, willing him to fight as he kept Julia crushed against his chest like a human shield. "You can't fight me without risking her life, Laird."

Ian focused on Basil's sword, attempting to strike it hard enough that he could tear it away from Basil's grip. But grabbing Basil's arm, Julia twisted her body, using her hip to catch Basil off balance. While Basil lost his grip on her as he fought falling, Duncan rushed in and yanked Julia away, and Ian went in for what he wished could be the kill.

Angered beyond reason, Ian slashed and thrust his sword at Basil, who tripped over a bench and backed into a table, cursing Ian in Gaelic.

"You can't have her," Ian warned in his native language. "She's already my mate."

"When you're dead," Basil threatened, "she will be free to be mine."

Ian continued to advance on Basil in such an aggressive manner that the bastard had no recourse but to continue to retreat and defend himself with his sword.

Then Heather climbed onto a table behind Basil, a clay pitcher used to serve mead during the feast clutched in her hands, and she slammed the pitcher on top of his head. Amber liquid poured down his face as the once fierce warrior crumpled to the floor.

The filming only lasted a couple of minutes more as the hero laird and his archenemy fought each other, and then the laird, with a final killing blow, took the life of his enemy.

"Cut! That's a wrap!" the director called.

For the movie, it was over. But the trouble was far from over between Ian and Basil, as his men carried their dazed leader out of the hall, cursing under their breaths and swearing vengeance.

After celebrating a real feast with his clan and Julia's friend, Maria, Ian had put Cearnach and Duncan in

charge of watching the film crew while they cleaned up
the last of their mess.

Now, Ian cuddled with Julia, naked, in his bed—
theirs, rather. In the past, as laird, this had been his bed.
The one in the adjoining bedchamber was his lady's. But
for Julia, this was *theirs*.

With pride in her voice, Julia said, "Your mother, she
came to my rescue."

His heart had nearly quit beating when he'd seen his
mother come into the great hall carrying the *sgian dubh*,
his father's gift to her in earlier times to use for protection. He stroked Julia's bare shoulder. "Aye, lass."

"I think she might even kind of like me."

He smiled and kissed Julia's cheek. "She does."

"Maybe someday she will think of me like the daughter she's never had. I mean, if she doesn't think of me
writing werewolf romances. Or that I'm American."

"She was furious with me for agreeing to the scene
in the great hall in the first place, worried about your
safety. I never thought she'd come to defend you and
risk her own well-being, though."

"You didn't tell me she felt that way."

"I didn't want her upsetting you."

Julia kissed Ian's throat and shifted her leg over his,
spreading herself to him, claiming him, and making
him hard and horny. "Will Basil return, do you think?"
she asked.

"He'll not get in again," Ian assured her, his voice
bordering on a growl.

Nothing else mattered after that. Just that Julia and
his people were safe and that she was his to love and
to hold.

As the faint glow of sunlight disappeared from the sky, he kissed her willing mouth, loving how restless she became as he moved her onto her back and pressed more kisses across her jaw and down her throat, his fingers kneading a handful of breast.

He loved how she urged him to take her, loved the feel of her hands sliding over his skin, the touch making him hot and needy—ravenous to take his fill. He ached for her, craving her and hating how possessive she made him feel, how out of control when he had rarely felt that way at any time in his life.

Her breathing quickened as she combed her fingers through his hair with a tender touch, her eyes like shimmering jade focused on his, her lips parted, full and luscious, and his for the taking. She licked them as if anticipating tasting a sweet treat, and he cradled her head in his hands and kissed her mouth deep and hard, the soft, wet touch and the spicy, sweet taste intoxicating to his senses.

Her hands shifted to his arse, squeezing his flesh, her touch sizzling, and making his breath raspy with need.

He moved over her, his hand on her breast, kneading the soft feminine globe. The rigid tip stretched out to him, so he kissed it and licked it, and then the other, too.

She murmured something under her breath. He thought she said, "Hurry," but he couldn't be sure. Or maybe it was the little voice in his head pushing him to take her fast and furious.

His fingers stroked her soft belly, moving south, while he trailed kisses down her rib cage, and then he found the center of her sweetness in the bed of red curls. He touched the swollen nub, and she moaned and writhed under his strokes.

A soft gasp and ripples of climax met his questing fingers, and then he was inside her, buried to the hilt, thrusting and meeting her as she arched against him. Her eyes were clouded with desire, her lips full and swollen, her skin flushed with the friction as their bodies glided against each other. Her nipples were dark and rigid. And the sweet, sexy scent of her clung to her like a fragrant invisible veil.

"I love you, Ian," she mouthed against his lips, her expression one of love and lust.

"Bonny lass..." was all Ian managed to get out as the tension of sweet anticipation built higher and higher until he was reaching for the peak and couldn't hold back any longer. Letting go, he released his seed deep inside her willing body, pumping until he was spent.

She murmured, "I love you," again.

"Aye," he said, lying on his back and pulling her against him, as she pillowed her head against his chest, feeling satiated and satisfied and on top of the world.

Only he knew the situation with Basil was bound to come back to haunt him.

—∞—

"Ian," Cearnach said low, trying to wake him, and in the recesses of his mind, Ian realized it wasn't a dream as his arms tightened around a naked Julia in his bed.

He opened his eyes and saw his brother frowning down at him, his looked worried. Ian slid out from under Julia's naked body, still covered in the blanket.

"What is wrong?" he asked, getting to his feet and quickly grabbing a pair of boxers from his chest and then pulling them on.

"Heather's been taken."

Ian stared at him slack-jawed for a moment and then seized his trousers hanging off the back of a chair and swore under his breath. "Are you sure?"

"Aye." Cearnach handed him a piece of paper.

Ian quickly scanned the typed note.

I want Julia. We'll make a trade. Your woman for your kin. For now, Heather's safe.

"How the hell did they get her?" Ian asked.

"That John Smith turned out to be a minor actor in the film. Basil paid the guy to send her a note. She believed she was seeing him, and when she left the holding, Basil and his men grabbed her."

"John Smith?"

"Not his real name, but aye, the one she tried to see earlier and you put a stop to it. According to the note, he was not leaving Scotland until tomorrow and wanted to see her tonight if she could sneak away."

"Get our men—"

Cearnach's look fierce, he nodded. "They're ready. We smelled their scents in the woods. They're wolves tonight."

"Then we'll greet them in kind."

———

The first thing Julia was aware of was that something cold pressed tightly against her arm. Her eyes shot open. The bedchamber was cloaked in darkness, but despite her night vision, she saw nothing. Her heartbeat picked up, and she quickly sat up in bed. Ian was gone, but something, someone was in the room with her.

A man, a specter of a man, loomed over her beside the bed.

"Flynn?" she whispered.

His wild red hair and closely trimmed beard made him appear like a warrior of old. He was tall like Ian and his brothers, and wore a kilt and a sword as if he were ready to do battle, but he held his finger to his lips, warning her to be silent.

That's when she heard movement in the lady's chamber adjoining Ian's. A rush of cold penetrated her bones as alarm spread through her.

Flynn tugged at her arm to get her to come with him, motioning to the door, but she wasn't dressed.

Everything happened so quickly after that. Two men, one of them Basil Sutherland, burst into the room from the lady's chamber adjoining Ian's. She opened her mouth to scream, but the black-hearted Basil silenced her with a blow to the head.

Stars sprinkled across her eyes briefly before darkness blotted out her night vision.

―∽―

As wolves, Ian and his men searched for Heather after they'd discovered her missing. He felt as though he and his men had been chasing shadows all night long. As soon as he'd spied a wolf of the Sutherland ilk, Ian raced after him, but each gray beast melted into the fog like a demon phantom.

Duncan joined him, and with a shake of his head, told him he hadn't had any more luck chasing the bastards down than Ian had.

Then a yip of fear came from near the falls. *Heather.*

Ian and Duncan raced toward the stream, as Ian's heart lodged in his throat. If any of Sutherland's kin had harmed his cousin, the whole lot of them would die.

Soon he was joined by five more of his men all running as wolves at top speed to reach Heather in time.

A Sutherland wolf dodged deeper into the woods off to Ian's right, but nothing would distract Ian from reaching Heather. Two of his men took off after the wolf, though.

The falls grew closer, and a chilly rain was spilling from the clouds when he spied her, trussed up like a lamb for the slaughter, only in wolf form, legs tied and her snout muzzled so she couldn't howl.

She was here alone.

First, relief flooded his veins to see her unharmed, although her eyes were wild with fear. Duncan quickly shifted and removed her restraints.

Something was wrong. The way Sutherland's wolves had drawn them out but hadn't engaged them in combat. The way they had taken Heather as a hostage and left her behind.

Ian looked back in the direction of the castle. Julia was who Basil had his sights set on. Not Heather. *Bloody hell*. It was a diversion. A means to get him away from the lass. Ensuring Heather was all right, Ian motioned with his head to the castle and gave a low growl.

"Julia," Duncan said with full clarity.

Aye, Julia. Ian had made the gravest mistake. In rescuing his kin, he'd left his bonny mate unprotected.

"They can't successfully storm the castle, Ian," Duncan called after him, as Ian bolted for home.

They might not be able to storm the castle, but he had no doubt that Basil had other plans in mind.

Chapter 24

HUSHED, ANGRY VOICES ECHOED OFF WALLS IN THE distance as Julia tried to make sense of where she was and what had happened. Her head throbbed with a vengeance, and focusing took an inordinate amount of effort. She was rewarded with more mind-splintering pain and blurred vision. But in that fuzzy awareness, she thought she saw Flynn crouching beside her, his icy grip on her bare arm.

She realized then she was naked, wrapped in a sheet, lying on the rocky floor of the secret tunnels below the castle. She took a deep breath of the chilly, damp air and shivered.

"Shift, my lady," Flynn whispered. His ghostly voice shimmered in her brain, the words unable to penetrate her fog-filled mind.

"Shift into the wolf, lass. Hurry."

"Wolf," she said, and closed her eyes.

A rough, icy yank on her arm pulled her out of the cocoon of darkness where she wished to remain until the pain in her head went away.

"You can fight them—as a wolf," he urged, his voice dark and insistent.

"Wolf." She closed her eyes, trying to recall what had happened. Where was Ian? Why was she in the tunnels?

"Julia," Flynn said, shaking her roughly.

Her eyes fluttered open.

"My lady, you are in grave danger. Until Ian returns, only I can protect you." He looked saddened at the thought.

"Protect me," she whispered. He couldn't protect her. Not as a—ghost. "Ian," she said, her voice hushed.

"Searching for Heather. They took her."

She groaned, raising a hand to her head. "Heather." But she couldn't summon the need to shift. She tried again and again. Each time, the pain ripped through her brain, short-circuiting what little thought she could dredge up, and the blackness crept over her.

Angry voices reached her again.

"How the hell do I know how the trapdoor got locked?" a man's voice said.

Her breathing suspended. She vaguely recognized his voice. Where had she heard that voice before? The dark, threatening tone. *Basil Sutherland*. And he was down here. With her. She was naked and unable to fight back. Unless she could shift.

She pressed her hands against her temple, trying to stem the pain. Flynn was right. She had to shift. As a wolf, she had wicked teeth, a growl, and a vicious bite. She could howl, letting anyone who was in the castle know where she was.

"We have to go up through the castle. Take our chances at leaving through the postern gate. We have no other choice," the other man said.

Footfalls headed her way. Lengthy, hard strides echoing off the rock walls.

Shift, damn it, Julia said to herself. She concentrated, commanded herself to shift. Pain streaked like needles through her brain, and the footfalls died.

Until that damnable icy cold hand shook her awake again. "Julia, they're coming."

She meant to say, "I know." But she couldn't get the words out. Knowing and doing were on opposite sides of the scale. Just keeping focused on the rapidly encroaching footfalls was effort enough.

"I will die fighting for you, my lady," Flynn said. He gallantly saluted her with his sword flat against his chest and then strode forth.

At first, alarm filled her as she worried Basil would kill the lone Scotsman, her brain still barely able to hold on to any reasonable thought. Then she reminded herself that Flynn could no longer feel any pain. Not like she could.

"Damn it to hell," Basil cried out.

"It's Flynn," another man said. He gave a dark laugh. "He's protecting the castle while Laird MacNeill is searching the countryside for his cousin."

The footfalls that had stopped so suddenly began again.

So close. Too close.

She tried to shift gain. Her head split in two.

"Julia?" Flynn yelled. The sound was hauntingly deep and cut through the darkness that swallowed her whole.

Her eyes opened to see Basil round the corner and stalk toward her, black eyes glittering with menace, face red with fury, stout, determined, and menacing. "You are awake, lass. This won't do."

He meant to knock her out again.

"I may not ever get the castle back, although I have plans since Silverman didn't succeed in financially ruining the MacNeills, but I vow an oath to my ancestors,

I *will* have the MacPherson lass promised to my kin to call my own. Besides, she's a direct descendant of the Duke of Argyll, Chief of the Clan Campbell."

"Ah, that's why you want her. Think you can get special concessions from the Duke's family then?"

"No, you fool. I want her because it's my God-given right." Basil didn't say anything for a minute and then added, "Although the fact she's a Duke's descendant sweetens the mead a wee bit."

But her family, knowing the truth of the matter as the history was orally passed down from generation to generation, had no written proof of the connection to the Duke, also known as the Marquess of Kintyre and Lorne. Did Basil?

She summoned the urge to shift. It was like the electrical current to a light switch was turned off. She had her fingers on the switch, but when she pushed it up, nothing happened. Except for the damnable pain. She wished she could turn that off with a flick of a switch.

Basil was nearly on top of her now. Flynn moved to stop him, swinging his claymore and cutting Sutherland in half, but the ghostly sword had no effect.

Julia prayed that she would shift. And then without realizing she was changing, her blood and bones melted in a comfortable heat, wrapping her up, and instantaneously her bare skin was covered in fur, her teeth long and sharp, but her eyes blurry.

She was now a wolf tangled up in a sheet, and her head hurt just as much as before.

She made a panicky little woofing sound that couldn't have gone any further than a few inches from her nose.

"Hell," Basil said, reaching her. "Shift back."

She growled, but the sound seemed stuck in her throat. Still, Basil didn't strike her like she thought he would. He must not have realized how out of it she still was.

"I don't have another muzzle with me," the other man said.

"Knock her out then," Basil ordered.

So he didn't have the courage to do his dirty work this time. When she had been a helpless woman, that had not been a problem.

The man hesitated.

Basil shoved at him to do it. She bared her teeth. She didn't think she looked very scary. She didn't think she was wrinkling her nose as much as she would have because every hair on her head felt excruciating pain.

"Now."

She snarled, a deeply threatening sound. At least it sounded scarier to her this time.

The man wouldn't draw any closer. "She'll bite."

"Omega wolf," Basil said with hate, then drew back his booted foot, and she feared he'd kick her in the head and knock her senseless.

She struggled violently to get loose of the sheet. Basil jumped back.

She freed herself and wanted to lunge at Basil's throat, but she swayed so unsteadily on her feet, she was sure she'd collapse instead. Just a feather of a touch against her shoulder and she'd topple right over.

Basil cast her a sickly evil grin that told her she'd had it. That even as a wolf—a half brain-dead wolf—she stood no chance against him.

"She's pretty out of it," the other man said, yet he still didn't draw any closer.

Basil took a step toward her, hands clenched in meaty fists. "You're mine, lass, as it always should have been. Only I didn't learn of the contract until it was almost too late."

She wanted to tell him it *was* too late. That she was mated to Ian. That he could do nothing about it. Unless he killed Ian. Her heart stuttered. Had he planned to ambush Ian in the woods?

"Strip off your shirt," Basil ordered the other man.

So focused on Basil, she'd barely paid any attention to the other man. But now that she watched to see if he'd obey Basil's commands, she noticed he was just as tall and broad-shouldered, but his hair was several shades lighter brown, his nose more pronounced, and his chin less prominent.

"What?" he asked in surprise.

"Hurry, you fool. Give me your shirt."

The man yanked off his plaid shirt and then handed it to Basil. He pulled out a dirk and sliced the shirt into strips, glancing with a sneer at her at one point. When he was through, Basil said to his cohort, "Grab her muzzle."

The man didn't move toward her. Even though her head was clearing, she was still groggy and not in really great shape to fight them, but she would do her damnedest.

"If I have to tell you again..." Basil left the threat hanging between them.

Looking ill at ease, the man stalked toward her, and she snarled and snapped her teeth at him. His eyes huge, he jumped back and glanced at Basil.

"She's all growl. *Do* it!"

The man swallowed hard and inched his way toward her. She'd never bitten a man before, never even fought with a werewolf before. It seemed unfair that she had such big teeth and he was sorely disadvantaged, but the way her head was hurting meant she was just as disadvantaged, and whatever ill deeds Basil planned for her would make her even more so. She lowered her head, bared her teeth, and with every muscle filled with tension like a tightly wound spring, she readied herself to attack.

Basil moved around behind her so fast that she turned quickly to see what he was up to. Her vision blurred, and a wash of inky blackness filled her mind. With a piece of the torn shirt, he tried to encircle her snout, but she snapped at him and her teeth clicking hard echoed off the walls. He jumped back, cursing.

The other man grabbed her around the back, and she swung her head, biting at him and connecting with his shoulder.

He cried out. The iron taste of blood stained her mouth, and she quickly let go, knowing it would only take a little more pressure to crush the bones in his shoulder. But she couldn't do it.

His hand clasped over the injury, he collapsed on his butt, screaming in pain. With the distraction, Basil got the upper hand, looped a strip of cloth over her muzzle, and tied it tight.

She jerked her head, trying to free herself to no avail.

Basil struck her in the head with a powerful fist. With a jolt of thunderous pain, the darkness again claimed her.

Draped in the sheet and slung over Basil's shoulder, Julia woke to find she'd shifted and was human. A piece of fabric was tied around her mouth to keep her quiet, and two more strips bound her wrists and ankles. She tried to discern where she was and what was happening.

"The postern gate is closed, damn it," Basil whispered to his henchman.

The man groaned in pain.

"Shut up or I'll kill you, you fool," Basil warned him. Then he stalked off past the stables.

She couldn't keep a clear head, but she could smell the horses and the hay as Basil carried her near the stables. They were headed toward the main gate, she thought. How come they didn't take another way out? Surely, the main gate would be watched.

The trapdoor to the secret tunnel beyond the moat was blocked, the injured man had said. That's why they had to chance leaving through one or the other of the gates.

Then they walked into the stables. "Saddle a couple of horses... *forget it*. You watch her." Basil laid her down on a stack of hay and then led a horse from one of the stalls and began saddling him.

"They're back," the man warned.

Basil let go of the horse's reins and peeked out the stable door. "Hell. All right. We'll get the horses, and as soon as they've entered the keep, we'll ride out of here."

Julia closed her eyes against the pain in her head. Then she tried to roll off the stack of hay, intending to make her way out of the stable any way that she could. She successfully rolled off the haystack but hit the ground hard, her head splintering again, and succeeded in knocking herself out.

Groaning with pain, she came to when Basil hoisted

her onto the saddle on her stomach. To his credit, he helped the other man up into his saddle with a few muttered curses, and then he mounted the horse she was riding and nudged it toward the door.

"They're searching the inner bailey, and several are headed inside the keep," Basil whispered, beads of sweat clinging to his forehead. "Only two are at the gatehouse now. It's our only chance."

They walked their horses out of the stable. Then as the two men at the gate glanced in their direction, Basil kneed his mount and raced for the open gate.

"It's him, the bastard!" redheaded Oran shouted. He looked big and angry, like he could take on a horse and rider both with his bare hands. "And he's got our lady! Close the portcullis!"

Julia envisioned being skewered as the metal grate dropped on their heads. She heard the metal grinding as it was lowered on the outer gate and felt Basil kicking the horse, attempting to get him to gallop faster. She could barely hold onto her wits, the jarring making everything in her brain hurt like the blazes.

The horse suddenly reared up, and Basil cursed aloud. She thought she was going to fall, but the horse settled back down and twisted around, the metal grate grinding as it closed behind her. What was happening?

Trapped! The men and horses and she were trapped between the first and second portcullis.

"Tell Ian that Basil's got her at the main gate! We've got them trapped," Oran told someone on his cell phone.

It wasn't long before Julia saw them—wolves and Irish wolfhounds headed in her direction from the keep, running at a full gallop in hunting mode.

She worried the horses might shy and rear again. But they recognized these wolves. "Laird MacNeill," Oran shouted.

As soon as the wolves and dogs stood in front of the portcullis, one of them looked her over. He had a dark brown stripe of fur between his eyes that lightened as it went down his nose, becoming crème-colored under his chin and on the sides of his face, which made him appear regal. His eyes were nearly black with anger, as he turned his head slightly to Oran and lifted it with a nod.

The innermost portcullis made its way down behind the wolves and dogs. And now they were all trapped together.

Then the wolf raised his head to Oran again and this time, the middle portcullis was raised.

The wolf let out a dark "woof," and the hounds raced in to unseat the riders. To Julia's amazement, the horses didn't rear, but the dogs snapped at the men's legs, threatening to bite, and the men quickly dismounted. Basil attempted to grab Julia from the saddle, probably to use her as a shield again, but the wolves got between the horses and the men and waited.

Someone clucked behind Julia at the innermost portcullis, and the horse she was riding and the other turned and walked over to it.

"Hold on, my lady," Oran said. He reached through the gate and grasped for her tied hands, but no matter how much he tried to unknot the shirt strip, he couldn't.

Then the growling began in earnest. Low growls and barks and yips and snarls.

"Wait," Oran said to Julia, who felt helpless and sick to her stomach and not at all like a heroine was supposed to feel in one of her stories. She was supposed to get free and help her mate. *Damn it.*

Oran pulled out a dirk and cut the ties on her hands, careful not to injure her. He reached up to remove the gag keeping her silent.

But her head pained her so much that she couldn't manage to move in any direction. As much as she wanted to know what was happening, she couldn't see Ian and his men and what was occurring behind her. Oran made the horse come around so that her feet were now facing him, and then he worked on the tie binding her ankles. She raised her head a little to see one wolf dead, now in the form of a naked man, and the other fighting for his life against Ian. *Basil.*

The bastard didn't stand a chance against an infuriated Ian. He stalked him, and Basil backed himself into a corner against the outermost portcullis. He bared his teeth at Ian, his head slightly bowed, but that didn't concern the pack leader. Ian lunged, and their teeth connected in a clatter of enamel. Ian backed off and again attacked, this time with the two riding high on their hind legs, teeth clashing and growls erupting, the sounds vicious as they spilled across the dark night and were amplified by the stone walls.

As in the previous sword fights with Basil, Ian had the upper hand. He was cool and made the moves that would benefit him most, proving to his men and to her that he was their leader and why. He was not only *her* Highland hero, but theirs.

Footfalls ran toward the portcullis from inside the holding, and it sounded like the whole of Ian's clan had been alerted to the trouble.

"Can't we open the gate to get to Julia?" Heather asked.

Julia moaned with relief. Heather was back and safe.

Oran said, "No, not without Ian's permission. If we open the portcullis, Basil may try to escape into the courtyard and injure any number of people before Ian takes him down."

Julia wanted to slip off the horse, but the way she was feeling, she figured she'd slide, fall a hundred feet from the tall horse, hit her head like she'd done when she'd rolled off the haystack, and then pass out.

She kept telling herself she had to do something that was more heroine-like than this. How could she write heroic scenes if in a crisis the heroine couldn't do something for herself or for her mate? Not that her mate needed her help. In truth, she'd probably be a horrible hindrance.

But at least she could stand and cheer him on instead of lying on her belly on the back of a horse wearing only a damnable sheet.

"Julia, are you all right?" Ian's mother asked, her voice laced with concern.

They couldn't see her except for her backside hanging over the horse so they must have figured she'd passed out, which was another reason she needed to get off the horse. "Yes," she said weakly, but with all the growling the two wolves were doing, she wasn't certain anyone heard her.

"Someone help her down from the horse," Aunt Agnes said.

One of the wolves looked in her direction but then continued to watch the fight between Ian and Basil. She was safe, they figured, out of harm's way and not in need of anyone's assistance at the moment. And the fight was much more intriguing than Julia.

Ian and Basil continued to bite at each other's faces, each blocking the other from grabbing his throat and scoring a kill, but Basil was wearing down. Ian still had the fight in him, and he was relentless.

"He will never give up," Oran said. "Ian will not let him live this time."

"And he shouldn't," Ian's mother said. "The bastard dug his own grave when he tried to take our Julia."

Our Julia. Tears swam in Julia's eyes. Ian's mother had finally accepted her.

Basil attempted to go low and bite Ian's leg, maybe intending to break it so he could go in for the kill. Julia wasn't certain why, but Basil's movement gave Ian an opportunity. He jumped on Basil's back and bit into his neck, killing the wolf instantly.

Ian whipped around then and headed straight for his horse. She smiled weakly at him, feeling like a total idiot, perched atop Rogue on her belly wearing only the sheet.

But Ian's eyes were still black as night as he motioned with his head to Oran to raise the portcullis. Ian shape-shifted, and then mounted the horse, totally naked, and lifted Julia into his arms. He was hot and hard and protective and comforting. And loved.

"Are you all right, lass?" he asked, tightening his hold on her.

"Now I am." Her voice was shaky, and her eyes filled with tears. Her head throbbed with renewed pain.

He kicked the horse's flanks and rode her to the keep as his people hurried after them. "Did I ever tell you how transparent you are?"

She gave him a small smile and let out her breath. "How would it sound if I told you my head hurts so bad that I feel I'm going to pass out any minute? How heroine-like is that?"

He raised his brows. "But it is the truth, lass. And that's all I want to hear."

She only heard a muffled curse as the jolting of the horse sent her head into a spin and blackness overtook her once again.

Chapter 25

FOR THREE DAYS, IAN STAYED WITH JULIA IN THE BED-chamber until she was feeling well again, the shadow of a bruise still discoloring the side of her temple and cheek where Basil had struck her twice. But the head-aches and the ringing in her ears and seeing double had all vanished. Yet, she had not wanted to leave the cham-ber. Not for any other reason than she wanted to stay with him, alone, as if they were on a honeymoon, away from everyone else. It was blissful just to be with him. It was a heady feeling to be desired that much by one so desirable.

"Will you make love to me again?" she asked, stretch-ing her hand out to him as he stood in his boxers looking out the window, glad that the movie madness was done and Sutherland's people hadn't retaliated for the death of their pack leader and the other man who'd died.

He gave his bonny mate a smile. "You're insatiable, wench."

She smiled back, pulling the cover aside, baring her breasts, and encouraging him to join her.

"Whatever gives you pleasure, Julia." He was stalk-ing back toward the bed when a thump in the lady's chamber adjoining his sounded and made him go for his sword instead. His first thought—some of Sutherland's men had breached his underground tunnels again.

But when he entered the room with sword readied,

he saw Flynn standing near the massive bed instead. Ian frowned at him. "I have already forgiven you, you ingrate. After you tried to save Julia in the tunnels from that bastard Basil, I told you that you had my undying gratitude. So what is it that you want now?"

If there was one thing he wouldn't tolerate was Flynn's interruption when Ian and Julia had more intimate plans.

Wearing only a T-shirt, Julia peeked into the room. "Did you want something, Flynn?"

He bowed to Julia, scowled at Ian, motioned to one wall, and then vanished.

"What now?" Ian asked, more to himself than to Julia. "Don't you think we ought to see what he wanted?"

The chest had been shoved aside and behind it, two stones caught his eye. The grouting around both was slightly shallower. He would never have noticed if Flynn hadn't pointed out the area to him. Ian returned to his chamber, pulled a dirk out of his drawer, and crossed the lady's chamber to where Julia was crouched, examining the stones. "They're not loose," she said.

He chiseled at the grout between the stones, and then as the powder fell to the floor, he jiggled the topmost stone. "They are now."

He pulled the stone out, and the next one also. And in the opening sat a rosewood box.

"It's... it's got to be the one." But when Ian pulled it out from its hiding place, she touched the lock. "My grandfather said not to break the lock."

Not to be thwarted, Ian left her again and returned with a set of lock picks. She was running her fingers over the carvings with a gentle touch, her breathing light, her eyes wide.

What would they find in the box? He told himself it wouldn't change anything between them, no matter what was contained within.

He wiggled the lock pick in the keyhole as he felt Julia still and barely breathing beside him. Then, with a click, he unlocked the box, pausing before he opened it. He thought of letting her see the contents in privacy to prove he trusted her. But he was dying to see what was so valuable in the box.

Still, he wanted her to know that she was more important than anything the box could contain. He kissed her cheek and said, "I'll leave you to explore the contents. Then, if you'd like, we can see your friend Maria before she leaves. Flynn made a special appearance just to give her a thrill."

"Was she all right?"

"Aye. At first she was just stunned, but then she asked him so many questions that she wore him out."

Julia chuckled. "Sounds like Maria."

Ian ran his hand over Julia's arm in a loving caress. "Your father and grandfather are coming here in a week's time."

"Are they upset with me?"

"For mating me? The laird of Argent Castle? Your grandfather was resigned to it. Said as soon as I knew of the contract, I'd never let you go."

She smiled. "The contract had nothing to do with it."

"Nothing at all." Ian kissed her cheek and then rose to leave her, but she grabbed his hand.

"Stay. What's mine is yours. If it's nothing of

importance to us, we can let Grandfather have his box and all its contents."

He pulled her up from her crouched position on the floor, box still in her hands, and embraced her with heartfelt love. "*You* are all that is important to me, love."

She smiled and led him to the lady's bed. "I love you, too." Then, with shaking hands, she opened the box and set it down on the bed between them.

Five brooches embedded with rubies and emeralds sat next to a Bible on top of several documents. But it wasn't the jewelry that caught her attention. Or the papers, either. Her eyes had widened at the sight of the Bible, her mouth parting a little in surprise, and then her fingers had lingered on the leather-bound cover.

She set the Bible on the mattress out of the way and reached inside for the papers, quickly inspecting them— one, a household accounting of payments and receipts for every aspect of maintaining the castle. Another, the contract between the Sutherlands and the MacPhersons concerning the betrothal with Fiona MacPherson and, if that did not come to pass, with the next female heir and the laird of Argent Castle. Also, the earlier contract between the MacNeills and the MacPhersons for the betrothal of Fiona with the laird. That was all. Nothing new. Nothing riveting.

Julia looked disappointed. But then she smiled brightly. "It's good that there isn't any bad news in the box."

Ian wasn't so certain. He'd seen the way she'd revered the Bible, as if she knew something important about it, some tie to the past, something that she was afraid to reveal to him.

"Anything in there?" he prompted, motioning to the book.

She looked up at him and attempted the most innocent expression, which was the most telling. "An old Bible?"

"Aye. You never know what secrets could be contained within a Bible."

"Did I ever tell you of my great-uncle who listed all his children in his Bible, birth dates and death dates, only I couldn't figure out why he listed *H* by some and *M* by others and nothing for seven of them? A middle name, maybe? But what was it? Grandfather told me his brother loved his children as much as his livestock. The *H* was for horses, the *M* for mules, and the ones without were his children."

Ian smiled. "But who did *this* Bible belong to?" He thought by the look on her face that she knew, but it was almost as though she didn't want to know. "Julia?" he said softly.

She swallowed hard. "I... I think it might be the family Bible some of my ancestors were questioned about." She looked from the Bible to Ian. "My father's great-grandmother was a Campbell." She paused, as if waiting to see if perhaps his people didn't get along with a faction of the Campbells.

"Go on," he prompted.

She sighed. "She was the daughter of the Duke of Argyll. But the Duke's descendants swear that she didn't exist. She ran off with a commoner Highlander who worked for the Duke as a groom. While she was at finishing school, she fell in love with him and they eloped. Anyway, the Duke stated that he would disown her and wipe her name from all records."

"So if the lady had kept a family Bible…"

"It would be proof." Julia took a hesitant breath and opened the Bible, scanned the dates, the names, and breathed in a deeper breath. Tears filled her eyes as she cast Ian a small smile and then closed the Bible with reverence. "It appears, Laird MacNeill, you have mated with a descendant of the Duke."

With a stern expression, Ian shook his head, not believing the implications. "We haven't had good relations with the Duke and his family for centuries."

Julia gently replaced the Bible in the box. "You are making real strides in that regard then, my laird." She set the box on the bedside table and climbed onto the bed. "Is this my bedchamber?"

"Your family has higher rank than mine," he said, utterly astounded.

She gave a breathy little laugh. "My grandfather feared that if we ever could prove our ties to the Duke's family, a Scotsman may want me for only that reason. Now I'm wondering if that had been my grandfather's reluctance about anyone seeing the contents of the box. But we don't have titles in America, remember?"

He eyed her lying on her back, her T-shirt barely covering her feminine treasures. "But in Scotland we do. Should we have DNA testing to see if we can lay claim to their castle? In the event you are a more direct descendant than those who are running the place now?"

She laughed and tugged him close. "If we participated in those circles, we'd have to get married, you know. As werewolves, we don't bother."

"Since I am an earl, we must also."

She frowned at him. "Basil said you didn't really

have a title. That you could buy a little bitty piece of
land and call yourself laird."

"He did, did he? Well, he only said so because he
was a baron. But a duke's descendant is within our pack
now? How could I ever have gotten so lucky?"

"You truly didn't know it, did you, Ian? That isn't
the reason you wanted me? That's why I normally kept
the Campbell ties secret," she teased, running her finger
down his bare chest. "Well, that, and the fact I didn't
have any real proof."

Ian laughed. "You only had to be Julia for me to fall
in love with you, lass."

With that, he pulled off her T-shirt and shucked his
boxers. Her arms wrapped around his neck, and he plied
her with a deep, ravenous kiss, that she responded to
with a kiss that was just as voracious. Her legs wrapped
around him as she wriggled, trying to line herself up for
his penetration. And then he plunged into her hard and
fast and furious, only stopping briefly to stroke her until
she was moaning and writhing under his touch.

Their breathing was ragged, their bodies covered
in a light sheen of perspiration, when he thrust deeply
inside of her again and felt the fervor of their lovemaking gathering and growing—the spasms of contractions
deep inside her gripping him like a velvet sheath. And
in an upsurge of white-hot heat, he was blown away by
the combustion—the chemistry between them nothing
like anything he'd ever experienced. Then he felt bone
weary and satiated, and sank next to her.

Kissing her lightly on the mouth, he smiled at her as
she closed her eyes and drifted off to sleep. He sighed
and spooned her body with his.

Somehow, he had to figure out some other way to keep the castle afloat, or he could very well be a titled laird without a centimeter of land to call his own.

—⁓—

A couple of weeks later, when Julia had finished mapping out her schedule with her publicist for her signing tour, Ian didn't take the news well at all.

"Worldwide book tour?" he grunted. "You said there would be one signing in the States."

"It's scheduled, Ian. I'll be gone all next month. But you're welcome to come with me."

"To do what?"

"Wear a kilt, stand behind me, and look ferocious or sexy as hell."

That brought a small smile to his lips. He enfolded her in his arms. "I told you, lass, you would not traipse around the world without your mate at your side."

"I know—there are wolves all over the place out there. And I thank you from the bottom of my heart for going with me. We'll have fun. You'll see."

His eyes gleamed with intrigue. "Different beds every night. Could work."

She laughed and poked him in the chest with her finger. "But you *can't* make me miss the engagements." She reached up and stroked his cheek. "What about the movie premiere?"

He shook his head. "It is said that if anyone sees those shots of me fighting Oran and the others, women will be driven to climb the castle walls to get to me."

Julia laughed. "Ah, but they would not dare tackle you with me around."

And with that, she returned him to bed, a surefire way to get his mind off book tours and the like.

———ᴡ———

Within weeks, they were off on her worldwide tour, including stops in Australia and New Zealand and all over Europe, and then on to Canada and the States. Not only did Ian accompany her, but his brothers also. If he was going to protect her, so were they. But she knew it had to do in part with them using that as an excuse to see the world. She needed no one's protection from her fans.

On one leg of the journey, she sat behind a table set up at Powell's in Portland because Ian didn't want her greeting anyone unless she had a barrier between herself and her fans. He stood implacably behind her, arms folded and proudly wearing one of his kilts from a couple of centuries earlier that gave him an old-world appeal, even though her historical book featuring Highlanders wouldn't be out until the next year. She still thought Ian could help market the upcoming books and was showing him off as the inspiration for her hero. Unfortunately, he could not wear his dirks or swords for total authenticity.

Her first customer was a beautiful redhead who Julia recognized at once as a *lupus garou*.

"I'm Cassie Wildhaven, wolf biologist," the woman said, her smile genuinely kind. She leaned over the table and spoke low, "Leidolf Wildhaven, my mate, is the pack leader here."

Which meant she was also.

"And we'd love it if you'd come and have dinner with us tonight at our ranch." She looked up at Ian and smiled. "And your friends here, too."

"My mate, Laird MacNeill," Julia said, motioning to Ian, "and his brothers Cearnach and Duncan." Guthrie had surprisingly made plans to be elsewhere and hadn't even accompanied them to the hotel that night when they first arrived.

Leidolf stood close to Cassie, eyeing Ian's brothers as if he worried that the men might take an interest in the winning redhead. But Ian's brothers were too busy ogling Julia's fans, who were talking to one another in line, some with books they'd already purchased while waiting to have them autographed, and others who were ogling the Highlanders right back.

Julia wasn't sure whether any of the brothers would show up for dinner with the Wildhavens, *or* from the looks of it, Julia's *fans* instead. Who knew? It might even help a few more sales.

All Julia knew was that when she retired tonight with the laird of the castle, he would be the only one for her.

"We'll be retiring early tonight," Ian said with a wink to Julia.

With books pressed to their hearts, the women standing in line started giggling when they overheard his delicious brogue, saw the sexy wink, and heard his words. They might want to go home with the laird, but he was all Julia's. She raised her pen to autograph the next book, still smiling. If she could drag the kilted MacNeill warriors with her to every event, one of her books might just make best seller on one of the premier lists, and then maybe their financial woes would—

Guthrie headed toward them wearing his kilt, looking just as daunting and handsome as the rest of the MacNeill clansmen. She swore the women all took deeper breaths of admiration at the sight of him. Three hunky Highland hunks to choose from, she imagined they were thinking.

Guthrie nodded to Ian and then handed an envelope to Julia.

She looked up at him, questioning what this was all about.

Ian leaned down and whispered in her ear. "The money your ex-boyfriend stole from you. Family takes care of family."

Tears filled her eyes. "But…"

Guthrie folded his arms. "He had a job. A good paying job. And the proceeds from the sale of several of his investments. He paid back every dime with interest, which is as it should be. I'm the financial advisor for the clan." He bowed his head slightly. "Anytime you need my assistance, just let me know."

Several of Julia's fans looked like they wanted to wave their hands and ask for his assistance.

Julia rose from her seat and gave Guthrie a hug. "Thank you from the bottom of my heart. And…" She handed him back the envelope. "…you can put that money in the castle fund."

Then the signing began in earnest because after dinner with the Wildhavens, Julia and Ian were returning to the hotel and renewing their vows. The small smile he wore and the sparkle in his dark eyes verified he was thinking along the same lines.

After romanticizing for years about what the perfect man in her life would be like, she'd finally found her storybook hero—rough around the edges, a little broke, and as sexy as any kilted warrior could be.

Acknowledgments

Thanks to Robyn, my co-worker, who suggested I have a "poor" werewolf hero this time around. Already fantasizing about Highland hunks because of my own Highland roots, I figured what could be better than a laird who is about to lose his ancestral home? I also want to thank Lynn Crain and Mary Curtis for fielding Highland questions for me.

And thanks to my editor, Deb Werksman, who has made the dream come true for me; to Danielle, my publicist, who is my marketing inspiration; and to the editorial staff and the cover artists who design such beautiful covers that they win awards and make me proud to say that these books are mine! And to the Rebel Romance Writers critique partners—Judy, Vonda, Tammy, Randy, Pam, Carol, and Betty—for always being there for me! And thanks to my fans who encourage me to write faster.

About the Author

An award-winning author of paranormal and medieval romantic suspense, Terry Spear also writes true stories for adult and young adult audiences. She's a retired lieutenant colonel in the U.S. Army Reserve and has an MBA from Monmouth University. She also creates award-winning teddy bears, Wilde & Woolly Bears, that are personalized and designed to commemorate authors' books. When she's not writing or making bears, she's teaching online writing courses.

Her family has roots in the Highlands of Scotland where her love of all things Scottish came into being. Originally from California, she's lived in eight states and now resides in the heart of Texas. She is the author of *Heart of the Wolf, Destiny of the Wolf, To Tempt the Wolf, Legend of the White Wolf, Seduced by the Wolf, Wolf Fever, Winning the Highlander's Heart, The Accidental Highland Hero, Deadly Liaisons, The Vampire... In My Dreams* (young adult), and numerous articles and short stories for magazines.

LOOK FOR TERRY SPEAR'S NEXT
WEREWOLF ROMANCE

DREAMING
of the WOLF

AVAILABLE FROM SOURCEBOOKS CASABLANCA
DECEMBER 2011

From *Heart of the Wolf*

1850
Colorado

AS SOON AS HE STRIPPED NAKED, HE'D BE HERS.

Unbraiding her hair, Bella's blood heated with desire while she observed the dark-haired boy. He looked about eighteen, two years older than she. He yanked off one boot, then another, at the lake's edge. It wasn't the first time she'd watched him peel out of his clothes, but it was the first time she'd join him. If he had a taste of her, wouldn't he crave her? Hunger to be like her? Wild and free?

She swallowed hard, longing to be Devlyn's mate—rather than some human's—but it would never be. Lifting her chin, she resolved to make the human hers. She untied her ankle-high boots, then slipped them off her feet.

The human boy's pet gray wolf rested at the shoreline, his ears perked up as he watched her. But the boy didn't see her—he was unobservant, as most humans were.

However, a boy who cared for his wolf such as he did would care for her, too, wouldn't he? He'd studied her when she swam here before, naked, splashing lazily across the water's surface, attempting to draw him to her. Though he'd tried to conceal himself in the woods, she'd seen him. And heard him with her sensitive hearing when he stepped on dried oak leaves and pine needles to draw closer, to see her more clearly. She'd smelled his heady man-scent on the breeze. He'd desired her then, setting her belly afire; he'd desire her now.

Tilting her nose up, she breathed in his masculinity. Masculine but not as wild as her own kind—lupus garou. A human who treated a woman with kindness, that's what she desired.

She tugged her pale blue dress over her head, struggling to shed her clothes as quickly as she could now. Wanting to get her plan into motion, before she changed her mind, or one of the pack tried to change it for her.

Adopted by the gray pack, she wasn't even a gray wolf. So why should it matter if she left them and chose the human boy for her own? Volan, the gray alpha pack leader, wanted her, that's why. Her stomach clenched with the thought that the man who'd nearly raped her would have her if she couldn't find a way out of the nightmare.

The human pulled off his breeches. A boy, still not well muscled, but well on his way. A survivor, living on his own, that's what intrigued her so much about him. A loner—like a rogue wolf—determined to endure.

Only in her heart, she desired the gray who'd saved her life when they were younger—Devlyn. Even now she had difficulty not comparing his rangy, taller body with this boy's. They had the same dark hair and eyes, which maybe explained why the human had attracted her. She wanted Devlyn with all her heart, but craving his attention would only result in Volan killing him. Best to leave the pack and mate with a human, cut her ties with the grays, and start her own pack.

She'd watched the human ride, run, hunt with his

rifle, but she admired him most when he swam. Her gaze dropped lower to the patch of dark hair resting above his legs and...

She raised her brows. A thrill of expectation of having his manhood buried deep inside her sent a tingling of gooseflesh across her skin. If her drawers hadn't been crotchless, they'd have been wet in anticipation. She smiled at the sight of him. He'd produce fine offspring.

He dove into the water with a splash. With powerful strokes he glided across the placid surface of the small, summer-warmed lake. She slipped out of her last petticoat, then her drawers. Without a stitch of clothes on, she stood on the opposite shore, waiting for him to catch sight of her. Wouldn't he yearn for her like her own kind did?

She had to entice him to make love to her. Then she'd change into the wolf and bite him. And transfer the beauty of the wolf to him in the ancient way.

Running her fingers through her cinnamon curls, she fanned them over her shoulders, down to her hips.

They'd live together in his log cabin, taking jaunts through the woods in their wolf states under the bright moon forever. His mother, father, and little sister had died during the winter, and none of his kind lived within a fifteen-mile radius. He'd want her—he had to. Like her wolf pack, most humankind desired companionship.

She stepped into the water.

Then he caught sight of her.

His dark eyes widened and his mouth dropped open. But he didn't swim toward her as she expected. He didn't come for her, ravish her as she wanted. His eyes inspected every bit of her, but then he turned and swam away from her, back to the shore and his clothes. What was wrong with him?

Her mind warred between anger and confusion. Didn't he find her appealing?

She swam toward him, trying to reach the shore before he dressed and headed back to his cabin. But by the time she reached the lake halfway, he'd jerked on his breeches and boots, not even bothering with his shirt or vest, and vanished into the woods with his wolf at his heel.

In disbelief, she stared after him.

"Bella!" the leader of her pack hollered, his voice forbidding and warlike.

She snapped her head around. Her heart nearly stopped when she saw the gray leader.

Volan stood like a predator waiting for the right time to go after his prey. His ebony hair was bound tight, and his black eyes narrowed. As a wolf, he was heavyset, broad-shouldered and thick-necked, the leader by virtue of his size, powerful jaws, and wicked killer canines. But now he stood as a man, his thoughts darker than night, his face menacing as he considered her swimming naked in the lake.

Did the boy get away in time, before Volan caught sight of him? How could she be so naïve as to think that Volan would let her have a human male?

She paddled in place and glared at him. "What do you want, Volan?" she growled back, unable to hold a civil tongue whenever he stood near.

"Come out at once!"

He turned his head toward the woods.

Had he smelled the human? Her heart rate quickened.

She swam back to her clothes, determined to draw his attention away from the boy.

Then she spied Devlyn, watching, half hidden in the shadows of the forest, as if he and the pack leader were maneuvering in for the kill. A pang of regret sliced through her that Devlyn might have seen her lusting after a human. Three years older than she, he still vied for his place within the pack. A strap of leather tied back his coffee-colored, shoulder-length hair, and she fought the urge to set it free, to soften his harsh look. His equally dark brown eyes glowered at her, while his sturdy jaw clenched.

He stepped closer, not menacingly, but as if he stalked a deer and feared scaring away his prey. She raised a brow. This time, he seemed to have Volan's permission to draw close.

She growled. "Stay away." Wading out of the water, she distracted Volan from considering the woods or who might have disappeared into them. Devlyn, too, eyed her with far too much interest.

She hurried to slip into her clothes, irritated to have the wrong audience. Still, the way Devlyn closed in on her, only keeping a few feet from her until she was dressed, while Volan remained a hundred yards away, sent a trickle of dread through her.

Volan never allowed males to get close to her when she was naked, and normally she wouldn't have permitted it either. So what were they up to? She left her wet hair loose, then Volan nodded.

From *Destiny of the Wolf*

WHY HAD LARISSA, HER LOVING SISTER, ENDED UP DEAD—
here, of all the godforsaken places in the States? Maybe
that was the reason—off the beaten path, surrounded by
wilderness, a place to hide from the harsh realities of the
forced marriage, safe from Bruin's retaliation should he
ever have located her. But she hadn't been safe. And
now she was dead.

Out of the corner of her eye, Lelandi Wildhaven
thought she saw her cousin, Ural, slink into the woods in
his wolf form, but she had to be mistaken. He wouldn't
be angry enough with her to shape-shift this close to
Silver Town and risk alerting the gray *lupus garou* pack
that a couple of reds had slipped into their territory.

Ignoring her gut instinct telling her this was a very
bad idea, she pushed open the Silver Town Tavern's
heavy door, the squealing of the rusty hinges jarring her
taut nerves.

Five bearded men sitting at a table turned to stare at
her, and at once she feared the worst—they saw straight
through her disguise.

She shoved the faux eyeglasses back into place, hating the way they kept sliding down the bridge of her
nose. The weather-beaten cowboy hat she'd picked up at
a resale shop half swallowed her head, making her look
like a little kid wearing her dad's Stetson.

Amber glass lights hanging from brass rods high above

softly illuminated dark oak tables and a long, polished bar. Slow-spinning wooden fan blades circulated the air, impregnated with the smell of gray *lupus garou*. Her nerve endings prickled with fresh awareness. Dingy antique mirrors covering the back wall behind the bar bore mute witness to the goings-on in the place, as she suspected they had for decades. If they had captured all the images of the bar's existence what a story those mirrors could tell.

Another bearded man crouching beneath the lip of the bar suddenly stood to his full six-foot-four height. The glass and dish towel he held nearly slipped from his grasp as his appraising glance took in every inch of her. His lips turned up at the corners slightly. Deep laugh lines were etched in his tanned skin and shaggy black hair extended to his shoulders, giving him the appearance of a rugged mountain man, unused to civilized trappings. What disturbed her most was that he was a gray, like the men drinking at the table. She'd anticipated it would be a human-run establishment frequented by *lupus garous*, like the bar back home.

"What'll you have, miss?" he asked, his voice warm and welcoming.

Expecting a chilly greeting—their kind didn't welcome strangers venturing into their midst, especially if she were human and this was an exclusively gray *lupus garou* tavern—she hesitated.

"Miss?"

"Bottled water, please." She'd meant to sound tough, to match the look of the place. She'd intended to be someone different, with her red hair dyed black and the high-heeled boots giving the impression she stood taller, more like *them*. The blue contacts she wore hid her green eyes sufficiently, but she still felt like Lelandi, triplet to Larissa, with barely any visible difference in appearance, except her eyes were greener and her hair more red and less golden than her sister's had been. Had her voice betrayed her?

The small smile on the bartender's face was more likely because she was a stranger who'd walked into a wolves' den without protection than because she'd given herself away. She cursed herself for not disguising her voice better, but the barkeep's warm demeanor gave her a false sense of security, which could be the death of her if she wasn't careful.

The bartender handed her a chilled bottle of water and tall green glass. "New in town?"

"Just passing through," she said, paying for the water.

"Sam's the name, miss. If you need anything, just holler."

"Thanks." Hollering for a drink was definitely not her style.

She chose a table in the farthermost corner of the room, half-hidden in shadows. Although any of them could see in the dark as well as she could, this location would keep her out of the main flow of traffic. She hoped she'd seem inconspicuous, not worthy of anyone's scrutiny, and most of all, human.

Lelandi glanced at the door. According to her information, Darien Silver—Larissa's widowed mate—should be here soon.

One of the men got up from his seat and gave Sam some cash. The man cast Lelandi a hint of a smile, then returned to his chair. Small for a gray, stocky, hair a bland brown, eyes amber, his clothes carrying a coating of dust, he had a soft, round baby face. Looked sweet, a beta-wolf type. Smudges of dirt colored his cheeks, and he wiped them off with the back of his denim shirt-sleeve. His eyes never straying from her, he smoothed out his raggedy hair and took another swig of his beer.

Sam joined Lelandi and handed her the cash. "Joe Kelly paid for your drink, miss. He works at the silver mine, which explains his slightly rough appearance. But he cleans up good." Sam gave her a wink, and returned to the bar.

Should she turn down Joe's offer? On the other hand, if he was interested in her, maybe she could discover the truth quicker.

"Thank you," she mouthed to Joe Kelly and his chest swelled.

The other guys started ribbing him in low voices. The tips of Joe's ears turned crimson.

Her stomach clenched with the notion that Larissa had had the audacity to mate with a gray, especially when she had a mate already. She'd said she wanted to find herself, and she did. Six feet under. Yet, Lelandi couldn't help feeling it was her own fault, that if she'd taken Larissa's place back home, or even run away with her, she might have kept her safe. But what about their parents? She couldn't have left them behind—not with her dad so incapacitated—but hell, she hadn't been able to protect them either. They had been murdered anyway.

She tamped down a shudder, hating that she hadn't stopped any of it. But once she learned what had happened to Larissa and put the murderer in *his* grave, Lelandi was going to locate her brother and their uncle—damn both of them for leaving the family behind.

The barkeep clinked some glasses, his gaze taking her in like a crafty old wolf's. He probably was on the younger side of middle age but due to the beard, he seemed older. The smile still percolated on his lips. Trying to figure her out? Or did he realize what a phony she was? Hunting in the wild was nothing new, but hunting like this...

She twisted the top off her bottled water and glanced down at her watch again. Only four twenty-five.

"Waiting for someone?" Sam asked, one dark brow cocked.

She shook her head. Her hat jiggled, her glasses slipped, and the annoying earrings danced.

Two men appeared in front of one of the dingy tavern windows and then the door jerked open. Her heart skittered.

"Hey, Sam! Bring us a pitcher of beer," one of them called.

About six-foot—as tall as her brother—with windswept shoulder-length dark hair and a newly started beard, his amber eyes hinted at cheerfulness and good-humor rang in his words. Both men wore leather jackets, plaid shirts, denims, cowboy hats, and boots, and they appeared to be twins. Multiple births abounded among *lupus garous*, so no surprise there. They looked like they were mid- to late-twenties and walked into the place like they owned the joint.

"Jake, Tom." Sam glanced in her direction, alerting them to the presence of a stranger.

She stiffened her back and gripped her glass tighter.

Tom—his hair the lighter of the two, longer, curling around his broad shoulders, his face smooth as silk—fastened his gaze on her and raised his brows, tipped back his Stetson, and grinned.

From *To Tempt the Wolf*

SUCKING UP OXYGEN, THE FLAMES SPREAD OUTWARD, devouring thirsty timber and underbrush, perfect fuel for the firestorm. The winds picked up force, and Tessa Anderson's adrenaline surged again as she snapped the last of the photos for the magazine. The summer drought had continued on through the fall and winter, leaving the California forests desert-dry, and now either a careless camper or an arsonist had turned the woods into a fiery inferno.

What in the world was she doing risking her life to photograph this disaster?

Coughing, her eyes filled with smoke, she reminded herself she needed the money to help defend her brother. Then in the haze, the silhouette of a wolf appeared—gray, like the smoke, a phantom. Watching her. Stalking her? Wild animals knew better than to linger with danger threatening. Only a human would be dumb enough to stay put.

His uncharacteristic actions made her back toward her vehicle. Having been fascinated with wolves all her life, she knew his behavior wasn't natural.

A tremor stole up her spine. He looked just like one she'd seen before. The one who'd attacked before.

Snapping a picture of the wolf, she bumped against the passenger's side of her Escort. As soon as she fumbled for the door handle, he crouched, readying to spring like a coiled snake.

Heart thundering, she jerked her door open and jumped inside. Before she could shut the door, the wolf's hulking body slammed against it, knocking it closed. She jumped back.

Snarling, he bared his wicked canines. She scrambled over the console and twisted the keys in the ignition, her skin prickling with panic. Tires spun on gravel as she whirled the car around and headed for the main highway.

A half mile later, she came across a home in the direct path of the fire. An SUV was parked in the driveway. Its trunk lid was open and the back filled with boxes. Reassured that the occupants were leaving, she tore on past.

Her main concern now was returning to her brother's trial and praying he would be found not guilty.

―――∽∾―――

Hunter Greymere shoved four more suitcases in the SUV while his twin sister rushed out of the house with another box of dishes, her face and clothes covered in soot.

The air was so thick with smoke, Hunter choked, fighting to draw in a breath of fresh oxygen. "Meara, enough! Get in the vehicle. We leave now!"

Black plumes of smoke spiraling upward indicated fire had claimed another of his pack member's homes and was growing ever closer to his own. Ash rained down like a light gray snow flurry. The smoke blocked out the sun, but the flames lit the sky with an eerie orange glow.

Meara shook her head and dashed for the house. "We have to get the safe."

Seizing her arm, Hunter pushed her toward the vehicle. "*Get* in the SUV! I'll grab the safe."

The look of mutiny on her face meant she would disobey him. He didn't have time to make her listen. Running in a crouch so he could breathe, he grabbed the steel box from his bedroom closet and carried it through the hazy living room. He crashed into Meara, stooping low, her arms filled with another box.

"Out, now!" he growled.

The blaze crackled, incinerating the old forest and homes in its path. The emerald green woods, already rusty with trees that had died from insect infestations and drought would soon be blackened. And the home they had lived in for two hundred years would vanish in a roaring ball of fire. No time for regret now.

The super-heated gases singed Hunter's throat and lungs, and he chided himself for staying as long as they had. After climbing into the vehicle, he turned the fan on high, but the car was already so filled with smoke, his eyes and throat burned. Meara's amber eyes glistened with tears as she covered her mouth and nose with a wet towel.

"We'll be all right, Meara." Hunter gunned the accelerator and sped toward the highway that would take them to Oregon, nearly hitting a Ford Escape in the fog-like smoke in front of them. The driver apparently had the same notion, but was not driving fast enough for Hunter's liking.

"Hell, who is that?"

"Oregon plates. Some idiot human camping out here? Who knows."

"A woman? By herself?"

He peered harder into the smoke and made out a crown of flame red hair cascading over her shoulders. Intrigued, he wondered if her face was as enchanting as the waterfall of red curls. But then he scowled. She shouldn't have been here in the first place.

He followed her as she hightailed it out of his territory in an attempt to keep ahead of the eye of the firestorm, and *him*. And for an instant, he felt like a predator stalking his prey. "At least we got all our people out."

Meara didn't reply.

She didn't adjust well to change. Moving from the Scottish Highlands over two hundred years ago to the untamed California wilderness hadn't set well with her. But change was inevitable for the *lupus garous*. Meara had been lucky they hadn't had to move as much over the years as many of their kind, hiding the fact that once they reached eighteen, they aged only a year for every thirty.

"Where are we going?" she asked, staring out the window at the vast ancient pines that would soon suffer the fate of their steadfast companions.

"To Oregon. Uncle Basil called earlier this morning while you were helping others pack. He's retiring to Florida. The cabins on the Oregon coast are ours now."

"Florida? Are there any of our kind there?"

"Real red wolves on St. Vincent Island off the Panhandle of Florida."

"*Real* red wolves?" Meara snorted. "I didn't think he liked mixing it up with red wolves, *period*. But *real* wolves?"

"He said he found a pack of gray *lupus garous* near the Everglades."

She shook her head. "So what's he going to hunt there? Alligators?" She let out her breath. "I don't want to move to the Oregon seacoast."

LEGEND *of the* WHITE WOLF

BY TERRY SPEAR

"A steamy, action-packed romance set within a complex and deadly werewolf society. This delicious alpha hero will leave you wild for more." —Nicole North, author
Devil in a Kilt

IN A WORLD OF SNOW AND ICE, THEIR PASSIONS BLAZE

Private Detective Cameron MacPherson arrives in the icy wilderness of Maine in search of his lost partners, who mysteriously disappeared on a hunting trip. Faith O'Malley joins Cameron on his quest, hoping to find her father's stolen research and discover just what he saw in that same region so many years ago—a sight that would lead him to lose all touch with reality. With or without Cameron, she won't be stopped. But in the wilds of the icy world around them, they encounter a mythical creature whose bite changes everything...

"*Action-packed romance and suspense-filled plot add up to pure magic. I couldn't turn the pages fast enough. Terry Spear is a great addition to the paranormal genre!*"
—ARMCHAIR INTERVIEWS

"*I love Ms. Spear's* lupus garou *society. She creates a world that makes you believe werewolves live among us.*"
—PARANORMAL ROMANCE REVIEWS

"*Tantalizing, action-packed romance... with all the magic of fantasy.*" —THE PEN & MUSE

978-1-4022-1905-4 • $6.99 U.S. / $8.99 CAN / £3.99 UK

A CERTAIN
WOLFISH
CHARM

BY LYDIA DARE

REGENCY ENGLAND HAS
GONE TO THE WOLVES!

The rules of Society can be beastly…

…especially when you're a werewolf and it's that irritating time of the month. Simon Westfield, the Duke of Blackmoor, is rich, powerful, and sinfully handsome, and has spent his entire life creating scandal and mayhem. It doesn't help his wolfish temper at all that Miss Lily Rutledge seems to be as untamable as he is. When Lily's beloved nephew's behavior becomes inexplicably wild, she turns to Simon for help. But they both may have bitten off more than they can chew when each begins to discover the other's darkest secrets…

"A Certain Wolfish Charm has bite!"

—SABRINA JEFFRIES, *NEW YORK TIMES* BESTSELLING AUTHOR OF *WED HIM BEFORE YOU BED HIM*

978-1-4022-3694-5 • $6.99 U.S./$8.99 CAN/£3.99 UK

TALL, DARK AND WOLFISH

BY LYDIA DARE

REGENCY ENGLAND HAS GONE TO THE WOLVES!

He's lost unless she can heal him

Lord Benjamin Westfield is a powerful werewolf—until one full moon when he doesn't change. His life now shattered, he rushes to Scotland in search of the healer who can restore his inner beast: young, beautiful witch Elspeth Campbell, who will help anyone who calls upon her healing arts. But when Lord Benjamin shows up, everything she thought she knew is put to the test...

Praise for *A Certain Wolfish Charm:*

"Tough, resourceful, charming women battle roguish, secretive, aristocratic men under the watchful eye of society in Dare's delightful Victorian paranormal romance debut."

—*PUBLISHERS WEEKLY* (STARRED REVIEW)

978-1-4022-3695-2 • $6.99 U.S./$8.99 CAN/£3.99 UK

THE WOLF
NEXT
DOOR

BY LYDIA DARE

REGENCY ENGLAND HAS GONE TO THE WOLVES!

Can she forgive the unforgivable?

Ever since her planned elopement with Lord William Westfield turned to disaster, Prisca Hawthorne has done everything she can to push him away. If only her heart didn't break every time he leaves her. Lord William throws himself into drinking, gambling, and debauchery and pretends not to care about Prisca at all. But when he returns to find a rival werewolf vying for her hand, he'll stop at nothing to claim the woman who should have been his all along, and the moon-crossed lovers are forced into a battle of wills that could be fatal.

"With its sexy hero, engaging heroine, and sizzling sexual tension, you won't want to put it down even when the moon is full."

—SABRINA JEFFRIES, *NEW YORK TIMES* BESTSELLING AUTHOR OF *WED HIM BEFORE YOU BED HIM*

978-1-4022-3696-9 • $6.99 U.S./$8.99 CAN/£3.99 UK

T OF THE WOLF

BY LYDIA DARE

REGENCY ENGLAND HAS GONE TO THE WOLVES!

Lord Dashiel Thorpe has fought the wolf within him his entire life. But when the moonlight proves too powerful, Dash is helpless, and a chance encounter with Caitrin Macleod binds the two together irrevocably. Though Caitrin is a witch with remarkable abilities, she is overwhelmed and runs back to the safety of her native Scotland. But Dashiel is determined to follow her—she's the only woman who can free him from a fate worse than death. Caitrin will ultimately have to decide whether she's running from danger, or true love...

Praise for Lydia Dare

"**The authors flawlessly blend the historical and paranormal genres, providing a hint of the lycan lifestyle with a touching romance... lots of feral fun.**" —ROMANCE NOVEL NEWS

978-1-4022-4437-7 • $6.99 U.S./$8.99 CAN/£4.99 UK